Praise for T.

'An impressive start in
The

'A page tuner that will appeal to fans of *Broadchurch*.'
Adele Parks, *Platinum*

'Packed with authenticity.'
Mail Online

'Fresh, vivid and totally engrossing: this is gold-standard crime
writing bearing the unmistakable hallmark of authenticity.'
Erin Kinsley, *Sunday Times* bestselling author of *Found*

'This could turn into a gem of a series.'
Sunday Post

'Fiendishly clever plotting. I was hooked from start to finish.'
Sarah Stovell, author of *Other Parents*

'A tightly-plotted, well-paced story with a disturbingly
manipulative, evil villain at its core.'
Country and Townhouse

'I genuinely found it hard to put down. The writing is beautifully
paced and the double viewpoint creates great tension.'
Alex Gray, *Sunday Times* bestselling author of the DCI Lorimer Series

'It's difficult to accept that *Breakneck Point* is a debut novel as
T. Orr Munro's writing is exciting, genuine and convincing.'
My Weekly

'T. Orr Munro has weaved such an intricate story,
she'll have you guessing right until the end. CSI Ally
Dymond is a brilliant and relatable protagonist.'
Sophia Spiers, author of *The Call of Cassandra Rose*

'Shot through with wit and peopled by characters you care about.'
Gill Perdue, author of *If I Tell*

T. Orr Munro was born in Aldershot in Hampshire to an English mother and a Greek-Armenian father who moved to deepest Devon after recognising it would be a great place to raise their children. She has a degree in Economic and Social History from Liverpool University and a PGCE in History and English. After university she trained as a CSI, then later became a secondary school teacher. She changed career at thirty-three to become a police and crime journalist and is currently freelance. She has since returned with her family to live in North Devon, the setting for the Ally Dymond series, but heads to Greece as often as she can. Her time as a CSI provided much of the inspiration for her novel, shining a light on what happens behind the crime scene tape.

Also by T. Orr Munro

Breakneck Point

Slaughter House Farm

T. Orr Munro

ONE PLACE. MANY STORIES

HQ
An imprint of HarperCollins*Publishers* Ltd
1 London Bridge Street
London SE1 9GF

www.harpercollins.co.uk

HarperCollins*Publishers*
Macken House, 39/40 Mayor Street Upper,
Dublin 1, D01 C9W8, Ireland

This edition 2023

1
First published in Great Britain by
HQ, an imprint of HarperCollins*Publishers* Ltd 2023

ISBN: 9780008479862

This book is produced from independently certified FSC™ paper to ensure responsible forest management.

For more information visit: www.harpercollins.co.uk/green

This book is set in 10.7/15.5 pt. Sabon by Type-it AS, Norway

Printed and Bound in the UK using 100% Renewable Electricity at CPI Group (UK) Ltd, Croydon, CR0 4YY

For Frank, Rosie, Joe and Alice
To the moon and back

Prologue

Miriam

At first, she couldn't work out why she was here. She hadn't been back since that night, years ago, when he had taken her hand in his and led her through the darkened farmyard and up the hill until the soft grass underfoot became thick gnarls of heather and she knew they were on the moor.

There his torchlight fell upon a huge, flat boulder, and he stopped to sit on it, patting the cold grey stone next to him. She wasn't sure what was happening, but she did as she was told, as always.

He switched off his torch and told her to look up. Despite the strangeness of his request, she didn't say anything. Instead, she cast her gaze skywards. The sight made her gasp in wonder. So many stars stretching across the horizon, the sky seemed to sag under the effort of holding them all. Someone once told her everyone has their own star and if we live a good life our souls will return to it when we die. She used to like the idea of being watched over by the souls of her kin, but that was before.

He pointed out the patterns and the constellations: Auriga, Cancer and the Plough. Did she know the Arabians believed the bowl of the Plough was a coffin and its handle of

I

stars the mourners condemned to follow it forever more? She said nothing and, realizing he'd careered from the romantic to the morbid, he stopped his chatter, and the silence engulfed them.

The torch came back on. She heard a rustle and turned to see him fumbling in his jacket pocket, mining its corners in panic. Finally, his face relaxed and he held up his hand. In the pale, shaky light, dwarfed between a thick callused thumb and forefinger, was a tiny diamond ring.

'Marry me, Miriam,' he said.

She knew this was coming because her father had told her. Now it was here she felt only despair. And guilt. For he was a good man, but she didn't love him, and she never would. Not because she didn't want to, but because she'd already given her love away. It didn't matter that it was a long time ago. She had used it up and she was certain she had none left to give.

If it had been up to her, she would have said no, but it wasn't; it was up to her father. He couldn't believe it when he asked him for her hand in marriage.

'I thought I'd have to beg some hairy lump to take ye off my 'ands, and then this farmer turns up asking to marry ye.' But her father's darkness was never far away. 'Now, you be a good girl and get wed quick, maid, before he finds out what you are.'

So she did as she was told. She said yes. She had been good. And look where it had got her.

***

'Jo, stay back! She's got a knife.'

'Oh my God.'

'Why does she keep looking up at the sky, Mum?'

2

'I don't think she's well, love. Stay close to me, Natasha. Dean, we have to call the police.'

'The police? Hold on, she's probably just a bit lost. Where do you live, love?'

'Hello. Yes. The police and ambulance. We're on Exmoor. On the B1583, I think. We were just driving home after our holiday, and we came across an old lady in the middle of the road. It's so foggy we nearly ran her over. I don't think she's hurt, but she seems a bit confused. She's wearing a nightdress and she's holding a kitchen knife. No, no she hasn't threatened us. It's like she doesn't even know we're here. She's just standing there, staring up at the sky. Can you hurry? Right. Thanks. OK . . . The police are on their way.'

'Let's get going then. We've got hours of driving ahead of us.'

'We can't leave her, Dean. We're in the middle of nowhere.'

'But they'll be ages and I've got work tomorrow.'

'No, they might want to talk to us. We have to wait until they get here. Natasha, can you please stop filming her?'

'Wait. She's trying to speak.'

'Where's Billy?'

'Who's Billy, Mum?'

'How should I know? Put that phone away. Can't you see she's upset? I think you should just get back into the car.'

'Mum.'

'Natasha, just do as you're told.'

'But what's that on her nightdress?'

'I don't know – I can't see from here.'

'Oh my God, it's blood.'

1

I hit the brakes hard, launching Megan at the dashboard.

'What was that for?'

'Sorry. I thought something ran out in front of me,' I lie.

She peers nervously over the side of her window for evidence of roadkill.

'Can't see anything. Whatever it was, I think you missed it.'

But I'm not listening. The real reason for my unexpected stop is the small white van in the corner of the car park. It isn't marked, but it doesn't need to be. I'd know it anywhere. Christ, there were days when I spent more time in that vehicle than at home. Not any more. I haven't driven it in eight months, not since that rainy day in the hospital car park when a police officer told me someone had tried to murder my daughter. Seeing the van now is a jolting reminder that my compassionate leave ends in just three weeks, but I'm not ready to face my colleagues. Not yet. Maybe not ever.

'Maybe we should go elsewhere for the paint.'

'What? Where? This is the only paint shop in Bidecombe.'

At least she's talking to me now after slipping into a monumental sulk when I refused to let her stay in the cabin alone.

'OK. Let's go in.'

I slap the car into reverse and manoeuvre it into a space between a tractor and a Land Rover.

'I'll stay in the car.'

'No, you won't.'

'You'll only be a few minutes.'

'Come in anyway, just to be on the safe side.'

Megan delivers her signature huff and unclips her seatbelt.

'God, I can't wait till you're back to work.'

'Thanks.'

'It means you'll stop breathing down my neck 24/7.'

'I think you'll find it's called parenting.'

'Yeah, well, I preferred the type where you're not around so much and it means I can go back to school.'

'We haven't made any final decisions about that.'

Megan pauses at the entrance to the shop. 'Look at me. I'm so obviously better.'

In some ways she is. The bulging purple bruises that bloated her face have long faded, restoring her freckles, beloved by me but hated by her, and her auburn hair has grown back enough to conceal the deep track running the length of a skull that had to be reconstructed fragment by fragment. You wouldn't know she was brutally attacked eight months ago.

'Not all scars are skin deep.'

'I'm good up here too,' she says tapping her temple. 'Just ask Lisa. She thinks I'm well enough to go back to school.'

Lisa is Megan's counsellor. I don't agree with her, but it's a conversation that's going to have to wait as a familiar voice calls my name and the first thing I notice when I turn around is an unmissable shock of red hair belonging to Jake Harris, a crime scene investigator and the van's driver.

'Hi, Jake.' Not yet out of his twenties, Jake was new to the job last summer before it all happened. I was looking forward to mentoring him – he has the makings of a great CSI – but that was then. Things are different now. Now I just want to get the hell out of there.

'I'm here for a break-in,' he says.

'I noticed the security alarm had been foamed.'

'Yeah. Not that anyone takes any notice of them. Second time I've been out this way this week.'

'Right.'

'Yeah, some old dear found wandering on the moors. She had blood all over her nightdress – only get this, it wasn't hers. They've no idea who she is or whose blood it is. She's got dementia or something, but she's not talking. I went up to the moors to examine where she was picked up, not that I found anything.' There was a time when I'd be all over this, interrogating Jake for the tiniest, most seemingly innocuous details, knowing that any one of them could unlock the mystery of the woman with someone else's blood on her. After all, crime scenes are my game. Or they were. 'Anyway, I couldn't borrow you for a minute, could I?'

'Not really, Jake. I'm with my daughter.' I glance at Megan who's trying her hardest to look anything but related to me. 'I don't like to leave her on her own.'

'Sorry. I didn't realize.'

'Go, Mum. I'll be fine. Nothing's going to happen to me.'

'I could really do with a second pair of eyes, Ally,' pleads Jake. 'Can't help thinking I've missed something.'

Backed into a corner, it would be churlish to say no. Besides, none of this is Jake's fault.

'OK but stay where I can see you, Megan.'

'Thanks. I really appreciate it,' says Jake, leading me to the back of the shop. 'It happened a couple of days ago. The place was closed over the weekend. They got in via a window in the back. Nothing taken other than some money left in the petty cash tin in the office. I've dusted the point of entry, the cash till and the counter for prints. Nothing but woollen glove marks which, I know, is par for the course.'

'It sounds like you've done everything you can.' I check Megan's whereabouts. She's browsing the photography books.

'I'm just not sure. It doesn't feel right.'

'What makes you say that?'

'This for a start.'

He stops and points at a wall at the back of the shop. Sprayed across it, red paint trickling from its blurred edges, is the word 'bitch'.

2

'So, what do you make of all this then, Dymond?' I don't need to turn around to know the voice belongs to PC Bryan Rogers. He and I go back years, and in all that time he's never called me by my first name.

'Well, it's no Banksy, is it?'

'We've missed you.' He grins. 'Life's a lot duller without you around.'

I guess he's right. There can't be many CSIs who have blown the whistle on police corruption during a murder trial.

'Have you come across anything like this before?' asks Jake.

'Not often, no,' I say, checking Megan is still in my line of sight. 'Most thieves don't hang around long enough to write expletives on walls. Unless it's personal.'

'Any idea who might want to break into your shop and leave that for you to find?' PC Rogers turns to the woman next to him. We've met before, several times. Some businesses are broken into so often that I'm on first-name terms with the owners, including Karyn Dwight, who has that same weary acceptance that comes with being burgled multiple times. But it's the first time someone has sprayed 'bitch' across her wall.

'Not offhand no. We have a few farmers who owe us money. I've threatened court action and even doorstepped some of them, which didn't go down well, but none of them would resort to this.'

'It's obvious who it is,' says a man in grey overalls emerging from the paint aisle looking like someone who had the option to retire some years ago. Judging by the expression on Karyn's face, she wishes he had. 'It's those kids from the care home down the road. They get up to all sorts.'

It's only been eight months, but I'd almost forgotten the sweeping accusations from members of the public who think they're being helpful. Christ, if we convicted people on the basis of them getting up to 'all sorts', we'd fill the prisons ten times over.

'Ray, you can't go around accusing people. Those kids at Whitebeam have enough to deal with, and Geoff does wonders with them.'

'A leopard never changes its spots, Karyn, but I know you have a soft spot for them.' He turns to PC Rogers whose look of honed disinterest fails to dissuade Ray's hypothesizing. 'Karyn fosters kids so she's a bit biased, but I'll bet you anything it was one of the little buggers.'

'We're not all bad, you know.'

'What?' Ray stares at PC Rogers, unable to square the idea that a care home kid could become an officer of the law. 'You went there?'

'For a while, when my mum couldn't cope. I loved it. It was like a holiday camp. Anyway, I'll pop in and make some inquiries. I quite fancy a trip down memory lane.'

'So what do you think, Ally?' asks Jake.

I check Megan again. This time she catches me, treating me to an eye-roll. I guess she'll be OK for a few minutes longer.

'Karyn, is it possible the spray can used to do this is one of yours?'

'Yes, we stock that colour. It's not out on the shelves at the moment though.'

'Even better. Do you have some weighing scales and something like BBQ tongs?'

'Er, yes, we do. Ray, can you show the lady where the spray cans are kept in the stockroom?'

Ray takes us to the stockroom. A few seconds later, Karyn joins us with scales and tongs.

Using the tongs, I pick up the first canister and place it on the scales.

'Two hundred and ninety-five grams – keep that number in mind, Jake.'

The next canister weighs the same, as do the next two. Losing faith and not feeling so clever, I place the fourth canister on the scales and read out the numbers.

'Two hundred and twenty.' I look up at Mrs Dwight. 'Is there any reason why this can would weigh less than the others?'

'No. Unless it's been used.'

I offer it to Jake. 'You might like to dust this one.'

Surprised to be asked to do anything and suddenly the centre of attention, Jake fumbles the lid on his pot of aluminium powder, reminding me he's still a rookie.

'Take your time, Jake.'

He nods, and carefully loads his squirrel-hair Zephyr brush with the fine silver powder, taking care to tap off the excess.

Swirling it across the shiny plastic spray can lid, several silvery fingerprints immediately make themselves known. It doesn't matter if the crime is big or small, the sight of those whorls and ridges, unique to the individual, still gives me the biggest buzz.

'You can't date fingerprints, but these look fresh. Now we just have to hope their owner is on the fingerprint database.'

Jake grins at me. 'How did you know?'

'You ever tried taking one of those tops off with woollen gloves on?'

'The sooner you're back off compassionate leave and back on the job, Dymond, the better,' PC Rogers says with a laugh. 'Three weeks, right?'

'Something like that.'

His radio fizzes into life: there's a fight on Bidecombe high street. 'Right, looks like I'm needed elsewhere. I'll pop back for—'

But he's interrupted by a huge crash that echoes around the hangar-like store as if it has been struck by lightning.

'What the hell is that?' Ray frowns. But I already know.

'Megan!'

'Who?'

But I'm already sprinting towards the book aisle.

***

I hadn't planned to raise my daughter in a log cabin on a holiday park in Bidecombe, but when we escaped my ex-husband Sean on Boxing Day eight years previously, my options were limited. Penny, the owner of Seven Hills Lodges, found Megan and me shivering on a bench in the local park and invited us to stay in one of her cabins. We've been here ever since. Penny is like a second mum to Megan, which is why she's sitting with me on my sofa in the living room whilst the doctor examines Megan in her bedroom.

'I knew something wasn't right.'

'Really?' says Penny. 'She seemed fine to me, and it might not be as bad as you think. Have you told Bernadette?'

'God no. The last thing I need is my so-called mother telling me how this is all my fault. Besides she's in the middle of some fjord somewhere.'

The doctor appears in the hallway and the two of us stand to attention.

'It's possible Megan has had a mild seizure, but it's difficult to say without further tests. She could just have fainted, but I'm sure you were warned that seizures can happen after a traumatic brain injury.'

'Yes, but that was eight months ago.'

'It can happen at any time, but let's not get ahead of ourselves. We need to confirm if it was a seizure or not first, so I'll refer her to a specialist immediately. You should be able to see someone in the next few weeks. Then we can take it from there.'

'Thank you.'

'There is one more thing. Megan is very keen to go back to school but she's worried that this latest setback will delay that. I told her that there's no reason why she shouldn't go back, if she feels well enough, but I'll leave that with you.'

Penny shows the doctor out before joining me on the lumpy brown sofa that dominates the living room.

'She can't go to school. Not until we're sure what we're dealing with.'

'We don't know if there's anything wrong with her yet. You heard him. She might just have fainted, and in any case, school might be the best place for her. You'll be at work; I'm at Will's a lot.' Will is Penny's boyfriend – two words I never thought I'd use in the same sentence. 'There's no one here to look after her.'

'What if she has another seizure?'

'You being there isn't going to make any difference, is it? And you can't stay off work forever. Your leave ends in a few weeks.'

'I know.'

My lack of enthusiasm draws her concern.

'You are going back, aren't you?'

'Honestly, I'm not sure.'

'But you love your job.'

'I love Megan more and she needs me. She's just had a seizure.'

'For which she can be treated. There's no need to resign, Ally; we can work something out.'

'I just don't think I can do it any more; you know? I'm tired.'

'This isn't like you. Are you sure this is about Megan?'

'What else would it be about?'

'Megan was attacked. She nearly died. No one would blame you for wanting to keep her close and not let her out of your sight, but he's gone, Ally.'

'I know that.'

'Do you? Look, I get it. I still have nightmares about that day too. I wake up in the middle of the night, drenched in sweat, my heart pounding and I don't why but I know it's to do with him.'

'God, I had no idea,' I say, laying my hand on her arm. 'I'm so sorry, Penny. I should never have involved you.'

'I don't regret any of it and I'd do it all over again in a heart-beat. What I'm trying to say is that I'm still struggling too.' She takes my hand. 'You wouldn't be normal if you didn't have bad dreams after what happened, but that's just it. They're only dreams. He can't hurt you, or me, or Megan any more. Don't let him stop you and Megan living your lives.'

I smile and nod. 'You're right. Thanks.'

I don't tell her that the nightmares never came for me.

3

A thick grey fret shrouds the bottom of the narrow path leading down to the edge of the cliff. Overhead, the plaintive cries of the gulls pierce the mist as if searching for a way out.

This is Breakneck Point. This is where I killed Simon Pascoe. The man who attacked Megan. That day, he thought he'd lured his latest victim, a young girl, to her death, but he got me instead. We fought and he almost took me over the cliff edge with him, but I broke free and watched him tumble to his death on the rocks below. I have no regrets. It was him or me.

My hand slides into my hoodie pocket and searches for the small black button. I take it out and hold it up against the greyness. It belongs to Pascoe. After he fell to his death, I scoured the area to make sure there was no evidence that could place either Pascoe or myself at Breakneck Point. Forensic evidence is often the first domino in a police investigation. Once that falls, everything else follows. I wasn't going to risk that no matter how slight the chances were of the police working out Pascoe's life ended on the rocks below Breakneck Point.

I didn't want to kill him. Not at first. I tried to persuade the police that he had already murdered two women and had tried to kill Megan, but they wouldn't listen. When I realized

Pascoe was going to kill again, I had no choice. I had to stop him. For good.

Penny was in on it. She was waiting in her boat nearby to take me the short distance to my car, which was parked in an isolated cove, in a time that couldn't be achieved by road. I had bet on the police not factoring in a sea getaway. I needn't have worried. They never got close, accepting the suicide note that I'd forged for Pascoe with indecent haste. His body finally washed up several miles down the coast. The police still don't know where he entered the water.

I stare down at the button in the palm of my hand, but I still feel nothing. Just like I felt nothing then. When I watched Megan battle night terrors, her brain releasing memories of the attack that it couldn't bring itself to reveal to her during her waking hours, I knew it was only a matter of time before my own torment would begin. But that's just it. There have been no horrors crashing my dreams, nor flashbacks derailing my day. Sense tells me that for some it's not immediate; for some it takes months, even years, but that doesn't lessen my unease that I killed a man and I walked away, my mind entirely undisturbed by what I had done. Like Penny said, it isn't normal.

The buzzing phone in my pocket interrupts my thoughts. It's Megan. Penny is watching her after she insisted I go for a walk to clear my head. In other words, see things her way and let Megan go back to school while I go back to work.

'You OK, Meggy?'

'It's Jay.'

Jay Cox, our friendly neighbourhood drug dealer, but that's only one of the reasons I dislike him.

'What about him?'

'He's been arrested.'

***

God knows how Jay persuaded the custody sergeant he was vulnerable and needed an appropriate adult but he did, and I've spent the last four hours watching two police officers extract no more than two words from him: no comment. They could have asked him if he had a pulse and I swear they'd have got the same response. Anyway, the incident PC Rogers was called away to when we were at Bidecombe DIY Supplies turned out to be a fight between Jay and his father Tony in the middle of the high street. Jay's been charged with ABH and bailed to appear at the magistrate's in three weeks. Jesus, Megan, you don't half pick your friends.

'So, what's really going on with your dad?'

I figure the least he owes me is the truth. The last time I saw him I threatened to lamp him if he didn't tell me where Megan kept her second phone – the phone she used to secretly communicate with a boy who wasn't a boy at all, but a grown man and a killer: Simon Pascoe. Jay had given it to her after I banned her from seeing him. I only agreed to be his appropriate adult because Megan badgered me into it, telling me I owed him because it was Jay who kept her going during those long days in hospital, sending her funny and, no doubt, inappropriate videos.

'Nothing.' He shrugs.

If I had one word to describe Jay, it would be pointy: pointy chin, pointy nose, pointy hair. And he's thin, not in a genetic way, but in a sorely neglected way, but any sympathy I might have quickly ebbs in the face of his surliness. God knows what the girls, including Megan, see in him.

'Bollocks. You don't attack your dad up in the middle of the high street over nothing. It's drugs, isn't it?'

'It's not drugs.'

He's so affronted by this, it's laughable. The truth is, just like his dad, he's made his living selling drugs for years. He's been caught a few times too, but each time he's wheedled out of it, trotting out the 'personal use' excuse, but Christ that's some level of personal use. I don't know how he's got away with it, but unbelievably he doesn't even have a police record.

'Yes, it is.' I hand him a can of Dr Pepper. Megan told me he lives off the stuff. He takes it without thanking me. 'What happened? Your dad try to muscle in on your territory now he's out of prison?'

He opens the can and takes a gulp. 'You don't know nothing.'

'So tell me. Because I've spent half the night freezing my arse off in that interview room just so you can have a glass of water and take a piss.'

'I'm clean.'

'If you say so.'

'I'm serious and it's got nothing to do with the pigs.'

'Thanks.'

'You're not a real pig.' Technically, he's right. I'm a civilian CSI, although criminals rarely trouble themselves with that distinction.

'And this has everything to do with the police. You assaulted your father. Unless you at least attempt to explain why, you don't stand a hope in hell of getting off.' He shrugs again and it takes all my resolve not to slap him. 'So, what are you going to do now? You can't go home – your dad's taking you to court.'

'I'll stay with mates.'

It occurs to me that I've never seen Jay with friends. Customers, yes, but none of them ever struck me as mates. I wait for him to leave, but when he doesn't, I weaken. It's gone midnight and although Jay can look after himself, I don't want him roaming the streets at this hour.

'Can I drop you somewhere?'

'Nah, I'll walk.'

But he still doesn't budge. Whoever his mates are, he's in no rush to join them.

'Have you eaten anything today?'

'Nah.'

I pull out a ten-pound note from my jeans pocket.

'Take it.'

'No, it's OK.'

'Take it, Jay. Go down to Kebabulous and get yourself a Jemmy Twitcher.' A Jemmy Twitcher – a local speciality that looks like some grotesque offspring of a kebab and a pizza – is the only food known to defeat the appetite of a teenage boy. 'You must be starving.' This time I get a mumbled thanks. 'Take care of yourself, right?'

'Yeah, I will. It's good to see Megan is better.'

'I'm not going to ask how you know that.'

He grins at me. 'I cheered when I heard the guy who hurt her killed hisself. What was he called?'

'Simon Pascoe.'

'Fucking nutter. He was an ambulance man too. He topped

Janie Warren and that lady that lived on the estate, didn't he? I knew Janie. She didn't deserve that.'

'The lady was called Cheryl Black and, no, neither of them deserved it.'

He nods solemnly and looks me in the eye, which takes me aback and I realize how rarely he does this, but he has my attention now.

'If I'd known he was talking to Megan online, Ally, I'd have killed him meself. Honest I would've. I still feel really bad about it. You know, when I heard Meg might not pull through, it choked me right up. I haven't felt like that since my mum died.' I didn't know Jay's mum, Sharon Cox, but Penny did. A nice woman who loved her boy, by all accounts, but no one can compete with a love of heroin, not even your own kid, not once you're in its grip. She died of a drug overdose when Jay was twelve. 'I'm made up Meg's OK.' He looks away. I'm not going to like what's coming next. 'I went to see her in hospital.'

'What?'

'Yeah, I'd wait for you to leave and hang out with her. I made a playlist for her, and we'd listen to it together. It was cool,' he says, smiling at the memory.

I had no idea but thinking back now there were times when I'd walk into Megan's hospital room and her mood would be considerably lighter than when I'd left her. She'd talk excitedly about her plans for when she got out of hospital and I'd listen, enjoying glimpses of the old Megan. I assumed one of the nurses had had a motivational chat with her or that it was just part of her recovery and she was having a better day. It turns out it was all down to Jay Cox. 'Thank you.'

'No probs.'

'Do yourself a favour, stay away from your dad, OK?'

'Will do,' he says, saluting me. 'And thank you for what you did in there.'

'I didn't do anything.'

'Yeah, you did.' He aims a sneer at the police station behind us. 'I'd have gotten a rough ride if it hadn't been for you. That's why I made them call you. I knew you wouldn't take any crap from them. I knew you'd be there for me.'

'Maybe if you kept away from the drug dealing, people would treat you better.'

'I told you. I'm done with all that.'

'Whatever, Jay. Just make sure that tenner goes on a kebab.'

4

I get up the next morning to find Megan is already back from Penny's. She's perched on a stool at the breakfast bar that separates the kitchenette from the living room, chomping through a large bowl of cornflakes.

'How are you this morning?'

'Fine,' she says, her suspicions aroused. When you have a teenage daughter, there's no such thing as an innocent question.

'How did it go with Jay?'

'He's been bailed to appear in court in three weeks.'

'The police charged him?'

'Yes.'

Her spoon clatters against her bowl.

'Why didn't you stop them?'

'It doesn't work like that. I'm an appropriate adult, not his solicitor. He refused one of those. The most I can do is make sure he stays hydrated.'

'It's not fair. His dad totally deserved it. He started it. Why can't the police see that?'

'They didn't have any choice. Repeating "no comment" for two hours didn't give them much to work with.'

'He should have told them the truth.'

'Which is?'

'His dad's new girlfriend took down the only picture of his mum and threw it away. She's half his dad's age too. Cassie Warnock. A right cow. Jay was gutted. He misses his mum loads still. Did you know that he found her?'

'No, I didn't.'

'The needle was still in her arm.'

'Oh God.'

'Yeah. His dad swears blind the drugs never came from him, but Jay doesn't believe him.'

'So why did Jay get into drug dealing if he's seen first-hand the grief it causes?'

'You know what his dad's like.'

'Unfortunately I do. By the way, Jay told me he visited you in hospital.'

Megan blushes. 'I didn't tell you because I knew you'd ban him.'

'That's OK. So are you two . . .' I can barely bring myself to ask, 'an item?'

'No,' she says, irritated that I don't magically know the answer. 'We're just mates. I know you and Penny can't cope with the idea that a boy and girl can be just friends, but we are.'

'He told me last night he doesn't do drugs any more.'

'Yeah, he gave them up for me,' she says casually, scooping a spoonful of cornflakes.

'He did what?'

'He knows I hate all that stuff so when it looked like I was going to die, he stopped because he knew that's what I would have wanted. Hasn't touched them in eight months.'

'So he says.'

She looks at me. 'Why can't you give him a break? He's trying his best. That's a good thing, isn't it?'

Maybe I am being too harsh on him.

'Of course it is. Take no notice of me. I don't meet too many reformed characters in my line of work, but at least he's found himself somewhere else to live.'

'What d'you mean?'

'He said he was staying with mates.'

Megan puts her spoon down. 'Oh, Mum, he's not with mates. He's living up in Bidecombe Woods beyond the rec. In a tent.'

***

The Beatles' 'Hard Day's Night' blares from Penny's soundbar as she pries the lid off the paint tin, wafting chemicals into the cold morning air.

We're painting the fence that runs the perimeter of Seven Hills Lodges as part of a general sprucing up that happens every March in preparation for the holiday season, although this is the first time I've helped out. Until now, I've always been too busy with work. I enjoyed it at first. It was a complete change from being a CSI where people are relying on you to find answers at some of the worst moments in their lives. My only responsibility now is to avoid paint drips, but as time has gone by the attraction has waned.

I've positioned myself so I can keep an eye on Megan who is spending the morning photographing the site. Penny has told her if the photos are good enough she'll put them on the website.

'She seems well,' she says, handing me a paintbrush and nodding at Megan composing an upward shot of the pine trees.

'Well enough to give me a hard time about Jay.'

'What happened?'

'He's been charged with assaulting his dad. He'll appear in court in three weeks. I don't know which is worse, being prosecuted for beating up your dad or living in a tent in Bidecombe Woods.'

Penny shakes her head. 'Really? That's sad. Maybe it's just as well his mum isn't here to see this. She loved her boy and she tried so hard to do the right thing. She'd be heartbroken if she saw him now. If he's not careful, he'll go the same way as she did.'

'I can't help thinking that with a bit of help, he could straighten himself out. Megan says he left home because his dad wanted him to sell drugs but he's trying to get away from all that. Apparently, he's not touched them since she was in hospital, but he's got no chance living in a tent in the woods, has he?'

'You can't save everyone, Ally. Speaking of which, I have some good news.'

'Oh?'

'I've sorted a minder out for Megan tonight, so our double date is back on.'

'What date?'

Penny tuts at my memory lapse.

'You, me, Will and Will's new tenant, remember? I did tell you. Anyway, Emma – Will's sister – said she'll look after Megan.'

'Emma?'

'Yeah. You met her at Christmas when she was home from uni?'

'Right,' I say, vaguely recalling a chatty young girl at a Christmas drinks do at Penny's. It was the first time I met Will too, but he was far more reserved than his younger sister. He'd only been seeing Penny a few months, but already he'd become a fixture in her life. I asked her recently what she liked about him so much and she gave me three reasons: his calmness, his predictability, and his dependability. When you've been stalked by your crazed ex, I guess those are the things you value the most. 'You'll be doing Will a favour. She's just broken up with her long-term boyfriend, Ollie, and he's a bit worried about her. He doesn't like to leave her on her own. She'll be round at six-thirty.'

'I don't know, Penny. Emma's only what? Nineteen? Twenty? What if Megan has another funny turn?'

'She's doing an agricultural degree and she's done loads of health and safety, including first aid, so Megan'll be fine. Problem solved. You shall go to the ball, Cinderella, or the Albion, anyway. It'll do you good. Help you get over all that business with Liam.'

'There's nothing to get over. He asked me out; I said no. I'm not looking for a relationship. Megan's my priority. End of story.'

'If you say so. So, what are you going to wear?'

'What I always wear: jeans and a jumper. Why?'

'Don't you think you should make more of an effort?'

'No.' I grin at her. 'It just raises expectations.'

Penny sighs. 'Something tells me you're not really entering into the spirit of this.'

'I'll play nice, I promise, but I'm not going to get dolled up for a few ciders in the Albion with a bloke I've never met before and am likely to never meet again.'

'Well, I'm pushing the boat out. I've picked up some gorgeous pink feather earrings from the Bidecombe Bazaar.'

'Sounds lovely.'

'I could lend—'

A woman's voice cuts across Penny's.

'Ally Dymond?'

Penny and I both look up from the fence with a start. Standing over us is a woman, early forties, I'd guess. Dressed in a camel-coloured coat, beige palazzo trousers and kitten heels, hair styled into a photo-shoot-ready pixie crop, she looks like she's come straight from a FTSE 100 company AGM, which is why I assume she's lost and wants directions until I remember she knows my name.

'Yes.'

'I'm Detective Inspector Harriet Moore.'

Horror briefly flashes across Penny's face. I know what she's thinking. The police have found us out. But there's no chance of that. If they had, I'd be facing the heavy mob now, not a DI wearing a hopeful smile.

5

Penny turns the music down while I wipe the excess paint off my paintbrush and lay it on a paint tray.

'What can I do for you, DI Moore?'

'Call me Harriet. I'm hoping to enlist you.'

Penny and I exchange glances.

'I'm on compassionate leave.'

'I know and I'm sorry to doorstep you like this.' Her accent is definitely more Brixton, London, than Bidecombe, Devon, and I wonder if she's recently transferred from the 'smoke'. 'But I wanted to run something by you.'

'I don't follow.'

'You might have seen the news reports of the old lady found on Exmoor.'

'No. I can't say I have,' I say truthfully. I've avoided the news these last eight months, but can guess this is the woman Jake was talking about. The woman with someone else's blood on her nightdress.

'Well, we managed to identify her yesterday. A retired community nurse recognized her from the TV appeal and called in.'

'That's good, but I don't see what that's got to do with me.'

'When we went to her address this morning, a farm, we

found the body of a man. Her son, as it happens. He'd been stabbed. So, we now have a murder inquiry on our hands. It'll be all over the news later.'

I wonder briefly if I know the victim, but I doubt it. North Devon stretches for miles and is home to dozens of farms, most of them completely hidden from the world, including criminals, which would be my only reason to visit them.

'And you think this elderly lady did it?'

DI Moore smiles, having snared my attention with the mention of murder.

'Yes, I'm fairly certain she did, not least because she was found covered in his blood and holding the knife that delivered the fatal wound, but fairly certain isn't good enough for me.'

'You've got CSIs. They know what they're doing. You don't need me.'

'You're right, and they're currently at the scene doing a great job, but I've been told you know this area better than anyone, and you spent years on Major Investigations. I'm after your knowledge and your experience.'

'Honestly,' I reply, shaking my head, 'I doubt I can add anything to what you've already got.'

'Maybe, maybe not. Ally, all I'm asking is that you pop up to the farm and take a look around, to see if there's anything that doesn't add up, anything we might have missed. I just want your opinion, that's all.'

'I can't.'

'Just a few minutes of your time, that's all I'm asking.'

'No.'

'OK, but if you change your mind, the address is Narracott Farm.'

'You mean Slaughterhouse Farm? That's not far from here.'

DI Moore sighs at her surroundings. 'What is it with Devon? No one uses the names actually on the map.'

'It's Gabe Narracott's place, but it's always been known as Slaughterhouse Farm. There used to be a slaughterhouse there, but it was pulled down years ago.'

'Gabe Narracott is the murder victim. The old lady is his mother, Miriam Narracott. Did you know them?'

'Not really. The farming community keeps to itself, but I attended a job there about five or six years ago. It was an odd one. Gabe's flock were almost completely wiped out in a dog attack.'

I remember it clearly. CSIs are used to horrific sights, but it's not often we're confronted with a field full of dead and dying sheep, their bellies ripped apart, spilling their unborn lambs. Life over before it even fully began.

'Why was it odd? Sheep attacks must be quite common around here.'

'Not really and when they do happen the owner normally gets their dog under control. You're looking at a couple of deaths at most, but Gabe lost around thirty sheep. It was a massacre.'

'Did we ever find out who did it?'

'There was someone in the frame for it, but they couldn't make it stick.'

'See, this is why I need you on board.'

'I doubt it has anything to do with Gabe's murder, especially if you think Miriam killed him.'

'Did you meet Miriam Narracott when you were there?'

'Briefly, she was too distressed to go into the fields and

I couldn't blame her. It affected all of us, which is why Gabe, me and PC Ingham, the police wildlife officer at the time, went back to the farmhouse where she made us all a cup of tea.'

'What was the relationship like between Gabe and Miriam?'

'Good. They seemed fond of each other. Gabe was very worried about how much it had upset his mum.'

'Any suggestion she was suffering from dementia?'

'No, but I'm really not qualified to say.'

DI Moore smiles. 'Thank you, Ally. I've learned more about the Narracott family in the last five minutes than I have all morning.'

'But you have your killer.'

'Yes, I think I do, but I just like to dot the i's and cross the t's. Is there any chance you'd reconsider? It won't take long.'

'I can't leave my daughter.'

'I understand, but here's my card if you change your mind.'

It would be churlish not to take it, so I slip it into my back pocket without looking at it and watch DI Moore totter back to her car parked a little way down the road.

'What a bloody cheek,' I say when I'm sure she's out of earshot. 'I'm not even at work.'

'I don't know why you're so testy. She was only asking for your opinion. You're returning soon anyway. It'll help you get back into the swing of things,' says Penny.

'I was kicked off Major Investigations, remember? I'm going back to division.'

'You know what I mean.'

'And they weren't interested in my opinion when Megan was attacked last year, were they?'

'No and that DI was put out to pasture as a result. I get

31

the impression DI Moore does things differently. Maybe you should give her a chance.'

She turns the music back up and George Harrison asks me to listen if I want to know a secret. I slap my paintbrush against the fence, channelling my irritation with Penny and her lack of understanding and DI Moore's presumptuousness, but it soon subsides, and my mind turns to the kind but timid lady I met at Narracott Farm all those years ago.

Fragile and nervous, with large brown eyes that seemed fixed with fear, Miriam Narracott reminded me of an injured dormouse. When I tried to make conversation with her, she froze, hoping to make herself invisible, allowing Gabe to step in and answer for her. As he spoke, she smiled at him with a love bordering on adoration. There's no faking that. Miriam worshipped her boy. So, why did she stab her beloved son to death?

6

Lisa Kendrick's dazzling smile greets me from the large poster in the window of her ground-floor office on Bidecombe high street, opposite Kebabulous where Jay hopefully spent my tenner on Ali's famous Jemmy Twitcher.

She's something of a local celebrity in North Devon. Her YouTube channel on youth mental health issues took off some years ago and she now has a regular slot on Moors and Shores FM, our local radio station, which is where I first came across her.

I caught her weekly mid-morning show on my way to the hospital to see Megan and instantly warmed to her soothing voice and thoughtful manner. Everyone told me Megan would need counselling, so I called her that day and Megan's been seeing her regularly since she came out of hospital.

I hoped Megan would forget about going back to school after her seizure at the DIY store, but if anything, it seems to have strengthened her resolve. She clearly sees Lisa as an ally, and she has nagged me to go and see her, so I agreed – not that I'm expecting to change my mind.

Lisa's assistant Fran welcomes me over intercom and the door opens, but before I can step through it a young girl appears in the doorway. It takes me a few moments to register that it's Emma, Will's younger sister, who I met at Christmas and who is looking after Megan whilst I reluctantly go out with Penny, Will and Will's mysterious tenant. Not wanting to embarrass her, I don't say anything, but the young are more open about mental health and therapy and when she sees me her face bursts into a smile.

'Hi, Ally.'

'Hi, Emma.'

'I'm looking forward to hanging out with Megan this evening.'

'Thank you, it's really kind of you to come over, but if you've got better things to do, I'm happy to cancel my night out.'

'Not at all. It'll do me good to get away from the farm. It gets a bit lonely up there on my own, especially when Will's out in the fields.'

'I guess it would.'

'See you later then and don't worry about a thing. I'm first-aid trained. Megan will be as safe as houses with me.'

I watch her disappear into the newsagent's. Penny said she'd just broken up with her boyfriend, Ollie. She must have taken it badly to seek counselling, but I admire her for getting help. Maybe I would have benefited from therapy after Julian, Megan's father, ran out on me when I was two months pregnant with his daughter. Maybe it would have stopped me stumbling into a violent marriage with Sean, a man of few words, but many fists. And maybe it would have stopped me turning Liam down. But it's too late now.

***

Lisa Kendrick slides out from behind a wide desk, extending a long, slender hand that feels oddly dainty in my clumsy grip. Her moon-shaped face, devoid of make-up and framed in an abundance of chestnut curls, gives her an outdoorsy look.

'How are you, Ally?' She speaks to me like we're close friends who haven't seen each other in a while, when in fact we've only ever met once at Megan's first appointment. After that, Megan insisted I wait in the car until she'd finished.

'Fine.' I sit down on a sofa covered in a colourful blanket of crocheted squares. At the other end, curled up asleep, is Lisa's Dachshund, Freud. 'I understand you told Megan she's well enough to go back to school.'

'Yes, I did.' She smiles, seemingly unaware of the annoyance in my voice. 'She's made great progress.'

'Did she tell you about the seizure she had when we were out shopping?'

'No and I'm sorry to hear that. Is she OK?'

'She seems better today. We haven't had a proper diagnosis yet. We're waiting for an appointment with the specialist, but obviously school is out of the question.'

'Not necessarily. Schools are well set up to accommodate children of all needs. If you spoke to them, I'm sure they'd be happy to put a plan in place for her.'

'What if she has another seizure?'

'That's always a risk but keeping her at home isn't going to stop that from happening. And . . .'

'And what?'

'Well . . .' She searches for the right words. 'Maybe a bit of space between the two of you would do you both some good.'

'Sorry, I don't follow.'

'Social interactions are vital at Megan's age. Also . . .' She pauses. Whatever she plans to say next clearly requires careful thought.

'Also, what?'

'The last months have been . . . er very challenging for you as well as Megan.'

'I guess so.'

'You'd already been through the horror of having an abusive ex-husband and then for this to happen to Megan. That's a lot for anyone to process.' I shift uncomfortably in my seat at the mention of Sean.

'I really don't think my ex is relevant to anything. We divorced a very long time ago. This isn't about me. It's about Megan. I think we should focus on her.'

She smiles and nods as if she was expecting me to say this.

'It's actually about you too.' She points to a sliver of a scar on her forehead. 'I'm a survivor as well. Not a husband. A step-dad. Your ex, what happened to Megan – these are traumatic experiences, Ally. I just wonder if you might benefit from some counselling too.'

Me? Counselling? Jesus, where would I even start? But I know when I'm being fobbed off.

'Lisa, is there something you're not telling me about Megan? Something I should know?'

7

It's late morning and the fog has retreated from the town and now lies in wait just outside the harbour, like a sinister presence that we can't seem to shake off. Even the usual sea breeze is more subdued, barely making an impression as I search out a patch of the steps to sit on that aren't streaked with seagull shit.

Towering over me is Cherish, a huge bronze of a serpent coiled tightly around the body of headless woman, compressing the life out of her, which is exactly what Pascoe did to Janie Warren. Poor kid. She was only nineteen. Her life over before it even started. She thought she was running from an abusive boyfriend only to career into the arms of a killer. The same killer who tried to end my daughter's life.

It doesn't escape my notice that I'm sitting in the exact same spot where Pascoe took Janie's life, but if I avoided every crime scene I'd ever attended, I'd never leave the cabin and, right now, that's the last place I want to be. Unsurprisingly, Lisa used client privilege to bat my question about Megan away, but the thought that my daughter tells her therapist things she can't tell me unsettles me. The last time she kept something from me, it almost killed her.

'You look deep in thought?'

'Liam.' I look up, startled by the intrusion.

'Didn't mean to make you jump. I spotted you walking along the quay. I thought I'd come and say hello.'

'It's good to see you.'

'Everything OK?'

'Yes, I'm fine.' It's then that I notice he's wearing a smart blue suit. I've only ever seen him in khaki shorts and shirts that look like paint pots have been spilled on them and his hair is shorter and darker, the sun-bleached ends lopped off, giving him a serious, business-like air. 'What's with the suit?'

'I'm meeting a potential buyer for the Coffee Shack in the Albion.'

The Coffee Shack is a silver, bullet-shaped caravan converted into a mobile café, what the Americans call an Airstream, on Morte Sands, just down the coast from Bidecombe that Liam has run for years, but he's also an ex-cop who hacked a girl's social media account for me so I could get to Pascoe. He doesn't know that because he never asked me why I wanted access to the account and I never told him.

'You're selling up?'

'Yes.'

Liam and his Coffee Shack have been a fixture at Morte Sands for years, but it's more than that. He's been a fixture in my life too, and Megan's.

'What will you do?'

'I'm heading up north, to be nearer to my kids.'

'You're moving away?' I look for something positive to say. 'That's great. I'm sure they'll be pleased to have their dad nearby.'

'Hopefully. How's Megan?'

After Megan left hospital, Liam taught her to surf again, which worked wonders for her rehab. I'd sit and watch them from the rocks, marvelling at his endless patience as Megan regained her mobility and her confidence. She loved hanging out with him. The day she stood up on her surfboard, their whooping reached the dunes.

'She's getting better, thank you.'

'That's great to hear.' He lingers for a few moments as if he has more to say, but thinks better of it. 'I best be off then.'

'Yes.'

As I watch him amble back towards the Albion, I can't help thinking what could have been. I haven't seen him since the night he asked me out. Megan had gone to Bernadette's for tea, and I was sitting on the veranda when he wandered unexpectedly up the path. We shared a cider, he told me he couldn't ignore his feelings for me, and if I felt the same then maybe we could be more than just friends. He'd taken me by surprise. I hadn't realized until then how much time we'd spent together; how easy his company was and how much I looked forward to seeing him and how feelings of friendship had seamlessly tipped into something else, something deeper.

But I still said no. He asked me if it was because I was worried what Megan might think and I said yes, but the fact is Megan adored him and, looking back now, she probably told him I'd be alone that evening. Megan isn't the reason I turned him down.

***

Penny and I are unfashionably early for our double date at the Albion pub on Bidecombe Quay with Will and his new tenant, but it means we've bagged our favourite corner with the wooden divider, sectioning it off from the other drinkers, affording an unusual amount of privacy in a town that has little respect for it.

Penny returns from the bar with a couple of pints of Sam's Cider, which tastes like the apples were pressed yesterday. She's wearing her brand-new pink feather earrings, which would stand out against her abundant greying hair were it not for the stiff competition from the thin plaits threaded with multi-coloured beads and rainbow-striped jumper. Penny nods over her shoulder as she sits down with our drinks.

'They're all talking about the murder up at Slaughterhouse Farm. Someone told Bill that Miriam Narracott was found on the moors, her nightshirt dripping with blood, so they all know she did it.'

I glance at the bar. Bill, the landlord, is regaling several of the regulars with his theories on the crime.

'Isn't Will's farm next door to the Narracotts' place?'

'Yeah. He says the place is crawling with police and journalists. They've already spoken to him, but he didn't see anything. He was with me all night, although apparently they questioned Sammy Narracott for six hours.'

'Who?'

'He's a cousin or something who works on the farm, but Will says he was out with his wife, trying to make up to her.'

'For what?'

'Apparently, he has a wandering eye.'

I laugh. 'There can't be much for the eye to wander over in the fields.'

'Maybe not, but Will says he can't keep it in his trousers.'
She takes a drink. 'So how did you get on with Megan's
counsellor?'

'Not great.'

'Oh?'

'She said Megan was OK to go back to school.'

'That's good, isn't it? Megan must be jumping for joy.'

'Don't say anything, but I told Megan Lisa said she should
stay off school at least until she's seen a specialist.'

OK, it wasn't my finest hour. I hated lying to Megan, but
it was for her own good.

'Why?'

'Aside from the fact she's not well enough, I think there's
something else going on with her. I need to keep her close
until I get to the bottom of it. Actually, I bumped into Will's
sister, Emma, leaving Lisa's. She must be pretty cut up about
this guy to be in therapy.'

'Yeah. Will told me she'd . . .' Penny leans in and lowers
her voice '. . . self-harmed so Will insisted she get counselling.
Said he didn't want her to end up like Caroline.'

'Caroline? His sister? But she died years ago, in a car accident.' I remember. I was at uni at the time. Bernadette told
me she lost control on a bend heading into Bidecombe and
skidded headlong into a tree. She died instantly. I can still
remember Bernadette's scolding voice: *If only the silly girl had
been wearing a seatbelt she'd have survived.* Only Bernadette
would tell off the dead.

'She got her heart broken too.'

Before I have time to ask her any more, dressed in jeans
and a red checked shirt, with ruddy-tanned cheeks that speak

of a life lived outdoors, Penny's boyfriend Will appears at our table. Penny's boyfriend, a phrase I'm still getting used to. After what happened with her ex, Penny swore off men for good until she answered an advert for free manure. When she pulled up at Will's farm, he emerged from the milking shed to the sound of the Beatles' 'Yesterday', his cows' favourite, apparently. His too. Deep in the Devon countryside, Penny had discovered someone as obsessed with the Beatles as she is and the two of them have been inseparable ever since.

'Evening, ladies.' His smile is surprisingly shy for a grown man, but I've come to realize there are two kinds of farmers: jovial or reserved. Will is definitely the second type. 'This is Gavin.'

He steps aside to reveal said Gavin, dressed in baggy beige walking trousers that unzip at the knees to convert to shorts. They have at least six pockets, as has the khaki waistcoat he is wearing. So that makes two of us that didn't make any effort.

'Hi, Gavin,' Penny and I chorus, shuffling along the padded seats to make room for them both.

Penny and Will instantly lose themselves in a private conversation, engineered by Penny, leaving me no choice but to talk to Gavin. *Best behaviour, Ally. You promised.*

'So, what brings you to North Devon?' I ask.

'I'm a financial adviser doing some work locally.' He rolls his eyes. 'Hashtag dull.'

I smile awkwardly. Do I agree with him that his job is dull or not? This is why I hate dating. I say nothing but wait for him to ask me what I do, which is when I quickly learn that Gavin doesn't really understand the concept of dialogue.

'Still, the birds will make up for it.'

'I'm sorry?'

He throws his hands up to ward off some perceived verbal attack that might be coming his way.

'It's OK. I'm not a sexist pig, I'm a twitcher. It's why I've rented a cottage on Will's farm. I'm hoping to see some of the spectacular birdlife you have around here.'

'Lots of early starts to catch the dawn chorus then.'

He grins and takes a glug of his drink.

'Quite the reverse. Can you guess why?'

'No.' I resist adding: 'How could I? I only met you five minutes ago.'

'I'm particularly interested in the nightjar which, as the name suggests, only comes out at night. It flies silently, which makes it very difficult to spot. It has quite a reputation too. Do you know why?'

'Yes, I do.'

I grew up here and on his days off my dad, a keen amateur wildlife photographer, would take me out with him. We'd photograph pretty much anything that moved. Mostly sheep and ponies and occasionally stag and birds including the nightjar, but the idea that I might have prior knowledge of this mysterious creature doesn't register with Gavin.

'Legend has it, it feeds on the milk of goats, directly from the udders,' he continues. 'It belongs to the group, Caprimulgiformes, which literally means goat sucker. Hashtag weird. All nonsense, of course. It actually feeds on the black dor beetle, which also flies at night.'

Hashtag I can't believe I let Penny talk me into this. I catch her eye across the table. Quite rightly, it's full of apologies, but Gavin is in full flight.

'Others see the nightjar as the harbinger of doom. The manifestation of the souls of unbaptized children, roaming across the night sky.'

Honestly, from where I'm sitting it feels more like the harbinger of boredom.

As Gavin continues to detail the habits of the nightjar, my attention is caught by raucous laughter coming from the now crowded bar. Over Gavin's shoulder, I spy what at first I think is a father and his daughter enjoying a lively drink, but as the man turns side-on to speak to the barman, I see that it isn't. It's Tony Cox.

8

Tony Cox is Jay's father, if you could call him that. He's spent more years in prison than he has at his son's side. I'm assuming the slip of a thing next to him is the infamous Cassie Warnock, the girl who chucked out the photo of Jay's mum.

I watch her eyes dance over Tony's face as she sucks at a straw, flicking her waist-long black hair extensions over her shoulder. He laps up the attention, but something doesn't ring true. When he leans forward and whispers in Cassie's ear they both laugh but hers sounds forced, not that he notices. Anger simmers inside me at the sight of them both. Tony Cox is here in the pub pawing at this young girl while his son is freezing his nuts off in the woods.

I volunteer to get the next round and Gavin follows me to the crowded bar. It's lined with drinkers but there's enough space for me to slide in between an old boy nursing a brown ale and Tony Cox's back.

'Just tonic water for me. I just got my purple chip.' He offers up a small medallion around his neck with the words 'Unity, Service, Recovery' written on three sides of a triangle. 'It's taken me five years so I don't want to blow it, although it's tempting. I'm having a really good time,' he says, shouting to make himself heard over the music and the hubbub.

'Good.' I lean over the bar to catch Bill's eye; he's busy down the other end, but I'm not in any hurry. I tilt my head towards Tony's back, catching fragments of his conversation with the girl.

'You've got a beautiful pair.' I can't hear Cassie's response, but Tony laughs loudly. 'I meant eyes, of course. What d'you think I meant? You're a bit of a minx, aren't you?'

For fuck's sake. He makes my skin crawl.

'Actually, make mine an orange juice and lemonade,' shouts Gavin.

'Sure. Just give me a moment.'

It's now or never. I tap Tony on the shoulder. With great reluctance, he hauls himself around. Unlike his son, he's thick-set and broad-jawed with a healthy mop of dark wavy hair and cobalt blue eyes, one of which is ringed in a purple-black bruise, so at least one of Jay's punches landed. Pity it wasn't more.

'Hello, Tony. You might not remember me.' Of course he does. I've faced him enough times in court. 'I'm Ally Dymond. My daughter Megan is friends with your son, Jay.'

'I know who you are. What d'you want? I'm busy.'

'I acted as your son's appropriate adult last night at the police station.'

'Then you know the little shit attacked me. Totally unprovoked, it was. Me and the missus were coming out of the Anchor on the high street, and he flew at me.'

The missus? Give me a break. And unprovoked? I sat in on the police interview with Jay. The police told Jay witnesses

46

had said that Tony goaded him. Told him he was soft in the head. That his mother couldn't keep her legs shut when he was doing time. But showing Tony up to be the arsehole he is isn't going to get me what I want.

'I know and I'm not going to defend what he did, but he's really sorry. He's not had it easy with you being . . . away.'

'That's life, innit? Don't see what it's got to do with you?'

'I wanted to ask you to withdraw your statement.' Tony laughs, which is a cue for his girlfriend to laugh too. Me? I've had a humour bypass. 'Please, Tony. If this goes to court, Jay could go to prison.'

'It'll do him some good. Toughen him up a bit.'

'For Christ's sake. He's your *son*.'

'What son attacks his dad in broad daylight in front of his missus? He was lucky she was there otherwise I'd have given him a right hiding.'

'Withdraw your statement, Tony, and you, Cassie.' I glance at the sulky girl next to him. 'If you do, there's a chance the CPS will drop it.'

Tony looks at me like I'm working some angle he hasn't seen.

'Why d'you care? You've spent most of your time trying to get him banged up.'

'He was really kind to my daughter when she was in hospital.'

'Oh yeah, the kid that got attacked on the trail near Barnston. I heard about that. She was yours, weren't she?' A sly smile crawls across his face. 'Seems you're not really best placed to give parenting advice.'

Nice try, but I'm not biting.

47

'Maybe not, but you and I both know that if Jay ends up in jail, he'll never shake that off.'

'You got a problem with that?' Great, that's all I need, a paid-up member of the 'prison never did me any harm' brigade. 'And who are you?' Tony glares over my shoulder at Gavin who visibly shrinks.

'No one. Just an acquaintance, not even that really.'

'Look, Tony, I'm asking you to do the right thing for Jay. Give him a chance.'

'No one gave me any chances.'

'So don't let history repeat itself.'

'I done all right for myself.' He places his hand on the girl's bare thigh. The salacious look in his eyes is enough to make my stomach heave again. Maybe I imagined it, but I'm sure she flinched and I want to tell Cassie, whoever she is, to get as far away as possible from this man before he drags her down to his level, but I don't. I'm here for Jay and I need to change tack because I'm getting nowhere.

'But Jay isn't you. He doesn't have your . . . inner strength. He won't survive prison.'

Tony nods. 'Yeah, that's true. Takes after his mother. She was soft an' all.'

Christ, he's utterly loathsome.

'So, what do you say? Why not let this one go, just this once? Be the bigger man.'

That thought appeals to him. He's considering it and I think he's about to relent when Cassie tugs at his shirt.

'I'm bored, Tone. Let's go.'

The interruption snaps him out of his momentary flirtation with humanity.

'Yeah, you're right.' He turns back to me. 'You know what? I don't take advice from the pigs, and I definitely don't take advice from people who can't even look after their own kids. So why don't you just piss off back to where you came from?'

'Tony, listen.'

He shoves his face into mine. 'I said leave it,' he snarls, holding me in his stare, daring me to respond. I don't and his lips press themselves into a victor's smile. 'Come on, Cassie. Let's go. There's a nasty smell in this place.'

He pushes past me and Gavin. Cassie slides off the stool and follows him, but not before giving me a defiant look. What is her game? Because whatever is going on between her and Tony, it sure as hell isn't a love match.

9

My run-in with Tony Cox killed off any amorous intentions Gavin may or may not have had because he suddenly remembered he had some important accounting to do and left. It comes to something when I can't even compete with a profit and loss sheet. Ten minutes later, despite Will and Penny's protestations, I left too.

The clatter of my keys on the kitchen counter attracts Emma's attention. She and Megan are on the sofa, watching some reality TV show; a young woman is pressing her ring finger to the corners of her eyes to stop her tears ruining her mascara.

'Did you have a nice time?' asks Emma.

Where do I start? I was set up with the dullest man in England and then almost came to blows with a middle-aged thug.

'It was fine, thanks, Emma. What about you two?'

I look hopefully at Megan, but her gaze is fixed on the muted screen now showing a young man vehemently shaking his head in the face of some accusation or other.

'We had a lovely time, didn't we, Megan?'

Megan nods vaguely, eyes still on the television.

'Nice to have a bit of company nearer my own age. Will hates reality TV.'

'How's things going for you? I'm sorry to hear about you and your boyfriend. Penny told me you'd broken up.'

'Thank you. I'm OK. It just takes time, doesn't it?'

'Yes. It does, but it gets better.'

'Anyway, I should be going.'

'Will said he won't be long. He'll see you back on the farm.'

The door has barely closed behind Emma when Megan finally speaks.

'It'd take a whole lot less time if she didn't keep messaging him. She was texting him all evening, but he didn't reply. He's clearly not interested. It was pathetic. And . . .' Megan points at the TV '. . . she made me watch that crap.'

'I'm sorry you didn't get on.'

'It's not that. She's nice enough. But she's not my friend. My friends are at school. If I still have any.'

When Megan first came out of hospital, they were around all the time, but then school started and with it new classes, new students, new alliances that made Megan feel more and more on the outside until she was a silent spectator in her own home. They sensed it too and their visits drifted off as their lives moved on without her.

'You'll see them soon enough when you're better.'

'I'm better now.' She frowns. 'I don't understand how Lisa could have changed her mind about me going back to school. She said I was fine the other day.'

'It's only for a little while longer. Your appointment came through to see the neurologist early next month.'

'It'll be too late by then. I'll have missed prom and anyway you'll probably find some other reason to keep me here.'

'That's not true. Megan, is there something else going on here? Something you're not telling me?'

She turns back to the screen. 'I just want to go back to school – that's all.'

'I know.'

'No, you don't. You don't know anything.'

She throws the remote onto the sofa and stomps off to her room. She's right. I don't know anything. That's the problem.

**

I could follow her, but it will only make things worse, so I flop onto the sofa with a sigh and pick up the TV remote. On the screen, the boy previously shaking his head is now crying so I switch over and restore the volume. It's local news and full of the murder at Slaughterhouse Farm or Narracott Farm for those recently arrived from London. The report cuts to the farmhouse and I'm about to turn it off when I'm amused to see a very bored-looking PC Bryan Rogers on scene-guarding duty.

The farmhouse, which lies at the end of a short track, hasn't changed at all since I was there a few years ago taking photos of dead and dying sheep. Peeling white paint, slipped roof tiles, a front lawn overgrown and weed-filled – makeovers are the last things on most farmers' minds. The land takes all their time and money, although Slaughterhouse Farm is gloomier than most, squatting in the shadows of a deep, narrow valley.

In the foreground, the reporter tells me that the body of Gabe Narracott was discovered earlier that day after his mother, previously found on the moor, was identified and police and social workers went to the farm to notify her next of kin.

Police believe Gabe was murdered and are appealing for anyone who might have seen anything suspicious. They'll be lucky. Even by Devon standards the farm is remote. The narrow road running in front of it is practically the Narracotts' private drive it's so little used.

The reporter makes no mention of Miriam being found in a nightshirt stained with her son's blood and that she is the only person in the frame for his murder. Instead, he pads out his report with a few more details about the family, stalwarts of the local community who have farmed the area for generations, but my attention is firmly on the muddy white farmhouse.

It's in the style of a Devon longhouse. When it was built it would have housed the family on one side and their prized animals on the other where they could be kept safe and provide additional heat during the bitter moorland winters. But, looking at it now, something doesn't sit right with me. Before I can work out what it is, the film cuts back to the studio so I rewind and press pause on the frozen image of Narracott Farm and that's when I see it. Surely someone else has noticed too; but what if they haven't?

Father

It started when Ms Winters offered her a job. She should have turned it down, but she didn't want to. It was a chance to make something of herself, but the decision wasn't hers. It was her father's, a man she had long since stopped asking anything of for fear of his fists.

'Why are you coming to me with all this nonsense about becoming a teacher when I already told you no? I thought you were a good girl.'

She was a good girl. She barely asked anything of him. Always did as she was told. Never got into trouble, never gave him or her mother a moment's cause to worry, but she wanted this job more than anything she'd ever wanted before. She decided it was worth risking his wrath.

'Ms Winters saw me talking to a little boy who was crying. She said I was a natural. She wants to give me a job.'

Ms Winters ran the Ladybird Nursery where Miriam and her mother cleaned. She radiated glamour in her capri trousers and kitten heels, blonde hair swept up into a beehive, like that actress Audrey Hepburn. Mother said the Ms meant she was one of those bra-burning feminists she'd read about in the *Daily Express*. She'd even kept her maiden name when she married and her husband was likely a doormat, not like her dad. A proper man. Miriam didn't even know Ms Winters had noticed her with the boy until she spoke.

'You're Miriam, Barb's daughter, aren't you?'

'Yes.'

'Didn't you go to the girls' grammar school?' She looked at the cleaning cloth in Miriam's hand. 'Barb said you got all As in your O levels?'

'Yes.'

'Well, you're wasted as a cleaning lady, and you clearly know how to care for an upset child.'

'I have three little sisters. I often look after them.'

'Ah yes, that probably explains it. Well, I have a position for a trainee nursery nurse and it's yours if you want it, Miriam.'

She couldn't believe what she was hearing. Her ambition was to become a secondary school teacher, but her father had scorched that idea. They couldn't afford for her not to be earning, he told her, and anyway there was plenty of work around so why bother wasting years at college. Oh, how she'd wanted to tell him that if he didn't drink so much and visited the bookies less, they'd easily have enough money, but she didn't. Truth or not, insolence resulted in a fat lip. But Ms Winters' offer wasn't going to cost a penny.

'Ms Winters will pay to train me too,' she told her father. 'I'll be qualified in a couple of years.'

'No point. You'll be married with your own babbers by then.'

He had spoken and that was the end of it.

'Maybe we should let her, Harold. It's more money.'

Her mother's intervention shocked Miriam. She never crossed her husband, not where the children were concerned. It was enough to take the punches for herself; she couldn't take them for her kids as well. It had taken courage for her to speak out, probably because they were desperately short of money, but Miriam didn't dare risk the smallest of smiles to show her gratitude. Instead, she held her breath as her father seethed, the voice in his head telling him he couldn't back down now. That's what weak men did, and he wasn't weak. He was in charge, master in his own home, and nobody – least of all his daughter – told him what to do. It was Robbie, her older brother, who saved her, and Miriam wondered if he had been listening in to their conversation all along as he breezed into the room and handed his dad his coat.

'Come on, Pa. First pint's on me.'

Her father hesitated before snatching his coat. 'Nothing good will come of it, mark my words,' he said, slamming the door behind him.

The next day she accepted the job. Miriam loved working with the pre-school children, helping to prepare them for school. She loved their openness and their innocence. She wished she could be like them instead of being so scared of saying the wrong thing that she often said nothing at all, and the things they came out with made her and Rachel, the other nursery worker, crease with laughter.

Rachel was a good sort, but she wasn't like Miriam. She left school with no qualifications and no ambition, but her dad, Councillor Montgomery, was the mayor and Ms Winters took her on as a favour to him. She was quite open about it, as if it was something that happened to everyone, but Miriam didn't resent her for it. She was fun to be around, and she loved the children as much as Miriam. They'd all sit in a line on the floor, pulling pretend oars and singing 'Row Row Row Your Boat' until they lost concentration and collided with each other, collapsing into giggles. Those were the happiest times of her life. If only things could have stayed that way.

Some months later, Ms Winters called her into her office again.

'I'm very impressed with your work. You haven't put a foot wrong since you started.'

Miriam's heart lifted at hearing this. She craved Ms Winters' approval. Over the months, she'd come to idolise this glamorous businesswoman in her matching pink and purple flower brooch and earrings, who seemed so composed, so in control of her life. No man told her what to do – she was sure of that. If only she could be more like her.

'Thank you.'

'And now I have a favour to ask.'

She was confused. People like Ms Winters didn't ask favours from people like Miriam.

'My son needs to pass his maths O level to get into university. I'm looking for a tutor and you have the patience of a saint. I think he'd listen to you, someone nearer his age. I'll pay you, obviously.'

'But I'm not a teacher.'

'No, but you're good at maths and you're good at explaining things – I've seen you with the children – and right now my son needs all the help he can get.'

'Well, if you think I can help.'

'I thought you could teach him after your shift. You can lock up after the last child leaves and meet in the community centre over the road. I've cleared it with the manager, Mr Sykes. Just don't put up with any shenanigans from my son.'

And that is how she met Ralph Foxton.

10

'Megan, come out of your room please.'

My ear is up against her bedroom door, but there's no noise. Perhaps she's still asleep. Lucky for her. I've barely had any myself. After I switched off the news and went to bed, I lay in the darkness, unable to sleep. All I could think of was Lisa telling me I needed to give Megan some space, but how do I do that when I'm sure she's hiding something from me? And the last time I took my eye off my daughter, a fucking serial killer slid into her DMs. My mind churned these thoughts until black skies faded to grey. It wasn't until my usual audience of tall pines outside the window emerged from the darkness that the answer finally came to me.

Megan doesn't respond and I'm about to call her again when her bedroom door opens by a fraction and her face, still puffy from yesterday's tears, appears in the gap.

'What?'

'I have a surprise for you.' I smile. Our idea of what constitutes a surprise rarely tallies these days and the prospect fails to lift her mood, but I'm not going to be fobbed off. 'Come on. I'll show you.'

'OK,' she says, closing her bedroom door.

For a moment I think she's gone back to bed, but she reappears dressed in her grey dressing gown adorned with white stars. Hood up, head down, hands in pockets, she shuffles into the living room behind me. When I stop, she lifts her head and takes a sharp breath. Standing in the middle of the room, a filthy torn sleeping bag gorging white stuffing dangling over his arm, is Jay Cox.

'Jay!' Her hood falls back as she flings her arms around him. 'You OK? I was really worried about you.'

'Wasn't so bad.' He grins. The harsh coastal winds have cracked his lips and his discoloured teeth haven't seen a toothbrush in a while. 'I wouldn't get so close though. I'm minging.'

Megan releases him and steps back.

'Ew, yeah, you stink.' She laughs. 'But what are you doing here?'

Jay looks to me to explain, but I let him do the talking.

'Your mum asked me to come and stay for a bit. Keep you company.'

Megan turns to me. 'Is that right, Mum?'

'Yes. But he took some persuading.' This isn't true. When I spotted Jay outside his tent, he was breakfasting on a can of Dr Pepper. Unsure of what I was about to do, I almost bailed. After all, Jay is a drug dealer. Then I noticed his shoulders shaking in the bitter cold, but as I drew closer, I realized he wasn't shivering. He was crying. Over a photograph. For the first time I wasn't looking at a petty criminal, I was looking at a boy, lost and vulnerable.

I don't know who it was a photo of, but I guessed it was his mum, possibly the photo Cassie threw out. I could also guess that before the drugs supplanted Jay in her affections, this is not the life Sharon Cox imagined for her boy. Maybe Jay did just need a lucky break to get his life straight. Just like the owner of Seven Hills had given Penny. Just like Penny had given Megan and me all those years ago.

A twig snapped underfoot, alerting Jay to my presence. He wiped the snot from his nose with the back of his sleeve, rammed the photo into his jeans' pocket and stood up. When he saw it was me, he was defensive at first, thinking I'd come to gloat. But when I told him I wanted him to come and live with us until he got himself sorted, he couldn't pack his stuff up quickly enough. Not that I'll tell Megan; we all deserve to hang on to some pride.

'Yeah, that's true, but your mum insisted, said you were lonely, and you needed some company.'

He rubs a patch of stubble on his jaw. Elsewhere it's smooth, reminding me he's in that netherworld between boyhood and manhood. Really, he's just a kid.

Megan looks at me. 'How did you find him?'

'With difficulty.' Bidecombe Woods is a hangout for the homeless, the number of tents slowly increasing over the years. I came across a black tarpaulin slung over a low branch to create a makeshift shelter but the black jacket I found inside wasn't Jay's. 'But I tracked him down eventually.'

'How long are you staying?'

'Ally said I could stay until I got myself straight. At least until after my trial, that's if I'm not locked up. She reckons it'll play well with the judge if I've got a proper address.'

'There are a few conditions, of course.'

Megan's eyes perform a playful roll. I haven't seen her this happy in months.

'Of course.'

'Number one, Jay. No smoking inside.'

'I've given up.'

'Number two. Don't lie to me.'

'OK, but I've cut down.'

'Number three.' I waggle my forefinger at Jay. 'No drugs. Of any kind.'

'Easy.'

But I'm not finished. When I told Penny I wanted to take Jay in, she took a lot more persuading than he did. Seven Hills Lodges has a reputation for being a wholesome family holiday experience. Any hint of drugs would destroy its good name in an instant. To say she was reluctant is an understatement, until I told her his presence would allow me to give Megan some space.

'I mean it, Jay. I've gone out on a limb for you. If I get so much as a whiff of weed or anything else, you're out. Got it?'

Jay stands to attention and salutes me. 'Yes, ma'am, you can count on me, ma'am.'

Megan giggles and whilst I'm sorely tempted to tear a couple of strips off him for his cheek, I don't. I let him have his moment. Something tells me Jay Cox hasn't had many of those in his life.

'Good. Just as long as we understand each other. Now, can I suggest you take a bath before you do anything else? I'll put your sleeping bag through the wash too. Megan will make up a bed for you on the sofa in the living room.'

'Jay can sleep in my room.'

'No, he can't.'

She goes to protest but thinks better of it. 'OK.'

I grab the car keys from the kitchen counter. 'There's some cereal in the cupboard, but I'll pop out and get some more food for us all and then I'll take you to your appointment with Lisa, Megan.'

'Why can't Jay take me? It's not far to walk. Then you wouldn't have to rush back.' I look doubtfully at the dishevelled boy before me.

'Don't worry, Ally. She'll be safe with me.'

'OK, but don't go ruining lunch by getting yourself a kebab while you wait.'

He laughs. 'Nah. I only get those at night. Otherwise, I'd see what goes in them.'

'I won't tell Ali you said that.'

I leave them and drive to the supermarket on the outskirts of Bidecombe. It's the first time I've left Megan with anyone other than Penny, Emma or Bernadette, when she's around. She was so pleased to see Jay. I just hope he doesn't let her down.

Out of season, the supermarket is quiet like most of the shops, and it takes me no time to pick up the fixings for a late breakfast for the three of us as well as a few items to make Jay a more fragrant house guest.

As I pull away from my parking space, my mind returns to the news report from the night before. Did anyone on the investigation team see what I saw? It was such a small thing, perhaps they didn't. Christ, if they can miss a serial killer, they can certainly miss this. It may not mean anything of course, but there's only one way to find out for sure.

I reach the car park exit and pause. Left takes me back to Bidecombe and Seven Hills; right takes me away from the town and up towards the moors. Out there, deep in one of its darkest valleys, is Slaughterhouse Farm, where Miriam Narracott murdered her son, Gabe.

I check my watch. Megan will be at counselling for at least an hour. I have time.

11

A tin of tomatoes falls out of my shopping bag and clunks onto the floor as my battered red Volvo bobbles over the cattle grid, signalling I'm in Exmoor National Park. The hedges soon give way to dry-stone walls as I follow the thin grey scar of a road that cuts through it.

A sharp right turn takes me into an even narrower road that curls back down into a valley where the sheltered land is lusher. Another turn and the road, now little more than a lane, suddenly thins and dips, the high banks either side seeming to close in on me, like the moving walls and floors of a horror movie. What light there is dims the deeper I drive into the valley. Finally, just as I think I've taken a wrong turn, I spy the grey slates of a farmhouse above the tall hedges – Slaughterhouse Farm.

After pulling up next to the five-bar gate, I get out of my car, slamming the door behind me. Its echo dissipates, and an eerie silence reasserts itself. There are no chirping birds, no trickling brooks, no rustling hedgerows. It's as if life has abandoned this corner of the world. In a distant field behind the house, a red tractor trailing a plough chugs noiselessly up and down the hillside, carving great black wounds in its wake.

It's too far away to identify the driver, but I'm guessing it's Sammy Narracott, Gabe's cousin, farmhand and – according to Penny – all-round lothario. There might have been a murder, but the land still needs tending to.

Outside the gate leading up to the house, PC Bryan Rogers, the officer I met at Bidecombe DIY Supplies, is still on scene-guarding duty and is as pleased to see me as I am him.

'All right, Dymond,' he says, using the standard Devon greeting that sits somewhere between a question and a statement.

'All right, Bryan. How come you get all the best gigs?'

He shrugs. 'Must be my devastating charm.'

'I bought you this.' I hand him the coffee that I picked up from the burger van parked outside Bidecombe DIY Supplies on my way here.

'You're a star.'

'Forensics finished?'

'Yeah, I'm just waiting for a joiner to come and make it secure. I'll be glad to get going if truth be told. The place is enough to give you the creeps. DI Moore said you might be dropping by.'

'Did she now?'

'Good job too. I've worked with a few CSIs in my time, but none as thorough as you. Nothing escapes those eagle eyes of yours.'

'You telling me I've got beady eyes?'

He laughs.

'Seriously, you can't come back soon enough as far as I'm concerned and not just because we're short-staffed. Jake's good, but he's still wet behind the ears, that one.'

'Speaking of Jake, did you ever follow up on that burglary at Bidecombe Supplies?' I say heading off further talk of me returning to work.

'Yeah. I dropped by the care home but the manager said it wasn't any of his kids as they were on an outward-bound course so there's not really a lot I can do unless the fingerprint you found comes back with something. I'm assuming you want to go in and have a look around then?'

'Er, no. I don't. Thanks. Actually, I just wanted to check something with you.'

'Well, as you can see I'm a bit busy right now.' He chuckles, throwing a glance over his shoulder at the farmhouse. 'But because it's you I'll make an exception.'

'Do you know who was first at the scene?'

'Me as it happens.'

'You do get around, don't you?'

'Sometimes, I think I'm the only one on. God knows where the rest of the shift is half the time.'

'How did you enter the farmhouse?'

'By the front. Just walked in. The victim was in the kitchen, lying on the floor by the back door.'

'You just walked in?'

'Yep.'

'So, the door was open?'

Bryan eases the lid off his coffee and, like all police officers whose taste buds and sensitivity to heat have long been deadened by constantly eating and drinking on the hoof, doesn't hesitate to gulp back the steaming liquid.

'Ah, that's better. Yes, it made me a bit cautious at first. I knew something was up. People don't go around leaving their doors open even in places like this, do they? Anyway, I went in really slowly. The door to the kitchen was open and I could see a body lying by the back door. I'll be honest, I forgot myself at that point and ran over to check for signs of life. I probably touched all sorts of things. Sorry.'

'Don't worry. You wouldn't be the first.' It's why officers at crime scenes automatically have their fingerprints checked against any that are found. 'So what happened next?'

'When I saw he was dead, I got the hell out of there and waited for the cavalry to arrive.'

'How did they enter the building?'

'Everyone went around the back.'

'Did anyone mention anything about the fact that the front door was open?'

'No. Only that it meant that the perpetrator escaped via the front not the back which, if I remember rightly, wasn't locked.'

'So, just to be clear, the front door to the farmhouse was definitely open when you arrived.'

'Wide open.'

Bryan takes another glug of coffee. 'You sure you don't want to take a look around inside? I've never seen so much blood, although your lot are used to that of course.'

'I'm good, thanks. I best be getting off.'

'OK. Thanks for the coffee. And, Dymond?'

'Yes.'

'It's good to have you back. When you turn up, I always feel that we're at least in with a chance of catching the bad guys.'

'Thanks.'

What PC Bryan Rogers doesn't know is that I am the bad guy.

I leave Bryan and stroll back towards my car. Before I get back in, I take a final look at the farmhouse. Do I say something to DI Moore or not? This isn't my crime scene. Christ, I'm not even meant to be at work. But someone needs to know.

'Can I help you?' I look around to see a man, about my age, striding up the lane towards me. 'Are you with the investigation?'

His regulation checked shirt, jeans and green wellingtons tell me he's farmer, but I don't recognize him.

'Sort of. I'm a CSI. Ally Dymond.'

'What do you mean, sort of?' he snaps, ignoring my outstretched hand. 'You either are or you aren't.'

'What I mean is, it's not my crime scene. DI Moore asked me to come up and take a look around. I'm just leaving.'

'You think Mum did it, don't you?'

'Mum?'

'Yes. I'm Kit Narracott. Miriam Narracott is my mother. Gabe is, was, my brother.'

I see it now. He shares the same mass of dark curls as Gabe, but his face is slimmer, his jaw sharper.

'I'm so sorry for your loss.'

But he isn't interested in my sympathy.

'It's a joke. There's no way she would or could have killed Gabe. She's seventy-one, for God's sake, and barely five foot tall. Gabe's over six foot.' I notice his use of 'is'. He can't yet accept the present has ceased to exist for his brother and Gabe is now only his past. 'And while you lot hound my poor old mum, the real killer is still out there.'

I don't tell him it's perfectly possible for a small, elderly lady to kill a large man. I've been here before. In the absence of answers, it's not unusual for the victim's family to direct their ire towards the police when all we're trying to do is get to the truth. Christ, I did it myself when I thought I'd lost Megan. Only in her case, they really did screw it up.

12

As I turn in to Seven Hills Lodges, the sight of Penny painting the perimeter fence sends a dart of guilt through me and I pull over and wind my window down.

'Pen, I'm sorry. I'll be back at it with you later.'

'Good, because Will is useless.' She laughs just as Will rounds the corner of the entrance. 'I've never known anyone take so many tea breaks.'

'Painting is thirsty work,' he says picking up his paintbrush from the tray and flicking paint at her, which she returns in kind. There's a lot more going on here than a bit of DIY, but I've never seen Penny so happy. She's found a good 'un in Will.

'Sorry about last night, Ally.'

'Last night?'

'Gavin and his complete guide to the birds of the British Isles.'

I'd completely forgotten about him. 'No apologies needed. He's harmless enough. Can I ask you something, Will?'

'Sure.'

'I just met Kit Narracott.'

'Gabe Narracott's brother?'

'Yes. Not the nicest encounter I've ever had, but that's not surprising. He's had a shock.'

'We all have,' says Will. 'I still can't believe Miriam killed Gabe.'

'That's what he said. Does he live at the farm too? I went to a job there years ago, but I don't remember seeing him around.'

'No. He left a long time ago to go travelling. He came back and then I think he ended up managing a big estate in South Devon.'

Penny looks at me slyly. 'So where exactly did you bump into this Kit Narracott?'

I hesitate, embarrassed by my U-turn since yesterday. 'I just popped up to Slaughterhouse Farm to check something out and I met him there.'

'Check something out? Does that mean you've changed your mind about helping that DI?'

'No. I just noticed something, that's all.'

'What was it?' asks Will.

'Nothing major. It probably isn't even relevant, but I'll let the investigations team know in case they missed it, and then that's it. Back to painting fences.'

'Great, because Will's just about to get his marching orders – although if he nips to the shops and gets me a packet of Hobnobs, I might keep him on.'

Will throws his brush into the tray. 'Consider it done.'

'Any excuse not to work,' she calls after him as he ambles down the hill towards the corner shop at the bottom.

'You like him a lot, don't you?'

'He'll do. For now,' she says, affecting an air of indifference.

'Give over with your fake disinterest. The two of you are besotted.'

'We are a bit, aren't we?' She grins.

'I'm pleased for you, Pen, and thanks again for letting Jay stay.'

'Just make sure he stays out of trouble.'

'I will. Promise.'

'I mean it, Ally. It doesn't take much to get a bad rep in the holiday business.'

'I know.'

'Lucky for you that boy thinks you walk on water. Wouldn't stop going on about you when they got back from Megan's counselling. Said he's going to prove to you big time that he was straight. Said he always had you down as a massive bitch, but you're actually all right.'

'High praise indeed.' I laugh.

'Yeah, well as long as he understands how much you're doing for him. Which reminds me, I'd prefer it if he didn't invite his friends over.'

'Friends?'

'Yeah, a girl with long black hair turned up a few minutes ago, asking for him. Apparently, Jay had already asked you and you said it was OK for her to come over.'

'Did I now?'

'Ah. I take it you said no such thing.'

'You're right – I didn't.'

'Sorry, I should have realized that and sent her away.'

'Did she give you her name?'

'No, but she had lots of attitude and a face like a smacked arse. I don't know her.'

I do.

***

I park my car in the designated space next to the cabin and retrieve my shopping from the boot. I'm already formulating my lecture to Jay about boundaries when a slight movement catches the corner of my eye. Out of season, deer occasionally wander onto the site, so I pause to see if I can catch further glimpses of our elusive intruder. Instead, through the pine trees, I spy a different kind of intruder wearing jeans and a pink puffer jacket and peering into the window of one of the other cabins.

'Oi! What do you think you're doing?'

My voice carries across the valley and Cassie Warnock turns to look at me. Worried she might make a run for it, I drop the shopping bags and start striding towards her, but she stays exactly where she is and is all smiles.

'I'm looking for Jay.'

'Well, you won't find him in there.'

'Number 27 is where he lives, right?'

'Who told you that?'

'He did.'

'Well, you won't get very far there. That's 72.'

Cassie rolls her eyes at her scattiness. 'I'm shit at numbers. I've got dyslexia.'

'It's dyscalculia when you get your numbers mixed up.'

'So which one is he in?'

'What do you want with Jay, Cassie?'

'I wanna make sure he's OK.'

My mood shifts from irritation to incredulity. 'Are you serious? He beat your boyfriend up, remember?'

'I know and I feel really bad about it,' she says, twisting a long black tendril of artificial hair around her forefinger.

'You've a funny way of showing it.'

'I just want him and Tony to make it up. They shouldn't be fighting.'

'Bit late for that, isn't it? This is going to court.'

'I know, but if I could speak to Jay, make him see sense, I can sort it out between them.'

'Look, this isn't an episode of *EastEnders*. Jay is on bail for assaulting his dad. If Tony wants to fix this, he needs to start by withdrawing his statement. And you, for that matter.'

'He will if Jay says sorry.'

'There's no way Jay is going to do that.'

'Anyway, which one is your cabin?'

'I'm not telling you and I'm also not going to let you see him.'

'Why not?'

'Because you shouldn't be here at all, that's why. You were there when Jay attacked his dad, which makes you a witness.' She doesn't understand the significance of this, and I don't have the will to explain it to her. 'I haven't had breakfast yet and I'm hungry, so you need to leave. Now.'

'You can't make me.'

'Oh, but I can.'

She checks over my shoulder. 'That's Jay there, isn't it?'

Jay is visible through my cabin window although he hasn't seen us.

'I mean it, Cassie. Leave now.'

She matches my stare but then her face relaxes into a smile, as if she's just conceded the contest and this is all a game. Maybe it is to her.

'OK,' she sings. 'Just tell Jay I came by.'

She dawdles towards the exit, so slowly it's laughable and childish and entirely for my benefit. I might have told her to leave, but in her head, it's on her terms. That's OK. I can wait.

***

'You OK, Ally?'

Jay is walking towards me, carrying the shopping.

'I am now. Let's go have breakfast.'

'Great, I'm starving.'

We walk back up towards the cabin.

'Can I ask you a favour, Jay?'

'Sure.'

'I know people know that we live at Seven Hills, but no one knows which cabin number. Because of my job, I'd like to keep it that way, if you don't mind.'

Jay shrugs like it's no big deal. 'Sure. Your secret is safe with me.'

'OK, but I just found your dad's girlfriend wandering around the site. She said that you gave her my address.'

He stops and looks me in the eye. 'Not me. I haven't seen her since I got a kebab with that tenner you gave me.'

He's either lying or someone else told Cassie Warnock where I live.

13

The last time I was at police headquarters it was to do the walk of shame. Not the fun one where you've stopped out all night, but the one where you've blown the whistle on corruption right in the middle of a murder trial and those who haven't been jailed or sacked refuse to work with you.

Detective Inspector Jon Stride didn't have enough evidence to put a murderer away, so he made it up. An approach that found more sympathy than it should have in the Major Investigations Unit. By the time it came out that the accused was innocent, it was too late. I'd already been unceremoniously redeployed to examining shed break-ins in the north of the county.

That day, I'd come to collect my personal belongings – well one, a photo of me and Megan at Morte Sands that I kept on my desk. Today, I'm not even sure why I'm here. It's nothing more than a niggle, but in this game even a niggle can lead somewhere.

Ida, who has been manning the front reception forever, smiles warmly when I stroll into the reception area.

'Ally, lovely to see you back.'

Not everyone finds police corruption acceptable.

She does the paperwork and hands me my badge.

'You know where you're going. Parking's got much worse around here since you left, but there's usually a free space around the back of the dogs section.'

When I texted DI Moore to tell her I thought there was something she ought to know about the crime scene at Slaughterhouse Farm, she insisted I come to the briefing, an unorthodox move given I'm not on the investigation, but as senior investigating officer she can have who she wants at her briefings.

I follow Ida's instructions and am met by a cacophony of barking from a huge aircraft-carrier-sized building as I get out of my car. To my relief, the briefing is in the conference room above the canteen, a little away from both the dogs section and the Major Investigations Centre. The reasons why it's being held here become clear when I get there. The seats around the large oval table are already taken and it's standing room only. Harriet is clearly an SIO who likes to have as much input from as many people as possible at her briefings. I find a space next to a young man in a dark suit who I don't recognize, but we exchange smiles and I prop myself up against the window ledge that runs the length of the room.

Of those faces I recognize, some smile at me, most frown, but I don't know if that's because they're confused by my presence, or they object to it. A man sitting at the table offers me an unreadable stare. Maybe he knew the beloved DI that my testimony sent to jail. I don't know. I've had worse so I shrug it off. I'm here on an invite.

DI Moore sweeps into the room, taking up her place in front of a large white screen. Detectives don't wear a uniform, but navy is often the colour of choice, especially for female detectives, and it's a confident DI who turns up in a pair of mint green trousers and jacket. DI Moore is looking to make her mark.

'Morning, everyone. Thanks for taking time out to come to what I call my general briefing.' There's a rumble of responses. 'The more heads we have on this the better. I know you've all got lots to do, so I won't take up too much of your time.' She looks in my direction. 'I'm sure some of you know Ally Dymond, but for those of you who don't, Ally is a CSI attached to the North Devon Division. She's currently on compassionate leave but she's agreed to come along in an observational capacity, as she lives close to the murder scene and attended a crime at the farm a few years back – sheep rustling. There's a crime I thought only happened in Westerns.' A few people nod, but overall, the response is one of disinterest. I'll take that. 'So, let's see what we've got so far, shall we?' continues DI Moore. 'Can someone drop the blinds? Lights please, Henry.'

Henry turns out to be the young man standing next to me. He flicks the light switch on the wall. Harriet immediately clicks the controller, and a grainy headshot of Gabe Narracott smiling shyly into the camera comes up on the screen. It looks like it's been cropped from a larger photo, probably taken on the farm judging by the fields in the background.

'OK. Our victim is Gabriel Narracott, thirty-five. Home address Narracott Farm, near Upper Farleigh in North Devon, known locally as Slaughterhouse Farm because there used to be a slaughterhouse there, but it was taken down.' DI Moore gives me a knowing smile. 'Anyway, at the time of his murder, Gabe was living at the farm with his mother, Miriam. He also employs a full-time farmhand, his cousin, Sammy Narracott.' This was almost certainly the person I saw driving the tractor in the field yesterday. 'So, what do we know about Gabe's movements on the day of his murder?'

Henry raises a hand. 'According to Sammy Narracott, he and Gabe spent the morning working on the farm. It was Friday so Sammy finished at midday as always, and he and Gabe went for their usual pie and pint at the Stag Inn in the village. As far as he knows, Gabe went back to the farm at 1 p.m. to continue mending a fence. Sammy stayed for another pint and then went home. He lives in the village. We don't know how Gabe spent the rest of the day, but Sammy said he and his mum loved their soaps, especially *Emmerdale*, and they often spent the evening in front of the box. Then sometime around 11 p.m., Gabe was stabbed to death. Our prime and currently only suspect is Miriam Narracott.'

Harriet clicks the controller and Miriam's face appears on the screen. She's wearing a hospital gown. Her hair hangs over her face like damp straw and all life has emptied from her eyes, the face of a mother who just murdered her son.

'At around 11 p.m., Miriam was found by tourists wandering about on Exmoor about a mile from the farm. She was holding a kitchen knife and had blood on her nightshirt.' A slide shows a crumpled nightshirt, reddy-brown patch down one side followed by another with a knife smeared with blood, next to a scale that tells me the blade was 15 centimetres long. 'It's been confirmed that the knife was the murder weapon and the blood on her nightshirt is Gabe's.'

'Sounds like the case is closed. His mum did it,' says a voice from the back.

DI Moore nods. 'Yes, but why? We've no motive as yet. It seems the two of them got on well.'

'What's his mum saying?' says the same voice.

'Still nothing. We're not sure what the issue is. When the ambulance arrived, she apparently asked them where Billy was. We've no idea who this mysterious Billy is and I'd feel a lot happier if we could identify him. Her other son is called Christopher, or Kit for short. He doesn't know who Billy is either. Since then, she hasn't said a word.'

'Dementia?' inquires another person who I don't recognize.

'It would seem to be the obvious answer, but there's nothing in her medical records to suggest she was suffering from this. The doctors are still doing tests.'

'Maybe she's undiagnosed,' says Henry.

'Maybe, but it means we haven't been able to interview her yet. Until we can, I'd like to keep digging. So, what did we get from the crime scene?'

An image of Gabe's body slumped by the back kitchen door, soaked in a pool of blood appears on the screen. Bryan was right – there's a lot of blood.

A hand goes up and it's the first time I notice Jim Dixon is in the room. He was a CSI when I was on the unit. I'm guessing he's now the crime scene manager. He's also one of the many who refused to have anything to do with me after DI Stride's corruption trial. I could forgive the detectives, just, but Jim and I had worked scenes together for years. We've not spoken since.

'Not much from the farmhouse. The kitchen had very few fingerprints.' He hesitates. 'It was surprisingly clean actually. The ones we found belonged to either Gabe or his mother.'

'Too clean? Could it have been wiped down?'

Jim tilts his head from side to side. 'Possibly. Or maybe the Narracotts just kept a very clean house.'

'Anything else?'

'We're still analysing the blood spatter patterns, but what we do know is that he was stabbed first near the fridge but stays upright. He's stabbed there again only this time he goes down. He then manages to get up and make his way towards the back door before he's knifed for the third and final time. The third stab wound is the one that killed him.'

'Sounds like he was trying to get away.'

I picture Gabe clutching his chest, trying to dam the blood, stumbling towards the back door to seek help, but by then it was already too late.

'What about outside?' asks Harriet. 'Any forensics there?'

'We recovered a lot of tyre tracks. We're currently analysing what we've got.' Jim seasons his voice with disappointment. 'But it's a working farm. People come and go all the time. We also recovered a lot of shoeprints. There's a public right of way across the farmyard and out the front that ramblers use all the time. Walking boots, trainers, wellingtons. It's like Clarks out there. You name it, we found it.'

That's the thing with forensics. People assume it's a struggle to recover evidence when mostly we're overwhelmed by it, especially murder scenes where everything is filmed, photographed, cast, lifted or 'bagged'. We're talking multiple haystacks here.

'OK. Thanks, Jim. Keep at it and if anything unusual pops up, let me know. I'm guessing there's no ANPR in the vicinity,' says Harriet.

Henry shakes his head. 'Nothing, boss. The nearest ANPR is ten miles away. Same with CCTV. It just doesn't exist out there.'

'Really? You can't move ten metres in London without being filmed scratching your arse.' The room ripples with laughter. 'What about witnesses?' There's a sea of blank faces. 'I'll take that as a no, then.'

Henry pipes up again. He has 'accelerated promotion scheme' written all over him.

'We've tracked down the people there on farm business. A farmer from up country came by to collect some rare-breed sheep he'd bought. The manager of Bidecombe DIY and Farm Supplies dropped in to discuss an unpaid bill – a Karyn Dwight. They had a thing a while back, apparently. She says it was just a bit of fun and it fizzled out after a few months. Seems like there were no hard feelings on either side. No one saw Miriam. That wasn't unusual. The locals say she was a very quiet lady, kept herself to herself, and rarely left the farm. All the callers said Gabe was his normal upbeat self.'

'OK, apart from this Karyn Dwight, what do we know about Gabe's personal life?'

'He's got a younger brother, like you said.' Henry checks his notes. 'Goes by Kit Narracott. He identified Gabe's body. He works in South Devon as an estates manager. He walked away from the farm some years ago after they fell out over how it was being managed.'

'Sounds like a possible motive to me. At the very least, I'd want my share.'

'Maybe, but his bank account is a lot healthier than his brother's. He lives rent-free on the estate, drives a Range Rover. The guy's loaded.'

'What about their relationship?'

'Seems they got over their disagreement. They weren't close, but they'd go for a pint if they bumped into each other at the markets. That kind of thing.'

'What about the night Gabe was murdered?'

'He was ninety miles away, tucked up in bed with his girl-friend. It was her birthday, so they'd partied hard. Car never left the drive. It all checks out.' He shakes an imaginary glass in his hand. 'He wasn't going anywhere that night.'

The image of Kit Narracott the party guy is a long way from the broken individual I met outside the farmhouse.

'OK. Did our victim have any enemies?'

Henry is on a roll. 'No. Seems he got on with everyone. A bit of a fixture at the local sheep markets, quite an easy-going character. His nearest neighbour, Will Sneddon, lives over a mile away. They didn't socialize, but if they ran into each other, they'd chew the fat, that kind of thing.'

'OK what about this Sammy Narracott? Tell me about him.'

A young woman goes to speak, but Henry cuts across her, earning himself a filthy look.

'Not much to tell. He's helped out since Kit Narracott left. He and Gabe got along well. He was out with his missus that night, celebrating their fourth wedding anniversary with a meal back at the Stag in Upper Farleigh. A bit of a make-up meal, according to the landlady.'

'Oh?'

This time the young woman won't be denied her chance to shine.

'Yeah. It turns out Sammy's a bit of a one with the ladies. His wife found out he was having an affair. She forgave him and decided they should make another go of their marriage.'

Harriet raises an eyebrow.

'She's a better woman than me. OK. What about the victim's girlfriends besides this Karyn Dwight?'

'He wasn't seeing anyone.'

'What about his finances? Any unusual activity?'

'Not really. Not much in the bank, but enough. He took a big hit when he almost lost his entire flock a few years ago, but he seems to have recovered from that. Mr Sneddon said that he'd recently gone in for rare sheep breeds and seemed to be making a good living from those.'

'What about his phone records?'

Harriet glances at a bespectacled young man in jeans standing by the door: digital forensics would be my guess.

'He took a couple of calls from people inquiring about his sheep. That's about it. The landline records show that his brother called from time to time.'

'What about a computer?'

'There was a laptop in the kitchen, but nothing of any note on it. His browsing history was mostly related to farming, machinery, rare breeds, the weather, that kind of thing.'

Harriet nods, taking it all in. 'OK, so does anyone else want to throw anything into the mix?'

Looks are traded and notes rifled through, but no one says anything, and I feel suddenly reluctant to contribute. In among the hard evidence before me, my minor observation is little more than supposition, but the option to keep it to myself ends when I catch Harriet's eye.

'Ally, what do you have?'

All heads turn towards me. I have no choice but to share my theory and hope I'm not laughed out of the room.

'It may be nothing, but I spoke to PC Rogers who was first

on the scene, and he told me that he found the front door wide open.' A few people nod.

'Yes, that's correct. We believe Miriam stabbed Gabe and left through the front door.'

She says this as if it's the most natural thing in the world and, in another world, it is, but not in rural Devon.

'I see that, but farmers rarely use the front doors of their houses and the Narracotts were no exception. This is a working farm. Everyone uses the back door to the property because of all the er . . . mud.' I just about refrain from saying shit. 'No one uses the front door. It's almost just for show. When I went to photograph what was left of Gabe's flock, we walked straight past it and went in through the back. That's the normal way of things here.'

'So what are you saying?'

'What I'm saying is I don't think Miriam would have left the farmhouse through the front door.'

Harriet tosses the remote controller onto the table in front of her.

'So, if it wasn't Miriam, then who the hell was it?'

14

It's only a little after midday, but the vast hill that lurks behind Slaughterhouse Farm has already cast its long shadow and ambushed the valley, trapping the farm in a never-ending twilight. A shiver runs the length of my spine. There's something unnatural about this place. The air is too still, too silent. I tell myself it's because the farmhouse is the scene of a horrific murder, but I've been to dozens of scenes and never felt this unnerved before. Whatever it is, it predates Gabe's demise. I glance at the hillside where a dog butchered Gabe's flock, the sight of their bloodied carcasses and the sound of their plaintive bleating as clear as if it were yesterday. And what of the slaughterhouse the farm is named after? Maybe that amount of death never leaves a place. I shake off the thought and check the road.

When Harriet asked me to go with her to Narracott Farm, I told her I didn't have time, but she insisted she needed my take on things. Henry, also known as Detective Sergeant Henry Whitely, was too busy to accompany her and besides she'd never find the place on her own. She's right there. The complex web of roads, lanes and sheep tracks woven through the moors regularly defeat the savviest of satnavs and there are few reference points. One dry-stone wall looks very much like another, so I relented.

The sight of Harriet's car rounding the corner brings a surprising sense of relief. She pulls up and gets out, her pristine snakeskin court shoes stabbing the thick layer of dark-green dung coating the road.

'Do you ever get used to the smell of cow shit?' she says, wrinkling her nose. 'I never knew there could be so much of it in the world until I moved here.' She tiptoes her way to the back of the car and releases the boot from which she produces a pair of mid-calf pale blue wellingtons decorated with pink roses. 'I know, I know, I'm a massive townie,' she says, catching the look on my face, 'but I wouldn't be seen dead in those horrible black things that come up to your knees.'

'Devon County Police must seem a world away from the Met,' I say, making conversation as we stroll up to the front door.

'To be honest, crime is crime. The biggest thing is the lack of resources. I reckon the Met's coffee budget is bigger than what I'm expected to work with here. Still, we can only do what we can do, eh?'

We approach the farmhouse, now boarded up, releasing PC Bryan Rogers from the tedium of scene guarding. Harriet unlocks the plywood outer door, opens the front door and lets us both in. She surveys the entrance.

'So, you're saying farmers don't use their front doors?'

'Not as a rule. They use the back because it takes them straight into the kitchen, so they don't traipse shit through the house. Like you said, there's a lot of it around.'

'Makes sense. And they keep the front door locked at all times?'

'Yes. They're out on the farm all day. Anyone could walk in.'

'Couldn't they just walk around the back?'

'They could, but you'd risk coming across a farm dog or two.'

'I see.'

She looks up at a large hook, almost level with the top of the door.

'I'm guessing that's where they kept the front door key. Miriam can't be more than five-two. There's no way she could have reached it without a chair. Assuming it was locked in the first place, which we don't know for sure, why would she kill her son and then carry a chair to unlock the front door, then put the chair back before she left?'

'I don't know.'

At the back the kitchen runs the entire width of the farm-house. On one side is a standard-issue Aga, a jumble of units and, in the centre, a large oak table. On the other is a tattered cream sofa covered in a crocheted throw and an armchair positioned either side of a wood burner. The heart of the home. Or it was. Now it's a murder scene.

Staying put, I take a long slow breath and scan the room. Two-dimensional murder scene photos never do justice to the sheer quantity of blood spilled. It's something that still shocks me. That and the smell, a distinctive metallic odour, not too dissimilar to rust, such an innocuous comparison, but to me it means only thing only: a bloody death.

Like everyone, I'm initially overwhelmed by the horror of it all. The grisly pictogram of a person's violent last moments and the cross trail of teardrop bloodstains with their elongated streaks make no sense at all. Only when that feeling passes can I begin to tease out patterns that point to behaviour and work out what might have happened. And it's always a might. Blood spatters can only give us a few chapters. Only Gabe and Miriam will ever know the full story and one of them is dead, the other mute.

I push aside what has taken place to concentrate on its aftermath.

'Gabe's body was found just about there.' Harriet points to a thick pool of congealed blood on the floor by the back door.

On the wall next to the door, Gabe's blood has trickled down its surface in parallel lines, known as a spine. For a brief second, it reminds me of the graffitied 'bitch' on the wall at Bidecombe Supplies. Only this isn't paint, it's blood, caused when a major artery is severed and the still-pumping heart forces the blood to gush or spurt from the wound, creating a new pattern each time.

'He bled out,' says Harriet. 'Even if Miriam had called an ambulance, he didn't stand a chance.'

I nod, only half listening. Above the arterial spurt is another spatter. This one is also linear, but much smaller, a cast-off pattern made by the knife. It suggests the perpetrator flicked the knife upwards as they pulled it out of Gabe's chest. There's another cast-off pattern on the side of the kitchen unit. This time it looks like the knife has been pulled out downwards. Knives don't always produce cast-off patterns and the most it can tell me is the minimum number of blows the victim received, not the maximum.

'Gabe was stabbed the first time by the fridge. The knife block on the side housed the murder weapon,' says Harriet.

I track the blood patterns from the fridge to the back door.

On the floor near the fridge there are round drops of blood: passive bloodstains that dripped straight down from an object or a person.

'So, after he was knifed the first time, he just stood still? He didn't try to escape?'

'Maybe it was the shock of being attacked by his mother.'

I point to some other passive bloodstains and hand smears on a kitchen cabinet a little further away. 'These drips are larger. So, I'm guessing he's stabbed again, but this time, he goes down.'

'Yes.'

'And he's there for a little while.'

'Seems so.'

'Then he finally gets up and this time he tries to make it to the back door where he's stabbed for a final time, but with greater force.'

'Yes. We think that Miriam thought she'd done enough with the first two stabbings and then when Gabe got up, she really went for him to make sure she finished the job.'

'That makes sense.' I cast an eye around. 'I don't see any void marks.'

In CSI land, what's not there is as important as what is. Void marks are gaps in the blood patterns. Sometimes they indicate something has been moved after the killing. Or someone, meaning there was more than one person present.

'That's because there aren't any. Miriam was alone when she stabbed her son and went walkabout.'

'What are these marks here?' I say, pointing to some streaks on the ground a little distance away from the kitchen counter.

'We think she dropped the knife after the second stabbing,

believing she'd done enough; then when Gabe got up again, she picked it up.'

I'm by the back window examining the white frame. It sheens with silver that pales into small rectangles where the CSI has lifted a fingerprint with fingerprint tape. Every conceivable surface in the room is covered in a layer of aluminium powder, but few marks have been 'lifted'.

'Jim's right. This is clean. I'd have expected there to have been a lot more prints even if they all belonged to Gabe.'

'Yeah, that's an odd one.'

'Any sign of forced entry?'

'None. If it's not Miriam, and that's a very big if, then Gabe let his killer into the house and then, it seems, let them stab him to death.'

***

Harriet draws the lapels of her camel coat around her neck in a wasted attempt to ward off the damp and cold. We are standing in a field a little way from the farmhouse, having navigated a barbed wire fence.

'Remind me again what we're doing here.'

'If mistakes are made, they're often away from the crime scene. Perpetrators relax and that's when they get careless.'

Harriet nods. 'That's assuming our perp isn't Miriam.'

'Yes, assuming that.'

Harriet surveys her surroundings. While we were in the farmhouse a mist has capped the peaks and is seeping down hillside.

'It's all a bit too *Wuthering Heights* for me.' She shudders.

'I couldn't live anywhere as remote as this. I only agreed to move here on the condition that we live in Exeter. If I'm more than twenty metres from a shop, I come out in hives. You know the first night here, I didn't sleep a wink. Too quiet.'

'So why did you move here?'

'My worst half comes from Devon, and he got a headship at a school in Exeter. Plus we've got three kids. Trying to keep tabs on them when we both have demanding jobs was impossible in London. When they're little you know exactly where they are, but when they're teenagers, my God, it's a nightmare. I thought about jacking it in, doing the mum thing full-time, but that's not me. Just the way we're made, isn't it? I was off for six months with a broken leg once. The kids said I was unbearable and if I didn't go back to work, they'd put themselves up for adoption. So, anyway, when Andrew got the job in the school, I put my transfer papers in. I reckon I doubled the force's diversity figures overnight. I'll be coming to a police recruitment poster near you soon, no doubt.'

'Yeah. We're not great on diversity. We're trying though.'

'I think they were hoping I'd have a nice Indian name too, but no can do. I'm a proud Anglo-Indian. First name Harriet, second name: Moore. That's the way we roll. So, here I am, standing in a field literally up to my eyeballs in shit.' She runs her hand down her coat sleeve. 'And how come my coat is wet when it's not even raining?'

'Welcome to Devon.' I shrug.

Harriet grins. 'Sorry. Didn't mean to rant. I'll grow to love it, I'm sure. So, Miss Local, what can you tell me about this place?'

'Well, one side of the farm borders Exmoor, which is where

Miriam was found, and on the other side is Sneddon's Farm, owned and run by Will Sneddon. The road in front of the farmhouse is a back road to Upper Farleigh. There's a row of houses a bit further along, which are converted farm workers' cottages. The only people using the road are those who live around here, but that's not many. The road joins another road, which then feeds the main road to Bidecombe. There's not much on it other than the Heale retail park, which has Bidecombe DIY and Farm Supplies and a few other units on it.'

'Yeah, I'm beginning to learn retail park down here doesn't have quite the same exciting ring to it that it does in London. Bidecombe Supplies? Isn't that the shop Gabe's ex-girlfriend Karyn Dwight runs?'

'Yes, it is. Most farmers have an account there. I'm guessing that's how they met.'

Harriet nods. 'So, from what you're saying, Narracott Farm isn't the kind of place you stumble across?'

'Not really. It's deep in the valley. You'd have to know it was there. Unless you're a rambler. The area's popular with walkers.'

'Miriam was found on the B1583. What direction is that?'

I point behind the farmhouse. 'It's just over the hill, about a mile and half away.'

'So, in the middle of the night this old lady walks a mile barefoot, in a nightdress, holding a kitchen knife. Poor dear.'

'But this poor dear had just killed her son. Only . . .'

'Only what?'

'The route to the road is quite straightforward if you leave the farmhouse by the back. You just cross the farmyard and take the gate next to the big barn and it goes straight up and over the hill. By coming out of the front door, Miriam would have had to walk along the road, go through that gate, cross a stream and then go up the hill.'

'So, now you're saying she didn't leave by the front door?'

'No, I'm just saying it's more complicated.'

Harriet shrugs. 'She's old and possibly senile. Maybe she got confused.'

I don't say anything.

'That's starting to sound like an excuse, isn't it? OK, tell me straight. Do you think Miriam killed her son?'

'I don't know, but every question seems to have a convenient answer. I don't like convenience.'

'Neither do I.'

'Did the CSI team examine that?' I point at a barn in a dip between fields, and invisible from the farm.

'I don't think so.'

To my surprise, a figure emerges from the side of the building. They're too far away to make out and if it hadn't been for their bright yellow jacket, I'd have assumed they were a farm animal of some sort.

'Hang on. There's someone over there.'

'So there is. Oi! You! Stay right where you are.'

Despite her petite frame, Harriet's voice packs a punch, echoing around the valley, startling a few sheep as well as attracting the attention of the figure who turns to face us, pauses for a moment, and then bolts in the opposite direction towards the woods.

'Shit. They're doing a runner.'

Giving chase is a reflex action for cops and Harriet immediately breaks into a run, but I'm a CSI and it takes me a few seconds to decide I may as well join her. I'm guessing this is the first time she's ever run in a pair of wellingtons because I quickly overtake her, but by the time I reach the barn, the person has already been swallowed up by the woods and they're nowhere to be seen. Harriet arrives behind me, gasping for breath. She leans against the barn door, wincing at the tightness in her lungs.

'What the hell was that all about?'

'No idea.'

'Did you get a good look at them?'

'No.'

'Me neither. Maybe it was Sammy Narracott, the farmhand,' she says, inspecting the green-tinged mud on the sole of one of her boots with some distaste.

'I'm not sure why he'd be wearing a yellow coat. Farmers' overalls tend to be green and why would he run away?'

'Perhaps it was this mysterious Billy who Miriam was talking about when those tourists found her in the road.'

'Well, whoever it is, they've gone now. Shall we see why they were so interested in the barn?'

Inside, the haybarn is like every other: farm equipment stored on the ground floor and hay bales in the loft above it. Harriet takes one look at a wooden ladder and begins to scale it. For someone so immaculately turned out, she's surprisingly happy to get her hands dirty. Two rungs from the top, she takes a pen from her inside jacket pocket, and prods the hay before hooking something.

'Looks like we'll have to get forensics back out here again,' she calls down to me.

'Why?'

She holds her pen up. Dangling off the end is a used condom.

15

Whitebeam House is a large stone building tucked away in its own grounds on the other side of the woods. Once the pride of some local gentry, death duties forced its sale decades ago when it was bought by a charity and turned into a children's care home, which it has been ever since. I told Harriet about the place after she found the condom and began to muse that having sex in a barn felt a bit 'teenage'.

Geoff opens the door to us and immediately smiles at me. 'Ally, hello, how are you?' He looks at Harriet. He knows a cop when he sees one, even ones dressed to the nines, and his thick, grey-flecked brows mould themselves into a frown. 'We didn't call you, did we?'

Geoff and I go back a long way for all the wrong reasons. Over the years, I've been called to the home a few times, usually when Geoff's patience has run out and he no longer feels he can or should protect a particular child from the law.

'No. We're just here for a chat. This is Detective Inspector Harriet Moore.'

'Detective inspector?' He rubs his thick grey beard. He knows enough about policing to know the higher the rank, the more serious the crime. 'What's going on, Ally? Is it to do with the break-in at the DIY place? The police officer has already spoken to me about it.'

Harriet offers Geoff her hand, which he takes warily.

'It's nothing to worry about, just routine inquiries.'

He doesn't believe her. Nothing is routine in the life of a children's care home manager and just to prove the point, a child pushes past him and runs towards a large oak tree on the edge of the car park, closely followed by a harassed young woman in green dungarees.

'Keifer, come back, let's talk about this.'

As Keifer passes Harriet's car, he thumps the driver's door. Geoff apologizes but she shrugs it off.

'Don't sweat it. I've got teenagers. Been there, done that, paid for the respray. Now, is there somewhere more private we could talk?'

'You'd better come to my office.'

Geoff leads us down a long corridor, the walls of which are adorned with photos. Geoff is a keen photographer, not just of the children, but also the surrounding area. If Harriet wasn't with me, we'd doubtless be discussing the merits of the latest telephoto lenses. Whitebeam is his personal gallery. Misty shots of stags on Exmoor, interspersed with photos of the children past and present, some smiling, some sullen, cajoled into neat rows, alongside framed letters from grateful employers praising the politeness and work ethic of youngsters who have left the care home and gone on to work for them. In the distance, children are laughing and shouting against the canteen din of cutlery clanging against plates. Many of these children have witnessed terrible things in their short lives, but all I hear is hope. Whatever Geoff does, it works.

We take a seat in his office.

'Right.' He clasps his hands on the desk in front of him, ready for an onslaught of accusations. 'What is it you think they've done this time?'

'You've probably heard about the murder at Narracott Farm a few days ago. We're just following up on a few things,' says Harriet.

'You don't seriously believe one of my kids is involved, do you?'

'Not at all. I was thinking more in terms of potential witnesses. Do the children ever stray onto the farm's property?'

'They're care home kids. Most of them don't know the meaning of boundaries, but they've had a tough time and, sometimes, you know, they need a bit of space; so, yes, they probably do go onto the Narracotts' land. They also hang out at Bidecombe Woods.'

I frown, not understanding the appeal of Bidecombe Woods, given it's a good few miles from here and there are other woods nearer to the home.

'It's a dead spot,' Geoff obliges. 'You can't get a phone signal there so they know we can't get hold of them, but they're just being kids. I don't see what that's got to do with this murder. I heard it was the mother.'

'We're just ruling everything out. There's evidence of sexual activity in a barn on Narracott Farm. Could it be possible that some of your older children are using it as a place to meet to have sex?'

Geoff's gaze switches between the two of us. We're all thinking the same thing. The kids at the children's care home leave at sixteen so if they're having sex, they're underage and they're breaking the law.

'Geoff, I'm not interested in prosecuting anyone for unlawful sexual intercourse; I'm only interested in the truth,' says Harriet.

'I knew Lee and Madison were up to something,' he huffs. 'They kept telling me they were going for walks. Walks my arse. They must have been nipping off to this barn.'

'Ah, so you know who's doing this?'

'Yes, I followed them one day, but they must have clocked me because they just did a circuit and came back to the house.'

'Can I talk to them? Just an informal chat?'

He hesitates for a moment.

'As long as I remain present.'

'Of course. Ally, are you OK to wait outside?'

'Sure.'

Geoff makes a call and a few minutes later a couple of surly teenagers traipse past me in the corridor. Madison is much bigger than Lee, who looks too young to be capable of any sexual act. But looks can be deceiving.

To fill the time, I scrutinize the photos on the wall, searching for a certain PC Bryan Rogers who had spent time here as a youngster. From flares to skinny jeans, the passing fashions of the children indicate the home has been here for a good forty years. Geoff has been here for at least half that time. I remember playing hockey against Whitebeam when I was at school and Geoff refereed.

I don't find Bryan, but one face in a photo of a group of about twenty children, taken several years ago, catches my eye. It belongs to a young girl, and I wouldn't have noticed her had she not turned her head away from the camera towards the boy next to her. They're grinning at each other like they've just shared a joke. She looks around fifteen; her face is rounder and her hair shorter and light brown, not black, but it's definitely Cassie Warnock, Tony Cox's girlfriend. There's a lightness about her, an openness, an innocence, I guess, that's at odds with the girl I saw in the pub and near my cabin. That girl was closed off and hostile. What ever happened to her to make her like that?

I move closer to the photo. There's something in the way she is looking at the boy that tells me they were more than just friends. She doesn't look at Tony Cox like that.

16

Harriet emerges from her meeting with Geoff, and Lee and Madison.

'Well, that's cleared that up.'

'They confessed then?'

'Yep, rather pleased with themselves too.'

'Were they there at the time of the murder?'

'No such luck. In fact, they're adamant they haven't used it in a while.'

'So, who was it that we saw just now?'

'No idea. Anyway, I'll send a CSI down to the barn to bag everything and get it tested. I don't know how we missed it the first time around, but I'm not sure it gets us anywhere anyway. I hear what you're saying about the front door, but other than Miriam, we have no other suspects and it's highly unlikely that a complete stranger walked in, killed Gabe and framed his mother.'

'That's true.'

'You know what? If it walks like a duck, quacks like a duck, maybe it is a duck.'

'You're probably right. Anyway, I ought to get going.'

'Of course.' Harriet gets back into her car and winds the

window down. 'Thank you for your time today – you've been invaluable. Can I beg one more favour off you?'

Somehow, I don't think it will make any difference if I say no. Harriet is the kind of person who seems to get her own way, one way or another.

'What is it?'

'I'd like you to look at the forensics on this for a second opinion.'

'I thought you decided Miriam did it.'

'I have, but I'm seeing a few loose threads here and I'd like your input. If you could just run your eye over the crime scene evidence from the comfort of your own home, I'd be really grateful.'

Unsurprisingly, her request raises an eyebrow. This isn't my case. There's no legitimate reason for me to have access to this information. Harriet knows this.

'I'm the SIO. This is my call and I want you in on this.'

'OK.'

'Thanks. I'll sort out access for you.'

'Can I ask you a question?'

'Sure.'

'Why me? You've got your own CSIs working on this.'

'Because you know the area better than anyone on Major Investigations.'

'You didn't call me in just because I know North Devon.'

She lets go of the sigh of knowing when you've been had. 'No, I didn't. I've not been here five minutes. It takes time to get to know a new team, to know who to . . . trust. You blew the whistle on corruption. That takes guts. I figured if I could trust anyone it would be you. Plus . . .'

'Plus what?'

'The force screwed up the investigation into your daughter's attacker but still disciplined you over some of the methods you used to prove Simon Pascoe attacked Megan and killed those other women. If I were you, I'd be seriously pissed off and I'd definitely be thinking twice about coming back, but we need you, and I get the impression you need us.'

'What do you mean?'

'Painting fences is the perfect job for a lot of people, but not you, Ally. I saw you in the briefing today. It's where you belong. It's who you are. If they cut you in half, they'd find CSI running right through you. I know you're not on Major Investigations any more, but I thought if I brought you in, I could show you things have changed in case you had reservations about returning.'

Reservations. That's one word for it.

My phone rings. I take it out of my pocket. It's Lisa Kendrick, Megan's counsellor. 'I need to get this.'

'Sure.'

She winds her window up and drives away.

'Lisa, what is it? Has something happened to Megan?'

'No, not at all. Megan's doing really well. Nothing to worry about.' Which means there almost certainly is. 'I was wondering if you could stop by my office this afternoon.'

'Sure. Can you tell me what this is about?'

'I'd rather not say. It's a little sensitive. It's probably best that you don't mention this to Megan.'

***

Fran, Lisa's assistant, guides me into her boss's office. Lisa is seated behind her desk but emerges to give me a warm handshake and a dazzling smile. Freud is curled up on a blanket at her feet.

'Ally, thank you for coming in at such short notice.'

We move to the sofa, but this time Lisa sits next to me, and I wonder just how bad this is going to be.

'I've been thinking about our conversation the other day,' she says without breaking her smile.

But there's something she needs to know first.

'I should tell you that I lied to Megan. I told her that you said that she wasn't well enough to go back to school.'

'I know and, in hindsight, I think you made the right call.'

'Really?'

'Yes. She has a lot going on. I think she should stay off school for a little while longer, at least until you have a diagnosis.'

'OK. Thank you.' I feel vindicated, but I can't help feeling there's more to come.

'I also understand that you've taken in a young lad.'

'Jay. Yes. He's a friend of Megan's. I'm just helping him out. He doesn't get on with his dad.'

'So I hear. He's had quite an impact on her mood.'

'Yes, he has. She's much happier when he's around and it's allowed me to put some space between us whilst keeping an eye on her.'

'That's good.' She nods. 'Hopefully, he'll also distract her from . . .'

'From what?'

Freud hauls himself from his basket and ambles towards Lisa, his elongated body swaying slightly. He sniffs at her feet, and she bends down and strokes his silky coat. When she looks up, her smile has slipped.

'I've agonized over whether I should tell you this or not, Ally, because I have to respect Megan's right to privacy, unless I think her personal safety is at risk.'

'Her safety? Oh God. What has she been up to?' A screenshot of Pascoe and Megan's online conversation flashes before me. 'She hasn't been talking to strangers on the internet, has she?'

'No, I don't think so.'

'Then what is it?'

'Has Megan ever spoken to you about her dad?'

'Sean?'

'Not your ex-husband, no, her biological father.'

'Julian? She's never met him. He walked out when I was a couple of months pregnant. I haven't seen him since. I reached out a couple of times when Megan was little to see if he wanted a relationship with her, but he wasn't interested.'

'What have you told her about him?'

'Not much, but who her real father is has never been a secret. If she'd asked about him, I'd have told her, but she never has.'

Lisa nods like I've said something significant, like I've given something away, but I've no idea what.

'Could that be because she doesn't want to upset you?'

'Why would it upset me? It's all in the past. I got over Julian a long time ago.'

'She may still feel she's being disloyal.'

'Disloyal? Lisa, what's this all about?'

'The thing is . . .' She lifts Freud up and places him on the sofa between us. Instinctively, I run a hand down his sleek back. I know this is a deliberate tactic. Stroking animals has a calming effect. I'm not going to like what's coming next. 'Megan is talking about getting in touch with her father. Her real father. Julian. For all I know, she might already have contacted him.'

***

When I walk into the cabin, Megan and Jay are sitting on the sofa watching television. Megan cranes her neck at the sound of my keys against the kitchen counter and waves at me.

'Did you catch the baddies?' She laughs.

Jay grins in my direction. ''Course she did. Your mum's a badass CSI.'

I don't feel very badass, but I play along anyway. 'Too right, Jay Cox, and don't you ever forget it.'

He salutes me. 'No, ma'am.'

'And thank you for clearing up. I take it you're responsible for doing the dishes.'

'No probs.'

I collect my laptop from the breakfast bar. It wouldn't feel right to do this in front of Megan. Weirdly, I think she might sense what I'm up to and then all hell would break loose.

'You guys OK if I leave you to it? There's something I need to do.'

'Paperwork, right?' says Jay. 'Cops always have lots of paperwork.'

'A fair amount of it caused by you, my friend.'

Megan scowls. 'Mum!'

'It's a joke.'

'It's okay, Meg, your mum just called me her friend. I'll take that.' He laughs. 'Anyway, I'm one of the good guys now, Ally. You'll see.'

I take myself off to my bedroom and make myself comfortable on my bed. Opening my laptop, I go into my mail. An email from Harriet. My hand hovers over it. She's right. I did get a buzz working with her today but investigating the murder of Gabe Narracott is not on my to-do list, which is currently occupied by Megan's fixation with Julian.

There aren't many Julian Winstanley-Joneses in the world, and it takes just a few clicks to discover the Facebook page of the man who loved me, but only on his terms, which didn't include a clause about standing by me in the event of an unplanned pregnancy. When I told Julian I was two months gone, he assumed I'd get an abortion and even offered to pay for it. Certain it was shock talking and he'd come round, because stupid me believed him when he said he wanted to spend the rest of his life with me, I said no. But it wasn't shock. He just wasn't ready for the responsibility, so I decided to go it alone.

It was a terrifying time not least because Bernadette's response was to throw me out and pretend I didn't exist. The council saved me from homelessness, housing me in a flat, stippled with black mould and reeking of tobacco, but it was better than being on the streets. I won't lie, there were times when I wondered if I'd made the right decision – maybe there were even times when I regretted keeping my baby – but as soon as Megan was born, I knew I'd made the right choice for me. Having been adopted myself, giving her away once she had entered this world was never an option. Since then

I've come to realize she's often been the only good thing in my life.

I click on Julian's profile picture and allow myself a shiver of *schadenfreude* at his near bald pate. The thick clump of hair that would hang over his eyes was his most prized possession and he'd spend hours teasing it into place with gel. What's left is wisely cut short, accentuating the angularity of his features, which could err on the skeletal were they not softened by full lips and a boyish grin radiating confidence. He's as attractive as he ever was.

Megan looks like him. Of course she does, because she doesn't have my dark hair or Mediterranean skin. The pale red hair, the hazel eyes, even the freckles – they're all Julian's. There's no such thing as a single parent no matter how much I wanted to forget Julian ever existed.

I scroll through his feed, and what a life he is having. So different from mine. After uni, he went to work in the City, the fruits of which appear to be a house in West London and a thatched cottage in Cornwall. He has a wife too, who shares his sharp cheekbones, but hers are framed by loose, large curls that suggest weekly blow-drys in a local salon. And he has two young boys. Megan's half-brothers. That thought hits me hard. Megan has siblings. She shares half of her DNA with them, and there's a look of her in both of them.

As I scroll Julian's gallery of grinning family selfies in various locations around the globe, I find myself wondering if Megan has already found him. Julian's name isn't on her birth certificate, but I've never hidden it from her. She probably doesn't know his surname, but she knows he was in the year above me at my college in Oxford. It wouldn't be difficult to track him down. What if she's already contacted him? What if he rejects her? He didn't want to know her when she was a baby; why would he want to know her now? Lisa advised me to wait until Megan came to me, but I don't know if I can stand by and watch Julian destroy her, like he destroyed me.

17

The reception at Seven Hills Lodges is really just a converted living room, occupying the front half of Penny's house, facing the entrance to the site. As I walk past, I glance through the large window. She's smiling at someone, but they have their back to me.

Penny called to tell me there was someone in reception for me. Firmly wedged down the luxurious rabbit hole of Julian's perfect life, I was grateful for the interruption. I was sure I detected amusement in her voice, so I'm assuming my visitor is Gavin and Penny has decided I need to give it another go. God save me from friends in couples who believe I need to be in one too.

The bell above the reception door jangles, announcing my arrival, and immediately attracting the attention of the person standing by the counter. It isn't Gavin.

'Mr Narracott.'

'I hope you don't mind me dropping in on you like this. DI Moore told me where you lived.' He speaks quickly, and I realize he's nervous. 'I-I wanted to apologize for my rudeness the other day. And it's Kit.'

'That's OK. You're going through a terrible time.'

'Still, it's no excuse when you're only doing your job. I should be thanking you, not making things harder for you.'

'There's really no need.'

'I think there is. DI Moore said you'd come back early from compassionate leave to help out with the investigation and that you'd introduced a new line of inquiry.'

He says this like it lets his mother off the murder hook. It doesn't. Harriet is pursuing these lines of inquiry to eliminate them not because she thinks someone else killed Gabe, but, at times like this, it's easier to fall back on clichés.

'Just doing my job.' I smile.

'Look, I'm staying at the Albion. Can I buy you a drink tonight to say thank you properly?'

'A drink?'

'Yes, or a coffee?'

Before I can tell him that won't be necessary Penny pipes up from behind the counter. 'What a great idea. You're not doing anything tonight, are you, Ally?'

'No, but . . . ?'

'Oh, Ally, don't be such a stick-in-the-mud.'

'It's not that.' I glare at Penny. 'I'm a CSI. It wouldn't be appropriate for me to socialize with the victim's relative.' I don't mention he's also the suspect's relative.

'It's just a drink.'

'Just say yes, Ally.'

An image of Julian and his flawless life comes to mind.

'OK then. Coffee, it is, but I can't talk about the case.'

'Suits me. See you in the Albion at eight.'

Penny waits for Kit to close the door behind him.

'You're a dark horse.' She grins.

'Stand down, Penny Fields. He's got a girlfriend.'

'He didn't give me that impression at all. Not by the way he was looking at you with, might I add, very sexy blue eyes.'

'The man's mother is currently accused of killing his brother; romance is the last thing on his mind and, in any case, he's not my type.'

'So how come you blushed when you saw him?'

'I didn't.'

'I don't know why you're so reluctant. I'd have snapped his hand off.'

'Don't let Will hear you speak like that.'

'He's got nothing to worry about. That man knows I adore him. Anyway, all I'm saying is that you need to get back out there. Liam was a great guy, but you have to put him behind you and move on. Kit Narracott could be just what you need.'

Ralph

Ralph wasn't like any of the boys Miriam had met before. The boys she knew wore jeans and dull beige jumpers and had their hair cut short like Robbie's. Ralph turned up to the community centre dressed in purple bell bottom trousers and a shirt covered in eye-aching orange and purple swirls. His hair was long and shaggy. He was the kind of boy Robbie and Dad shouted 'poofter' at as they walked past the building site, but to Miriam, he came from another world where everything was vivid and alive, like the colour TVs in the Radio Rentals shop window.

It didn't bother her when Rachel, her friend from the nursery, warned her Ralph had a terrible reputation with girls because she knew he would never be interested in someone like her. But he was.

The first few lessons, he spent watching her, smiling, as she jotted down equations, trying to ignore her burning cheeks. It unnerved her and she wanted to ask him what he found so funny. During their third lesson, he heaved a huge sigh and leaned back in his seat, putting his hands behind his head. His shirt lifted, revealing a smooth torso still bearing a tan from a family holiday to Majorca that Ms Winters hadn't stopped talking about. Miriam tried not to look, but they both knew she had.

'What's the point? When will I ever need algebra?'

'You need your maths to get into university.'

'I'm not going to university. It's full of idiots who don't know anything about life but just do what Mummy and Daddy tell them. I want to get a proper job on a building site or a farm. Do some real work instead of all this poncy learning.'

'You sound like my dad.'

'Well, he's got a point. Where's uni going to get me? A dull nine-to-five job in an office full of stuffed shirts. No thanks.'

'I'd love to go to university, become a proper teacher.'

He leaned forward. 'Maybe if there were more people like you there, I'd go.'

'What do you mean?'

'You're the real deal, babe.'

No one had ever called her babe before. She liked it. She liked him.

'What do you mean?'

'You know, working class. You're authentic. You don't have any pretensions, not like my family, sipping Mateus Rosé with their cheese fondues, pretending everything is fine when it's so obviously not.'

'Don't your parents get on?'

'God no. They hate each other's guts, but they'll never divorce – far too unseemly. All the neighbours would know so they just seethe in silence unless they're in public and then they pretend they have the perfect marriage. It makes me sick. Whereas your people are different.'

She didn't know what he meant by 'your people', but her parents sounded just like his.

'My parents argue all the time.'

'Sure, they fight, and they fuck, but they don't care who knows it.' His language shocked her, but she hid it; she didn't want him to think she wasn't worldly. 'Like I said, you're the real deal. This is your time, Mir.'

She smiled; she liked how he shortened her name too, like they were already close.

'It doesn't matter anyway. My parents won't let me go to university.'

'Forget them. You need to get out of Barnston before you end up with ten sprogs at your feet.' He shuddered at the thought. 'You're a million times better at maths than I am. You could do your A levels at evening classes. Let's ditch this *for the pub. I want* to hear more about your ar—

'We're meant to be doing algebra.'

'Oh come on. Don't be a spoilsport. One won't hurt.'

She should have said no. She should have put *her* foot down, but she didn't. She told herself it was because he was the boss's son, but it wasn't that. She never stood up for herself. Not until it was too late.

He bought her a Dubonnet and lemonade because she'd seen an advert for it and it sounded sophisticated, but she must have drunk it too quickly, because she started talking and didn't seem able to stop. She told Ralph that she had wanted to go university and become a maths teacher but she wasn't sure now because she loved it so much at the nursery. Some days, she thought she had the best job in the world. As she chatted, he just listened in a way that no one had ever done before, his head cocked to one side *with a smile on his face and a look in his eyes* that made her feel she was the most fascinating person in the world.

By the time they left the pub, it was dark. Ralph helped her with her coat. As she swung back round to face him, he planted a kiss on her lips. She wasn't sure if it was the shockwaves his lips on hers sent through her, but she jerked her head backwards.

Ralph laughed. 'It's OK, silly. It was your fault anyway. Has anyone ever told you that you have very kissable lips?'

'No,' she said earnestly, and he kissed her again.

This time it was longer and harder and the pleasure of it pulsed through her body in a way that unsettled her because she wanted it to last forever. In the end, it was Ralph who pulled away from her, a smirk on his face that made her think he knew something she didn't.

'... ...west I like about you, Mir. You've no idea how beauti-

She didn't know what to say to that. Her dad always told her she had a face that could curdle milk and couldn't afford to be choosy when it came to courting. Now Ralph Foxton was looking at her like she was Miss World or someone. 'Look, it's probably best if I don't walk you home. You know what gossip is like in this place. If my mother finds out we've skived off, she'll stop my lessons with you.'

She nodded, still dizzy from their kiss.

'You're such a good girl, Mir.' He smiled.

She didn't care that she had to walk home alone; she was bathed in feelings she'd never felt before, feelings that were so strong that if they didn't wear off before she got home, she was sure her parents would notice. She'd read about this in Jackie magazine. Rachel would bring her issue into the nursery and they'd devour it in their lunchtimes. Her dad said it was filth, but it was the only way to find out things to do with boys, things her parents would never talk to her about. In the letters pages, girls would write in, saying that when a certain boy kissed them, it made them tingle all over and was that normal? *Jackie* said it was perfectly normal and just showed you had feelings for them. That was when Miriam realized she was falling in love with Ralph Foxton.

After that night, Ralph cooked up a plan to come to the nursery when Miriam worked the later shift, after his mother and the others had gone home. He said it would be more private, away from the prying eyes of Mr Sykes, the community centre manager. She wanted to say no. It was one thing to skip lessons to go to the pub, but to let someone who wasn't a staff member into the nursery was completely out of order. Boss's son or no, Miriam could lose her job over it, a job she adored.

'I know I shouldn't ask, Mir, but you drive me crazy. I honestly can't stop thinking about you. No one will find out and if they do, I'll tell Mum it was all me. I made you.'

So, she gave in. Ralph would sneak in after everyone had left and it was just Miriam taking care of the last remaining children. Once their parents had picked them up, Miriam would begin their lesson and Ralph would pretend to listen, nodding solemnly as she explained quadratic equations. Then he'd tickle her ribs, blow on her cheek or steal a kiss and Miriam would dissolve into shy giggles. The lesson would be abandoned, and they'd end up necking on the same sofa where Miriam consoled distraught children.

Ralph's hand would slide higher and higher up her leg but each time she would grab it and remove it, because she knew what would happen if she didn't. They hadn't talked about doing it. It was too embarrassing. She'd always been taught that good girls waited until they were married, but that wasn't the reason. She knew from the letters page in *Jackie* that girls only stopped boys going further because they were terrified of getting pregnant, even though they wanted to carry on. She felt this too. They didn't tell you that at school. At school, it was always about the boy wanting to have his wicked way and the girl fending him off, but she wanted it too, only she wasn't stupid. The fear of getting in the family way was greater than her desire for him. Or so she thought.

Her first time was the night her father found out she'd enrolled for evening classes. It was Ralph's idea. He said it was the only way she'd ever get out of Barnston. She'd get bored of working at the nursery eventually, but by then she'd be stuck forever.

A family friend had seen her leaving the college campus and told her father who flew into a rage at her. He didn't recognize her any more. Working at the nursery had changed her, turning her into a sly, stuck-up, ungrateful girl who thought she was better than the rest of them. Well, he'd show her. And he did. He curled his hand into a fist and punched her. It felt like her cheek had exploded as she went down. He didn't wait for her to get up or see what damage he had done. Instead, he announced he was going to the pub and left.

She could tolerate the physical pain, but as he left, her father told her he'd called the college and withdrawn her application and it was in that moment that her world narrowed to nothing. She looked at her mother who said it was her own fault for letting that Ms Winters put silly ideas into her head. Miriam couldn't bear to be in the house any longer. After he left, she ran, still cradling her throbbing face, to the phone box at the end of the street, where she rang Ralph.

Ten minutes later, he picked her up in his mother's Rover and drove her out to Morte Sands car park where, in between sobs, she recounted the injustice of it all. He kissed her bruised cheek lightly so as not to hurt her and told her that her dad was a fucking bastard and she needed to break free of his patriarchal grip. She knew he'd understand, but he'd stopped listening.

His lips had moved to hers, but his kisses became harder, rougher, their teeth colliding as he pressed his tongue deep inside her mouth. Still distraught, she didn't want this, but he'd been so kind she didn't want to hurt his feelings, so she kissed him back and before she knew what was happening, he was undoing her shirt buttons. She knew she should stop him, but her row with her father had sapped her resolve, and, in some ways, it felt like a way to get back at her parents, a rebellion. They were furious that she wanted to make something of herself. Imagine how they would be if they found out she'd had sex?

Miriam discovered she was pregnant four weeks later. She'd read in Rachel's magazine that doctors took an oath of secrecy, and she prayed that Dr Willis would stand by that oath and not tell her mum. The results came back positive, and he called her a stupid girl who'd ruined her life because she couldn't say no. She left the surgery white with shock, but at least Ralph loved her and would do the right thing.

Father would get him work on a building site, like he wanted, and they'd be married before she began to show. They might have to live with his parents for a while – there was definitely no room at her house – but they'd get themselves on the list and get a council house soon enough, maybe one of the new ones being built on the edge of Barnston. It would all work out in the end.

It was late. They were parked at the far end of Morte Sands car park. They'd made love. That's what Ralph called it. She really didn't want to because she thought it might harm the baby, but Ralph wasn't the kind of boy you said no to.

'Guess what?' he said, pulling up his fly. 'I passed maths and my A levels, and I got into Birmingham Uni. I couldn't believe it when I saw my results. Was sure I'd failed. Perhaps you are a pretty good teacher, after all.'

'I thought you said you weren't going to uni.'

He checked his hair in the mirror. 'Got no choice. Mum's making me. I'll be back at Christmas.'

She couldn't imagine Ralph being made to do anything he didn't want to, but she had other things on her mind. She couldn't keep it to herself any longer, but she was nervous. He'd never shown anything but intense dislike for the children at the nursery, but surely it was different when it was your child.

'I'm pregnant.'

'What?'

'I'm pregnant.'

He didn't say anything for a while then lit up a Woodbine, blowing a smoke ring at the car's windscreen. 'You'll have to get rid of it.'

'What? How?'

Someone at school had gotten pregnant and rumours flew around that she'd ended up in hospital because she'd drunk a bottle of gin in a hot bath. She never came back to school, but Miriam heard her baby was born eight months later.

'I've got some money saved. It's not much, but it might be enough.'

'For what?'

He took another drag on his cigarette. 'An abortion, of course.'

Fear forced the air from her lungs. She'd heard about back-street abortions. They were dangerous. Mrs Arthur on the next street got ten years in prison for killing a girl who'd gone to her. Her mum said it served the girl right because that's what you get when you throw yourself at a man. She didn't know what happened exactly because no one ever spoke about it other than to say it had been dealt with, but Miriam did know one thing about abortions: they were illegal.

'I could go to jail.'

But Ralph wasn't listening. 'You can't do it here, though. It would get out. People would know and that nosy mate of yours, Rachel, would guess it's me. No, you'll have to go to London and do it there.'

'I don't know anyone in London.' She couldn't believe she was even thinking about doing it, but she went along with him just like she always did.

'In that case, you'll have to tell your mum. She'll know what to do.'

'I can't tell her. She'll be devastated. Dad'll throw me out.'

'Well, you'll have to.'

'They'll want to know who the father is.'

'You can't say it's me because Mum'll find out then.'

'But you are the father.'

He blew another smoke ring and watched it disappear. 'Are you sure about that?'

'What?'

'Well, you dropped your knickers pretty quickly for me. What's to say you're not doing it for other boys?'

'How could you say such a thing?'

'If you say anything to my mum, I'll just deny it. She's hardly going to believe a nursery worker over her own son.'

He flicked his cigarette butt out of the window and they drove home in silence. He pulled up at the end of her street in Barnston and told her to get out.

'Please, Ralph. I love you.'

'I'm not going to ask again, get out of my car.'

She never saw him again, but that didn't mean he was out of her life. There would come a time when Miriam wished she'd never laid eyes on Ralph Foxton.

18

Kit Narracott is already at the bar in the Albion when I arrive. He's swapped his checked shirt and wellies for a dark blue jacket, jeans and brown shoes, and attempted to brush his curls into some semblance of order. I tap him on the shoulder to tell him to make my coffee black and that I'll bag us a table. I catch a waft of aftershave, leading me to wonder if he always puts in this amount of effort to say thank you.

Kit joins me with our drinks. He takes a sip of what looks like a G&T and scans the pub.

'It's better than I remember it.'

'Nothing stands still, not even in Bidecombe.'

'I used to come here when there was a nightclub in the back room.'

'I remember that. All sticky floors and condensation running down the walls.'

'That's the one. I'm surprised we never met.'

'I'm guessing you went to Delderfield Hall.' Delderfield Hall is the local public school on Exmoor where farmers send their offspring. 'You were probably too posh for us.'

'I doubt that.' He takes another sip of his drink. 'What about you? Are you local?'

'I guess. I've lived here all my life. I've no idea where I'm from originally,' I say, heading off the question my dark brown eyes and complexion can invite sometimes. 'My parents adopted me when I was a baby. I never knew my real parents.'

'Was it hard growing up here?'

'Not really. People from Barnston are considered foreigners in Bidecombe and that's only sixteen miles away.'

Kit laughs. 'That's true. Look, I'm sorry I was such a dick the other day. I'm not normally that rude.'

'It's OK. I get it. You've lost your brother in the most terrible of circumstances. How are you managing?'

'It doesn't feel real.' He wipes the condensation from his glass until it's clear. Another distraction to stop the pain getting in. 'I keep expecting to see Mum feeding the chickens in the yard or Gabe steering the John Deere through the farm gates. It just hasn't sunk in.'

'It takes time to come to terms with something like this. I'm not even sure people ever do.'

'I don't remember feeling like this when Dad died, and that was really sudden. He had a heart attack down the local pub. We didn't have time to say goodbye. I remember being upset, but Gabe and I accepted it and just got on with it.'

'When did you last see Gabe?'

'Last year sometime. We spoke on the phone from time to time. We were close as kids but when Dad died, other things got in the way.'

'Like what?'

I've already heard the police version, but I'm curious to hear what Kit has to say.

'I wanted to modernize the farm, take it in a different

124

direction, diversify, maybe into tourism. Gabe wanted to keep things the same.'

'Wouldn't the farm have gone to Miriam after your dad died?'

'Yes, but she's not from a farming family. She pretty much left it to me and Gabe to manage. I thought it would be a new start for us all, but Gabe would have none of it and the truth is he always loved farming more than I did. Without the farm, he'd have been lost. Leaving seemed the right thing to do, for all of us.'

'What did you do?'

'I travelled. I went everywhere. It was brilliant.' His face lights up at the memory. 'For the first time in my life, I felt free. Till then, I'd never realized what a burden being a farmer's son was, how you're just expected to take over the farm without question. What I wanted didn't matter. The farm came first.'

'What did you want?'

'For a time, I was obsessed with flying. I wanted to be a pilot, but my parents swiftly put paid to that idea. I was needed on the farm. That was the end of it.'

'That's a real shame.'

He shrugs. 'Not really. My grades weren't good enough anyway.'

'So you didn't miss the farm then when you were travelling then?'

'No. I spent quite a lot of time in the Far East and then I ended up working at Stathmore Station, one of the biggest sheep farms in Oz, for three years. When I got back, I got a temporary job on an estate in South Devon. Been there ever since.'

'But it's farming.'

'It's the only thing I know, but the difference is I don't have any of the risk and I can walk away any time. Anyway, what about you?'

'Not much to tell, really. I went to uni, had big plans to see the world, got pregnant with Megan and did the one thing I swore I'd never do – came back to Bidecombe. Been here ever since.'

'Are you happy?'

'Happy enough.'

'I heard about what happened to your daughter last year. It sounds horrific.'

'It was. She's still got some way to go, but we're getting there.'

'We? So there's a Mr Dymond?'

'No. He didn't make it to the first scan. Probably a good thing. It wouldn't have worked. I got married to someone else a few years later. Big mistake. We broke up. I've been pretty much on my own ever since. How about you?'

'Divorced. A bit of a whirlwind romance. We were great while we were travelling. Soon as we stood still, it all fell apart. Unfortunately, we didn't find out until we were married. No kids though so it meant we could have a clean break.'

'And now?'

'I was seeing someone, but it's over now. It was nothing serious. More of a fling really. Do you want another coffee?'

So what happened to the woman Kit Narracott got drunk with the night Miriam murdered Gabe?

I pick up Kit's glass along with my coffee cup. 'Another would be great, but it's my shout.'

'You might want to wait until the rush has died down though.'

I glance over at the bar, crammed with people waving credit cards at the barman. 'Good point. So, what will happen to the farm now?'

'I don't know. Sammy, the farmhand, is doing a pretty good job; maybe he'll take it on as a manager. Even when she's better, there's no way Mum can run the place on her own and I'm not interested in coming back. I've made a life for myself elsewhere.'

I don't remind him that if Miriam gets better, she's almost certainly facing a murder charge. 'How is Miriam?'

'Still hasn't spoken a word. She just lies in the hospital bed staring up at the ceiling. They're testing her for dementia, but they're not sure if it's that or something else. Can I ask you something?'

'Sure.'

'You've been to the farm, you've read the case files, do you think Mum killed Gabe?'

'I haven't read them, Kit. And even if I had, I can't discuss the case with you.'

'Yes, of course. Sorry. I forgot. The thing is I just don't see it. Mum loved Gabe. She loved us both. We were her world, but she especially looked out for Gabe.'

'Why was that?'

'He was a bit slower than most kids. Nothing major, he just took a bit longer to process things, but it was enough for the bullies at school. The thing is, despite his size he never fought back. He just took it. I was always stepping in to defend him. Not that I minded. He was my brother. The other kids soon got the message but Mum constantly worried about people taking advantage of him. That's why I know she'd never have hurt him. Sorry, I didn't mean for us to have such a maudlin conversation.'

'That's OK. She's on your mind; that's understandable.'

'Can I ask you a favour?'

'Depends what it is.'

'I'm going to the hospital tomorrow to see her. Would you come with me? I could do with a bit of moral support, and it's been really good to talk to you. I feel like I've known you for ages.'

His candour takes me aback, but he's right – ours is one of the easiest conversations I've had in a while.

'Yes. It's been nice, but I don't think I can go to the hospital with you.'

'I know she's a suspect but she's still my mum. I can't leave her. I just don't think I can face her alone.'

I look at Kit. His brother is dead. His mother almost certainly murdered him. He has no one.

'How about I meet you at the hospital entrance at about 1 p.m.?' I check the bar. 'The queue's died down now. I'll get us that drink.'

'Best leave the gin out of my G&T; I need to go to the farm later.'

I return his empty glass and my coffee cup to the bar where I wiggle in between two drinkers and catch the landlord Bill's eye.

'Be with you in a sec, Ally,' he says, expertly flicking a beer tap just as the frothy head reaches the top of the pint glass.

'No rush.'

While I'm waiting, I idly scan the pub. Like any coastal town, Bidecombe has its fair share of pubs, but the Albion has been a favourite with locals for years and tonight is no exception. It's no surprise to see PC Bryan Rogers throwing darts at a board, cheered or commiserated with by those around him. He notices me and waggles his darts as an invitation to join him. I smile and shake my head. At another table, Megan's counsellor Lisa Kendrick is tapping away on a laptop. I've warmed to her since she gave me the heads up about Julian. And even Karyn Dwight from the DIY shop is here, enjoying cocktails with a female friend. It's a small world, but in Bidecombe it's minuscule.

'Same again, Ally?'

'No, just a tonic this time, and I'll have a Sam's.'

He looks at Kit and is about say something, after some juicy gossip to share with his customers no doubt, but he knows me better than that, so he just smiles. 'Right you are.'

I watch Bill amble off to the chiller at the other end of the bar and it's then that I spy a crown of spiky hair over the top of the bar. Suspicions aroused, I shift along for a better view. Sure enough, it's Jay, sitting by the other window. But he's not alone. His arm is draped over the girl sitting next to him: Cassie Warnock.

'Jay!' I shout, loud enough to a attract a glare from the man next to me, but Jay can't hear me above the din, so I abandon my drinks and zigzag through the crowded bar towards the two of them. They don't notice me until I'm standing right in front of them.

'What the hell do you think you're doing?'

Jay's arm beats a hasty retreat. 'Nothing. We're just having a drink.'

My phone rings, but I ignore it. Whatever it is can wait.

'For Christ's sake. She's the girlfriend of the man you're accused of beating up. Your dad in case you've forgotten.'

'I haven't forgotten and we're just chatting.'

I ignore Cassie's smirk.

'There is no "just chatting" with the person who is a prosecution witness in your own trial, you idiot.'

'There's no need for that.'

'There's every need for it, if you don't want to go to jail. And, who's with Megan?'

'No one.'

'What do you mean, no one?'

'She said she was fine on her own.'

'For fuck's sake, Jay, you're meant to be looking after her.'

My phone rings again. I check to make sure it doesn't need answering, but it's Penny, which means it could be Megan.

'Pen, what is it? Is it Megan?' Her voice is tight, her Liverpool accent stronger when she's excited or stressed, but I can't make out what she's saying. 'Hang on a mo. I'll take this outside.' I point at Jay. 'You stay right where you are. I haven't finished with you.' I leave the pub and go out onto the street. 'Sorry, Pen, say that again.'

This time I hear her loud and clear.

'The police have just turned up. They think Will killed Gabe Narracott.'

19

Will is sitting at Penny's kitchen table, cradling a mug of steaming tea in his huge hands, disbelief writ large across a face drained of colour. Next to him, Penny rests her hand on his arm, her consoling eyes locked onto her boyfriend.

I open the door and relief washes over her.

'Thank God you're here. You just missed them. It was awful, Ally.'

'What happened?'

'They were so rude and aggressive. We were watching TV and they practically barged their way in.'

I turn to Will. 'Are you OK?'

'It was my own stupid fault really,' he says, his eyes still trained on his mug.

'Will, you've done nothing wrong,' says Penny, 'and they'll regret this. You can't go around accusing innocent people of murder.'

'OK, can we just rewind a bit?' I need Penny to dial down the hysteria so I can make sense of what has actually taken place. 'Why were they even here?' If guilty expressions met the bar for a conviction, Will Sneddon would be looking at life without parole. 'Will?'

'Tell her,' says Penny.

'Tell me what?'

'I went to Gabe's farm the morning of the day he died.'

'You did what?'

He winces slightly at my incredulity, but it's his own fault. How could he be so stupid?

'And you didn't tell anyone?'

'I didn't think it was relevant. It was first thing in the morning. The news reports said Gabe was killed late that night. He probably saw dozens of people that day. He wasn't even in. Miriam said he was out in the fields.'

'So how did the police know you were there?'

'Another farmer passing on his tractor spotted my Land Rover parked up on the road and told the police.'

'What were you doing there?'

Penny tuts loudly. 'Christ, Ally, you're as bad as the, she says, her Scouse accent becoming more pronounced the minute.

'If you want me to help, I need to know the truth.'

Finally, he looks at me. 'I went there to discuss fly-tipping.'

'What?'

'Someone's been dumping rubbish in the lay-by next to the woods on Gabe's land and I went there to ask him if he wanted help clearing it.'

'That was it?'

'Yes, but I don't think the police believed me. They asked me a lot of questions about whether Gabe and I were friends, if we'd ever argued, that sort of thing.'

'And what did you say?'

'We weren't friends, but we weren't enemies either. We

saw each other occasionally on market days and in the Stag in Upper Farleigh. Sometimes we'd help each other out during lambing season or borrow each other's machinery from time to time.'

'Anything else?'

'They asked me what I was doing on the night of his murder, and I told them I was here at Seven Hills with Penny.'

'They couldn't have made it more obvious they thought Will was lying.'

'I'm sure that's not true, Penny. What did they do then?'

'They asked me if I saw Miriam Narracott when I was at Gabe's, or anything that looked suspicious. It was Miriam who opened the door to me. She told me Gabe was out in fields.'

'And you didn't think to tell the police this?'

'No, she seemed completely fine to me. If I'd thought something was up, I'd have said something. They asked if I could go to the station to give a statement tomorrow and then they left.'

'Why does Will have to give a statement when he didn't see anything?'

'It's a murder inquiry. They're just covering all the bases.' By now, I'm struggling to understand Penny's ire. 'It all sounds routine to me. If you'd have told them you were at the farm in the first place and that you'd spoken to Miriam, this wouldn't have happened.'

Penny folds her arms in disgust. 'That's right – blame Will. I'm surprised you're on their side. You of all people know how incompetent they are.'

'I'm not blaming Will. I'm just telling you how it works.'

'Well, they've a funny way of doing things,' she says, sitting back in her chair.

'I get that it isn't a pleasant experience to be questioned by the police, but as long as you tell the truth, you've nothing to worry about.'

Will looks away, but Penny isn't letting this go.

'Of course he's told the truth. I thought people were innocent until proven guilty in this country.'

'They are. Look, I've got to get back to Megan. Jay left her on her own tonight, but I'll speak to the DI and find out what's going on.'

'Good, because someone needs to say something.'

There's nothing more I can do to placate Penny or reassure Will, so I leave just as Penny launches into a rant about invasion of privacy and living in a police state whilst Will, the wronged party, just stares down at his mug. It's then that I realize he hasn't touched his tea.

20

The thick fog that has hung around for weeks amplifies the sound of my key turning in the front door lock of the cabin, announcing my return. The lights are off, and the stillness of the cabin tells me Megan has turned in for the night and Jay is fast asleep on the sofa. Good, because I don't want her to hear this.

Switching on the kitchen light, I rummage in the cupboards for the largest vessel I can find, unearthing a huge German beer glass with a map of the Rhine on it that Bernadette brought back from a cruise several years ago. I let the tap water run ice cold before filling the glass to the rim. Carrying it in two hands, I march over to Jay and fling it over his face. He wakes with a terrified start.

'What the fuck?'

'Keep your voice down. I don't want to wake Megan. I told you to stay away from Cassie Warnock.'

'I'm sorry, all right. She called me. She wanted to talk and you said I wasn't allowed to have people round.'

'It didn't look like a lot of talking was going on to me, just a lot of canoodling.' He pauses dabbing his chest with the duvet and frowns at me. God, I feel old. He doesn't know what canoodling means. 'Snogging.'

'It wasn't like that. I swear.'

'Actually, I don't care. The courts are probably the least of your worries because if Tony finds out he'll kill you and I can't say I blame him.'

'Like I care what that twat thinks.'

He's no more convinced by his words than I am. Son or no son, only a fool crosses a man like Tony Cox, and the fear in Jay's eyes is so palpable that I can't help but soften towards him.

'I'm trying to help you out here, Jay' – I hand him a towel from the radiator – 'but I can't if you're going to do shit like this.'

He nods. 'I thought I was doing the right thing.'

'You left Megan on her own too. What if she'd had another seizure?'

'She said it was OK, but I know I shouldn't have done it. I won't do it again, not without your say-so. I'm sorry, Ally. Please don't throw me out. I've got nowhere else to go. And I'll make it up to you, I promise. I'll prove to you I've changed. Just give me time.'

I let my anger slide away on a sigh. 'Just keep away from Cassie Warnock. At least until the trial is over.'

'I will.'

'Does Megan know about you and her?'

'There is no me and her.'

'Well, there fucking better not be because if there is, I'm the least of your worries.'

***

136

I make myself comfortable on my bed and open my laptop to check my mailbox. Harriet's email is still there, unread. I click on it. It's little more than a thank you for attending the briefing and Slaughterhouse Farm. She tells me she's arranged access to the case files in the cloud, as discussed, before finishing with a pre-emptive thank you for going through them.

I want to ignore her email. I'm on leave, for Christ's sake. This isn't even my case, but the words 'kid' and 'candy store' come to mind and I can't help myself. I go into SHINE, the police records management system, and navigate my way to the investigation. Sure enough, I'm allowed in. I immediately notice a MP3 file, labelled Narracott Farm, plus the date and a reference number and click on it. It begins with a wide shot of the Narracotts' kitchen. Gabe's body is on the floor by the back door, but the camera doesn't home in on him, not straightaway. This isn't the movies. CSIs are not wannabe filmmakers. Our job is to record a crime scene in as much detail as we can, which means crime scene footage involves a lot of slow panning, zooming in and lingering shots of anything that might be evidence. Think of an exceptionally bad home-made horror movie: only everything you see is real.

After taking a tour of the room, the camera arrives at Gabe's body. In close-up, his face is serene and unmarked. He could be sleeping until the camera shifts downwards to his blood-soaked green overall and the dark viscous pool that has bloomed underneath him. I don't need a pathologist to tell me that Gabe Narracott bled to death.

The camera pans out to show the kitchen cabinets, a few metres from Gabe's body. There's a pause so the viewer can examine the blood patterns, their position and distance from the corpse, which could be crucial to a court case. The camera isolates several blood spatters of interest before tracking to the back door where it lingers on more blood patterns, including the arterial spurt high up the doorframe that I noticed, and a spatter caused when the knife was pulled from Gabe's body, which stretches across the wall and top of the doorjamb.

Rewinding the film, I go through it again frame by frame, checking the position of the body and the blood spatters. There's something about them. The shape, the quantity, the position – I'm not sure what it is. Maybe nothing. I continue to stare at them for a little while longer, cross checking them against the findings in the blood stain pattern analysis report, hoping for inspiration, but none is forthcoming, so I click out of the film and it's then that I notice another film file. This one is entitled: Exmoor B1583 plus the date and reference number.

Assuming it's film taken by Jake or another CSI, I press play, but it isn't. It's footage from inside a moving vehicle. It's dark; the only light comes from the car's dashboard, illuminating two air fresheners in the shape of roses attached to the air vent and the headlights, which barely cut through the curtain of fog drawn across the road.

A woman in the front passenger seat asks why the person is filming the road at night. A teenage girl by the sounds of it responds, mumbling something about wanting to be ready in case the Beast of Exmoor leaps out at them. The beast, allegedly some kind of black panther, is a local legend that rears its head from time to time, normally, the cynic in me says, when tourism is sluggish and needs a boost. The driver, the girl's father presumably, laughs. Then, from nowhere, a woman in a white nightdress – Miriam Narracott – emerges from the mist like an apparition and the driver slams on the brakes, swearing loudly and throwing both his passengers forward. The car comes to an owl-screeching halt just a couple of metres from her. She doesn't react straightaway, but eventually she turns her expressionless face towards them.

The driver and passengers unbuckle themselves and get out of the car, all the while the camera is on Miriam. Their concern for her welfare quickly turns to fear when they spot the knife in her hand. The driver, called Dean, wants to leave her, but the woman – Jo – says they should wait for the police. Then the teenage girl, Natasha, informs Dean and Jo that the wet stain on Miriam's nightshirt is blood and the filming ends. The prime suspect caught holding the murder weapon, soaked in the blood of her victim. As evidence goes, it's as damning as it gets.

Reeled in by the two films, I can't resist the other files. I hesitate for a moment before reasoning that if Harriet didn't want me to see them, she wouldn't have given me access. Considering this is a murder inquiry, there aren't many witness statements yet and there's nothing from Miriam, as she's still in no fit state to give one. Most are from people who visited the farm that day, including Karyn Dwight, the manager of DIY Supplies who Gabe had a fling with, who was there to collect an unpaid debt, and the dealer in rare breeds. It's mundane stuff, a snapshot of farm life. No one saw anything suspicious, and Gabe was his usual convivial self, according to those who saw him.

Kit's statement takes me by surprise. I don't know why. He's Gabe's brother and only living relative in possession of their faculties; of course he's given a statement. I feel uneasy at the thought of reading it, like I'm prying into his personal affairs, which I am, but that doesn't stop me.

On the night of Gabe's murder, Kit was at home waiting for his girlfriend who had arranged to drop by at 8 p.m. to celebrate her birthday. They shared three bottles of Champagne and went to bed around 9.30 p.m., not waking until around 9 a.m. the next morning with a hangover. Pretty standard stuff, really. I check the other statements and there's one from Kit's now ex-girlfriend confirming all of this. The police have either been ultra-thorough or they're scraping the bottom of the barrel. Maybe it's both.

I'm about to come out of the file when I notice Kit's girlfriend's name at the top of the statement. It has a familiar ring to it, so I go onto the website for the Bellworth estate that Kit manages and click on 'Our Story'. The first thing that comes up is a picture of the estate owner, Mike Clevedon, Kit's boss. Next to him is a woman in black riding boots and a hacking jacket, her hair swept up into one of those expertly teased messy buns. According to the caption, this is Georgina Clevedon, Mike Clevedon's wife. She's also the woman Kit Narracott slept with the night his brother was murdered.

21

A night's sleep and an early start to the dulcet sounds of 'Hey Jude' appear to have calmed Penny after last night's visit from the police, and she hands me a paintbrush with an apologetic smile.

'Sorry. I went off on one a bit, didn't I?'

'Don't worry. I've met enough detectives to know that, for some, their skills set is more kicking in doors than talking to people. I left a message for the DI to call me. How's Will this morning?'

'I think he's more upset about it than he's willing to show.'

'I don't understand why he didn't tell the police he'd been to Narracott Farm that day. Gabe's murder was all over the news. The police were going to find out sooner or later.'

'It honestly didn't occur to him. He literally dropped in on the off chance to talk to Gabe about fly-tipping on his land. He wasn't even in.'

'It just doesn't look great.'

'I know. I told him that. You don't live with a CSI for eight years without some of that police stuff rubbing off on you. I'm sorry I interrupted your date with Kit. How did it go by the way?'

'It wasn't a date, but it was good. I enjoyed myself. He's a nice guy.'

'Wow, that's high praise coming from you. I told you Kit Narracott could be the just the person for you.'

My phone rings before I tell Penny that men who knock off their boss's wife aren't really my type. It's an unknown number: Harriet.

'Thanks for returning my call, Harriet.'

'Er. It's not Harriet. It's Jake.'

'Oh, hi, Jake. What can I do for you?'

'I hope you don't mind me calling while you're still off, but I thought you'd like to know the fingerprint you found at Bidecombe DIY got a match.'

'You're kidding. That's great news.' I'm surprised at how much of a thrill this still gives me, but a fingerprint match is a fingerprint match. I once read somewhere that the chances of two people sharing the same fingerprint are one in sixty-four trillion. The population of Bidecombe is around 12,000 people, which means one of its residents is about to have their collar felt. I already have a few culprits in mind.

'So, put me out of my misery – who is it?'

'We don't have a name.'

'I thought you said you had a match.'

'We do, of sorts. The fingerprint matched fingerprints found at another burglary.'

'Ah, a new player in town.' Criminals have to start somewhere. Often there'll be a spree of burglaries where offenders will leave copious fingerprints, but it makes no difference if they're not on the database. That changes the moment the police get them into custody and their prints are taken for the first time. After that, the gloves are off for the police, but definitely on for the criminals. 'Good luck with that.'

'Yeah, but here's the weird thing, the other burglary took place a couple of days before the one at Bidecombe Supplies.'

'So?'

'It was in London.'

'That is unusual.'

'That's what I thought.'

'Maybe it's a thief on an away day who just couldn't help themselves.'

'Maybe. Anyway, when I've got a bit of time, I'll drive out to Bidecombe and tell the manager.'

He doesn't sound keen, and I don't blame him. There's a reason Bidecombe is considered a punishment posting. It's on the tip of the North Devon coast which means it's not on anyone's way to anywhere. Unless a crime has been committed, there's no reason for Jake to be out this way.

I look down at the empty paint pot.

'Tell you what, I've got to go to Bidecombe Supplies to buy some more paint.' Penny gives me the thumbs-up. 'Why don't I tell Karyn Dwight for you?'

'But you're not officially back at work until the end of the month.'

'It's no problem. I'm there anyway.'

'Thanks, Ally. I owe you. When you get back, I'll buy you a pint. Actually, I'll buy you a pint anyway. We've missed you.'

'Thanks. One more thing though. Was "bitch" scrawled across the wall in the London burglary too?'

'Already ahead of you.' Hearing this makes me smile.

Jake has the makings of a great CSI. 'I called the officer in the case, and he said no it didn't.'

'Really?'

MOs are MOs. Burglars, like the rest of us, are creatures of habit and that goes for their modus operandi; some will trash a place, some will defecate all over it, and some will spray offensive messages on walls, and they'll do this at each and every break-in. It's like a signature. Only not in this case, it seems.

***

Bidecombe Supplies is deserted so I grab a large tin of white paint from the shelf and go in search of life, which I eventually find in the form of Ray, the deputy manager, who is at the back of the shop pricing spades. He scowls at the paint pot I'm holding.

'Is there no one on the cash desk?'

'I don't think so.'

'I'll kill that boy. Bloody useless. If you want something doing, Ray, do it yourself.'

'Actually, Ray, I was hoping to speak to Karyn.'

Recognition dawns in his eyes. 'You're the CSI who found the fingerprint on the spray can lid.'

'Yes, that's right.'

'Sherlock Holmes eat your heart out, eh?'

'Is Karyn around?'

'I was right, wasn't I?'

'About what?'

'About the break-in here. It was one of the little beggars from the kids' home, wasn't it?'

'The police haven't arrested anyone and from what I understand the children at Whitebeam have all been accounted for on the night of the burglary. Anyway, is Karyn here?'

'No. She's taken the day off.'

'Oh. OK. Perhaps, I'll come back tomorrow then.'

'Not sure she'll be back then. She won't mind you dropping by her house though. She lives at Hillside cottage. It's the first one on the left as you go down the hill into Bidecombe.'

'OK, thanks.'

'It'll do her good to think about something else. She's been struggling a bit since, you know, the murder of that farmer.'

'Gabe Narracott?'

'Yes. She's devastated. Poor woman.'

'It's been a shock for everyone.'

'Some more than others.'

'Oh?'

Ray leans on a spade. 'The two of them had a bit of thing going.'

'Right.'

'But he broke it off.'

'Why was that?'

'His mother didn't approve apparently.'

'His mother? But Gabe is . . . or was a grown man.'

'You know what these farming families are like.' Ray places a spade on the rack and selects another. 'Anyway, I don't know the ins and outs of it, but, one day, Karyn comes into work all red-eyed. Then I find her in the back office, sobbing her heart out and she tells me he's dropped her.'

'Just like that.'

'Yep. Sent her a text, saying it was over. She was distraught.

Poor thing. I felt quite sorry for her. She really thought he was the one.'

'Sounds rough.'

'It was. She was in a terrible way for weeks. You'd think she'd hate him, wouldn't you? Hell hath no fury and all that, but when she heard he'd been murdered, she burst into tears.'

'I didn't realise she liked him so much.'

'Enough to have been secretly engaged to him.' He looks down at the paint pot in my hands. 'Do you want me to ring that through the till for you?'

22

Karyn Dwight takes so long to answer the door that I assume she's out. I'm just about to leave when I hear a key in the lock and the door opens to a narrow crack, but it's wide enough to catch a glimpse of her. Still in her dressing gown, dark shadows circle her bloodshot eyes, and her fair hair hasn't seen a straightening iron in a few days. The woman before me couldn't be further from the Karyn Dwight I met a few days ago.

'What is it? I'm not well.'

'Hi, Karyn. It's Ally Dymond, the CSI. I helped out with the burglary at your shop the other day. I have some news for you.'

'The burglary?' she says absently. 'Oh yes, of course. I suppose you'd better come in.'

The door opens onto a low-ceilinged, beamed living room in keeping with the style of the seamen's cottages built several centuries ago when people were a few inches shorter. The single blue sofa in the middle opposite an open fire appears Gulliverian in such a confined space.

Karyn doesn't invite me to sit down, and we stand awkwardly next to a sideboard covered in bird ornaments.

'Sorry to drop in like this. Ray said it would be OK.'

'That's no problem. What is it you wanted to tell me?'

'Actually, there's something I'd like to ask you first.'

'Oh?'

I deliberated over whether I should say something about her relationship with Gabe or just phone it into Harriet and let her deal with it, but what if Ray got it wrong? I'd be wasting everyone's time.

'Why didn't you tell the police you were engaged to Gabe Narracott?'

I get straight to the point. It's a deliberate tactic. It throws people off and in the split second it takes them to recover, they often give themselves away, including Karyn, but that doesn't stop her giving it her best shot.

'What do you mean?'

She knows exactly what I mean but I oblige her with an answer anyway.

'Ray said the two of you were engaged to be married until Gabe broke it off.'

She thinks about denying this before surrendering with a sigh. 'Ray had no business telling you that. It's personal.'

'It's also relevant to the murder inquiry. You should have told the police.'

'I didn't deliberately hide it. I just didn't want to go over it again. It was painful and I didn't see what it had to do with Gabe's murder.' She picks up an ornament. It's of a nightjar. 'I know what you're thinking – I'm pathetic, falling for a man ten years my junior.'

'I wasn't thinking that at all.'

'I thought he really loved me. He told me he did all the time, then out of the blue he finished it.'

'Ray said Miriam, his mother, didn't approve.'

The ornament bangs the sideboard when she puts it back in its place.

'Yes, that's true. I thought it was because I was so much older than him, but Gabe said she was odd about any woman he took home. She was just really possessive over him. It was weird. I think she was terrified he'd leave her, like her other son had. But Gabe would never have left the farm. The stupid thing is I still love him.'

'Is that why you went to the farm that day, to tell him?'

'No. I didn't lie to the police about that. Gabe owed Bidecombe Supplies £15,000 and I went to tell him to pay up otherwise we'd take him to court.'

'How did he take it?'

'He said he had some money coming in from the sale of some sheep and he'd settle his bill the following day.'

'Anything else?'

'Yes. He said he was sorry for the way things had turned out between us and that he missed me. I had the impression he regretted breaking up with me. I said I was sorry too and I left.'

'OK. Karyn, you know I have to tell the investigation team all this, don't you? And they'll probably want to interview you again.'

'I'm sorry. I should have said something before. I'm still in shock, I guess.' She frowns. 'But this isn't why you're here though, is it?'

'No. It's not. I got a call from my CSI colleague who examined the burglary at your shop. The fingerprint came up on the national fingerprint database.'

This surprises her. 'Oh? So, you know who did it then?'

'Not exactly.' Did I imagine it, or did Karyn just let go of a tiny breath she was holding on to? 'We don't have a name, but it matched a fingerprint found at another burglary. In London.'

'In London?'

'Yes.' I let that thought ferment in anticipation of further questions, but there are none. She couldn't be less interested. She doesn't have a single question for me. She doesn't ask me if 'bitch' was scrawled across the wall in the other burglary.

23

Wiping her paint-splashed hands on her overalls, Penny stands back and nods approvingly at the bright white fence in front of her.

'Good job. I think we've done enough for one day. I reckon we'll have this finished by the end of the week. Then the place will be just about ready for the new season.'

It's mid-afternoon and we've been hard at it for hours. I stand up, legs protesting at crouching for too long, and join her in admiring our handiwork.

'Is there anything else left to do around the site?'

'Not really. The cabin windows need cleaning, but I can do that.'

'Looks like I've just been made redundant.' I smile.

Penny grins at me. 'Given I wasn't paying you in the first place, I wouldn't hold out much hope for a redundancy package.'

'You've refused to let me pay rent these last eight months. I've no complaints.'

Penny, once again, has been a godsend. After six months off work on full pay, my wages were halved. If I'd had to pay rent, my finances would be in a far worse state than they already are.

'The least I could do. I'm going to miss having you around when you go back to work.' I don't respond and she looks at me, the same concerned look on her face as before. 'You are going back, aren't you?'

'I don't know if I can, Pen.'

'We talked about this. Megan will be fine. She's got Jay and I'll make sure I'm around for her. I know you won't be returning to Major Investigations, but being a CSI is who you are.'

'That's what Harriet said. She told me not to throw away my career just because I'm pissed off with the force.'

'And she's right.'

'I don't think it's that—'

But I'm interrupted by the roar of a man's voice.

'Come out here, you little shit!'

Penny frowns. 'Who the hell is that?'

'I don't know, but it's coming from somewhere on the site. I didn't think anyone else was staying here at the moment.'

'They're not.'

'Get out here now!' The man's voice echoes around us. 'I'll teach you to mess with my missus.'

'Oh shit. It's Tony Cox.'

'He must have climbed over the fence.'

We throw our paintbrushes into the tray and sprint back through the gates to Seven Hills and towards my cabin where a track-suited Tony is on my veranda, pounding on the front door. Standing on the grass below is Cassie, in her pink puffer jacket. No doubt, she showed Tony exactly where he could find his son.

'Tony! Stop!'

'And you can fuck off.' He spits the words at me, his face twisted in fury. 'Come out here, Jay, and face me like a man.'

'Leave him alone.'

I take the three steps onto my porch in one bound and grab Tony's arm.

'Get off me, bitch.' He swats me aside and I land on my arse. I think he's going to turn on me, so I scrabble backwards into the corner of the veranda. Once clear of his fists and feet, I get my phone out and punch it three times.

'I've called 999, Tony.' I hold my phone up knowing he can't see the screen from where he is. 'When they find out I'm one of them, they'll have a fucking SWAT team here in minutes.'

I haven't called them. The last thing I want is the police finding out a suspected drug dealer is living in my cabin. Besides, Devon County Police doesn't have a SWAT team. Hopefully Tony doesn't know that. He wavers, unsure if I'm telling the truth. Maybe this will convince him.

'Yes, police please. An intruder has broken into my house. I'm scared for my life.'

He thinks for a moment. He's almost certainly on some kind of probation. The last thing he needs is the cops nicking him for threatening behaviour. He puts his hands up.

'OK, OK,' he says, stepping away from my door.

'Wait,' I tell the imaginary call handler. 'I made a mistake. Sorry to have wasted your time.'

I get to my feet and look Tony Cox directly in the eye just so there's no misunderstanding between us.

'Now get the fuck off my property and if I ever see you here again, you won't get a second chance.'

He puffs his chest and clenches his fists. I think he's going to take a swing at me. He wants to. I'm guessing Tony Cox isn't used to women telling him what to do, but even he isn't stupid enough to punch a CSI in full view of witnesses.

As he slopes passed me, he turns to me.

'This ain't over, bitch.'

24

Breakneck Point. I used to come here after a particularly diffi-cult job. There was something about the high-pitched bickering between the gulls that provided the perfect distraction, and the constant breeze seemed to cleanse me of the stench of human depravity that sometimes lingered long after I left a crime scene. I would sit on the bench dedicated to Rex Gordon, who also loved this view, look out over the vast, dark stretch of empty water between North Devon and South Wales, open my mind and just let all that space flow into it.

Thankfully Megan was at counselling when Tony decided to give Jay a hiding. Tony's gone for now, but he isn't the only one feeling violent. God, how I wanted to slap Jay's sheepish face. Instead, I sent him to collect Megan and I headed here, to cool off.

The cabin is my refuge. I've worked hard to make it a safe place for Megan and I, and to see a thug like Tony Cox trying to kick my door in has shaken me. Maybe letting Jay move in wasn't such a good idea after all. He's lied about seeing Cassie, which makes me wonder what else he's lying about, but it's too late now. Megan would never forgive me if I threw him out.

A voice makes me start. 'I didn't expect to see you here.'

I look up to see Liam making his way down the path from the direction of Morte Sands.

'I could say the same thing to you,' I joke.

'Can I join you?' he asks, nodding at the space next to me.

'Sure.'

He sits down and stretches his legs out in front of him. He's swapped his suit for jeans and a red and white Hawaiian shirt spills over the collar of a battered brown jacket. His chin is stubbled, and his hair all mussed up. Normal Liam resumed.

'I thought I'd come and say goodbye to the old place. I'm going to miss it. It's been good to me over the years.'

'You sold the Coffee Shack then?'

'Yes.'

'Congratulations.' I try to infuse some sincerity into the word, but I don't feel like celebrating. 'I hope everything works out for you.'

'You too. You must be returning to work soon.'

'So everyone keeps telling me.'

'You thinking of leaving then?'

I shrug.

'I wouldn't blame you if you did.'

'Why do you say that?'

He looks at me and I think I see something flicker in his eyes, but maybe I'm imagining it because when I look again it's gone. 'The investigation was a dog's dinner and then to give you a final warning for doing their job for them was totally out of order.'

'So you think I should quit?'

'Absolutely not.' He smiles. 'You were born to do the job.'

'Megan still needs me though.'

'I didn't get that impression when I saw her the other day in the high street. She looks great.'

'She's getting there slowly. You know, I never thanked you for everything that you did for her. You made such a difference to her recovery.'

'I wanted to do it. She's a great kid, Ally, and everyone knows surfing is the best medicine there is.'

I nod and let the squabbling gulls fill the growing silence between us. It never used to be like this. Our conversation flowed as naturally as a spring tide, but not any more.

'Well,' I say finally. 'North Devon is going to miss your chococinos.'

It's the best I can manage. Liam looks at me, a smile playing on his lips.

'Is that all North Devon is going to miss?'

'No, we'll miss your flapjacks too.'

He laughs. 'I'll let you have the recipe then.' He pauses. 'Aren't you going to ask me what I'm going to miss? Although' – he looks directly into my eyes – 'it's probably obvious, isn't it? I'm going to miss you, Ally.'

'I don't know what to say, Liam.'

But that's a lie. I know exactly what to say. I want to tell him I'll miss him too. Christ, I want to tell him not to go, but I don't. I know he wanted there to be an us. I did too, but he doesn't know I killed Pascoe and I can't tell him, which means our relationship would be built on secrets. It would have no future and we'd destroy each other pretending it did. This way at least Liam has a chance of happiness.

My phone buzzes. I take it out of my pocket. It's another unknown number. 'Sorry. I should probably take this.'

'Of course,' he says, getting up from the bench. 'Take care, Ally. And, if you need anything from me, anything at all, just call.'

Hands in his jacket pockets, he strides back up the hill and there's a part of me that wants to run after him, to beg him to stay, but I don't. Instead, I take the call. It's Harriet.

'Did you find anything in the files I sent you?'

'No. Your team did a really thorough job. I've got nothing to add.'

'OK. Thank you for trying.'

'There is something you should know about though.'

'Oh?'

'I saw Karyn Dwight today, as a favour to Jake. He got a fingerprint match at a burglary at Bidecombe DIY Supplies which, as you know, Karyn manages, so I went to give her the news.'

'Ah yes.'

'You know about it?'

'Yeah, because of Karyn's association with Gabe, we had a look to see if it was connected to his murder, clutching at straws really.'

'Or dotting the i's.'

'Precisely, anyway the print matched one found at a burglary in London, which, granted, is unusual, but we don't think it's related to Gabe's case.'

'Right, well, you might want to look again.'

'Why?'

'When I went to the store, the deputy manager Ray said Karyn had taken the day off as she was really cut up about Gabe.'

'Why?'

'They were secretly engaged.'

Harriet sighs. 'You know, our jobs would be a whole lot easier if people told us the truth from the start. We get there anyway. It would just save everyone a lot of time.'

'She didn't want to bring it up because it's still quite painful and she didn't think it was relevant to Gabe's murder.'

'I'll be the judge of that.'

'There's something else. Ray said Miriam didn't approve of their relationship so maybe it was Gabe and Karyn having sex in the barn.'

'Maybe. The DNA results haven't come back on that yet. I'll send someone to take a swab from Karyn and we'll get that checked as well. I don't think it will change things. We've already looked into her. She was doing a stocktake with at least one other person on the night of Gabe's murder. The CCTV shows her car parked in the car park until 1 a.m., but thanks anyway. Was there anything else?'

'Yes. Two detectives came to Seven Hills Lodges last night to speak to Will Sneddon. He's going out with the owner, my friend Penny Fields.'

'Yes, that's right. A farmer saw his Land Rover parked outside Narracott Farm, the morning of the murder. We just wanted to find out what he was doing there, see if he saw anything suspicious. Is there a problem?'

'I'm not sure, to be honest. Penny says the detectives were very aggressive and it just sounded a bit odd. She might have been overreacting, of course.'

There's a silence at the end of the phone.

'I take it you don't know about Will Sneddon's past.'

25

Kit and I walk to the hospital ward in silence. I sense his mind is filled with anxiety at what awaits him. I remember that feeling when I visited Megan in hospital. I'd pretend to be upbeat and positive whilst all along strung out by the tension of not knowing if this would be the day that she came back to me or the day she left me for good. Fake it until she makes it, that's what one of the nurses once said to me, but that's easier said than done when you're consumed with fear.

Kit and I are shown to a side room on the geriatric ward. There's no police officer on guard. There doesn't need to be. Miriam Narracott isn't going anywhere.

'Do you want me to wait outside for you?'

Kit thinks about this for a moment. 'I think I'd find it easier if you came in with me if that's OK with you. It's not like Mum is going to object.'

Miriam is lying on her bed, her thin mottled arms by her sides and her legs poking out from underneath her hospital gown. Her pale-yellow hair has been smoothed back from her face, which is calm, almost serene. She would look like she was lying in state, were it not for the disconcerting sight of her eyes, wide and unblinking and fixed to the tiled ceiling above her.

'Mum. It's Kit . . . Your son?' he says, sitting down in the chair next to her. 'I brought you some daffodils. They're your favourite, remember? I picked them this morning. They're early this year.' Instinctively, he holds the tiny flowers up for her to admire and when she doesn't, he looks at them with disappointment. 'Um, I don't think we're allowed to bring flowers into hospital anyway, so I'll take them home and put them in a vase for you.'

He shifts awkwardly in his seat. He's running out of things to say. My heart goes out to him. I know how foolish and rejected you feel talking to someone you love who doesn't respond, your words not enough to haul them out of themselves.

'So, um . . . how are you, Mum?' He cringes at his crassness and pinches the top of his nose between his thumb and forefinger, pressing his eyes closed, either to relieve the tension of the situation or to search for something to say that doesn't require a reply. Probably both. Finally, he speaks. 'So . . . lambing is going well. Sammy has it all in hand. He says not to worry. He's got some extra help from someone in the village. Apparently, we've had quite a few multiple births this year so that's good . . .' The topic exhausted too soon he scrabbles to keep talking and turns to me. 'Oh, and I've brought a . . . friend with me today. Her name is Ally. She lives in Bidecombe, Mum.'

I step towards the bed and smile at Miriam.

'Hello, Mrs Narracott. It's nice to meet you.'

Miriam continues to stare at the ceiling, like a petulant child determined to ignore our presence.

Kit looks up at me. 'Sorry, I shouldn't have brought you.'

I squeeze his shoulder to comfort him. 'That's OK. You're doing great.'

'Thanks.' He smiles and turns back to Miriam. 'Mum, Ally works with the er . . . um . . . she's helping with the, with the . . .' He realizes he's about to refer to his brother's murder investigation and stops himself.

'I'm helping Kit around the farm just for a few days, Mrs Narracott, keeping the place tidy for when you come home,' I say stepping into the silence. 'The weather isn't great at the moment though. There's still a lot of fog on the moors. It's quite treacherous in places. I can't ever remember it being this bad. Thankfully, they're forecasting better weather next week, which is good for the tourists planning to come down for the Easter break, so I expect you'll be getting your fair share of ramblers coming through the farmyard in the next couple of weeks. I understand it's a popular route with walkers.'

Kit mouths 'thank you' at me. What he doesn't know is that I've had a lot of practice. Last year, I spent hours at Megan's bedside, babbling away about anything and everything, trying to pull her out of her unconscious state. Only Miriam isn't in a coma. She's lying on her bed with her eyes wide open.

***

'Is it dementia?'

We're sitting in Kit's car in the hospital car park.

'No. They think it's some kind of catatonic state brought on by trauma.'

'Gabe's death?'

'Possibly. But the doctor said it could be something else,

something going way back to her early life. She said that people in catatonic states also often have other mental health problems, but apart from being a bit of a worrier Mum wasn't mentally ill.'

'A worrier?'

He looks at me. 'Yeah, she was always terrified something would happen to us. She once caught me sneaking out in the middle of the night to play with some friends when I was about ten.'

'Ten?'

'I know. I was a fearless little so and so.' He grins at me. 'Me and some mates had some madcap idea about holding a séance in the graveyard in the church at Upper Farleigh. Mum caught me and went ballistic, totally over the top, telling me I could have been kidnapped or anything, as if she didn't have enough to worry about with Gabe. It was the one and only time she ever hit me. God, it hurt.'

'Why did she fret so much about Gabe?'

'She was convinced people were out to hurt him. She wouldn't let him out of her sight when he was little. When he was older he wanted to come out with me, of course, but she refused until I promised her I'd look out for him, which I did. I didn't mind. He was my brother. Maybe Mum never really trusted me with him, I don't know, but I don't see how that would make her like this.'

'Then it sounds like it was Gabe's death that did this to her.'

Kit slaps the steering wheel in frustration. 'What the hell happened that night, Ally?'

'I don't know, Kit, but you said Miriam wasn't capable of killing Gabe.'

'She isn't but seeing her in hospital, a face like stone. I don't even recognize her. What if she did do it? What did Gabe do or say to make her go at him with a knife? I don't get it.'

'I'm sorry, Kit,' I say, taking his hand in mine. 'This must be so hard for you.'

'I should never have left. She begged me not to go, but Gabe wouldn't listen to my ideas and Mum sided with him. In the end I felt I had no choice, you know, but I should have stayed. Then none of this would have happened.'

I've seen this before, the irrational 'what ifs' that people go through, the belief that their actions, no matter how distant or disconnected, somehow played a part in the death of their loved one. If they'd just done things differently, none of this would have happened. It's not true. Kit isn't to blame for his brother's death, but nothing I say is going to dislodge that idea from his head, so I change the subject.

'Will Miriam recover?'

'I hope so and the doctors seem to think there's a good chance she'll come out it. It's just a case of when.'

'Then she'll be able to tell you what happened herself.'

'Yes, that's true.' He smiles at me. 'Thanks for coming.'

'That's OK.'

He looks down at my hand on his. 'I don't think I could have done it without you. I've been avoiding seeing her and you being there really helped.'

He leans towards me for what I think is a thank you peck on the cheek. Instead, he kisses me on the lips. I snatch my head and my hand back.

'What are you doing?'

'Oh my God. I'm sorry. I thought—'

'It's OK,' I say, cutting him off. 'I need to go.'

I get out of his car and walk briskly towards my own, trying to ignore the lingering sensation of Kit Narracott's lips on mine.

***

By the time I pull up outside the cabin and check my phone, there's a text from Kit apologizing for his behaviour, insisting he didn't know what came over him, maybe the high emotion of the last few days meant he wasn't thinking straight but he'd like to buy me a drink to thank me more appropriately for accompanying him to the hospital. I text back telling him to forget it ever happened and that a drink really isn't a good idea.

I don't give it another thought. I have other things on my mind. I've been dreading this moment since Harriet's phone call at Breakneck Point. I went to look for Penny immediately, but she was nowhere to be found and I realized it would have to wait until I got back from the hospital, but I can't put it off any longer. Penny needs to know exactly what her boyfriend is.

She looks up from her computer and greets me with a smile when I walk into reception.

'Guess what? We're already fully booked for August. It's looking like it's going to be a good season for Seven Hills.'

'That's great.'

'How did it go at the hospital with Kit and his mum?'

'As well as can be expected. The police haven't interviewed her yet. She's in some kind of catatonic state. They're not sure when she'll come out of it.'

165

'Poor woman, but it's Kit I feel sorry for. Imagine having to deal with your mum killing your brother.'

'He's bearing up well.'

'Ably assisted by you, by the sounds of things.' She grins.

But the memory of Kit's kiss is still fresh and I bristle at the inference. 'I'm just giving him a bit of support,' I snap.

'OK. It was just a joke.' She pulls a face that suggests I've overreacted. 'Anyway, how's our teenage lothario? Still knocking off Tony Cox's girlfriend?'

'Honestly, I don't know. He tells me there's nothing going on between him and Cassie and that he didn't invite her to the cabin and then he's all over her in the pub.'

'I don't know why you bother with him.'

'I just feel with a bit of help, away from Tony, he could get himself straight.' I smile at her. 'Someone once helped Megan and me, when we needed it. Guess I'm just paying it forward.'

'OK, but I can't have Tony coming round here screaming blue murder.'

'I know and Jay has promised me he'll stay away from Cassie.'

'Good.' She looks at me. 'What is it? What's up? You seem a bit on edge.'

'DI Moore got back to me about those detectives who visited you the other night. There's something I need to tell you. About Will.'

'Will?'

'Yes.'

'OK. Sounds serious.'

'It is. She said that the reason why they were so rude to

Will the other night wasn't just because he hadn't told them he went to Gabe's farm the day he was murdered.'

'Oh?'

'It was because ... dn't tell them that ten years ago, he viciously ass... Gabe Narracott at the Stag Inn in Upper Farleig...

26

I arrive at Sneddon Farm to find that someone has already opened the five-bar gate, saving me the trouble of getting out of my car in the drizzle. I drive the short track to the farmhouse and park next to Will's Land Rover.

Dinner was Penny's idea. She decided that if I just got to know Will better, I'd see for myself that what he did to Gabe was a one-off and that he isn't capable of hurting anyone. I'm not sure how much can be gauged about a man's character over a plum crumble, but Penny is my friend and I owe it to her to at least try.

I find her in the kitchen. Unlike the Narracotts' kitchen, Will's is ultra-modern, and I can't help but notice that the shiny white surfaces and an island that wouldn't be out of place in a trendy townhouse are perfect for fingerprinting. It's a CSI thing.

'Thanks for coming,' she says, taking the top off a bottle of cider and handing it to me. 'What happened to Megan?'

Jay didn't receive an invite. She's still angry with him about his dad turning up.

'Sorry, I did my best but apparently she couldn't possibly come as a new game has just been released which, in her world, is a perfectly reasonable excuse.'

'I don't blame her. Look, I've been thinking about Tony's visit.'

'Oh?'

It's not the opening conversational gambit I was expecting.

'He obviously knows where you live so maybe now would be a good time to swap your cabin number.' I do this from time to time, just as a precaution. Few people know my exact address because all mail deliveries, along with visitors, go to reception. Unless, like Tony, they scale the perimeter fence. 'I'll give you one that isn't taken so it doesn't mess with the bookings.'

'OK. Thanks. That would be great.'

Our conversation lapses, but I can't avoid the metaphorical herd of elephants in the room any longer.

'So, did you speak to Will about what happened between him and Gabe?'

'Of course. I told him straightaway, including calling him an idiot for not telling the police.'

To her credit, she was horrified when I told her what Will did to Gabe, particularly as it was over something as trivial as non-payment for some sheep.

'What did he say?'

'He didn't say anything to the police because he'd forgotten about it. He was embarrassed, Ally. It was over something and nothing, and he accepts he completely overreacted.'

'Apparently, he gave Gabe a real pasting.'

'Then why didn't he report it to the police at the time? You said they only found out about it when they were inquiring about Gabe's murder and the landlady of the pub remembered it.'

'I don't know, but this isn't something you can ignore, Penny.'

'We all make mistakes when we're young.'

'That's a pretty big mistake. The second one was not telling the police about it now.'

She looks at me. She knows what I'm getting at.

'You think I'm making excuses for him, don't you?'

'Aren't you?'

'Will would never hurt me, Ally.'

'Are you sure about that? You haven't been seeing him that long. How well do you really know him? Violence doesn't discriminate – you know that as well as I do.'

She looks over my shoulder and back to her own past, one that contained a man, her ex, Ian, who almost killed her. A man she could only escape by running away and starting a new life under a new identity in a remote coastal town. Even now, years later, she's so terrified he might find her she keeps an 'escape boat' moored in the quay.

'Yes, I do and I also know the signs as well as you.'

'Meaning?'

'Meaning Will is nothing like Ian. What he did to Gabe was an isolated incident that happened years ago. Will doesn't have a nasty bone in his body.'

'But—'

She holds her hand up to stop me.

'I know this comes from a good place and that you're only looking out for me, but honestly, you've got nothing to worry about. I'd trust Will with my life.'

The back door opens and a rush of cold air deposits Will in the kitchen. He quickly closes it and removes his boots and boiler suit to reveal a checked shirt and jeans. Like all farmers, Will has an air that no task is too great for his strength, but I can't help wondering what else he has used that strength for.

We sit down to eat, our conversation never straying beyond the day-to-day mundanity of farming and running a holiday park. At the end of the meal, Penny clears the table and ushers Will and I into the sitting room, promising to follow us with coffee. For once, I'm happy to be the victim of a set-up. I'm interested in what – if anything – Will has to say, so I make myself comfortable on the red velvet sofas while he lights a fire in the grate.

'Penny told me that the fight me and Gabe had ten years ago was the reason the detectives were so hostile the other day,' he says, pressing the wood logs into position with his huge and apparently impervious-to-heat hands.

'Can you blame them? It doesn't look good, does it?'

Satisfied with his efforts, Will sits back on the sofa opposite me.

'No, but, as I told the police, me and Gabe put it behind us. We weren't enemies. We've been neighbours all our lives and sometimes neighbours have arguments.'

'But to attack him over some sheep?'

'I had a lot going on at the time. Not that that's any excuse. Look, I know about Penny's past. I'd never do anything to hurt her or anyone.' We both stare at the fire crackling in the grate. He's waiting for me to respond, but it strikes me he's the one who needs to do the talking. He gets the message. 'Penny said you've been helping the police with the murder investigation,' he says, changing the subject.

'Not really.'

He's the last person I'm going to discuss Gabe's killing with.

'I can't believe Miriam would hurt him. She doted on him and Kit. The boys were as thick as thieves, but they couldn't have been more different. Gabe was a bit slower than the rest of us kids and a bit gullible, which made him an easy target with the bullies. Kit would launch himself at anyone who went near him, fists flying, all sorts. He was suspended from school a few times, but he'd do anything to protect his brother.'

'Did you play together as children?' I ask, moving the conversation to safer ground.

'When we were little. I didn't like going onto their farm. I always preferred it when they came to ours.'

'Why was that?'

'Their grandad ran a slaughterhouse there. That's where the farm got its name. It was pulled down years ago. You could hear the animals squealing right across the valley. Didn't matter if you put your hands over your ears, you could still hear it, feel it. It went right through you. Sometimes, at night, when the wind's in a certain direction, I think I can still hear their cries.'

He shudders at the memory.

'It sounds horrible.'

'It was. Dad always suspected old man Narracott secretly enjoyed it.'

'So, did you and Gabe hang out when you were older?'

'No,' he scoffs. 'There's no free ride when you're a farmer's son or daughter. As soon as we were big enough and strong enough to be useful, Dad had us out on the farm. It was the same for the Narracott boys.'

'Us?'

'Me and Caroline. Emma was still a babber then, of course.'

'It must have been a terrible shock when you lost her.'

'It was.' He looks at a photo on the mantelpiece above the fireplace. Sitting next to a teenage version of himself, in the driver's seat of a car, is a young woman. Their ruddy-cheeked likeness is unmistakable. 'That was taken the day she died. She was a brilliant horsewoman. She'd just moved up to the intermediates for British eventing. Her dream was to compete in the Olympics. And then she was gone.'

I remember the crash was on a deceptively sharp corner that had already claimed the lives of the inexperienced and the out-of-towners and still does. Caroline would have known it well, but something happened that day, a combination of speed and a wet surface meant she misjudged the bend and collided with a tree.

'I miss her. Every day.' The fire spits out a tiny spark on the beige rug. Will watches it die. 'Mum and Dad were never the same afterwards. All the joy had left them. They carried on for another five years for Emma's sake as much as anything, but it got to them in the end. Dad had a heart attack and cancer took Mum.'

'I'm so sorry. That must have been a very difficult time for you and Emma.'

'It's why I'm so protective of her. She's all I have left.'

'You have Penny.'

He brightens. 'Yes. I have Penny. I thought it was the bachelor life for me until she came along.'

As if on cue, Penny walks in carrying a tray with a cafetière and some mugs adorned with cartoon sheep with goofy grins.

'What are you two talking about?'

Will grins. 'I was just telling Ally how lucky you are to have me.'

She sits down next to Will and nudges him playfully. 'Is that so?'

Will takes his coffee, rewarding Penny with an affectionate smile, which she returns. I've never seen her so happy.

'Ally, I meant to thank you for having Emma over the other night.'

'That's no problem. You did me a favour too. I don't like leaving Megan alone, especially since her seizure. How's Emma doing, by the way?'

'She'll be OK. She's pretty cut up about this guy, Ollie, but I didn't mess around. I got her in to see a counsellor straightaway. Lisa Kendrick. Penny recommended her to me. She's the best around apparently.'

'Sounds like a good move.'

'I didn't want to risk her doing anything stupid. You never know what goes on in people's minds, do you?'

'I guess you don't.'

I finish my coffee and we say our goodbyes. Standing in the farmhouse doorway, arms wrapped around each other, Penny and Will wave me off into the dark night. God, I hope I'm wrong about him.

As I drive through the twisting lanes, my mind shifts from Penny and Will to Caroline, Will's sister. How terrible it must have been for him and his family to lose her like that. She was so young, her whole life ahead of her. How does anyone recover from that?

My headlights pick out the T-junction where the road joins the main road and I turn left and head back towards

Bidecombe, passing the spot where Caroline Sneddon's life ended. There's a ribbon tied around the trunk of the hundred-year-old oak and several bunches of wilting flowers placed at its base. They've been there for a year or so, a tribute to the latest victim. Maybe they should cut the tree down and then if a driver loses control, they'll end up in the field behind and at least have a chance of surviving. It's then that I realize what's been bothering me about the photo on Will's mantelpiece.

Billy

She didn't tell her parents; she didn't have to. Her mother found her in the toilet throwing up her Ready Brek one morning and guessed straightaway. Predictably, her father flew into a fury. She was a slut, a trollop, a whore, a scrubber, the town bike. There was an apparently endless stream of words to describe her, but at least he didn't strike her. Even he drew the line at pregnant women. And all the while, in among her father's insults, her mother kept asking her if she was sure the lad didn't force himself on her. The hopefulness in her mother's voice sickened Miriam. Her eyes urged her to say yes, yes, that's what happened. He forced me, like that was better than the truth which was she had willingly given herself to Ralph.

Even Robbie had his two penn'orth worth, pacing the small living room, hands curled in fists, declaring he would find the boy and kill him. Her parents demanded she get rid of it. It could be arranged. Her mother new someone in Exeter. Far enough away, no one would ever know.

It. That's what they called the baby growing inside her: it. Like some growth to be cut out, but it was too late for that. She was too far gone. She wouldn't have had a termination anyway. She wanted this baby more than she had wanted anything in the world.

Her parents nagged her to tell them who the father was. She was living under their roof, so they had the right to know, but she didn't tell them even though Ralph had abandoned her. That wasn't his fault. Like her, he was scared and confused, he just showed it differently. He hadn't spoken to her since the night she told him because he needed time to work things out, but she was sure he still loved her. Hadn't he once written her a poem about how their love was so deep, so special, it could overcome anything? And what more proof of their love was needed than the babber growing inside her?

For as long as she had him, Ralph would be in her life and, in time, their son would bring them together again. And it was a boy. She was so certain of it that she hadn't even thought of girls' names. She planned to call him William. Then he could call himself anything: Will, Bill, even Liam. But he would always be Billy to her.

Late at night, away from the disgusted gaze of her parents, she'd stroke her expanded belly and talk to her son, picturing herself holding him in her arms. She'd tell him how much she loved his father and that he would come for them when he was ready, because he loved them. She loved him too, with every beat of her heart. He'd always be safe with her. Then she'd gently sing 'Row Row Row Your Boat' as she rocked him to sleep. It was in those moments that Miriam was sure everything was going to turn out just fine.

Then, one day, her parents told her she couldn't keep Billy. She would go and stay with her father's sister, Aunt Beryl, in South Devon, until the baby was born. They'd arrange for the baby to be adopted there.

South Devon was beyond the reach of the gossips in Barnston, her father said, but everyone knew what it meant when a young girl suddenly disappeared for half a year. It was dressed up as working away or going to look after an ill or elderly relative, but they all came back sadder, emptier.

It was best for everyone, her mother said, but not for Miriam. She didn't want to give Billy up. She should have refused, stood up to her parents for once, but her father said he would toss her out on to the streets and where would she have gone then? She'd be destitute. So, she said nothing and clung to the thought that Ralph would do the right thing.

She pictured him appearing breathless on the station platform to claim her and their unborn child just as she stepped on to the train. Or she'd wake to the sound of stones against her window, and the two of them would disappear, laughing into the night, to make a new life a long way from Barnston. But it was all a fantasy. She knew from Ms Winters that Ralph was living uni life to the full while she got fatter. Ralph wasn't coming for her or Billy.

She left the nursery when she started to show. She told Ms Winters she'd got another job, but the way she kept glancing at Miriam's swollen belly, she was sure she knew the truth. She didn't say anything, just how very sad she was at how things had turned out.

The morning Miriam was due to catch the train to her Aunt Beryl's, her stomach cramped her so badly she threw up and she started to bleed, like it was her monthly, but it couldn't be. She told her mother, who couldn't hide her relief, and it was then that Miriam knew she'd lost Billy.

It was her fault, of course. It was all that fear and fretting she kept inside her. What baby would want to be born to a mother like her? She didn't deserve him and now he'd left her.

In the weeks and months that followed, Father told her to pull herself together. Robbie said she should be celebrating as she'd had a lucky escape. Mother told her it was for the best – no one wants a bastard around the place. At night, she'd sit by her window and stare up at the cloudless sky, wondering if one of those stars was Billy. But it couldn't be, could it? Because he'd never had the chance to live, the chance to prove he was good. Maybe the spaces in between the stars was for all the souls, like Billy's, that had never been born. There was a space inside her too, a cold, dark void that could never be filled. Even now, even after giving birth to her beloved Gabe and Kit, it's still there, waiting for the impossible, waiting for Billy.

To her shame, now there was no baby, she wondered if Ralph would come back to her, and things would return to how they were. She could still be his girl. This time, she'd be more careful, of course. To her amazement, Ralph did come back into her life, but there was no going back for either of them. He'd made sure of that.

27

When I get back to the cabin from my night with Will and Penny, I find Jay sitting on the sofa reading his phone, which he stashes as soon as he sees me.

'Don't stop on my account,' I say, draping my jacket over the back of the kitchen bar stool. 'I'm heading to bed. I take it Megan's already turned in?'

'Yeah, actually, I was waiting up for you.'

'Oh? Everything OK?' Megan's bedroom door receives an anxious glance.

'All good.' Jay pauses and swallows. 'Has Penny told you I have to leave? Is that why you went to Will's tonight?'

'What? No. She's angry about Tony, but she'll get over it. She just needs a bit of time, that's all.'

'I'm sorry.'

'You can't help how your dad behaves, I guess.'

'Not sure he was ever much of a dad.'

'Stay away from him, Jay, he's dangerous.'

He gathers the duvet around him. 'You think I don't know that?'

Bed can wait. I push the covers to one side and join him on the sofa. 'That means staying away from Cassie too.'

'Honestly, there's nothing going on between us.'

'So what's the story with her and Tony? He's all over her, but I get the impression she's not terribly keen.'

'She likes someone else, and it's not me before you ask. She'd been seeing this guy for years till he cheated on her.'

'So why's she with Tony? To make him jealous?'

'Dunno. Maybe. I don't think she has much choice.'

'He's forcing her?'

'Nah. He's just a dickhead.'

'There's a lot of it about.'

He nods at me. 'Yeah, Megan told me about her real dad.'

'Really?' I try not to make my interest too obvious. 'What did she say?'

'Not much. She's never met him, right?'

'No, he scarpered before my first scan. She hasn't talked about trying to contact him, has she?'

'Dunno, but why would she do that? He's no better than mine, is he?'

'No, I guess not.'

'Anyway, I told her she doesn't need him. She's got you.'

His words tease a grateful smile from me.

'I appreciate that.'

'She's lucky to have a mum at all.'

'You must miss yours terribly.'

'Yeah.' He grins at me. 'Soppy bugger, ain't I?'

'Not at all.'

'But it's OK, I've got you now.'

'I'm hardly Mum of the Year.'

'But you've always got my back even when you're having a go at me.' We both laugh, but his quickly fades. 'That's why

I got them to call you that night in the cop shop when I beat Dad up. I knew you'd come. You wouldn't let me down. And I won't let you down.' I'm touched by his words, and I wonder if I'm seeing what Megan sees: a sensitive young man who cares. 'And ta for letting me stay here. It's cool with you and Megan.'

'It's nothing special.'

'Maybe not, but there's no drama. No crying druggies on the doorstep or screaming cops battering the door down. It's just . . .'

'Normal?'

'Yeah. Normal. I didn't know what that felt like till I moved in with you and Megan. It helps I'm off the drugs too.'

'Really?'

He looks at me intently. 'Really. Swear on my mum's life.'

It's then that I notice he's changed. Nothing startling, just that his cheeks have plumped out a little and his complexion is clearer, less pasty, and his eyes less dull. For the first time, I actually think Jay Cox might be telling me the truth. He's off the drugs.

'You don't need to do that, but now you're back on your feet you can start thinking about what you want to do with your life.'

'Don't laugh, but I'd really like to work with birds. Maybe at one of those rescue centres.'

'A bird sanctuary?'

'Yeah. My mum loved nature, passed it on to me. Taught me the names of all the wildflowers in the hedgerows. They all mean something, you know. Snowdrops mean hope, daffodils forgiveness and violets innocence. But she really loved birds. She could tell what it was, just by hearing their song. So can

I. I heard a couple of sand martins the other day. Not seen them in a while.'

He moulds his lips together, leaving a small opening between them. A chitter-chatter sound, not unlike the sound crickets make, fills the cabin.

'That's incredible, Jay. I'll have to take your word for it that's what they sound like. A pigeon cooing is about my limit.'

'I'll teach you if you like.'

'You know what? I'd like that. Look, whatever you decide to do, promise me you'll stay away from Tony and Cassie.'

'Sure.'

But he can't look me in the eye.

***

I open my laptop on my bed and type Caroline Sneddon's name into Google. Dozens of links appear. I click on a local newspaper report, headlined 'Promising young horsewoman killed in horror crash' and start reading.

The accident happened mid-morning on a clear, dry day. It had rained the night before but there was no standing water on the roads and conditions were good. Caroline was on her way back from Bidecombe where she had just collected her dressage uniform from the cleaner's. As she approached the bend, police believe a pheasant, or something, flew out in front of her distracting her from the road, because she failed to turn the wheel quickly enough to negotiate the corner and ploughed headlong into the oak tree.

The subsequent investigation revealed there were no skid marks, so she didn't even have time to brake. She just drove straight into the tree. The local police commander calls the accident a tragedy that has rocked the community of North Devon. Having competed in horse shows since she was a little girl, Caroline was well known and well loved locally. The officer also takes the opportunity to implore youngsters to buckle up. If Caroline had been wearing a seatbelt, it would have saved her life.

I remember Bernadette telling me the same thing in one of her weekly phone calls to me when I was at uni. Only in the photo on Will's mantelpiece, which Will said was taken the day she died, Caroline is wearing a seatbelt.

28

The next morning I find Megan sitting alone on the sofa, tucking into a bowl of cornflakes. Her smile warms me and I join her with a mug of black coffee.

'How was it at Will and Penny's?'

'Lovely, thank you. How was your night? Good game?'

'Fantastic. I beat Jay hands down.' She laughs.

'Speaking of which, where is he?'

'Job interview. The council is looking for an apprentice to keep the parks looking nice.'

'Well, if anyone knows the parks in Bidecombe it's Jay. He's certainly spent enough time in them.'

'Mum!' she says, nudging me in the ribs.

'I'm joking. Seriously, it's great to hear he's finally getting his life together. You like having him around, don't you?'

'If that's code for *are you going out with him*, I already told you the answer is no, I'm not. We're just good friends.'

'It wasn't code for anything,' I lie.

'He hasn't got anyone else,' she says in an exasperated tone of someone tired of explaining themselves. 'His mum is dead. His dad's an arsehole.'

'Having the ability to manufacture sperm doesn't make you a great dad.'

'Yeah, well, I know what that feels like.'

'Are we talking about Sean or . . . Julian here?'

'Both. They're both losers, aren't they? Just in different ways.'

'I guess so. Do you ever think about either of them?'

'Sometimes.'

I put my empty coffee cup on the breakfast bar. 'Do you wish you knew Julian? He is your real dad. I'd completely understand if you did.'

'I thought I did, but I'm not so sure any more. I've got you and Penny, haven't I? That's enough parents for anyone.' She grins. 'And Jay's here now. I don't need anyone else. That's what I told Lisa, anyway.'

I want to ask her more, ask her if this means she's contacted Julian, but I don't. For now, it's enough to hear that whatever she has done or was thinking of doing, she's pulled back, so I change the subject. 'I've been meaning to ask you, how's the counselling going?'

'I'm not sure I'll need it much longer. In fact, I've seen a course at college in Barnston. It's in photography. I'd have to start at a lower level because I'll have missed my exams, but it looks really cool. It starts in September.'

'That sounds great. Maybe we can arrange to have a look around.'

'I'd like that. Jay and I are going to go out and take photos today. I thought I might put together a portfolio.'

'That's a really good idea. Megan, you do understand why I've kept you off school, don't you?'

'You're just looking out for me, I guess.'

'Once we have a diagnosis for what happened at Bidecombe Supplies, we can move forward.'

'Does that mean you'll let me go to the school prom in a few weeks? It's before the exams because of all the trouble they had last year. It's just for a few hours. Maybe I could take Jay as my plus-one. Please say yes.'

'Maybe, as long as you don't have another seizure before then.'

'Deal.'

The front door flies open and Jay bounds in, firing imaginary guns into the air. 'You'll never guess what? I got it! I got the job!'

Megan springs up from the sofa and hugs him. 'I knew it.'

Jay turns to me, reading the disbelief on my face. 'The guy who interviewed me knew my mum.'

'I'm sure that's not the only reason he offered you the job.'

'It is.' He laughs. 'But who cares? I told him no one knows the parks in Bidecombe like I do.'

I exchange smiles with Megan, and Jay slides his spare spindly arm around me and gives me a surprisingly strong hug.

'So, is this what you meant when you said you'd make me proud of you?'

'Nah, this is just the start.'

'Just make sure you turn up on time and do as you're told.' I want to tell him this is a real chance to leave his old life behind, to start afresh, but I don't as my throat feels suddenly constricted.

***

My entrance to the Stag Inn draws a predictable response from the sprinkling of locals nursing their lunchtime drinks; their curious eyes follow me all the way to Sammy Narracott, dressed in his farmer's overalls and standing at the bar supping his pint. I'm assuming his pie is on its way if the information at the briefing at Police HQ is sound.

After I read about her death, I couldn't get Caroline Sneddon out of my mind, more specifically why she wasn't wearing a seatbelt when she crashed, given she'd worn one earlier that day. Did she forget? Or did she not wear it for a reason?

Penny said that Caroline was heartbroken after breaking up with her boyfriend at the time. It wouldn't be the first time an emotionally distraught young woman unbuckled her belt and deliberately drove a car at high speed into a tree. Caroline's death was certainly tragic, but I'm starting to think it wasn't an accident.

According to the date on the newspaper, less than month after Caroline died and the day after her funeral, Will viciously attacked Gabe in the pub. Was Gabe Caroline's boyfriend? Was he the one who broke her heart? Was that the real reason Will went for him? And was that why Gabe, ridden with guilt, refused to report him to the police?

The problem was I had no way of finding out. Gabe was dead and, already wary of me, Will was unlikely to tell me anything. I couldn't ask Kit either; he'd just lost his brother. But then I realized there was one person who might know. One person I could ask about Caroline.

'Sammy?'

He turns his thickset body so slowly, he reminds me of

those oil tankers that are too large to manoeuvre quickly. He frowns at me before recognition dawns.

'You're that police lady Kit was talking to the other day.'

'Yes, that's right. I was wondering if I could have a word.'

'Fire away,' he says, thinking I'm on official business.

I'm about to suggest somewhere away from the landlady's undisguised interest before changing my mind. Maybe it was her who tipped the police off about the fight between Will and Gabe in the Stag that night, in which case she may have other things to say.

'I wanted to ask you about Caroline Sneddon.'

'Caroline?' He screws his face up in confusion. 'What d'you want to know about her for?'

'I wanted to know what happened the day she died.'

Apparently accepting that this must be part of the inquiries relating to Gabe's murder, Sammy nods. 'Well, as you know it was a long time ago so I was just a nipper when she died.'

'Lovely maid,' interjects the landlady.

Sammy nods at his pint. ''Twas a terrible way to go.'

'Especially given how well she knew those roads,' I add, hoping that by casually sliding into the conversation, I'll elicit some information, but it doesn't work and Sammy sees right through me.

'What are you saying?'

He's impossible to read and I can't tell if my words have angered him or not, but there's no turning back now.

'I heard that her death . . . wasn't an accident?'

'Who told you that?' He knits his thick brows into a deep frown.

'I heard that she deliberately crashed her car.'

'Now hold on a second,' says the landlady.

'It's all right, Carla.' He raises his hand surprisingly quickly. 'I got this. What do you want exactly?'

'Just some answers.'

'Is this official police business?'

'No,' I concede. 'It's got nothing to do with the police. It's personal and it won't go any further either, I promise. I'm not here to cause trouble, Sammy. I'm just trying to help a friend of mine. Please.'

He glances at Carla.

'You may as well tell her, Sammy. There's no shame in it, not these days.'

'OK. The police called it an accident, but we all knew she'd done it on purpose.'

'Why didn't anyone say anything?'

'Esme and Lawrence – Caroline's parents – and Will were going through hell as it was. No one wanted to say that it might have been suicide. It was a long time ago when plenty of people around here still considered it a sin.'

'Why did she do it?'

'No idea,' he says too quickly.

'It's just that I heard she was going out with Gabe Narracott at the time and that he broke up with her just before she died.'

'You hear a lot, don't you?'

'It's true then.'

Caught out, Sammy sighs. 'Yes. Gabe tried to keep it quiet. He was worried if his mum found out she'd put a stop to it. Miriam could be a bit possessive of him, but I'd seen them in the woods together.'

'Did Will know?'

'If I'd seen them, maybe he had too.'

'Is that why Will beat Gabe up in this pub? He blamed him for Caroline's death.'

Sammy shrugs at his half-empty glass.

'Who knows?'

'It was terrible,' says Carla, who has been itching to have her say. 'Like I told the police. He came marching in here and grabbed Gabe by the throat. He had him on the floor and he was just punching him in the face. It took Zac Coombes and a couple of others to drag him off. Poor Gabe was in a right state, but I felt for Will too. He'd just lost his sister.' Mitigating circumstances – that's what it's called, when something beyond your control affects your behaviour, and Will Sneddon had them in spades. It doesn't excuse his violence, but it does explain it. ''Course, it didn't stop with poor Caroline, did it?' says Carla.

'What do you mean?'

'Esme and Lawrence never got over her passing. The stress and grief of it all did for them both. The cancer got Esme first and Lawrence came in from the fields one night, sat down in his chair and never got up again.' She taps her chest. 'Ticker just gave out. I remember it like it was yesterday. It was lambing season. Poor Will was left to fend totally on his own. Emma couldn't have been more than twelve. He blamed Gabe for their deaths too.'

***

I leave Sammy tucking into his pie and return to my car, but as I pull out of the parking space, Will's Land Rover swings into the car park. I decide to hang back to say hello, but when the door opens, it isn't Will, it's Emma. Before I have time to wind my window down and shout hi to her, she slams the car door and hurries into the pub.

Through the pub window, I watch her march over to Sammy Narracott who is chomping enthusiastically on a pastry crust. Glancing at Carla, she says something to him, and he picks up his plate and pint and they adjourn to a table away from the bar. Sammy carries on forking his food into his mouth as Emma leans in close to talk. When she stops, he makes her wait until he's finished his mouthful and has another drink before he responds. He doesn't say much and what he does say is wrapped up in several shakes of his head.

Whatever it is, Emma doesn't like it, but she doesn't give up. She's asking him something, no, not asking, pleading, but he refuses to meet her eye. Finally, while she's still talking, he collects his glass and his plate and returns to the bar, leaving her sitting alone. Judging by the expression on Carla's face, she's as keen to know what they were talking about as I am, but I'm interrupted by my phone buzzing.

It's Kit, but I don't want to talk about me, him or that kiss, and I'm about to refuse the call when I stop myself. Maybe it's about Miriam. I take the call. At first all I can hear is the wind buffeting the line. Eventually, Kit's voice reaches me.

'Ally, can you come to the farm right away? I think I've found something.'

29

Kit and I trudge through the long, dew-soaked grass across the field towards the woods, passing the barn where Harriet discovered the used condom. He reaches the perimeter and climbs the low wooden fence into the dense swathe of woodland that divides Narracott Farm and Sneddon Farm. I ignore his outstretched hand, dropping down beside him, and we continue along an unseen path through the woods. The thick canopy of leaves casts an eternal gloom, sealing the pungent mustiness that rises from the soft damp earth, nourishing the pale-yellow clusters of death cap fungi dotting its floor. My spine registers the drop in temperature with a shiver and not because of the unusual stillness of the air and absence of any birdsong. At least that's what I tell myself.

'You should have called DI Moore,' I call out to Kit who is a good few metres ahead of me.

'It might be nothing,' Kit says, batting aside a thin errant branch in his way. 'I didn't want to drag her out here on a wild goose chase.'

'Ninety per cent of policing is a wild goose chase.'

At the edge of a clearing, he stops, allowing me to catch up with him. In the middle is a building, but I have no idea what it is for. Farmers don't usually house their animals in sheds in the woods and it's too small to be a hay barn. Besides, it's made of brick, and someone once took the trouble to paint it white, although judging by the green mildew, that was a long time ago. It could have been a labourer's cottage but there's no running water or electricity and then it dawns on me. This was never anyone's home. Hidden in the woods, away from prying eyes, this wasn't a place where lives were cherished. This was a place where lives were ended.

'It's a slaughterhouse, isn't it?' I remember Will saying he avoided Narracott Farm as a child because he couldn't bear the squeals of animals in their death throes. In a narrow, deep valley like this, their cries must have echoed for miles. 'I thought farm animals were meant to go to the local abattoir.'

'They are.'

'So why would you need your own slaughterhouse?'

'Farmers can kill their own animals if it's for their own consumption, but not all farmers liked the idea, so they'd bring the animals to my grandad. He was pretty good at it, by all accounts, and cheaper than the abattoir. He had quite the production line going at one point, too much to be eaten by one family. And they weren't all farm animals.'

'What do you mean?'

'People would bring him deer they'd shot on the moors, and he'd chop them up for them. They then sold it directly to the butchers in Bidecombe and Barnston.'

'Which is illegal.'

'Very. He had quite an industry going, big enough to build a new slaughterhouse. That one was pulled down years ago though.'

'So what am I doing here?'

But he isn't listening; his memories have already transported him elsewhere.

'I'd be playing on the farm, and it would suddenly start up, a high-pitched scream, like some kind of death siren which meant the killing had begun. It's like nothing you've ever heard before. It just seemed to go on forever. I'd run inside and hide in the cupboard under the stairs until it stopped. Gabe was different. He'd go down and watch. He even persuaded Grandad to teach him how to slaughter animals. Dad was furious. He hated the place. Had it knocked down as soon as Grandad died.'

'So what's this place then?'

'This is the original slaughterhouse. Dad probably forgot it was here. We all did.'

Kit takes the final few paces towards the front door.

'I thought I'd kill a bit of time and take a look inside.' He lifts the latch and tugs at the door, but it catches on the uneven ground. He gives it another yank and it opens. 'And then I saw this,' he says, stepping aside for me to go in, but I don't move. For a second, I think this is a set-up and I realize that no one knows I'm here. Kit reads my thoughts. 'It's OK.'

Of course it is. I put my head around the door and peer in. It takes a few moments for my eyes to adjust to the darkness. Ivy has slowly strangled the interior, lacing itself over an opening that once held a window frame, but there's still just enough light for me to make out a table made from thick wooden blocks hewn from English maple. Littered with different-sized saws, it's not a surface to eat off, but a surface for working.

A spectre of a shadow falls across the table and walls,

but I can't work out what's creating it until I realize it isn't a shadow: it's a huge dark stain. It looks like blood, but it's impossible to say without testing it.

In the corner furthest from the door, there's another table – the small, foldaway kind. On it, is a laptop. It looks oddly out of place in this centuries-old building, and, on the floor next to it, squats a large black holdall. I've seen enough. I step back from the doorway.

'Shouldn't we go in and take a closer look?' asks Kit.

'No,' I say, putting my arm up in case he's thinking of doing exactly that. 'We're not going inside this building.'

'Why not?'

'Because it's a crime scene.'

30

DI Harriet Moore is standing next to DS Henry Whitely, arms folded, scowling at the slaughterhouse as if deeply offended by its presence.

'How the hell did we miss this place? I mean the farm is named after it, for God's sake.'

Harriet looks at DS Whitely like it's his fault he didn't know there were two slaughterhouses, but it isn't. This was her call. She's running the show. She decides what gets searched, but any other SIO would have done the same. The moor isn't a city park. It's nearly three hundred square miles of mostly desolate uplands. You have to call it off somewhere, but I can tell Harriet thinks she stopped short, way too short.

'We did ask, Boss, but Mr Narracott said the slaughterhouse was pulled down years ago. This is the original slaughterhouse, apparently, before a newer one was built closer to the farm-house. The search teams didn't get this far.'

To his relief, she switches her focus to Kit.

'So what exactly were you doing in the woods, Mr Narracott?'

'Killing time until the industrial cleaners had finished cleaning the farmhouse.'

'I see. And what about you, Ally?'

'Kit called me when he saw what was in the slaughterhouse.'

'Did either of you go in, at any time?'

'No. I stood in the doorway and as soon as I realized what I was looking at, I called you.'

'I see. Well, thank you, Mr Narracott, I think we can take it from here. We'll be in touch about a statement.'

Kit hovers for a few moments before realizing he's just been dismissed.

'Right, yes, of course. I'll go and see if the cleaners have finished.'

He ambles off just as Jim Dixon, the crime scene manager who was at the briefing, approaches us. He doesn't acknowledge me.

'We've done a presumptive test on the substance on the walls which suggests it's blood,' he says to Harriet.

'Is it human?'

I can almost sense her holding her breath. She could be looking at another murder inquiry and no SIO wants more than one murder on their books; it means difficult decisions have to be made, especially in a rural force like this one where budgets are tight and resources thinly stretched.

'We won't know until it goes to the lab. All I can say is that looking at the layers of dust and dirt, it's not particularly fresh.'

'When you say it's not fresh, could it be twenty years old? That's when the place was last used to kill animals.'

'Sorry, I honestly couldn't tell you.'

I once read scientists can only predict the age of a bloodstain if it's less than two years old.

'OK.'

'What about the laptop?'

'We've lifted some fingerprints and we'll send it off to digital forensics to see what's on it. We'll let you know as soon as we hear anything. We've also got some shoe prints.'

'Shoe prints? Should I get excited?'

'Possibly. We found them on the other side of the slaughter-house. Whoever they belong to, it looks like they came from the road which is about a hundred metres away on the other side of the slaughterhouse.'

'So they don't belong to Ally or Kit. They came from the farmhouse.'

'No, they don't. And possibly not Gabe either. They're quite small and it's an odd route to take. He'd have had to walk along the road and then cut into the woods. It's far longer than just taking the route across his own land. There's also a lay-by where the woods meet the road.'

'So, you think someone parked in the lay-by and walked to the slaughterhouse?'

'It's a possibility.'

'OK. Let's get those shoe prints checked against the shoe prints recovered from the murder scene. Anything else?'

Jim smiles. 'On the floor was a black holdall. We estimate there's around £180,000 of used notes inside it.'

'You're kidding?' Harriet frowns at the building. 'What the hell is that doing there?'

'Drugs would be the obvious answer,' says DS Whitely, 'but £180,000 is a hell of a lot of cash. Do you think it could be a county line?'

'Could be, but Narracott Farm would be like no trap house I've ever seen.' She spreads her hands. 'Why turn to drugs when you have all of this?'

Harriet has fallen for the assumption that land equals wealth, but anyone in farming will tell you that isn't the case.

'The thing with farmers is that they can be asset rich, but cash poor and they need cash to run a farm,' I say.

'What do you mean?'

'Gabe lost his entire flock a few years ago. It almost ruined him. He would have been desperate for cash, desperate enough to turn to crime, maybe.'

'But how would he even know how to go about it? He only left the farm to visit his local and the sheep markets. It doesn't make sense.'

'This has to be connected to his murder though,' says DS Whitely. 'It's too much of a coincidence.'

'Believe me, I don't like coincidences any more than the next person, but it's still possible Miriam killed Gabe. The fact he might be running a drugs ring could have nothing to do with his death.'

'Or someone else was running a drugs op from the slaughterhouse and Gabe had no idea what was going on. The route the CSIs found goes straight down to the main road. They could have come and gone completely unnoticed.'

'So many maybes. I like maybes even less than I like coincidences.' Harriet tuts. 'Tell me about Kit's behaviour when you discovered what was inside the slaughterhouse.'

Her sudden interest in Kit takes me by surprise but I cast my mind back to when I told him I thought the stains on the wall could be dried blood, after we called the police.

'He was as surprised as I was when I told him it was a crime scene. Why?'

'Just asking.'

'Is he a suspect in Gabe's murder?'

'No. Not at all. His alibi is encased in lead. He crashed out after downing three bottles of Champagne that night.'

'So why the interest in him?'

She looks at DS Whitely.

'Henry, go ask the CSIs how much longer they'll be.'

He looks at me and leaves.

'Look, you can tell me to piss off, but you do know Kit Narracott is knocking off his boss's wife, don't you?'

'Thanks. Yes, I do, but there's nothing going on between us anyway.'

'You sure about that.'

'Positive.'

'OK. That's good to hear, but . . . ?'

'But what?'

'Kit Narracott is the son of a murder suspect and the brother of the victim; you'd do well to remember that.'

31

Ingham Farm lies in the heart of Exmoor, nestled towards the bottom of a gentle grassy slope where the light is brighter and the air sweeter. As I get out of my car, I can hear the stream gently chuckling its way through the valley floor. The low growl of chickens drifts over the stone wall circling the farm, and somewhere deep in one of the barns a lamb bleats in hunger.

Carla's words about Esme and Lawrence played on my mind long after I left the Stag Inn yesterday. Will's parents never got over the loss of their daughter, Caroline, and both died quite soon afterwards. If Will beat up Gabe because he blamed him for Caroline's death, what else was he prepared to do if he thought Gabe was responsible for his parents' death too?

Jonny Ingham is already at the front door of Greystone cottage; the throaty roar of my ageing red Volvo having already disturbed the peace. Alongside his small flock of sheep, Jonny rears Gloucestershire Old Spots and sells the pork at the local farmers' market. When I first met him, he only had a few chickens in a shed in his back garden in Bidecombe and he was PC Ingham, North Devon's police wildlife officer. He was good too, but the call of the land was too great, so he left the job, sold up and moved out here to become a full-time farmer.

'Hi, Jonny. I see you have a new addition to the farm since I last saw you.' I smile at the little girl of about three with blonde curls and red wellington boots he's holding in his arms.

'This is Daisy.'

'Hello, Daisy.'

She buries her face in her dad's shoulder and he gently lowers her onto the ground, making sure she finds her footing before he lets go.

'Off you go, back inside now. Noodles needs feeding.' Watching her march purposefully back into the farmhouse kitchen, I feel a pang for the days when Megan did as she was told.

'Noodles?'

'A lamb. Rejected by its mother. I thought she'd be a great mum too. She's even taken on other ewes' lambs, but when it came to her own, she wasn't up to it. Just goes to show you never can tell. That's what I like about farming. Full of surprises.' He smiles.

'Doesn't sound like you're missing your old job then?'

'No, I did my time, but this is my first love.' His eyes flow over the surrounding hills blushing purple with heather. 'Apart from Jayne and Daisy, of course. But how's things with you? I heard what happened to your daughter. You've been in our prayers.'

'Thank you, Jonny. I really appreciate that, and Megan is getting better every day.'

'That's good to hear. They're all that matters really, aren't they? So, what brings you out to these wild and desolate parts?'

'Do you remember a few years back you asked me to photograph the sheep killed on Gabe Narracott's land?'

'How could I forget? The worst case of sheep worrying I've ever seen. Terrible business.'

'If I remember correctly, we had someone in the frame for it.'

'Yes, that's right. A rambler saw a man with two dogs not far from the scene. Gave us a cracking description.'

'Can you recall who it was?'

'Of course. Lobby Rix. His real name is Bernard, but he's from Lobb, hence his nickname. He was notorious. We'd caught him badger baiting. He got twenty weeks for that so when his name came up, we thought we had him.'

'But you couldn't make it stick.'

'No. The descriptions matched him and his dogs, but he insisted he was just out walking his dogs on a public footpath like any other law-abiding citizen.'

'Didn't we take DNA samples from the sheep?'

'Yep. We brought in the Animal and Plant Health Agency and all sorts, but when we went around to Rix's house to seize the dogs, they were nowhere to be found. He said he'd sold them, but then couldn't remember who to, so we hit a dead end. The problem was we couldn't work out a motive. Even if it was an accident, Lobby would have got his dogs under control long before they killed thirty sheep.' Jonny frowns. 'Besides, this was deliberate.'

'What happened to Lobby?'

'We had to let him go. Actually, he's still around. Got himself straight. He runs a farm over at Dunkery Beacon. The only dog he has now is a collie, called Dilly.'

'So you still see him?'

Jonny smiles. 'This'll make you laugh. Not only do I see him, I'm related to him.'

'How?'

'He married Jayne's cousin a few years back. Best thing he ever did. Now I'm not wearing a badge any more, we get on quite well.'

'Do you think he'd be prepared to tell you the full story now?'

'Why would he do that?'

'Like you said you're not a police officer any more and Gabe's dead. It's not like anyone's going to press charges.'

'No, I'm sorry, Ally.' He glances back at the farmhouse. 'I can't. Lobby's turned over a new leaf. I should respect that and not go dredging up the past. I doubt he'd tell me anyway.'

'That's fair enough. You have my number if you change your mind. I have one more question.'

'Oh?'

'Could someone have hired Lobby to do it?'

'We thought about that but got nowhere. Gabe was well liked around here, a real gentle giant. Everyone thought well of him.' Not everyone, but I don't correct him. 'Gabe's only neighbours were the Sneddons and the Coombes and they'd never have done something like this. What people don't realize is that farmers are animal lovers.'

'Perhaps they had a good reason.'

'It'd have to be a pretty bloody good reason.'

32

The briefing room quickly fills. Jim Dixon, the crime scene manager, catches my eye. He doesn't think I should be here either. I'm not on Major Investigations or even officially back at work, but Harriet seems to like having me around, and I can't deny I'm flattered: ego trumps reality every time.

Harriet phoned me just as I was leaving Jonny Ingham's farm and asked me to attend the briefing in an 'observational' capacity. I'm pretty sure I don't have any observations worth sharing, but Megan and Jay have gone to photograph the quayside and I'm as curious as the next person to know what a laptop and a large stash of cash was doing in an old slaughterhouse on Exmoor.

Harriet joins us, and the chatter dies away.

'OK, I've called you together this morning because we may or may not have a development on the Gabe Narracott murder. Yesterday the deceased's brother, Kit Narracott, came across this place in the woods on their farmland.' She nods to the back of the room. The lights dim and a slide appears on the screen behind her. 'Apparently it's a slaughterhouse.' Harriet talks the room through the building and what was found there. 'The blood on the walls isn't human so that's something.'

'Best guess is that it's deer,' says Jim.

'There's quite a black market in venison in North Devon, but we're still firming that up,' says Henry.

'Enough of a black market to earn someone £180,000?'

'No.' Henry consults his notes. 'Wholesale deer costs around £3.00 per kilo and a deer carcass weighs around 55 kgs so, as a very rough estimate, that's around £165 per animal, but that's the legal trade. Under-the-counter meat would be less. Based on those figures, Gabe would have had to slaughter well over a thousand deer. There's only around three thousand deer on Exmoor so it just isn't possible.'

Henry's female colleague appears irritated by his familiarity with deer prices, but it's this kind of thoroughness that will make him a great detective.

'The £180,000 hasn't come from selling deer meat so where is it from?' continues Harriet.

'Drugs are the obvious route.'

'Yes, we know Gabe lost his flock of sheep a few years back and so would have been short of money, enough to threaten his livelihood, so we have motive, but it's one thing to be short of cash and another to be able to set up a drugs ring and, of course, none of this may be connected to Gabe's murder. What forensics do have we from the slaughterhouse, Jim?'

'The fingerprints on the computer belong to Gabe Narracott.'

'OK, so whatever was going on there, Gabe was involved in some way.'

'Looks that way.'

'Any other fingerprints?'

'No.'

'Anything from the shoe print at the slaughterhouse?'

'Yes. It matches the shoe print found near the farmhouse.'

'Really? Another rambler? They do get around.'

'Unlikely, there are no rights of way near the slaughter-house.'

'That is interesting. So whoever it belongs to visited both the slaughterhouse and the farmhouse? Which potentially connects them to the murder and whatever shenanigans were going on in the woods?'

'Yes.'

There's a knock on the door. A young woman puts her head around.

'Ah, digital forensics. Nice of you to join us.'

'Sorry, I'm late, ma'am, but we've only just got into the laptop recovered from the slaughterhouse,' she says, slightly breathless.

'Did you find anything?'

'Yes.'

'And?'

She hesitates, unsure that she should share her findings with a room full of people.

'It's OK. Go ahead. No secrets here,' says Harriet.

'We found several hundred indecent images of young children being abused.' There's an audible intake of breath from the room followed by a couple of utterances of 'Christ'. Murder inquiries are one thing, but murder inquiries that involve children in any way are on another level. The investigation takes on a different hue. The collective horror and grief for the child who has been hurt, or worse, will never see adulthood, fires a greater determination to bring the perpetrators to justice.

Harriet gives herself and the room a few moments to digest the news before taking a deep breath.

'Where are they from?'

'We don't know yet. They look like they're downloaded from some site. We've only just found them.'

'OK, well I won't keep you. Let me know as soon as you have something.'

The young woman leaves, and Harriet faces the room. 'Thoughts?'

'The £180,000 could be to pay off a blackmailer.'

'Yes. The question is how did this blackmailer know about Gabe? It's not the sort of thing you advertise, is it? And that's a helluva lot of cash,' says Harriet.

'He had a lot to lose.'

'But where would he get that kind of money?'

'These farmers have all sorts stashed away,' says Henry vaguely.

Harriet shakes her head. 'Are you saying he happened to save £180,000 for the day someone might attempt to blackmail him? That doesn't fly with me. I still think drugs are at the heart of this. What if someone found out about Gabe and was blackmailing him into using the shed as a distribution hub.'

'Why bother? Why not just use an abandoned barn up on the moors?'

'That's true. My hubby drags me out walking on the moors every Sunday; there are dozens of them all over the county. So why bring in Gabe and Slaughterhouse Farm?'

The room falls silent whilst we mull over her question. I turn to look out of the window. We're on the third floor, overlooking the helipad. Beyond, sheep dot the patchwork of hills rolling towards the horizon. It's lambing season and I watch a couple of lambs leaping around each other whilst their uninterested mother grazes nearby. In a few short months, they'll be off to market.

That's it. That's why there was £180,000 in a bag in the slaughterhouse at Narracott Farm.

33

Difficult conversations come with the territory in policing, but none are as difficult as the one I'm about to have with my closest friend, but she has to know the truth, for her own sake.

Dressed in red tie-dye dungarees, hair wrapped land girls' style in a yellow paisley scarf, Penny is easy to spot in among the pines at Seven Hills, furiously scrubbing six months of grime from the windows of cabin 214.

'How the hell can something get so dirty in such a short space of time?' She rolls her eyes and laughs as she sees me approaching.

'Do you want a hand?'

'No, this is the last one. Megan said you were at police headquarters. She and Jay have gone off to take pictures of the quay.'

'Yeah, the DI wanted my input on something.'

Penny wrings the water from her cloth. 'She must like you.'

'I guess so.'

'At this rate, you'll be back on Major Investigations before you know it,' she says, swiping her cloth across the glass.

'Maybe.'

'Is something up, Ally? You seem distracted.'

'There's no easy way to say this, Penny.'

She stops wiping. 'Say what?'

'Will didn't beat Gabe up over some sheep.'

'Oh?' Already, I can detect a defensiveness in her voice.

'It was over his sister, Caroline.'

'What?'

'Gabe was going out with Caroline, but he broke up with her. The crash wasn't an accident. She killed herself.'

'Oh my God. Poor Caroline.'

'Will never mentioned it to you then?'

'Why would he? He's not one to rake over the past or talk about his feelings, but, at least it makes more sense than fighting over some sheep. Will was obviously completely consumed with grief.'

'Yes, it does. But . . .'

'But what?'

'There's something else you should know. I don't think it was a one-off.'

'What do you mean?'

'Around two years after Caroline died, someone set their dog on Gabe's sheep, killing thirty of them. It was horrific. Most of them were in lamb. It was a terrible thing to do.'

'And you think that someone was Will?'

'I don't know for sure, but yes, I think it might have been. It seems his mum and dad never got over losing Caroline. They died quite close to each other. Carla, the landlady at the Stag, said Will blamed their deaths on Gabe. I think he might have gone a step further and destroyed Gabe's flock.'

'You don't know this for certain though?'

'No, I don't, but attacking someone's livelihood like this is personal and Will had a strong motive. He thought Gabe had effectively killed three members of his family.'

Penny shakes her head.

'There's no way Will would do something like that.'

'How do you know? He didn't tell you the truth about Gabe.'

'That's different.'

'Is it?'

'I know what you're thinking. I'm so besotted with the guy it's clouding my judgement but you're wrong about me and you're wrong about Will.'

'Yes, I admit I could be, but what if I'm not? I've been to too many jobs where the police have got there too late, Pen. You're my friend. I'm not prepared to risk that. I'd rather be wrong and piss you off for a few days than be right and be photographing your body in the mortuary.'

'Jesus, you're making him sound like some kind of monster.'

I don't say anything.

'For fuck's sake, Ally. This is Will you're talking about.'

'I know and I wish it wasn't, honestly I do.'

She stares down at the rag she's twisting in her hand. She's arguing with herself. Is Will just like her ex, Ian? Is it happening again? Is he going to hurt her like Ian did? Did she miss the signs?

'You said this sheep attack happened eight years ago?' she says finally.

'Yes.'

'Well, I don't believe he did it, but if he did, and it's a big if, he'd lost his mum, his dad and his sister. Don't you think he had every right to be angry?'

'Don't do this, Penny.'

'Do what?'

'Make excuses for his violence.'

She tosses the cloth into the bucket.

'Oh, come on, Ally, this isn't even about Will. Not directly.'

'What's that supposed to mean?'

'This is about you. It's like you're . . . stuck.'

'What are you talking about?'

'Where do you want me to start? You won't let Megan go back to school when her doctor and her counsellor both said she could. You're being really weird about returning to work even though they clearly want you back. You won't give Liam, or any man, the time of day.'

'What's that got to do with anything?'

'I think deep down you resent me for getting on with my life.'

'That's not true. I'm worried about the type of man Will really is.'

'Save it. I'm perfectly capable of looking out for myself. It's you who has the problem. You need to sort yourself out, Ally, before you lose everything that ever mattered to you.'

34

When I return to the cabin, Jay is propping up the breakfast bar in a way that suggests he's been waiting for me, but I'm not in the mood for him, or for anyone.

'What's the matter with you? The local Spar run out of Dr Pepper?' I snap before realizing my filthy mood isn't his fault. 'Sorry. Ignore me. Is something the matter? Where's Megan?'

'In her room downloading the photos she took this morning.'

I need a drink, so I amble into the kitchenette and retrieve a bottle of cider from the fridge, offering it to Jay first, but he shakes his head. Prising the top off, I take a few glugs. Now I'm ready for him.

'What is it then?'

'The council called and asked if I had any criminal convictions because they don't take on people with a criminal record.'

'You don't have a criminal record.' I take another swig. 'God knows I tried.'

'But I will have if I lose my court case.' Shit. I'd forgotten about that. Jay's shoulders sag. 'I knew it. They're going to find me guilty, aren't they? Then I'll have a record and no job.'

'Hold on a minute. Not necessarily. If you tell them the

truth about why you hit your dad, that he started it and you were defending yourself, they may take pity on you.'

'You're a shit liar, Ally.'

I go to take a drink, but suddenly I don't want it any more and put the bottle down.

'At least wait and see what happens.'

He shakes his head.

'No point.' He picks at an imaginary scab on the back of his hand. 'I may as well tell them now. Get it over and done with. The thing is I really wanted this job. It might sound funny, but it's my dream job.'

'It doesn't sound funny at all.'

'I couldn't believe it when they gave it to me. It felt like things were finally going my way.'

'I know.'

'And now it's gone. I need a fag.'

He grabs his jacket and goes out onto the veranda, closing the door behind him. I watch him through the window, pulling on the weediest roll-up, screwing his eyes up against the column of smoke.

This is the boy who found his mum dead when he was just twelve years old, the boy whose dad made him sell drugs, the boy who snuck into the hospital to keep my daughter company when I wasn't looking and made her want to live again. I finish my bottle and place it on the side. Jay Cox, I owe you.

***

Tony Cox is exactly where I expect to find him, stroking a beer in the Albion, and he's alone. There's no sign of Cassie. Just as I'd hoped.

Inserting myself between an elderly man and Tony, my arm brushes his and he glances sideways at me.

'I thought I could smell something.'

'Can we talk?'

'I've nothing to say to you.'

His words slur into each other; he's already one over the eight.

'Bill, can I get another pint for Tony, and I'll have a half of Sam's?'

'That won't make any difference.'

'Jay swears blind nothing is going on between him and Cassie and I believe him.'

'I know. She told me.'

'You two still together then?'

'Yeah. Why wouldn't we be?' he says, belching beery fumes into my face, daring me to recoil in disgust, but I don't give him the satisfaction.

'No reason. I'm here to ask you a favour.'

'I'm not withdrawing my statement.'

'I understand that you're angry and I don't blame you. Jay was out of order, but he's got himself a job now, an apprentice parks keeper with the council.'

I search his craggy face for a positive response. Any normal father would be delighted at his son's achievement. Not Tony. Unless it benefits him directly, he couldn't give a shit.

'So?'

'So, if he's convicted of assaulting you, he'll lose his job before he even starts.'

'He should've thought about that.'

'You're right. He's an idiot. We both know that. But he's young, Tony. The young are idiots.'

'Ain't that the truth?' He nods at the pint Bill slides towards him.

'So, will you speak to the CPS?'

'What will you do for me if I do?' he says, smearing his face with a sly smile.

'What?'

'You heard me.' He moors his piercing blue eyes to mine. 'What will you do for me if I tell them I don't want to go ahead with it?'

Christ. He's asking for a shag in return for his son's freedom.

35

The door of the Albion pub opens, noisily delivering Tony Cox in a shaft of yellow light onto the street. It closes and the dark and quiet quickly reassert themselves.

Tony tries to compose himself but misjudges the height of the pavement and his leg buckles, sending him veering from side to side. His hand flies out and he grabs the quay wall to stop himself falling over. He's paralytic.

He looks left to right, trying to work out which direction is home. He doesn't know I'm watching him from the shadows, my stomach knotted with loathing. He doesn't care about Jay. He resents him. He can't stand the thought that his son might just make a better life for himself than he has, that any respect Jay earns will be because he is a decent person not because people fear him. It was Tony who persuaded Jay to deal drugs for him in the first place, sending him down a one-way road that sooner or later ends in incarceration. Or worse. The police have spent years trying to put Jay Cox away, but it's his so-called father, not them, who will finally get him sent down because Tony knows that once that happens there's no turning back for Jay. His course is set.

'Tony.'

He frowns and turns towards me, swaying gently, squinting into the darkness.

'Ally Dymond? Is that you?'

'Yes.'

'I thought I told you to fuck off.'

'You did, but—'

'So fuck off then.' Christ, I'd like nothing more, but I can't because if I do that tiny spark of a chance that Jay has will be stamped out for good. 'What you waiting for?'

Yes, what am I waiting for?

'I-I've changed my mind.'

The words tumble from me before I can stop them. Tony frowns before the realization of what I'm saying hits him, and he lurches towards me.

'Knew you would.'

I feel his hot beery breath on my face.

'You'll speak to the CPS?'

'Course.'

'And if they go ahead with the court case, will you promise you won't turn up to the trial?'

If Tony is a no-show, the case will more than likely be dropped. Technically, this is witness intimidation, not that anyone intimidates Tony, but I'm desperate.

He holds up a couple of fingers.

'Scout's honour so what do you say?'

I look at him. *You can do this, Ally. It's not the first time you've had sex when you didn't want to.* What woman hasn't? It was always easier to give in to Sean's demands, to get it over and done with as quickly as possible, than it was to resist him.

'OK, but not here. It's too public. People will see.'

'Yeah. Yeah. Where then?'

'The other side of the quay.'

He nods and turns towards the quay, but his body doesn't respond so I jostle his dead weight of an arm over my shoulder and nudge him forward. He leans into me, his eyes tracing my body until they come to rest on my chest, repulsing every fibre of my being. How can Cassie bear to be anywhere near this man?

'I always knew you had a thing for me,' he slurs, his spittle spotting my cheek. 'I've always fancied you. Your ex said you were wild in the sack.' Jesus. Of course Tony knew Sean. They both drank in the Albion. 'Wassup now?'

'Nothing.'

I steer him away from the harbour, towards the other side of the quay facing the Atlantic where the paltry streetlights offer no defence against the great blackness of the sea sky. I pause for breath, which Tony interprets as the beginning of the proceedings and his gaping fish hole of a mouth comes at me. I palm his chest, but I can't hold him off for long.

'Not so fast. We've got all night.'

His eyes widen with expectation. 'What have you got in mind?'

I don't have anything in mind. Maybe I thought he was joking and wouldn't go through with it, maybe I hoped he'd be too drunk and would pass out. But neither of those things are going to happen. Tony wants sex and I've promised him he's going to get it. I slide my hand down his trousers. His hardness shocks me and I look up at him to find him grinning back at me.

'Never lets me down. I should get into a fight with Jay more often.'

My utter repulsion for him distils into a white-hot fury that a quick fuck is the price Tony Cox has set in return for his son's freedom. I close my eyes and take a deep breath. I can do this; I have to do it. I can live with that, but I don't know if I can live with seeing this vile excuse for a human being around Bidecombe, that triumphant smirk of his a constant reminder of what I let him do to me. There is an alternative.

I slide my hand through Tony's thick hair and guide his head into the curve of my shoulder. His warm, wet lips search out my neck and anchor themselves to the bare flesh. The sucking noises they emit make me want to heave, but I force aside the sensation and let him continue while I retrieve a pair of gloves from my pocket. No self-respecting CSI leaves home without them. Once they're on, I take Tony's head in both hands, prising him off me, hoping he doesn't notice the latex, but he's too busy staring at me.

'You've got beautiful dark eyes, maid.'

'Thank you.' I smile.

My hand searches for his belt which I unbuckle with ease, ignoring his eagerness. I begin to fumble with his trouser zip.

'It's stuck.'

Tony looks down, frowning. He tugs at it himself, immediately releasing it, but in his inebriation the movement unsteadies him, and he topples towards me.

'Whoa. Steady there,' I say, righting him. 'You nearly pushed me in then.' He has no idea we are less than a metre from the edge of the quay where black waters circle silently below us.

His trousers snagged on his hips, revealing bright red boxers, he lurches towards me, lips puckered. I step in between his outstretched arms. He thinks I'm going to kiss him, but I dodge his mouth, grab his jacket lapels, and swing him around. There's now nothing between him and the depths of the sea.

His brow furrows. He can't work out if this is all part of the game, but it doesn't matter because he's too drunk to resist. I lengthen my arms until I am holding his torso directly over the water. All I have to do is let go.

The latex gloves are just a precaution. The chances of the police finding any forensics connecting me to the crime are slight. Fingerprints on non-porous surfaces like glass can survive immersion but only for so long. Tony's clothing is fabric. It's too rough with too many spaces between the individual threads to hold a pattern. Leather might tell a different story, but Tony's wearing denim. The police will likely assume Tony ambled to the water's edge to take a piss and, in his paralytic state, toppled into the harbour. It happens surprisingly often.

But what if the police get suspicious? What if some go-getter like DS Whitely decides something doesn't add up? What if they suspect me? They'll examine Tony's clothing for any fibres that shouldn't be there. From that, they'll probably be able to work out what kind of fabric the assailant was wearing, maybe even the type of clothing and the make. But dozens of people saw me talking to Tony in the pub. It was crowded; I was pressed up against him. Of course, he'll have fibres from my jacket on his. That's what my brief will say. And what of the CCTV on the quay? It's trained on the Cherish statue to protect her from vandals, but we detoured to the other side of the quay before we reached its radius.

My alibi is a problem though. It's weak. I'll say I went for a walk after seeing Tony in the pub. I'll tell them the truth; Jay was worried about his upcoming court case, and I needed to clear my head before heading home. It isn't ideal, but there's nothing on the statute books that says solitary late-night strolls are illegal. Besides, this is Tony Cox. The local nick will be dancing on his grave. I'm in the clear on this one.

'Come on then, girl. Show me what you got.'

I take one last look at him.

'Fuck you, Tony.'

36

It may be March, but winter still has an icy stranglehold over the town and the streets feel empty and dark and hostile as I stroll down the hill towards Bidecombe and the Albion pub.

When I woke up this morning, I couldn't face anyone, so I told Megan I had a cold coming on and spent the day in bed. Kit sent me a text this afternoon and, for once, I welcomed the distraction.

'Can we meet? Please. I could really do with a friend right now.'

I was about to turn his offer down when I stopped myself. I didn't want to be alone either, not after last night, and the prospect of being with someone who didn't know me, someone whose problems could divert me from mine, if only for a few hours, appealed to me. Maybe that's Kit's attraction – I don't know, but I told him I'd meet him in the Albion at 8 p.m.

As I reach the quay, my phone buzzes. It's Harriet. The last time I saw her was at the briefing when I told a crowded room that I thought the reason Gabe had £180,000 in his slaughterhouse is because he was laundering the money through the sheep markets. It made sense. Gabe almost lost his entire flock a few years ago. It nearly wiped him out. He switched to rare and expensive breeds, which he bought and sold at markets all over the country. A lot of farmers still operate in cash. No one would look twice at Gabe handing over wads of money. Harriet went for it.

'Nice work,' Harriet told me as I left the briefing. I won't lie it felt good to be told by a DI, especially one I respect, that I'd done a good job, but that was then. Now, Harriet is the last person I want to speak to, so I let it go to voicemail and half listen to the recording.

'Sorry to bother you in the evening.' I notice how her London accent is less pronounced on a recorded message. 'I guess you're out having a life like normal people. Anyway, the good news is the blood recovered from the slaughterhouse is deer blood, so it looks like someone was using the place to dismember deer illegally shot on the Exmoor. I've got a couple of officers talking to local butchers and restaurants. Obviously, it may not be related to Gabe.

'We've also spoken to all known sex offenders in the area. Nothing on that front, but we made some inquiries, and it seems there was an incident involving Gabe taking photos of the children in their swimwear when he was eighteen. He was spoken to, and his parents were informed, but the children's care home didn't want to pursue it.'

Oh Christ. Gabe had form. Of course he did. This starts somewhere, often with some seemingly minor act that attracts a good talking-to and a hope that it goes away. It rarely does.

'Remember the shoe print we found? It's the wrong size to be either Gabe's or Miriam's. The pattern belongs to a trainer, a very expensive one by all accounts, one of those fashion trainers that's more for show than exercise. It matches the one found outside the farmhouse although of course there's no way of knowing if the owner was at the farm at the time of Gabe's murder.

'There are also some fingerprints on the holdall. They're not Gabe's either and, this is where it gets really interesting. They belong to the same person who burgled Bidecombe DIY Supplies and a property in London.'

My mind wanders back to Karyn Dwight and her indifference when I told her the fingerprints matched another crime scene hundreds of miles away. Harriet will certainly send a detective to reinterview her. I wonder how she'll react when she's told the fingerprints from the burglary match those on a bag found at the farm of her murdered ex-fiancé?

I reach the Albion. Harriet is still talking.

'Anyway, I thought I'd fill you in. If you've got any thoughts on any of this, give me a shout. I'd value your input.' There's a pause. 'I trust your judgement, Ally.'

Really? Because I sure as hell don't.

***

Kit is sitting at a small table by the window, staring into his gin and tonic, his ruddy cheeks paled by shock, his hair dishevelled. There's no sign of Tony Cox. He must be sleeping off the booze from yesterday after waking up to find himself slumped against the harbour wall, trousers around his ankles. I'm banking on him either not remembering anything or being too embarrassed to admit he was dumped on the quay.

I barely slept last night, replaying the scene over and over.

Me luring Tony to the end of the quay. Me promising to make it worth his while. Me holding his great hulk over the edge. Me pulling him back at the last moment when a car door slammed nearby.

I don't know what's happening to me, but I do know I nearly killed Tony Cox because he wouldn't withdraw his complaint against Jay, a boy who until a few weeks ago I'd spent my career trying to get put away. What if that car hadn't turned up when it did? What if I hadn't heard the door? Would I have let go of Tony's lapels and let him fall to his certain death in the black waters below us?

'Usual, Ally?' Bill, the landlord, calls over the heads of those lining the bar. I give him the thumbs-up and sit down on the stool opposite Kit.

'Are you OK?'

'I take it you already know about Gabe.'

'I'm sorry.'

He shakes his head. 'I can't believe it. He was a nice guy. A gentle giant. Everyone loved him. He had girlfriends, for God's sake. He . . . he just wasn't the type to . . . you know?'

'No one ever is.'

'When DI Moore told me I thought I was going to throw up. What makes someone even want to look at that stuff?'

'I don't know. Thanks, Bill.' The landlord delivers my drink. Kit waits for him to return to the bar and be out of earshot.

'There was this incident when he was eighteen, something to do with photographing girls in their bikinis in the park. The police were involved. Mum said the girls were making it up. Nothing ever came of it. Do you think it started then?'

'Honestly, I've no idea.'

'Sorry, I forgot – you can't talk about it. It's just that I didn't think it could get any worse and then I find out my brother . . .' he drops his voice '. . . is a paedophile. How am I going to tell Mum when she comes around?'

'How is Miriam?' I ask, changing the subject.

His horror subsides into sadness. 'No change. She just lies on her bed staring blankly at the ceiling. It's called akinetic catatonia apparently.'

'Will she recover?'

'The doctors have given her a sedative, which is meant to ease anxiety. They're hoping that will work. If it doesn't, they might try electroconvulsive therapy.' Kit's phone buzzes. 'That's the hospital now. Can you excuse me for a minute?'

'Sure.'

He takes the call outside. Through the window, the orange streetlights cast dark shadows, turning his eyes into hollows. First his mother stabs his brother to death; now he discovers his brother is a paedophile. How much can one person take? I'm so lost in the sight of Kit and the fishing boats, catching the streetlights as they bob silently in the harbour behind him that, by the time I realize my own phone is buzzing, it's too late and the caller has rung off.

I check the screen. Two missed calls from Jay. That's odd. He never calls, unless he's in custody and needs an appropriate adult. I phone him back, but it goes to voicemail and Jay isn't the kind to listen to his voicemails, so I don't bother to leave one, and call Megan instead.

'Megan, it's Mum. You OK?'

'I know it's you, Mum. Your name comes up on my screen.' She laughs. 'And yeah, I'm fine. Why wouldn't I be?'

'Jay tried to call me, but I missed him. Is he OK? He's been a bit quiet since the council told him he can't have the job if he has a criminal record.'

'He told me, but he seemed OK this evening. It's probably a butt call.'

'Where is he?'

'He's gone to get a kebab.'

'He's meant to be looking after you.'

'He'll be back soon.'

'I can come home.'

'No, don't do that. I'm fine; really, I am.'

'If you're sure.'

'I'm sure.'

I ring off just as Kit returns.

'Everything all right? Do you need to leave?'

'No. Is Miriam OK?'

'Yes. They were just returning my call to let me know she's had a comfortable day.'

'That's good.'

'So, you know all about my day. How's yours been?'

'Not great.'

'Try me.'

'I had a falling-out with my friend Penny yesterday.'

'Oh? Why?'

'She's going out with Will Sneddon, and I found out that he beat up Gabe about ten years ago.'

Kit pauses mid-drink at the mention of his brother. 'Gabe?'

'I take it you didn't know.'

'No. It must have been while I was travelling, but why would he do that? They've known each other since they were kids.'

'Do you remember Caroline Sneddon?'

'Of course. She died in a car crash.'

'Only it wasn't an accident. She drove her car into a tree on purpose.'

'She killed herself?'

'Yes, she was heartbroken after her boyfriend broke up with her.'

Kit looks at me. 'Are you saying she was going out with Gabe?'

'Yes. That's why Will beat him up. He blamed Gabe for Caroline's death.'

Kit shakes his head. 'I'm beginning to think I didn't know my brother at all. And I never had Will down as the violent type.'

'It doesn't end there. Two years after Caroline was killed, Lawrence and Esme Sneddon died within months of each other. Will says they never got over Caroline's death.'

'I remember Mum telling me.'

'Oh?'

'She used to fill me in on what was happening when I phoned although she never said anything about Will attacking Gabe.'

'So, you know what happened to Gabe's flock?'

'Yes. She was devastated. I offered to come back and help, but Gabe said they could manage.'

'Did she tell you it was deliberate? The police believe someone hired a local thug to set their dogs onto the flock. I think it might have been Will Sneddon?'

'Will? No way.'

'The attack happened about two weeks after Lawrence Sneddon died. I think Will was swallowed up by grief all over again and wanted to destroy Gabe like Gabe had destroyed his family.'

'Are you certain about this?'

'No and that's the problem. I can't prove it.'

'But you told your friend Penny anyway?'

'I couldn't not tell her.'

'Really?'

'I'm trying to protect her, Kit. I'm a CSI; I've spent years photographing the results of abusive relationships. People talk about how the person snapped, how the violence came from nowhere, how it's not who they are, but that's crap. Believe me, the signs are always there if you look hard enough. Will Sneddon viciously assaulted a man and probably paid another to let their dog massacre an entire flock of sheep. Those are fucking big signs in anyone's book.'

'Well, when you put it like that . . . but I take it Penny doesn't agree.'

'No. She doesn't.'

'Maybe you should trust your friend's judgement.'

'The problem with judgement is that it gets clouded by emotion. This is a story as old as time, Kit.' I take a sip of my cider. 'The trouble is the ending is so predictable.'

'So what will you do now?'

'I don't know. I don't have any real evidence so I can't go to the police, and she's convinced he's innocent. There isn't anything I can do except hope I'm wrong. Sorry, I didn't mean to offload onto you. You've got enough going on without hearing about my problems.'

'It's fine. To be honest, it's good to think about something else.'

'Thanks for listening. It helped.'

'You sound surprised.'

'I'm not one to pour my heart out.'

Kit downs the rest of his drink and takes his coat from the back of his chair.

'Come on. Let's get out of here.'

37

'It's the best seat in the house. I promise.'

'Are you sure?' I stare down at the large, flat stone slab, hemmed in by the damp heather, barely illuminated by Kit's iPhone.

Getting out of here meant getting into Kit's car. Maybe I should have said no, but I didn't want to stay in the Albion, and I didn't want to go back to the cabin either. I texted Megan and she said Jay was home. At first, I thought Kit was taking me to Narracott Farm until he drove past the turning and carried on up to the moors. When the road levelled, he pulled over and got out of the car.

'How about I go first?' He sits down on the stone. 'See. Apart from the fact it's freezing cold, there's nothing to worry about. I'll promise it'll be worth it.'

As soon as I sit down in the tiny pool of light offered by his phone, he turns it off, plunging us into near darkness.

'What are you doing?'

'Look up.'

The doubtful look I give him is wasted in the darkness, so I do as I'm told for once.

'Oh my God.' The sight of a billion stars, all jostling to outshine each other, makes me gasp. 'It's incredible.'

'It is, isn't it? That's the North Star,' he says, and I can just make out the outline of his arm against the sky pointing to the brightest and largest star directly overhead. 'To the left is the Cassiopeian constellation and directly above that is the Plough.' He turns his iPhone light back on, picking out his smile. 'This is where my dad proposed to my mum.'

'No wonder she said yes. It doesn't get much more romantic than this. He must have loved her very much.'

'I think he did once, but they drifted apart. There were no rows or anything dramatic like that. They just seemed to live separate lives. He had an affair with the landlady from the Stag.'

'Carla?'

'Yes. He died in her bed. A heart attack. Mum doesn't know that I know. Carla's daughter told me. You know what it's like around here. No secrets in North Devon.'

'I'm so sorry.'

'It's OK. Mum didn't blame him. Or Carla. I think she was pleased he found someone who could give him something she couldn't.'

'Didn't she love him?'

'I don't know. She once said she'd only ever been in love once. She wasn't talking about Dad and, whoever it was, I don't think she really ever got over him. First loves can be like that, can't they?'

Julian flashes across my mind.

'Sometimes.'

'She once told me she never wanted kids either, but women

didn't have much choice in those days. What about you? What about your parents?'

'I was adopted as a baby, so I never knew my real parents. My adoptive dad, Davy, was a lovely man, always playing practical jokes. Bernadette, my adoptive mum, used to tell him off, but not seriously. He definitely brought out her fun side. Maybe that's what she found attractive about him. I adored him. He was Bidecombe's harbourmaster. I used to spend hours down on the quay with him when I was little. He used to have his own boat and he'd take me out fishing.'

'What happened to him?'

'He died in a boating accident when I was fifteen.'

'Now it's my turn to be sorry.'

'It was a long time ago. Bernadette is still around. Let's just say our relationship is . . . complicated.'

'Did you never want to find out who your real parents were?'

'I did for a while, but I didn't get anywhere. They didn't want to be found. By the time I was nineteen, I'd had my own baby and other things to think about.'

'That must have been hard.'

'Yes, it was. Made harder by marrying an arsehole, but we're OK now it's just the two of us and Megan is nearly sixteen.'

'I guess she doesn't need you so much any more.'

I think about our phone call in the pub and how keen Megan was for me not to come home.

'I guess she doesn't.'

'So, you can get on with your own life now. Live a little. What is it?' He smiles.

'You reminded me of something Penny said, that's all. About

being afraid to get on with my life after what happened last year, which is why I won't . . .'

'Won't what?'

I look across the expanse of moorland but there's nothing but blackness. '. . . Give men the time of day, among other things.'

'But you're here with me now.'

I turn to look at him. 'Yes. I am.'

Kit leans over and kisses me. This time I don't pull back. Instead, I respond in kind because I want this as much as he does.

He stops and holds me in his gaze.

'I think we just proved Penny wrong, don't you?'

Silas

She only went to the disco in the back room of the Albion in Bidecombe that night because her father told her he was sick of seeing her moping around the place, and Bidecombe was far enough away that there was no chance she'd meet anyone who knew what she was.

After passing her half a lager top, Robbie turned his attentions to the barmaid, and Miriam found herself standing alone by the dance floor, sipping her drink. As soon as she saw Silas, his shapeless green tweed jacket taut across his broad expanse of back and a shirt so tight the collar looked like wings trying to take off, she knew he was a farmer.

He caught her eye and she quickly looked away, but it was too late, and he ambled over to ask her to dance. No, she said, but smiled when he told her he was relieved because he hated dancing anyway. He was only there because it was his cousin's stag do.

She warmed to his honesty and his shyness but that wasn't a good enough reason to marry him. Not that her father saw it like that after they started courting. 'Keep hold of this one, maid. No one in Barnston'll have you.'

And he was right. No one else would have her because they knew what she was. The truth didn't matter to Barnston's gossips.

No one should have known; it should have stayed private, but Barnston is a small town, which meant everyone knew. You'd have thought people would have gotten over it after two years, but they hadn't, and they hated her for it.

But Silas lived on a farm up on Exmoor. He hadn't heard the rumours and he had no idea about what had gone on. Maybe he would find out one day, but they'd be wed by then and there would be nothing he could do about it. And maybe, just maybe, she could explain in a way that wouldn't make him despise her. So when he asked her to marry him, she said yes.

No one from her family came to their wedding at Upper Farleigh Church. It was better that way. She couldn't risk her father or Robbie getting blind drunk and blabbing her shame at their reception at the Stag.

They honeymooned in Exmouth in South Devon, a little guesthouse – Sea View B&B. She didn't tell Silas that two streets away was her Aunt Beryl's; where she was meant to go while she waited to have her Billy. It had been five years since she'd lost him, but sometimes, if she woke up before Silas, she'd sit by the window overlooking the seafront and picture herself pushing a pram. People would stop her, charmed by such a bonny baby. They'd tell her she and her husband must be so proud.

Silas asked her why she was so quiet, and she told him she just enjoyed listening to the waves on the shore and the gulls overhead.

'Make the most of it.' He laughed. 'Everything'll change once we have little ones.'

But her smile took too long to arrive.

'You do want babbers, don't you?'

'Yes, yes, of course.'

What else could she say? She couldn't tell him about Billy, about any of it. Or that she was the last person who should have children.

'We can't wait too long. I'm not getting any younger and the farm doesn't run itself.'

'All in good time.'

But there never would be a good time for Miriam.

Neither of them mentioned children again on their honeymoon. Silas thought there was nothing to talk about and that it would just happen, but she knew different.

Nobody said anything for a while. Silas's parents lived with them, as was the way with farming families back then, and, at first, they were too polite to comment. But as months became years, hints about the 'patter of tiny feet' and 'not leaving it too long' firmed up into anxious mutterings about who would take on the farm and whether 'everything was OK in that department'.

One day, out in the fields, Silas asked her if they should see a doctor. She didn't know what to say. She couldn't tell him the truth, so she said that they didn't need doctors interfering in their lives. They just had to be patient and let nature take its course.

Then Silas found her pills. He'd gone upstairs to fetch her cardigan from the bedroom. When he didn't come down, she went looking for him and found him standing by her dressing table, a wedding gift from him, his eyes misted with hurt and confusion, a silver foil packet in his hand. He held it up.

'What's this?'

'It's the contraceptive pill.'

'So, all this time you've been pretending that you wanted children?'

'Yes.'

'You let me think there was something wrong with us, let my parents think there was something wrong with us?'

'I'm sorry. I thought I was doing the right thing.'

She shrank back towards the door, certain his hurt would explode into anger and violence, like her father. She wouldn't have blamed him if it had, but he just sank down onto the bed and shook his head.

'How can lying to me be the right thing, Miriam?'

'I'm sorry.'

'Why? Why would you do this? Children are a gift. Every woman wants children.'

'I was scared I wouldn't be able to keep them safe.'

'What do you mean? The farm's the safest place for them.'

'I just didn't think I'd be any good at it.'

'But you looked after your own sisters, and you were a nursery nurse.' He looked at her, his eyes filled with tears. 'You love children.'

She could have said something then. She could have told him the truth. Then maybe none of this would have happened. But she stayed silent.

'Is that it?'

She nodded and he let out a loud laugh, startling her.

'You'm a good girl, but you'm as maze as a brush, Miriam Narracott.' He threw the packet of pills onto the bed. 'No harm will come to you or our babbers and you'll be the perfect mum to them.'

38

The orange glow from the streetlight outside Kit's hotel room window guides me to my clothes, hastily discarded the night before. I tug my crumpled jeans on just as Kit stirs. He squints at me in the half-light and checks his watch.

'It's only five-thirty. Don't go yet.'

'I have to.'

He sits up in bed, watching me get dressed. Feeling suddenly self-conscious, I turn away from him to button my shirt.

'I'd really like to see you again, Ally.'

After pulling my sweater over my head, I release my hair from under the collar. 'That's fairly unavoidable in Bidecombe.'

'You know what I mean. We had a good time, didn't we?'

'Yes, we did.'

'There's something between us. I think you can sense it too and I'd like to see where this goes, wouldn't you?'

'I don't know. You should know I'm not very good at the relationship thing.'

'That makes two of us, but I'd like to try. We can take things slowly. I'd like to think last night meant something.'

'Well, it's not something I make a habit of.'

Not only was last night something I don't make a habit

of, but it's also something I've never done before. Since Sean, there hasn't been anyone else. The most I have to show for the last eight years or so is the odd awkward fumble, and, if it threatened to progress, I'd make my excuses and leave. But when Kit drove me back to Bidecombe and asked if I wanted to go back to his hotel room, I knew what he was asking, and I didn't hesitate. I guess that must mean something.

'So, what are you saying?'

He wants an answer. For some reason, I can't give him one, but I don't want to lose him either.

'Can I think about it?'

'Is that a polite way of saying no?'

'Honestly, if I wanted to say no, I'd say no. I just need a little more time. The police investigation into Gabe hasn't ended yet.'

'That's true. I don't want to make things difficult for you, but if we're not going to see each other for a while, maybe we should make the most of the time we have now.' He pulls me towards him. I don't resist, allowing myself to fall back onto the bed. He brushes aside a strand of hair that's fallen across my cheeks. His kisses feel good, right even, and I respond until he pulls back.

'Are you sure you can't stay?'

'Maybe just a little longer then.'

***

When I step outside the Albion Hotel, the day is starting for me but ending for the fishermen returning in their trawlers laden with their catches. There's fewer of them now than there used to be, but they still manage to eke out a living. As I stroll along the quay back towards the town, in the half-light, they grin and greet me in my night-before clothes with a knowing look. I return their smiles and waves. I knew their dads and they knew mine. Dad was Bidecombe's harbourmaster for years. I still expect to see his boat – *The Aloysia* – bobbing on the tide.

Aloysia is my full name. Apparently, it means famous warrior, but that doesn't make it any better. Only Bernadette uses it, but it's a good name for a boat. *The Aloysia* isn't there any more. Dad co-owned it with his friend, Howard, who sailed it away soon after Dad's death and never came back.

The low stone walls and brightly coloured boats are soon replaced by empty grey streets, their out-of-season shabbiness on full display, strewn with rubbish where the seagulls have pecked open the bin bags and feasted on their innards. In a few days, the cracks will be filled and sanded and freshly glossed in white paint in readiness for the tourists who will arrive in their droves to admire its bygone charm. Once I hated this place and couldn't wait to get away. Now, I have nothing but admiration for its ability to renew itself, to move on.

That's what I need to do. Move on. Leave the old me behind. Kit could be a part of that. The physical attraction between us is undeniable, but it's more than that. Last night our conversation flowed so easily it was like we'd known each other years. I realized he hadn't asked me about what happened to Megan last year. Maybe he felt it was too painful for me, but it meant that I didn't have to couch my words carefully or hide myself from him. Kit knows only what I want to show him, which means I have a chance to be a better version of myself with him, a version I can live with. Perhaps Penny was right after all. A bit of Kit Narracott is just what I need, and this is what moving on looks like.

I take a right where the road begins to climb upwards and out of Bidecombe. In the distance, a thick layer of fog hangs over Seven Hills Lodges. It's lingered for days now as if it's got caught up in the pine trees and can't unravel itself.

The houses fall away. I am almost in the countryside and nearly home. It's still early. Megan and Jay will be asleep. Maybe I can grab a couple more hours myself before they wake up. I'd rather Megan didn't know I was out all night.

As I get nearer home, an aroma of burning wood infuses the cold morning air. It's a funny time of day to light a fire and I scout the houses for a pale grey plume. There is none, even though the smell has become more intense, more cloying as I carry on up the hill towards Seven Hills. It's then that I realize, it isn't fog draped over the site, it's smoke. Something's on fire. Oh Christ, please don't let it be the cabin, but as I sprint through the entrance to the site, I already know that it is.

Through the pine trees, fire engines and ambulances cluster around the bonfire that is my home. By the time I reach it, one side of the cabin is already engulfed in orange flames reaching the height of the surrounding pines, silhouetting three firefighters and their hoses, cannoning gallons of water at the burning building, but it isn't making any difference. The fire has taken hold, devouring everything in its path. Megan.

'Megan!'

I race towards the cabin, frantically scanning the area for my girl. Surely she got out, but I can't see her anywhere, just people in uniforms. Firefighters, police officers, paramedics, but not Megan.

I run towards the cabin, but a firefighter's arm flies out and bars my way. 'It's not safe.'

'My daughter is in there. And her friend, Jay.' Did Jay get home? Maybe he stayed out all night too.

There's a cracking sound, followed by a loud whoosh. Part of the roof caves in.

'Oh God, you need to get them out.'

'We will. We already have a man in there.' He nods at someone behind me, and a paramedic appears with a blanket, which they throw around my shoulders. 'Can you take care of this lady for us?'

'Sure. Do you want to come with me, my love?'

'No. I'm staying put.'

So, I stand there, utterly helpless, the heat drawing the sweat from my pores, searing my unblinking eyes trained on the front door because I don't dare blink. A lifetime passes and all I can think of is what's taking so long? Where are they?

Thick, noxious smoke billows out of the front door and huge orange tongues begin to lick the edges. Momentarily, they're beaten back by the water hoses, only to return with renewed vigour when the firefighters switch their attention elsewhere.

Then there's a flash and a roar and the rest of the roof collapses. No one is getting out of there alive. Megan has gone. Jay has gone. I know that, but hope trumps reason. Always. I stare at the collapsing building in front of me, believing in miracles because it suits me to, but miracles aren't real.

A figure appears at the front door. It's a firefighter, a body slumped over their shoulder. Please God, let it be Megan and let her be alive. I run towards him, but he strides past me towards the paramedics and lays the body on a trolley. The paramedics immediately surround their patient, but I push between them. It's Megan.

Her eyes are shut and her smoke-smudged face passive, but I know what death looks like and this isn't it. Megan is alive.

The paramedic puts an oxygen mask on her.

'Megan. It's me. Mum.'

Her eyes flicker and open. She follows my voice and focuses on my face.

'Mum.'

'I'm here. You're safe.'

Disorientated, she tries to sit up. 'Jay.' Her voice is little more than a rasp.

The paramedic lays her hand on Megan's arm. 'Try to stay calm, love.'

'Is he in the cabin?'

She nods at me. She coughs and, exhausted by the effort, slumps back on the trolley and closes her eyes.

The paramedic looks at me. 'She's inhaled a lot of smoke. We'll need to get her to hospital and get her checked out properly.'

The paramedics wheel Megan to the back of the ambulance. I keep hold of her hand only letting go so they can lift her into the back.

'What about the boy?' I shout at the nearest firefighter.

He ignores me, transfixed by the sight of the cabin. The kitchen wall caves in and there's a boom – a gas canister exploding – forcing the firefighters to retreat. The air is filled

247

with burning debris. A thousand scorched fragments that used to be my life float down around us. But I can't think about that now. I need to find Jay.

Perhaps he's already being tended to by the other paramedics. I look across to the other ambulance. The back doors are open in readiness, but I already know the paramedics sitting inside aren't waiting for a patient, they're waiting for a body.

39

Megan is sitting up in her bed when I enter her room. I hug her tightly, squeezing a faint smile from her.

'How are you feeling, love?'

'OK.' Her voice is little more than a rasp that makes her cough.

'You inhaled a lot of smoke, so try not to talk too much. The doctors want to keep you in for a day, just to make sure everything's OK. You'll be out tomorrow.'

She goes to speak, but the words catch in her throat, making her wince with pain, so I pour her a glass of water and hand it to her. The cool liquid immediately eases the soreness, and she closes her eyes in gratitude. It's a moment that I want to last forever because I know what's coming next.

'How's Jay?' I look at her expectant face. 'What ward is he on?'

What wouldn't I give to tell her he's just down the corridor, trying to persuade the nurses to bring him a Dr Pepper for his breakfast. But he isn't on a ward, he's in the mortuary. Jay didn't make it out. The firefighters tried their hardest to reach him, but the roof collapsed and they were lucky to get out with their own lives.

'Mum?' she says as if I didn't hear her the first time, but I heard her. I just don't want to destroy what little happiness Megan has managed to carve out of her life these last few days she has spent with Jay, but I have no choice. I have to do this before grief overwhelms me, and I can't get the words out at all.

'Jay's gone, love.'

Oh God. I can't even bring myself to say he's died out loud because as soon as I do, it's real.

'Gone?'

I can tell from her hopeful eyes and the slight upturn of her mouth she wants my words to mean he's just left the hospital and he's waiting for her back at the cabin, but they don't.

'He didn't get out of the cabin in time.'

Her jaw falls open, but no sound comes out. The smoke and shock have stolen her voice. A frown masks her incomprehension of the situation as if I'm speaking to her in a foreign language. Her gaze shifts from me to the beige wall ahead of her. For a moment, she reminds me of Miriam Narracott, her eyes open, but unseeing, lost in her own mind. Finally, she looks back at me, searching for a different answer, but I have none.

'I'm so sorry, Megan.'

'No.'

'They tried, but they couldn't reach him in time.'

'No. No. That can't be right.'

She can't accept it, won't accept it.

'He would have been overcome by the smoke before the fire got to him.'

And that's supposed to fucking comfort her? I wince at my own attempts to try to move her on when she isn't ready, to console her when there is no consolation. She looks at me like I'm playing the cruellest trick on her.

'No. You're wrong.'

I swallow hard, trying to ram my own emotions back down deep inside me until this is done because I have to say it, I have to say the words so there can be no misunderstanding, but, my God, my chest aches with the thought of the pain I am about to inflict on my daughter.

'Jay died in the fire, Megan.'

***

Penny just phoned to tell me she's on her way. She arrived at Seven Hills as I was leaving with Megan in the ambulance. She was distraught on the phone, blaming herself for being at Will's and not Seven Hills. But I wasn't there either. I haven't rung Bernadette who's still cruising the fjords. A thousand miles between us isn't enough to dilute her disapproval and apportioning of blame – *this is your fault, Aloysia*. I'm quite capable of blaming myself without her help.

The double doors swing open, but it's not Penny. It's DI Harriet Moore and DS Whitely and they want to talk to Megan.

'How is she?'

'They're keeping her in overnight for observation.'

'She's lucky to be alive. Does she know about Jay Cox?'

She uses his full name. To her, he's a victim, not a friend.

'Yes.'

'How did she take it?'

'Not good. She's still in shock.'

'I'm sorry. For you both. I guess you know why we're here.'

'The fire was started deliberately.'

'Yes. We're treating Jay's death as a murder. I'm sorry to ambush you like this, Ally, but you know the score. The sooner we crack on, the greater the chance we have of catching the scumbag.'

'Sure.'

'I just have a couple of questions for you and Megan.'

'OK.'

'Can you tell me what Jay Cox was doing at your cabin in the first place?'

'He's a friend of my daughter's. He was staying with us, just until he got himself straight.'

'Even though he's rumoured to be dealing in drugs and he's on bail for assault?'

'I know how it looks, but he'd left that life behind. It was the only reason I let him stay.'

'And you believed him?'

'Yes, I believed him. Do you think he was the intended target?'

'We don't know yet.'

'He has plenty of enemies, but then so do I.'

'Anyone in particular?'

'No, but it wouldn't matter anyway because no one knows where I live.'

'I find that hard to believe in a place like Bidecombe.'

'People know I live at Seven Hills, but they don't know which cabin is mine. I swap the numbers around every now and then to throw them off.'

'Smart. So who knew which cabin was yours?'

'Penny, the owner. Her boyfriend, Will Sneddon, and his sister, Emma. Jay, obviously. His dad, Tony.'

'Who Jay beat up in the high street?'

'Yes.'

'We heard Tony paid you a visit a few days ago.'

'Yes, he heard whispers that Jay was seeing his girlfriend, Cassie.'

'This would be Cassie Warnock.'

'Yes, but Jay denied anything was going on between them, although I saw them in the pub together. Cassie knows where I live too.'

'OK. Anyone else?'

'No.'

'Right, well, until we're sure Jay was the only target, we have to consider the possibility of an ongoing threat to your life. I don't need to tell you resources are stretched, and police protection is going to be very difficult to arrange. Is there somewhere you and Megan can go where you'll be safe?'

'I'm sure I'll be able to sort something out.'

'Good. DS Whitely will stay and take your statement and Megan's when she's ready.'

'OK.'

'There is just one other thing though.'

'Oh?'

'I understand you were out when the fire started.'

'Yes.'

'So, who, apart from Megan and Jay, knew you weren't in?'

'No one except the person I spent the night with and anyone else who happened to see me in the Albion on the quay.'

'And who were you with?'

It's the one question I've been dreading since she arrived.

'Kit Narracott.'

40

It's already dusk when I pull into Sneddon Farm. Will's two sheepdogs amble over to greet us but when we don't get out of the car, they saunter off again. Despite the lingering tension between us, Penny insisted Megan and I stay at Will's farm until it's safe to go back to Seven Hills. I couldn't refuse. For the second time in our lives, Megan and I have nowhere else to go. Bernadette is still on holiday and, for reasons known only to herself, has never trusted me with a front door key. But once again Penny has come to our rescue, turning up to the hospital with armfuls of clothes bought from the local supermarket, which is why Megan and I are wearing matching red tracksuits.

'Where are we?' says Megan frowning at the farmhouse.

'Will's farm. I told you we were staying here.'

'But it's in the middle of nowhere. What am I meant to do here?'

'It's only for a few days. Just until we know it's safe to go back to Seven Hills.'

Megan folds her arms.

'But I don't want to stay here. I want to go home,' she says, her voice cracking.

I frown. There is no home. The cabin has gone. She knows that. What she really means is she wants to go back to her life before the fire.

'I know. So do I.'

'So how long do I have to be here for?'

'Until it's safe to leave.'

'What do you mean "safe"?'

'The police need to be sure Jay was the only intended target. It's just a precaution. A few days at most and then we'll go back to Seven Hills.'

'Doesn't matter anyway because Jay won't be there. What am I going to do without him, Mum?' She tries to clear the word as it catches in her throat.

'I don't know what to say to you, Megan.'

'I didn't see him for long when he came in that night because he said he was tired, but he seemed really happy. I asked him why he was in such a good mood, and he said because things were finally going his way and that we'd be proud of him.'

'We were proud of him already.'

I squeeze her hand, but it remains soft and limp, unaware of my touch, as she stares out of the car window, her cheeks a tributary of silent tears. A few moments pass and she tries to stem their flow with a hard sniff, wiping her face with the back of her sleeve. She turns to me. 'I don't understand why he didn't get out, Mum. He was nearer the front door than me, but he didn't even try.'

'The fire must have spread quickly. He was probably overcome by the smoke before he even realized what was happening.'

But the same thought had crossed my mind.

41

All that remains of cabin 27 are a couple of charred struts and a small section of the veranda, the same veranda Megan and I sat on to discuss her day at school, the same veranda where we built our own convoluted marble run and where she tied a bird feeder we'd made from a plastic bottle. It's the only physical marker of our lives left. Everything else is ash to be carried away on the breeze until there's nothing left, but a scorched rectangle. But homes can be rebuilt. Nothing can bring Jay back.

My eye strays to the corner of the cabin that once was home to the sofa that doubled as Jay's bed. I lose the battle with myself not to picture the Jay the firefighters found when they finally dowsed the flames, but I've been to too many fire deaths. I know too much. I know his hands were likely clenched, his arms raised, and his back bent over like a boxer ready to fight. People think it's proof the person was alive and trying to protect themselves from the flames, but it's simply the natural reaction of the body when the fire burns through its muscles and tendons. Oh God. Jay.

I press my fingers under my eyes to clear the tears that have escaped. In some ways, I'm surprised at the effect his death has had on me. I didn't know him that well and I spent much of the time being angry with him. It took me a while to see what Megan saw, but I got there in the end. She was right. Underneath it all, he had a good heart. He just needed a lucky break. Instead, he burned to death in my home.

I run a hand along the blue and white police tape tied taut between two pine trees. I don't cross it. It's there for a reason, and now I'm the victim, my place is on this side of the crime scene tape. A CSI in a white suit is photographing the smouldering carcass that was once my home but I'm too far away to see who it is.

I left Megan at Sneddon Farm still asleep. She's sharing a room with Emma who hopefully can provide some distraction for her via the medium of reality TV shows. By the time I came downstairs this morning, Will was already out in the fields. He's been avoiding me since I arrived. I'm guessing Penny has told him I think he's responsible for trying to wipe out Gabe's flock, but I can't think about that right now. All I can think of is Jay.

'Hi, Ally.'

The CSI is waving and walking towards me, but it isn't until he pulls down his white paper mask that I realize it's Jake. I haven't seen him since the break-in at Bidecombe DIY Supplies, which feels several lifetimes ago.

'I thought you were one of the MI team.' I smile.

'They finished examining the place yesterday.'

'So what are you doing here?'

'They decided they needed some more shots but weren't willing to travel up from Exeter to take them, so they sent me.'

I survey the charred remains that were once my home.

'Did the CSIs find much?'

I'm not hopeful. Fire destroys everything. CSIs know it. Criminals know it.

'There was a petrol can nearby, but it had glove marks on it.'

'Glove marks? Anything else?'

I can't help myself. I want to not care, play the role of victim I've been handed, let Jake and Major Investigations get on with it, but I can't. This is personal, after all.

'No.' His face is apologetic, but it's not his fault. 'How are you?'

'Relieved Megan is OK. Devastated a young man lost his life.'

'I heard it was Jay Cox.'

Jake is as familiar with Jay as I am. Even if we couldn't catch him, we all knew he was the go-to guy for drugs, especially among teenagers.

'Yes. It was.'

'That explains it.'

'Explains what?'

'I asked the guy from the Major Incidents Team how the investigation was going, and he said it's always difficult when the victim deserves it. No one wants to go the extra mile for those who had it coming to them, especially when they've plenty of worthier cases stacking up. Still, one less toerag for us to deal with.'

A sentiment that I probably would have shared until recently.

'He was beginning to turn life his around, you know, which is why I let him live with us.'

Jake is surprised at my response. Jay Cox's name has echoed

around the police station for years and until recently I didn't have a good word to say about him either.

'That's not what I heard.'

Before I have time to press Jake further, my phone rings. It's Penny. Given the only conversations we've had recently have been essential ones, I answer it immediately, but she doesn't give me time to speak.

'You need to come back to the farmhouse right away.'

'Why? What's happened?'

'There's a man in Will's kitchen. He says he's Megan's real dad.'

42

Julian Winstanley-Jones is sitting at the table in Will's kitchen, drinking a coffee, like he owns the place. He's wearing dark blue slacks and a cream jersey sweatshirt. I don't need the distinctive polo-player emblem to tell me his clothes are expensive. Megan is next to him. Her proximity to him unnerves me, like sides have already been taken.

As soon as Julian sees me, he gets up and hugs me like an old friend and not the pregnant girlfriend he abandoned sixteen years ago. My hands remain by my sides and he sits back down, finally allowing me to ask the only question on my mind.

'What the hell are you doing here?'

He glances at Megan who bows her head in guilt.

'Megan asked me to come.'

'What?'

I look to Megan for an explanation, but her eyes are fixed on the table, so Julian speaks for her. 'She messaged me about the fire, and I asked her if she was OK. She told me about her friend and that she was scared, so I asked her if she wanted to come and stay with me for a few days. She said yes, so here I am.'

'What are you doing even communicating with her?'

Julian squeezes Megan's hand. 'We've been talking to each other for a while now.'

'Is that true, Megan?'

Megan nods at the table.

'You make it sound like she's done something wrong, but Megan is my daughter too, Ally.'

'Don't even go there.'

Julian lets out an exasperated sigh like he's already explained things a thousand times. 'Look, whether you like it or not, Megan and I have built up a relationship over the last few months and now I'm here to help.'

'We don't need your help. Megan is perfectly safe with me.'

'She's not though, is she?'

He's not just talking about the fire. He's talking about last year, but he doesn't need to spell it out. The unspoken truth hangs in the silence. *It's your fault our daughter was attacked.*

'Megan, I won't let anything happen to you. I promise.'

She shakes her head. She still can't look at me. 'I'm scared.'

'There's no need to be frightened. We're safe here.'

'The point is, Ally, Megan doesn't feel safe. Why don't you let her come and stay with me for a few days?'

'You can't be serious. You actually think I'm going to let Megan, who you've never set eyes on until today, go with you?'

Julian leans back, bathed in a confidence and smugness that comes with knowing that you always get what you want in life.

'Yes, I do. I think it might be a good idea for everyone if Megan stays at mine for a few days until the police work out what's going on.'

'No and I can't believe you'd even suggest it. You need to

leave now and, Megan, I have no idea what you think you're playing at, but you are not going anywhere with him or anyone else.'

'Ally, let's talk about this.'

'You didn't want to talk about it sixteen years ago. Well, guess what? I don't want to talk about it now. I want you to go, Julian. You're not helping. What's happening here is nothing to do with you.'

Julian smiles at Megan. 'Well, I'm afraid Megan has made it to do with me.'

'You're a complete stranger to her.'

Julian laughs. 'Not quite. I am her dad, after all.'

'But you don't know her. You don't know anything about her.'

'I know she needs me.'

I'm trying hard to sound calm and reasonable, but Julian has already won that battle and my voice is tight with disbelief and a creeping panic that I'm also losing the war.

'No, she doesn't need you. She just thinks she does because she's angry with me because I wouldn't let her go back to school after . . . after what happened.'

'She says you're keeping her off for no reason.'

'She's playing you off me. That's what teenagers do. You'd know that if you'd hung around.'

Megan throws Julian a worried side glance. He nods at her. 'It's OK. We'll get this sorted.'

What the fuck does he think he's doing reassuring my daughter? Like I'm the one she needs protecting from.

'There's nothing to sort. Megan stays here.'

'No,' Megan says firmly. 'You might be able to stop me

262

going back to school but you can't stop me from going to live with my dad.'

Her dad. For fuck's sake. He's never been her dad.

'Megan, please.'

'Ally, I don't know why you're so resistant to the idea. Megan'll be absolutely fine with us.'

'You haven't been there for her.'

'I know that, so let me do this for her, for you, now. It'll just be a few days. She'll be safe with us. She can get to know her half-brothers, Josh and Noah, and my wife, Camilla. When the police give you the all-clear, I'll bring her back.'

'She's not well, Julian. She had a seizure last week. We're still waiting for tests. What if she has another one? And she has a doctor's appointment next week. And what about her counselling?'

'Megan says she doesn't need it any more.'

'She's not in a position to make that call. She was just beginning to deal with what happened last year and now she has the added trauma of almost dying in a fire that claimed the life of her closest friend.'

Megan's eyes shine with tears.

'She doesn't need any more upheaval in her life right now.'

'I understand that, but maybe you need to respect the fact that Megan knows what's good for her.'

'What?'

But he doesn't give me any time to channel my mounting fury into more words.

'I promise we'll have her back in plenty of time for her doctor's appointment. Cam's a stay-at-home mum so she's around if anything happens. She's a trained first-aider and we're two minutes from one of the best hospitals in London.'

He has an answer for everything. Some things never change. I look at Megan.

'Is this what you really want?'

She nods and my heart folds in on itself.

43

Tall, confident and with cheekbones to die for, Julian Winstanley-Jones was hard to miss and I'd seen him around our college long before I met him. I had no idea he'd even noticed me until he appeared by my side in the common room bar and insisted on buying me a drink. A drink became a date, which became a relationship. I was in love, and I was sure he was too. He had this ability to make me feel I was the most interesting person in the world. It was a long time since I had felt that special, not since before Dad died and Bernadette disappeared within herself, only emerging to disapprove of my life choices.

For a time, Julian found me endlessly fascinating. Being adopted was 'so cool' and having a mixed and undefined heritage made me 'mysterious and exotic'. After a while, I began to wonder if my novelty value was my only attraction and that I was just another uni experience to tick off. I was the 'go out with a girl from a completely different background to you' box. Then I discovered I was pregnant, and Julian suddenly found me a lot less interesting. He dumped me and refused to respond to any attempts to involve him in his daughter's life. Now, sixteen years later, he's telling me what a great girl she is. But how long before he tires of her? What happens when it gets difficult because difficult is a teenager's middle name. Will he reject her, like he rejected me?

A buzzing noise interrupts my thoughts. It's Megan, FaceTiming me to tell me she's arrived at Julian's house.

'Hi, love.' Unsure if I've forgiven her for leaving with Julian, she offers me a wary smile in return, but none of this is her fault. 'How are you?'

'OK.'

'Good.'

'Mum. I'm sorry. I couldn't stay. It's too . . . hard.'

'I know.'

She is in Julian's kitchen, which is all marble countertops and high-end appliances and is one of those that have been extended into the garden to increase the light, putting the cabin's poky, utility-room-sized kitchen to shame.

'Have you met your half-brothers?'

'Josh and Noah. Yes, they're really sweet.'

'What about Julian's wife, Camilla?'

'She's nice too.'

'Good.'

'Any news on Jay?'

'No. It's still early days.' A shadow passes over her face, grief creeping back in. 'Are you OK?'

She presses her quivering lips together until her sadness recedes. 'I still can't believe he's gone. I keep checking my phone to see if he's sent me a meme. He used to send me them all the time.'

A single tear escapes and I want to reach out and hold her close to me, take her pain away and make it mine.

'It might not feel like it right now, but it will get better,

I promise. How about when you're home we arrange a special service for him, maybe hold it in the park?'

She nods and glances to one side. There's someone else there, off camera.

'Julian wants a word.'

Only I don't particularly want a word with him. What I want is to carry on talking to my daughter, but I have no choice and the screen fills with his face. The similarity between him and Megan startles me all over again.

'Ally, hi, I wasn't listening in. I just want to tell you all's well. Cam loves Megan,' he says with more than a hint of relief. He moves the screen back to include a woman in a black cashmere sweater slicing carrots. I recognize her from the photos on Julian's Facebook page. She waves her knife at me.

'Hi, Ally, nice to meet you.'

'The boys adore her too.' Julian shifts the screen back to himself. 'She's so good with them, considering she's grown up an only child.' Next to him, Megan flushes with pride. 'Anyway, I just wanted to say, you've nothing to worry about. We're taking good care of her. She's welcome to stay as long as she likes.'

'Thanks, but—'

'Hold on a second.'

The screen is gate-crashed by two small boys who just want to say hello to 'Aunty Ally'. The eldest one, Josh, is dark-haired like his mother, but Noah looks like Julian. And Megan. The same eyes, the same cheekbones. They elbow each other in their enthusiasm to appear on screen. Julian laughs at their antics, which even raises a smile from Megan. Domestic bliss.

I return my phone to my jeans pocket. I don't think I've ever hated him more. Or myself.

44

Harriet is leaning against her car, arms folded, exchanging wary looks with Will's sheepdog, Jude, who is lurking near the haybarn. I spotted her drive into the yard after my call with Megan and came out to meet her. When Jude sees me at the kitchen door, she trots towards me for a ruffle of her head before slumping at my feet.

'It's OK,' I tell her. 'She won't bite.'

But Harriet stays where she is. 'I'm not sure about that. Me and dogs really don't get on. I have the scars to prove it.'

'How's the investigation going? I'm assuming that's why you're here.'

'No, it's not actually,' she says coolly. 'The FLO will keep you informed on that score.'

No surprises there. She's frozen me out since I revealed I spent the night with Kit.

'So why are you here?'

'I'll get straight to the point. I want to know what's going on between you and Kit Narracott.'

'Nothing is going on. We've met a few times, and it was just that one night. I didn't discuss his brother's case with him if that's what you're worried about. I'm not on it anyway. Technically I haven't done anything wrong.'

'You're right, but you know how the force frowns on this kind of thing.'

'Have you reported me to Professional Standards?'

'Not yet. I wanted to find out from you how serious it is.'

'It's not.'

She doesn't believe me, but I guess that's her job.

'Look, whatever it is you've got going on at least wait until the investigation is over. We're only talking a few months here. Otherwise, you could do your career some serious damage.'

Jesus, she doesn't know the half of it.

'Why are you so interested?'

'I'm just looking out for you, that's all. You're a damn good CSI and I don't want to lose you. You're already on a final warning, Ally. I just don't understand why you're risking everything for this guy.'

'I appreciate your concern, Harriet, but . . .'

I want to point out to her that she's not above taking her own risks. If the top brass found out she'd given me access to all the files on Slaughterhouse Farm, she too could find herself staring down the barrel of a professional standards investigation, but I don't say anything because I'm tired, tired of it all.

'But what?'

'You're too late. I'm resigning.'

***

The cabin has that fresh, newly built smell. The layout is identical to our previous cabin, but, unsullied by humans, its kitchen units are gleaming and pristine and its green velvet sofa taut and untested. It's as if someone has peeled back magic slate paper and erased any evidence of our previous life.

'Welcome to cabin 36,' says Penny, ushering me in. When I came down to breakfast this morning Penny was already waiting for me with the keys to our new cabin. It's a relief for all of us. Will has been largely absent since I moved in and when he is around there's an awkward atmosphere. Penny and my conversations are painfully superficial, neither of us wanting to discuss Will for fear that it will lead to an argument. Penny points at the living room wall. 'As you can see, these new cabins have different murals.'

Our old cabin had a tropical beach scene When we first moved in, Megan took her crayons to it, adding the two of us in starfish stick-figure form, our grins wider than our heads, holding ice creams in our outstretched hands. Our new mural is of the morning sun, star-bursting through a forest of pine trees.

'It's really lovely, Penny.'

Penny leads me down a short corridor into the bedroom on the left. She pushes the handle of a door, which swings open, revealing a small, grey-tiled bathroom.

'Both bedrooms have an en suite. Megan will love that.'

'It's great.'

We return to the kitchenette.

'I think we should christen the place, don't you?' She opens the fridge, already packed with food, and extracts a couple of ciders. After taking the tops off the bottles she hands one to me.

'Here's to a new beginning,' she says, clinking my bottle with hers, but neither of us are in the mood for celebrating.

She puts her glass down and looks at me. 'Something came in the post today.'

'What was it?'

She pulls a white envelope from her pocket and hands it to me. It's addressed to Jay.

'It's from the council,' I say, opening it and scanning the contents. 'It's his job offer. I'll call them and let them know what's happened,' I add quickly, pushing back a sudden swell of grief that threatens to overwhelm me.

God, I want to leave it there, just stuff the letter into my pocket along with my emotions and try to ignore it, but I can't. I care that a young man's life has been lost and I care that it is Jay's and not just because of how much he meant to Megan. I'm beginning to realize that he meant something to me too, and I need to honour that by talking about him. 'You know, he was so excited about his new job, Pen. It was his way out. He knew it, and he wasn't going to waste it. He'd have been brilliant too. Did you know he loved nature? His mother taught him the names of all the wildflowers. She even taught him to recognize a bird by its song. Isn't that incredible? It's just so fucking cruel. All of it.'

'I know. He didn't deserve it, Ally,' she says, rubbing my back. She lets the moment pass. 'I heard DI Moore came to the farm yesterday. Does that mean there's news on Jay?'

'No, not yet.' I put Jay's letter on the side. 'That wasn't why she came. She wanted to know what was going on between Kit and me. She's worried it might compromise the investigation into Gabe's murder.'

'What did you tell her?'

'I told her nothing was going on and even if it was, she didn't have to worry because I'm . . . quitting.'

'What?'

'She tried to talk me out of it, told me what a loss I'd be and how they needed me, which was flattering I guess, but my mind's made up.'

'But I thought we'd agreed. I can take care of Megan.'

'It's not about Megan.'

'Then what is it about?'

I pinch the bridge of my nose between my thumb and forefinger. Do I say anything? What difference will it make if I do?

'Ally? What is it? You know you can tell me anything, don't you?'

'The other night . . . I almost killed Tony Cox.'

'What?'

'After our argument about Will, I went back to the cabin. Jay was waiting for me. The council told him that they wouldn't take him on if he had a criminal record. There was no way he was going to win his court case, so I went to ask Tony to withdraw his statement.'

'What happened?'

'He refused unless I . . . had sex with him.'

Penny screws her face up. 'What? God, that man is disgusting.' She looks at me. 'You didn't, did you?'

'No, but I was so angry with him that I waited for him to leave the pub and then lured him to the end of the quay by pretending I would. I was about to push him into the water when I heard a car door slam. If it hadn't been for that, I'm fairly sure Tony Cox would be at the bottom of the Atlantic.'

'Oh God, Ally.'

'What's wrong with me, Penny? I nearly killed Tony Cox, for Christ's sake. And don't try and tell me he deserved it.' To her credit, she doesn't. In fact, she doesn't have any words for me at all. She just stands there looking at me like she doesn't know me anymore, but I'm a stranger to myself too. 'The point is I don't trust myself any more and that terrifies me.'

'I . . . I had no idea you felt like this.'

'I couldn't see it at first, but now I can and look where it's got me. I've lost everything I ever cared about: my home, my daughter, my job. It's all gone, and I don't know how I'm going to get any of it back.'

45

PC Wendy Blake and I have worked a few scenes together. She's great with victims, displaying natural empathy, so it was no surprise to hear she'd become a family liaison officer or FLO, but it is a surprise to find her on my veranda. I refused a FLO last year when Megan was attacked. I didn't need one. As a CSI and someone in 'the job' the senior investigating officer kept me informed, but by sending Wendy, DI Moore has sent a clear message: I'm on the outside now.

'Hi, Ally. DI Moore asked me to drop by. Sorry, it's just me. My colleague is sick.' Normally, there are two FLOs. 'So, how have you been?'

'OK.'

'And Megan?'

'She's not here. She's staying with her father.'

'OK. Is this your new place?' She surveys the outside of the cabin. 'It looks lovely. I always wanted to live in the woods when I was a little girl.'

A classic FLO move: establish a rapport with the subject as soon as possible. And Wendy is good, but I only want to know when Megan can come home.

'What's happening with the investigation, Wendy?'

'Right. Yes. The investigation. Did you see the reconstruction on *Crime Time* last night?'

'No.' I couldn't bring myself to watch it.

'Well, we had a few calls from people saying they saw Jay talking to a girl on the high street about 6 p.m.'

'A girl.'

'Yes.'

'Not Cassie Warnock by any chance?'

'Yes, but how did you know that?'

So much for me telling Jay to stay away from her.

'Lucky guess.'

'OK, well, a witness also saw him outside the kebab shop at around 8 p.m. when he bought a kebab. This is confirmed by CCTV footage of him passing a charity shop a few doors down from the takeaway place. He's then seen on CCTV crossing the car park on Anchor Road, with a can of Coke in his hand.'

'Coke? Jay was addicted to Dr Pepper.'

'We're not sure where he got it from because he didn't buy it at the kebab shop.'

'What time was that?'

'About 9 p.m.'

'Nine? Anchor Road car park can't be more than two hundred metres from the kebab shop. Where did he go for an hour?'

'Er . . . we're not sure at the moment.' Not telling me more likely. 'As you know he tried to call you twice at 9.30 p.m. and we now know he made that phone call at the bottom of Cliffside Road. He got back to the cabin around 10.30 p.m. We're hoping someone will come forward and confirm what he was doing in that missing hour but that's where we're at with the investigation.'

'Thanks for letting me know.'

'Is there anything else I can do for you? Like put you in touch with victim support services?'

'No. I'm fine, but there is something I'd like to ask.'

'Fire away.' Wendy blushes at her clumsiness. 'Oh God, sorry.'

'It's not a problem. Has the investigation been able to identify if Jay was the only intended target?'

'Didn't the DI tell you?'

'No.'

She pauses, unsure whether to proceed before deciding it's safe. 'You're a CSI, you understand the need for confidentiality, so I guess there's no harm in telling you.'

'I won't say anything. I just need to know.'

'OK, well, there was only one seat of the fire, directly under the window close to where Jay was sleeping. The CSIs found the petrol can that was used nearby. It was still a quarter full.' I can see where this is going, but I let Wendy have her moment. 'The area around the cabin was pitch-black. The team doesn't think the perpetrator was disturbed. They think they pretty much had all the time in the world to do what they wanted including pouring petrol elsewhere, through the letterbox, for instance. That's often a favourite. Sorry, you know that, of course. Anyway, the point is the person only poured petrol under the living room window.'

'And all the curtains were open so they would have known I was out; Megan was in her room and Jay was sleeping on the sofa below the living room window.'

'Which means, Ally, we're as certain as we can be that Jay was the only target.'

***

As soon as Wendy leaves, I FaceTime Megan immediately.

'Hi, Mum. What's up?'

'Nice coat.'

'Do you like it? Cam bought it for me. She thought it might cheer me up a bit. It's just like Emma's but red. Yellow makes me look ill.'

'It's lovely. Anyway, I have some news for you.'

'About Jay?'

'In a way. The police have just been. It's safe for you to return to Seven Hills. That's great, isn't it?'

'I suppose.'

'I can pick you up tomorrow lunchtime.'

'Oh.'

'Is there a problem?'

'It's just that I'm still getting to know everyone.'

'I'm sure you can visit them again and Penny has given us a lovely new cabin with en-suite bathrooms. We've even got a new mural in the living room – a pine forest – just waiting for you to draw all over.'

'I've grown out of all that.'

'I know. Look, Megan, you need to deal with what's happened and the only way you're going to do that is by coming home. Besides, it was only ever a short-term arrangement, a few days at most just until the police were sure we were safe. Julian, Cam and the boys, they've got their own lives to be getting on with.'

'That's just it.'

'What do you mean?'

'Dad, Julian, said I could stay as long as I wanted.'

***

Julian throws his hands up in surrender. 'Sorry. Sorry. I put my foot in it. Cam's always telling me off for my big mouth.'

I'd waited until I was sure Megan had gone to bed before I phoned him.

'That's not good enough, Julian. It's not what we agreed. You can't tell Megan she can stay with you without consulting me.'

'I know. I wasn't thinking. It's just been so great having her here. She's told us all about your lives in Bidecombe. It sounds like an idyllic place. And you're a CSI. That's a helluva job, Wish.' Wish, derived from Aloysia, was Julian's pet name for me at uni. 'Funny, I couldn't imagine the nineteen-year-old Ally doing something like that.'

'Maybe she was too busy being pregnant with your child.'

'You've still got the same caustic sense of humour I see.' He laughs. 'The truth is I, we, love having Megan here and, well, we'd really like to hold on to her for a few more days.'

'That wasn't the arrangement.'

'I know, but maybe it would be a good thing if she stays a little while longer. For both of you.'

'What's that supposed to mean?'

'OK, cards on the table.'

'That'll be a first.'

'Megan has told us that, well, you can be a bit overprotective. Since last year, you've barely let her out of your sight. Now, given what's happened that's totally understandable, but, well, it's making her life pretty miserable. So, what Cam and I were thinking is that we can keep hold of Megan a little longer and that will give you both some space to work through things. You could use the time to work on yourself.'

'Work on myself?'

'Yes, you know, a bit of self-care. Maybe Megan isn't the only one who could benefit from some counselling here, Wish. There's no shame in it. You've been through hell.'

'You've no idea what I've been through. You know nothing about me. This isn't just about space, Julian. Megan needs to grieve properly for Jay, and she can only do that here. This is her home. This is where all her memories of Jay are. The people who know and love her are here.'

'Yes, of course, we understand that too, but a few extra days isn't going to make any difference in the long run and, anyway, she really loves it here. She gets on great with the boys. She's fitted in so well.' He doesn't go as far as to tell me she's just like one of the family. 'Look, Wish, I'm not trying to muscle in or anything. You clearly have a great relationship with Megan. All I'm saying is I'm here now. I can pick up the slack while you get back on your feet.'

He rings off and I sit back on my new green velvet sofa, dazed by our exchange. This is what he does. It's what he always did. Take control of our conversation, twist it to suit himself with words that sound so sensible until he's walked away, and I realize I've been manipulated. I pick up my coffee mug and launch it at the wall. That's all the fucking self-care I need.

46

I open my front door, blinking into the dull morning light, to find the last person I expect or want to see on my veranda.

After I spoke to Julian last night, I went onto Megan's Instagram, hoping these people weren't significant enough to earn a place on her timeline, but there they all were: on a roundabout at a park, in the car eating McDonald's, standing in front of donkeys in a petting zoo, as if they have been a part of her life forever and the preceding sixteen years had never happened. Below the photos, the comments were sprinkled with heart emojis from Penny, which felt vaguely disloyal somehow, and Emma, Will's sister, declaring they all looked 'super cute'. There was even a remark from Cassie telling Megan she's so lucky to have a family, which takes me by surprise. I didn't know they knew each other. Maybe they don't. That's social media for you, a place with no rules, no boundaries.

I couldn't bring myself to write anything. Instead, I headed to the local Spar and bought six bottles of cider to deaden the questions plaguing me: how could I not see how unhappy Megan was at home? Why didn't I listen to her? Why didn't I just let her go back to school? But mostly, how do I get her home?

I must have drifted off to sleep because the next thing I knew someone was banging on my door. When I realized it wasn't going to stop, I hauled myself to my feet and was instantly punished with throbbing temples.

'Hello, Bernadette.'

Seeing Bernadette is shocking on so many levels. Firstly, I thought she was still on holiday and, secondly, she's never set foot in Seven Hills before, deeming it beneath her. She lives on the better side of town, high on a hill from which she can look down on us all. For her to deign to come here it must be serious.

'You look terrible,' she says, marching into the cabin. 'I can't leave you for five minutes, can I?' she adds, glaring at the empty bottles of cider on the coffee table.

'I thought you had another week of your holiday left.'

'I came home early. Penny phoned me and told me what was going on. She's worried about you. I can't believe you didn't tell me about the fire.'

'I didn't want to ruin your trip. Besides, Megan is fine.'

'If she's fine, what's she doing with that man?'

'By that man, I assume you mean Julian, her father. We decided his place in London was the safest place for her just until the police worked out who the target was.'

She presses her lips together to show my explanation is far from satisfactory.

'And did you know she's taken to calling him dad already?'

'There's not really much I can do about that. He is her father after all.'

She shakes her head. 'Well, I never thought I'd see the day when you'd let that man into Megan's life.'

'Like I said, it was for her own safety.'

'So when is she coming home?'

'Soon. The police now seem certain her friend Jay was the intended target.'

'What do you mean by soon? Because I've just spoken to her and she gave me the distinct impression she wasn't coming home.'

'Well, there's no rush,' I lie, but I don't want Bernadette to sense the panic in me. 'She's still getting to know her dad and her stepbrothers. It's all very overwhelming for her, but she knows this is her home, her real home, and she'll be back for her school prom. She won't want to miss that.'

'I wouldn't be so sure of that.'

'What do you mean by that?'

'I wouldn't trust that man as far as I could throw him and I'm surprised you do, but then you always have been a bit naïve when it comes to men.'

'I needed Megan to be safe.'

'That's as may be, but did you know they've been putting all sorts of ideas into her head about going to college there.'

'What?'

'I thought not. Aloysia, that man is used to getting things his own way. You, of all people, should know that.'

'That was sixteen years ago. We've all grown up since then.'

'Really? I wouldn't be so sure. And who was this boy, Jay?'

I press my fingers under my eyebrow to try and dispel the pain. 'He was Megan's friend.'

'I heard he was a drug dealer. What was he even doing in your cabin?'

'I was helping him get back on his feet.'

'Typical of you, taking in every waif and stray when it's your real family that needs you. Have they caught the person who did it?'

'No.'

'Well, he was a druggie after all.'

'What's that supposed to mean?'

'He lived by the sword and died by the sword. Why would the police bother themselves with someone like that?'

Her words trigger a vague memory of my conversation with Jake at the cabin the day after the fire when we were interrupted by Penny calling to tell me Julian had turned up unannounced to whisk Megan away. I had completely forgotten about it. Until now.

'Aloysia, are you all right?'

'I will be.'

Gabe

The doctor called it delayed development. He said it could be caused by trauma, but Silas insisted that nothing traumatic had ever happened to Gabe. His grandparents and parents loved him and kept him safe, but the doctor said that parents could pass on their own trauma. Silas dismissed this too, but Miriam knew she was the reason Gabe hadn't developed like he should. It was her fault, her trauma, and she had passed it on to him and she would have to live with that for the rest of her life. She was an idiot for thinking she could escape her past and now her beloved son would suffer, but she would make it up to him. She would prove them all wrong. She'd protect him, make sure no harm came to him. She would be a good mother.

Then Kit came along. He was everything Gabe wasn't. Quick-witted, lively, he could charm the birds out of the trees. She couldn't spend as much time with him as she wanted, not with Gabe the way he was, but he never seemed to mind. She promised him his time would come, but he just shrugged it off. He was the independent type, was Kit, and so protective of his brother.

When the children at school stole Gabe's dinner money or called him names, Kit would step in and right the wrong done to his brother. He got into so many fights she had to beg the school not to expel him. She told him he didn't have to do this, but he said someone had to look out for Gabe when she wasn't around. There was a time when she thought Kit would never leave his brother's side, but she was wrong about that too.

The best days were when it was just the three of them on the farm together. When Miriam first arrived at Slaughterhouse Farm, the big skies and empty hills made her feel uneasy. There was so much space, so many places to hide. Someone could be watching her, and she wouldn't even know they were there. But as time went by she realized there was no one there. She was alone and she came to love the isolation of the farm. It was her world. It was all she needed. Silas was right about that. They were safe as long as they stayed on the farm. By the time the boys came along, she rarely left the place, and it began to feel as if no other world existed beyond those hills, which suited her just fine.

She would take Gabe and Kit with her wherever she went. Mostly they'd help out on the farm, but in the quiet times when Silas didn't need them so much they'd build dens in the woods, dam streams and pick the crab apples to take back to the farmhouse to turn into chutney.

But she couldn't keep Gabe at home forever. He wanted to be out in the world like his younger brother. She couldn't make him see that he wasn't like Kit and the only way she could protect him was if he stayed close to her. Then there was all that trouble with those underage girls. Gabe promised her he'd done nothing wrong, the children said they didn't mind; they were just having fun. She was so certain he was innocent; she didn't question it. It probably was their idea anyway, she reasoned. The kids from the home were a rum bunch who got up to all sorts. Silas once found two of them in one of his barns. What they were doing was no one's business. It was so easy to convince herself that they had led Gabe on, but she was a fool to have believed him. The signs had been there all along; she had just chosen to ignore them, and now it had come to this.

After that, Gabe stayed close to home, for a while. She thought he'd learned his lesson and then he started seeing Caroline Sneddon. He tried to keep it secret from her, but she'd seen them holding hands in the woods. She wasn't surprised. Gabe was a good-looking boy, but he wasn't ready for girls. At least Caroline was the same age and Miriam had nothing against her personally, but she wasn't right for Gabe.

She was too ambitious, and Miriam knew that she'd tire of his slow ways. She assumed it would fizzle out, but one evening Gabe told her he loved Caroline and wanted to marry her. *Silly boy*, she said, allowing his feelings to run away with him. That never got anyone anywhere. He was much too young, but he was adamant, so she told him that she'd heard Caroline was moving up country to pursue a show-jumping career. He couldn't say anything to her as no one was meant to know. It was all very hush-hush, but she obviously didn't feel the same way about him as he did about her. It was better that he finish it then and there before it went any further. A clean break was best all round.

Caroline sobbed her heart out when Gabe broke it off, begging him to tell her why, but he kept quiet just as Miriam had told him to. When Caroline died in that car crash, he got himself in a right state, blaming himself. Then Will Sneddon attacked him in the pub. He said he deserved everything he got, but Miriam knew she was right to tell him to finish it before he got hurt.

There were others, but nothing serious. None of them were suitable, least of all that woman who runs the farm supplies shop.

Miriam didn't like her at all. She was at least ten years older than Gabe, running around making a fool of herself with younger men, making a fool out of her boy. It was obvious she was only after the farm. She'd marry and divorce him in the blink of an eye and take him for all he was worth. But Gabe insisted he loved her. That was Gabe. He could only see the good in people. She thought for a moment she'd lost him, but when she told him she was too old to have babbers and there'd be no one to take on the farm and it'd have to be sold, he finished it. Again, she was surprised at how upset he was. She told him he'd get over her soon enough, but he was very down about it.

Then, out of the blue, he told her he still loved this woman. He'd made a terrible mistake and he was miserable without her. The night he died he said he was going to see her, to ask her to give him another chance. Miriam couldn't have that.

47

When I arrive at police headquarters late in the afternoon, Harriet is pacing up and down in reception, impatient to get this over and done with. I don't want to be here either, and I'd have been here sooner if I hadn't been distracted by the father of my daughter reappearing after a sixteen-year absence to invite her to live with him. I have Bernadette to thank for reminding me of my brief chat with Jake when I met him photographing the remains of the cabin. Someone on Major Investigations had told him Jay's case would receive the minimum of attention. No one cared if it got solved because, as far as they were concerned, Jay got what was coming to him. It's an attitude I've come across before. Christ, there are times when I've had to steel myself to treat victims who are also criminals with the same level of respect and diligence as everyone else. But that's just how it is. Or should be.

'So, what was so important that it couldn't be said over the phone?' asks Harriet.

'I wanted to ask how the inquiry into Jay Cox's murder is going?'

She lets out an incredulous gasp. 'You've come all this way for that? I'm sure our FLO Wendy has told you it's proceeding well enough.' Proceeding. It didn't take her long to recede into the comfort zone of police 'speak'.

'Wendy said that you're now sure Jay was the target.'

'Yes. That's right.'

'Do you have any suspects?'

'None that I'm willing to discuss with you.'

'Wendy said Jay met Cassie the night he died. I take it you've interviewed her.'

'Yes, we have. She's in the clear.'

'And Tony Cox?'

'He's in the clear too.'

'What about the two missed calls I got from Jay the night he died?'

'What this all about, Ally? It's like you're checking up on us.'

'It's just something someone said to me, that's all.'

'Which is?'

'That Jay was a criminal who caused his fair share of misery so Major Investigations aren't taking it seriously.'

Harriet is genuinely offended by this.

'I don't know who told you that, but it's not how I work. Look, I know what you went through last year, Ally, and I don't blame you being a bit edgy, but I'm not Holt.' Holt was the SIO in charge of Megan's case. 'I do things properly. A victim is a victim. I'm not arsed about their CV.'

'It's not you I'm worried about.'

'I can assure you my team think the same way I do and anyone who doesn't will have me to deal with. We've got this. I promise you we'll find Jay's killer.'

Our eyes stay locked for a few seconds more.

'OK. Thanks, I needed to hear that. Jay made plenty of

mistakes in his life – I won't deny that – but he was a good kid who was getting his life straight and he certainly didn't deserve to die.'

She nods.

'You're right, he didn't, but—'

'But what?'

'He's not the saint you think he is either.'

***

Megan's tired and guarded face comes up on my screen as if she's braced for interrogation. Is that what I am? Her interrogator?

'How are you, love?'

'Fine.'

'Look, it's OK for you to stay at Julian's a little longer.'

'Really?' She lets go of a tiny breath of relief.

'Just for a few more days.'

'Thank you. It's just easier here. Nothing to remind me of Jay.'

'I know, but there's something I have to tell you about Jay.'

'Have they found the person who did it?'

'Not yet, no.'

'Oh.' Her shoulders sag. 'I miss him so much, Mum. He was my best friend, the only one who really got me.'

'He was a good guy.'

She frowns, detecting insincerity in my voice despite my efforts to remain neutral.

'What is it?'

'There's no easy way to say this, Megan, and I can't tell

you how much I don't want it to be true, but the post-mortem showed that Jay had taken drugs the night he died. He was on heroin.'

'What?'

'That's why he didn't get out of the cabin in time. He was out of it. I'm so sorry, love.'

She shakes her head. 'That's not possible. I spoke to him. He was tired, but he was OK. He wasn't on drugs. He can't have been.'

'Megan, it's true. He lied to you. He lied to us both. I've just spoken to the SIO. There's a missing hour in Jay's timeline on the night he died. They're fairly certain he met his dealer and took drugs.'

'No. He loved living with us. He wouldn't have done anything to spoil that, especially drugs.'

Her loyalty is touching. The only truth she can consider is the one that exonerates him, and I have to choose my words carefully so as not to alienate her.

'Look. Maybe he couldn't help himself. It's really difficult to get off drugs. Relapses are very common.'

She's shaking her head. 'You're not listening to me, Mum. I know for a fact Jay wasn't on drugs.'

'How could you possibly know that?'

She lets out an exasperated sigh. 'Because he tested himself every day to prove to me he wasn't.'

'What?'

'Yes. When he moved into the cabin, I had a right go at him about it all. I told him if I caught him, I'd tell you, so he bought some kits off Amazon and tested himself. They were all negative. He did one that morning.'

'Why didn't you tell me?'

'He told me not to. But that's how I know he wasn't on drugs. No way. He thought too much of me, and of you.'

'But the PM showed he had heroin in his system.'

'He's never touched heroin in his life. He refused to deal it too.'

'Really?' Drug dealers aren't that discerning in my experience. 'But why?'

She looks at me as if the answer is obvious.

'Because heroin killed his mum.'

48

Why am I here? Because I believed Harriet when she said she treated all victims the same. I saw it in her eyes. Just as I saw a flicker of uncertainty when she told me her team felt the same way she did. The truth is she doesn't know her team. She inherited them from Holt. She said herself she brought me in because she wasn't sure who she could trust yet. Well, she's not the only one with trust issues.

I duck down behind my steering wheel as Tony Cox emerges from his house. Striding down the street, a smile playing on his lips, he doesn't strike me as a man consumed with grief over the death of his son. He has the arrogance of a man who knows he's top dog. Even in a place like Bidecombe that counts for something, but it isn't Tony I want to talk to.

The doorbell goes unanswered and I'm about to give up when the door finally opens and Cassie's scowl appears in the crack. I know Harriet said she was in the clear, but I'm certain this girl is in it right up to her pencilled eyebrows and if Megan is right and Jay didn't knowingly take drugs then someone gave them to him. Someone he trusted.

'It was you, wasn't it?'

'Fuck off.'

But my foot is already wedged in the doorway and when she tries to slam the door on me, it bounces back, giving me time to grab it and barge my way into the hallway. She turns to run from me, but I grab her hair and slam her against the peeling wall, pinning her shoulders against it.

'Ow, you're hurting me.'

'You gave the drugs to Jay, didn't you?'

'What? No. Why the fuck would I do that?'

'I don't know. You tell me.'

'I didn't do it. I just saw him in the street, that's all.'

I stare at her for a while longer, reluctantly concluding she might just be telling the truth. It was a long shot anyway. Cassie met Jay at 6 p.m. If she'd given him drugs then they would have taken effect immediately, but it's clear they didn't kick in until after he got home. I let her go.

'So, if you didn't, who did?'

'I dunno,' she says, rubbing her shoulder.

'But you met Jay that night.'

'Yeah, by accident. In the street.'

'So what did you say to him?'

'Can't remember.' She shrugs.

'For fuck's sake, Cassie. Jay is dead. This is serious. What did you say to him?'

'Nothin'. Honest. None of this is anything to do with me.'

I let my anger slide; it's getting me nowhere.

'I just want to find out what happened, that's all. Only you and Tony knew Jay was living in my cabin. Did you tell anyone else he was there?'

'No.'

'Then how did the person who killed him know where to find him?'

'I dunno, do I?'

She blinks away her tears and I soften towards her. She's just a kid really, like Jay, caught up in the shitty end of an adult's world. All that anger masks a lifetime of being let down.

'You liked Jay didn't you?'

'Yeah. He was nice to me.'

'Why did you meet him in the pub that night I saw you together?'

'He called me. He wanted me to get Tony to drop the court case.'

Poor Jay. He wouldn't have known that it wasn't within Tony's power to do this. As soon as Tony made his statement, it became evidence. The most Tony could do is try and withdraw it, but the CPS could still prosecute Jay. Except this isn't the time for legal niceties.

'And what did you say?'

'I said I'd try, and I did, but Tony wouldn't listen.'

'Jay said something about you not having any choice. Is Tony forcing you to be with him?'

'No, I just had enough of living with that bitch of a foster mother, that's all.'

'What about this boyfriend who cheated on you? How does he fit into all this?'

Her shaded brows push themselves into a frown.

'How—?' But she stops herself.

'Cassie, Jay said you knew something. What was he talking about?'

'I dunno.'

'Do you know who killed Jay?'

'No, 'course not.'

'Did Tony hire someone?'

She puts her hands over her ears. 'No. Stop it. Stop going on at me.'

I pull back, aware I'm hectoring her. 'Cassie, if you're in danger' – I drop my voice few decibels – 'I can help you. I can protect you.'

'No you can't,' she sneers. 'I've had people like you tell me all my life they're going to look after me, keep me safe. It's all bullshit though, isn't it?'

'I'm sorry, but, please, if you cared anything for Jay, help me find his killer.'

She hesitates and then glances over my shoulder as someone walks by. 'I thought I already told you to fuck off,' she says loudly.

She rams her hand into my chest, catching me off guard, and I fall backwards through the open front door, which bangs shut in my face. I hear several heavy-duty bolts slide into place. She's scared and she's hiding something. Whatever it is, she isn't going to tell me or the police, but maybe she doesn't need to. Maybe I can find the answers much nearer to home.

49

The living room of cabin 27 is little more than a collection of soft peaks of grey-white ash, diminishing by the day. The chemical stench of burned treated wood still lingers, stinging my nostrils and catching in my throat.

My foot nudges a piece of wood to one side. Beneath it is a section of my old living room wall, charred and sodden, but I can just make out two smiling stick figures, Megan and me surrounded by blue sea. She drew them a little while after we moved in. I wasn't angry. I loved their huge grins. They were a mark of how far we'd come after we escaped Sean, my ex-husband. She never drew happy pictures when we were with him. It was the moment when I realized that I had finally freed us; we were safe. I slip the wood into my pocket and shake off thoughts of what I've lost. This isn't my home any more. This is my crime scene.

Before I begin, I take a moment to reflect on what's happened here. I would do this even if I didn't know Jay. I'm not religious and I don't pray, but over the years I've found myself holding silent conversations with murder victims. It's a mark of respect, an acknowledgement of what has taken place, that their life has been extinguished, that I'm here for them and them alone, and that I'll do all I can to find the person responsible. Normally I'm surrounded by other CSIs, murder detectives, search teams, the whole nine yards and so I keep this conversation to myself, but it's just me here now and this is Jay.

Kneeling on a cushion of ash, I scoop a handful and hold it up in front of me, letting the air currents lift the flecks from my palm until there is only smudged skin left.

'I'll find them, Jay, I promise.' In the distance, the distinctive sound of a pigeon cooing in the trees brings a smile to my face. Taking a breath deep enough to detach myself from the emotion of talking to my daughter's dead friend, my friend, I stand up and brace myself for the task ahead. I'm ready. 'Time to be a badass CSI.'

***

I start by trawling through what I already know. Jake and Wendy, the FLO, both referred to the near-empty petrol can, discarded some distance from the cabin. In a way, leaving it behind was a risky move. It could have the perpetrator's fingerprints on it. Plus the can could be traced back to where it was bought and there are few shops that don't have CCTV these days. So why did the perpetrator leave it behind? My guess is they knew it was clean and untraceable and decided it would be a bigger risk to be caught carrying a large petrol can in the middle of the night. That would be difficult to explain away to even the most gullible of police officers.

Wendy said the police had found glove marks on the outside of the can. It's glove-wearing season. No one would look twice so it's likely they wore them the moment they stepped out of their house.

My foot disturbs the ash, sending sooty white clouds into the air as I slowly make my way towards what was the end of the lounge. This is where the sofa was, where Jay was sleeping, but all that's left are a couple of coiled springs, already rusting.

It couldn't have been easier for the killer. The end of the sofa butted up against the wood cabin wall. The curtains weren't drawn here or in any other room. There's no need out of season when there's no one else on the site. The murderer simply looked in the window, saw Jay and emptied the petrol can underneath the sill. The cabin walls are so thin, Jay would have been less than a metre away from the seat of the fire, which would have caught immediately. There's no way a heavily drugged Jay could have escaped.

Rooted to the spot, I rotate slowly, scanning the burned-out cabin as I go, pausing to sift through the debris when I think I spot something, but everything has been destroyed. There's nothing for me here.

Stepping over the charred embers that once formed the back of the cabin, I make my way up the grassy hill, through the pines, towards the path that leads to the coast. Midway up I stop, turn around and survey the scene before me. A little way down the tarmac path from the cabin is Penny's white house and the reception at the entrance to the site. Tall pines puncture the ground between her place and mine and the nearest cabins are at least fifty metres away to help give visitors the illusion they have the woods to themselves.

As I told Harriet in the field next to Narracott Farm, I like to stand some distance from a crime scene to gain some sense of what the perpetrator would have seen and what they might have been thinking. When a criminal commits a crime, the adrenaline is pumping. Their senses are heightened. They know they have to cover their tracks but as soon as they leave what they think is the crime scene their minds tell them they've escaped. They're in the clear. They're free; no one will catch them now. They can relax. The adrenaline that coursed through them, keeping them alert and smart, drains away. They drop their guard. And that's when the mistakes are made.

Snippets of what I know sift through my mind, coupling and uncoupling, regrouping, linking. I analyse every possible permutation until I find what I'm looking for – a glimmer of a possibility, that might become a probability, that might become a certainty. My eyes fall on another cabin, a little way down the hill and to the left of my own. It's the same cabin where I found Penny cleaning the windows the day I accused Will of destroying Gabe's flock. Unlike ours, it's empty, so the curtains are drawn. I stare at it a little longer. I've found my possibility.

50

Fifteen minutes later I'm back in my cabin. I take my phone out and dial his number. He's surprised to hear from me, and I'm surprised to be calling him, but I don't want this to go through official channels, assuming Harriet would listen to me, and he's the only one I really trust. I talk him through what I've found. It's tenuous, to say the least, even laughable, but murder is no laughing matter and we both know not to dismiss anything, no matter how absurd it may seem.

He listens in silence. At the end, there's more silence before he tells me he thinks he can help, and someone will be touch. I want to talk for longer, ask him how he is, but I don't. It isn't fair on either of us.

As I ring off, my phone goes immediately. It's Kit. I haven't seen him since the night we spent together and I told him we might have a future. Right now, I don't even have a present, but I take the call.

'Ally, it's me, Kit' he says needlessly. 'It's Mum. She's confessed. She did it. She killed Gabe.'

***

Kit is waiting for me at the main entrance to Barnston hospital, dazed with the shock of hearing his mother admit she killed his brother. He's agitated too, shifting from one foot to another, scanning the car park, before the sight of me calms him.

'Sorry. I didn't know who else to call.'

'That's OK. What happened?'

'She came round. Just for a short while.'

'Oh my God.'

'The nurse and I were with her and she just suddenly started speaking. She was a bit difficult to understand and it was garbled at first, but she just started talking about Gabe and me and Dad. Then she turned to me and said she was sorry for what she did to Gabe, but she had to do it.'

'Does Harriet know this?'

'Yes, she and that other detective came straightaway.'

'Did she get to speak to Miriam?'

'Yes.'

'So, what did she say to Harriet?'

'The same as she told me. That she did it.'

'Did it? You mean killed Gabe?'

'Yes. DI Moore asked her outright. "Did you kill Gabe?" And she said yes.'

'Oh, Kit. I'm so sorry. I know you were hoping for a different outcome.'

All he can do is nod, his mind elsewhere, trying to make sense of the fact his mother has admitted killing his brother.

'At least I know now.'

'So what happened after that?'

'She didn't say much more so DI Moore said she would

return later to carry on interviewing her. Then, shortly after she left, Mum had a massive stroke. That's when I called you.'

'How is she now?'

'Difficult to say. She's in intensive care. The doctors are doing tests. They've warned me there might be brain damage.'

The waiting game: I know what that feels like.

'OK. I'm sure they're doing the best they can for her.'

Trite, meaningless words, but I learned to value even those when Megan was in a coma because I came to understand that when people don't know what to say they fall back on stock phrases, but in the end it doesn't matter. You'll take anything to fill the silence.

'Yes. You're right. It's just that I feel so bad. All that business between me and Gabe. It hurt her deeply. I shouldn't have left.'

'You left because you couldn't stay. You didn't have any choice.'

'But I could have been around more. Maybe I would have seen what Gabe was getting into. Done something about it.' He looks at me. 'I know he was a terrible person, Ally. I won't defend what he did, but he was still my brother. I could have tried harder.'

Nothing I say will persuade him he's wrong. He's trapped in a downward spiral of guilt and responsibility. All I can do is change the subject.

'Does DI Moore know about your mum's stroke?'

'Yes, I phoned her right away. She was really sympathetic. She said that they still had a few things to tie up but as far as they were concerned the case was closed.'

'So if Miriam recovers, they're not going to charge her?'

'No. She said Mum was too ill. The case will never go to court. At least that's something.'

'What about the slaughterhouse?'

'She didn't mention it. Whatever Gabe was involved in, they don't think it's connected to his death.'

I watch him for a few moments. His eyes are glazed, his mind fogged with thoughts, but he needs to understand what has happened in the simplest terms. I take his hands in mine.

'Kit, you do realize what this all means, don't you?'

He frowns at me, but I don't say anything. He needs to get there on his own.

'My God. It's finally over, isn't it?'

I enclose him in my arms and he buries his head into my shoulder, releasing the turmoil of emotions that have spun inside him these last few weeks.

'Yes, it is,' and, for a brief moment, I envy Kit Narracott.

51

Geoff Conway closes the office door behind him and invites me to sit down while he props himself up against his desk.

I stayed with Kit until daybreak. I couldn't leave him. He seemed so helpless. I know what that feels like, and I know how grateful I was to have Penny by my side when Megan was in hospital. The two of us kept vigil by Miriam's bedside and I listened as Kit held her hand and told her how much he loved her. At dawn, at the nurse's insistence, we went to the canteen for breakfast, which is when I told him I had to go.

Grief is easier in the daylight and so I headed for home, but as soon as I pulled onto the Bidecombe road, my thoughts swung away from Miriam and Kit and back to Cassie. I had got nowhere with her, but I was convinced she knew a hell of a lot more than she was letting on. I still needed to find out what she told Jay and if she wouldn't tell me, maybe someone else would, but who? Jay mentioned Cassie's ex-boyfriend, the one she'd been seeing for years and who had cheated on her, and that's when I remembered the photo on the corridor wall at Whitebeam House.

'This isn't about kids having sex in the Narracotts' barn again, is it?' says Geoff, folding his arms in expectation that he's going to have to defend at least one of the children in his care.

'No.'

'OK. Good. So, what can I do you for?'

'When I was here last time, I noticed a photo on the wall in the corridor.'

'Thanks' he says, assuming I'm referring to one of his landscapes. 'I managed to get out and take some shots recently. You guys still using Nikons?'

'Yes.'

'I don't think I'll ever be anything but a Canon man myself.'

'Nothing wrong with that.' I smile.

'Sorry, what were you saying about the photo?'

'Actually, this one was taken a while ago. Cassie Warnock is in it.'

'She used to come here from time to time, to give her foster mum a rest. Do you know her?'

'A little. In the photo, she looks like she's sharing a joke with the boy next to her.'

'Probably. That would be her—' He stops himself. 'Are you here on official business?'

I hesitate. I don't want to lie to Geoff. 'No. I'm not. I'm trying to find out who torched my cabin a couple of nights back.'

'I heard about that. Terrible loss of a young life.'

'Yes. It is.'

'I knew Jay Cox. Not well, but well enough to know that with a dad like his, he probably never stood a chance in life. What was he doing at your place?'

'It's a long story.'

Geoff nods. He's had his fill of long stories. He doesn't need to hear mine.

'And you think the fire had something to do with the boy in the photo?'

'Honestly, I've no idea, but I think Cassie knows something. She won't tell me. I was hoping this boy could help me. They looked close in the photo. Is he Cassie's boyfriend?'

'I can't tell you that, Ally – you know that.' Which means he is. 'If it was part of an official inquiry, it'd be a different matter.'

'I understand. Thanks anyway.'

Geoff knows me. I wouldn't be asking if it weren't important. He searches for something he can give me.

'Even if I could tell you anything, you couldn't talk to him because he doesn't live here any more. He went back to a children's care home in London a while ago.'

'He left?'

'Yes, over a year ago. Maybe longer. When Cassie's foster parent found out about their relationship, she kicked up a real fuss, so we got him transferred to another home.'

'You can't tell me where he went?'

'No, sorry. He's probably not there anyway. These kids come and go, but he was still seeing Cassie. I bumped into her foster mum in town, and she said they thought he was sneaking down here to see Cassie, but she couldn't be sure. Her relationship with Cassie broke down completely after he left. God knows how he could afford to travel back and forth from London.'

'What happened to Cassie after he left?'

'She left her foster home. I think the council set her up in a flat in Bidecombe somewhere.'

'Did you know she's moved in with Tony Cox? It's why Jay left home.'

Geoff shakes his head. 'Tony Cox? Really? That's depressing, but there's nothing we can do about it. Once they leave our care, we've lost them unless they ask for help. It's really sad.'

'I think she might be involved in some seriously nasty stuff, Geoff, but I can't prove anything.'

'Sorry I couldn't be more helpful.'

'It's OK. I understand. There is one more thing though . . . Who's Cassie's foster parent?'

Geoff looks at me. He's wrestling with himself, but we go way back. He knows I've always been fair with him. If I'm asking, there's a good reason.

'You say Cassie is in danger?'

'Yes, I think she might be.'

'OK. It's Karyn Dwight. She manages Bidecombe DIY Supplies but that didn't come from me.'

Karyn Dwight, the woman who is still in love with her murdered ex-fiancé, Gabe Narracott, and who seemed oddly indifferent to the person who broke into her store and daubed 'bitch' in red paint on her wall, is Cassie Warnock's foster mother.

52

Away from the coast, the fog has persisted, trapped between the high hedges that hem the lanes leading to Will Sneddon's farm. I cut my speed even though I know these roads inside out and I'm unlikely to meet anyone at this time of night, apart from the odd fox, their eyes reflecting in my headlights before they dart into the hedgerows.

After I left Whitebeam House I swung by Bidecombe DIY Supplies, but my conversation with Karyn Dwight will have to wait. She's on a training day in Exeter, according to Ray, who followed it up with a wink and a 'the cat's away so the mice doth play'. Just as I was leaving, Penny texted me, inviting me to the farm for dinner. I haven't seen her since she gave me the keys to our new cabin.

The food is already on the table when I arrive. 'Sergeant Pepper's Lonely Hearts Club Band' is playing in the background. There's no sign of Will, but the atmosphere feels charged and I sense I've stumbled into the aftermath of a row. I take a seat at the table and Penny joins me.

'No Will?'

'He's gone to help a mate with lambing,' she says, forking

roast beef onto her plate. 'How's Megan getting on? Now you're back at Seven Hills she can come home, can't she?'

'It's not as easy as all that,' I say, filling my plate as if I haven't eaten in weeks.

'What do you mean?'

'She wants to stay a bit longer at Julian's.'

'Well, he is her dad, I suppose.'

'Bernadette thinks he's got some grand plan to keep her there forever. She says they've been talking to her about going to college there.'

'That's a bit cheeky, isn't it? Have they said anything to you?'

'No, but Julian told me Megan feels suffocated by me. He suggested I get counselling.'

'Wow, where would you even start?'

'Exactly. Hi, I'm Ally Dymond. I murdered one man and almost killed another. Feel free to counsel the shit out of that.'

Penny laughs. It's been a while and it's good to see.

'I guess they're just being helpful.'

'Maybe.'

'So, what does Megan think about it all?'

'She's confused. She's still really cut up about Jay. Says she can't stand the thought of coming home and him not being here.'

'You can't blame her there. It took her mother to find her attacker last year, but she should come home, Ally. She needs to come to terms with what happened. Do you want me to have a word with her?'

'There's no need to do that.'

Penny clears our plates and fetches an apple crumble out

of the oven and puts it on the table. Taking a spoon, she hews a large portion out of the dish and transfers it to a bowl, which she pushes towards me along with a dish of clotted cream.

'I saw you the other day, going through the ashes at your old cabin, like you were looking for something.'

I top the steaming crumble with a dollop of cream.

'Just checking to see if anything had survived the fire.'

'So why did you go looking at the other cabin?'

'I didn't realize I was under surveillance,' I say, digging the edges of my crumble in search of a portion cool enough to eat.

'It looked like you were . . . working, but you're off work and you're leaving anyway so then it occurred to me . . .' She hesitates.

'What?'

'Are you investigating Jay's murder?'

I put my spoon down. 'Don't have a go at me, Pen.' Last year Penny was furious with me for going after Megan's attacker when I should have been with Megan in the hospital.

'I'm not. I think it's a good idea.'

'Really?'

'Yes. If it hadn't been for you, Pascoe would still be out there. It sounds to me like the police need all the help they can get, and it shows Megan that you care about Jay as much as she did.'

'That's what Bernadette said. Maybe she's right. Maybe if I help catch Jay's killer, it'll help Megan come to terms with it all and she'll come home. Then we can start to piece our lives back together.'

The door flies open and Will's sister, Emma, breezes in. She's surprised to see us sitting around the table.

'Oh, hi. Sorry, I didn't mean to interrupt.'

'Do you want something to eat? There's plenty left.'

'No, I'm just heading out.'

'OK.'

'Hi, Ally. How's Megan doing at her dad's?'

'Good, thanks.'

'I've seen her Instagram. Nice place he's got there. Anyway, I'll be back by 10 p.m.'

Penny waits until she's closed the door behind her.

'She's a lot better than she has been. The counselling seems to have done the trick. I know you're not a fan of Lisa Kendrick, Ally, but she knows her stuff.'

But I'm not listening. I'm still distracted by the bright yellow coat Emma was wearing when she walked out the door.

53

It's early. Bidecombe Supplies has only been open for a few minutes and judging by the effusive welcome I receive from Ray, I'm their first customer of the day.

'Ah, if it isn't our friendly neighbourhood CSI. Hello again.'

'Morning, Ray. Is Karyn back from her training day?'

'She is; she's in her office. You know the way, don't you? I don't want to leave the till unattended. You never know who's lurking around here, ready to swoop the moment my back's turned.'

Clearly where I see an empty car park, Ray sees a threat.

The office door is open, and Karyn is at her desk studying some spreadsheets, pencil in hand. Order has been restored since I last saw her: her hair is sleek and she's wearing a tailored black suit and cream blouse.

I knock to attract her attention and when she looks up from her desk and sees it's me she forces the corners of her mouth into some semblance of a smile. 'Hello again. What can I do for you?'

'I think I might know who broke into your shop, but I wanted to talk to you about it before I speak to the officer in the case.'

'Oh?' she says, putting her pencil down.

'I think it might have been Cassie's boyfriend, but I'm not telling you anything you don't already know, am I?'

She watches me for a moment, trying to work out how much I know before giving in. 'I knew it was him as soon as I saw "bitch" written on the wall. It's just the sort of thing he'd do.'

'Why didn't you tell the police?'

'Cassie is, was, my foster daughter. Our relationship broke down over Lenny. I've been trying to patch it up ever since. I thought I was getting somewhere with her. If I'd told you the burglar was Lenny, she'd know it was me and I'd have lost her for good.'

'Lenny?'

'Yes, his name is Lenny Russo. They met at the care home. Cassie used to go there for respite care when I needed a break.'

'Why did you object to their relationship?'

She picks up a pen again and taps the end on a pad of paper in a mini stabbing motion before putting it down again.

'Because he got her into drugs. I found some weed in her room. I let that go, but then I got a call from her school to say she was selling the stuff to the other kids. I couldn't ignore that, and I knew she'd got it from him.'

'So, Cassie was dealing drugs?'

'Not really. Just selling it to her mates.' I don't tell her that this is the very definition of dealing and that most low-level teenage dealers sell to those they trust, friends who won't snitch on them in other words. 'Anyway, I banned her from seeing him. She didn't take any notice, of course. She'd climb out the window at night and meet up with him so I told the care home. I kicked up a bit of a stink and got him transferred back to London.'

'Do you think Cassie is still into drugs?'

'I don't know. I hear she's hanging out with a guy who used to deal in town, Tony someone, but who knows? I don't know what she's up to. They're very clever at hiding it.'

'What happened when you banned her from seeing Lenny?'

'She turned against me. It was wasted effort anyway because he continued to come down and see her.'

'How often was that?'

'I've no idea. Every month or so, I'd guess, but he was obviously here a few days ago because he burgled my shop.'

'Why was he sent to the home in North Devon in the first place?'

'Because of all the trouble he was getting into up in London. It was meant to be a fresh start for him, but trouble follows kids like Lenny Russo, doesn't it?'

54

Winter is never kind to seaside towns. The harsh salty winds gusting off the sea strip the buildings of their summer sheen, leaving them tired and washed out under the unforgiving grey skies. This year it has stretched deep into spring and it's beginning to feel like it will never end. It's only ten in the morning but a bitter wind is already up, battling a tenacious seagull for a polystyrene chip carton discarded from nearby Kebabulous; but at least it's seen off the fog.

I shelter in a shop doorway, attracting a glare from the shopkeeper, so I return to the kerbside, rubbing my arms to keep warm. I've been here for thirty minutes already, but it can't be long now. Unless the timings have changed.

I discover they haven't when, five minutes later, the front door to Lisa Kendrick's office opens, and Emma Sneddon steps out. She doesn't see me immediately and, chased by the wind, she veers left and walks quickly towards the car park at the junction between the high street and Anchor Road. I cross the road to catch up with her.

'Emma, have you got a moment?'

Mild surprise at being accosted turns into a warm smile when she sees it's me.

'Oh. Hi, Ally. Sure. What is it?'

'It was you Harriet and I saw, running away from Gabe Narracott's barn the other day, wasn't it?'

She frowns. 'What? How—?'

'Your yellow coat gave you away. So why did you run when we called out?'

'You scared me. I didn't know it was you and I was trespassing.'

'What were you doing there?'

She rummages in her handbag for her car keys. 'I was just out walking,' she says without looking up.

'Odd place to go for a walk, given you live on a farm with plenty of its own land. It looked like you were waiting for someone.'

'I don't know what you mean.'

'Let me spell it out for you then. The police found evidence of people having sex in that barn. It was you, wasn't it?'

'Yes,' she sighs.

'I thought you were in a relationship with a guy from uni.'

'I was. This was someone else.'

I can guess who that someone else was.

'Going for the ones who are already spoken for never ends well.'

She looks at me, horrified.

'Oh my God, how did you know?'

'I saw the two of you together.'

'Don't tell Will. He'll kill him. It's over anyway. I've made a total fool of myself, Ally. I thought he cared about me. He told me he did. Turned out I was just a fling.'

'So what happened?'

'I texted him to meet at the barn again, but he didn't show up. Then I saw you and panicked. I tried to talk to him, but he wouldn't listen to me and I realized he'd just been using me.'

'I'm sorry, Emma.'

She shrugs. 'My own fault, really. He was the first person to show me any attention after Ollie finished with me and I fell for it.'

'Still, you were in a vulnerable state and he took advantage of that. He's older than you; he should have known better.'

'Maybe.' Her face flashes with concern. 'Are you going to tell Will?'

She looks terrified. I'm not surprised. Will would be furious if he knew she was sleeping with Sammy Narracott. It would feel like history was repeating itself. First Caroline and Gabe. Now Emma and Sammy.

'No. I won't tell him.'

'Thank you.'

I watch her get into her car and just as I get back into my own, my phone goes. It's an unknown number and so I answer it thinking it's Harriet. But the voice belongs to a man.

'Liam said you needed my help.'

55

Lenny Russo. The boy who broke into Bidecombe Supplies and scrawled 'bitch' on the wall to get back at his girlfriend's foster mother. The boy who left his fingerprints on a spray can lid. The same fingerprints that were all over a bag containing £180,000 in an old slaughterhouse on a farm in Exmoor, the owner of which has just been murdered. The same boy whose ex-girlfriend is Cassie Warnock, the current girlfriend of a convicted drug dealer, the father of a boy murdered in a fire. Whatever Lenny Russo is mixed up in, he's in deep and I need to find him.

Back at the cabin, I go into Megan's Instagram and scroll down to Cassie's comment on her being lucky to have a family. I click on Cassie's account. It isn't set to private. It never ceases to amaze me how cavalier kids are on social media, but today I'm grateful that Cassie prizes likes over privacy.

Her timeline chronicles her life, tracking her descent from a fresh-faced, plump-cheeked teenager to a young woman hoping thick layers of make-up can hide her grey pallor and blemishes. Eventually, I find what I'm looking for: a photo of Cassie and Lenny together. There's only one. Jay said he'd cheated on her so I'm guessing she's deleted the rest but missed this one. It doesn't matter. I only need one and, just as I'd hoped, Cassie has tagged him in it.

On Instagram, Lenny is Sickboy2006. His account isn't set to private either. Like Cassie's, it's innocuous stuff, mostly selfies: Lenny lying on a sofa, Lenny on a swing in a park, Lenny balancing rather precariously on a railway bridge. And so it goes on. As far as I can tell, Lenny's only crime so far is vanity.

Cassie also makes an appearance on his timeline, her pale arms wrapped around his neck at various locations in Bidecombe, including the Rec and Kebabulous, but also out at Morte Sands, up on the moors and in Bidecombe Woods. Lenny and Cassie get around. They're mostly of the two of them, grinning smugly into the camera, but in the shots where they're looking at each other, there's an unmistakable fondness in their eyes. Or there was.

Some of the photos are taken in places I don't recognize. I can't work out where and my initial enthusiasm that I might find some clues as to Lenny's whereabouts is fading rapidly when my phone goes.

It's Kit and my first thought is Miriam.

'Everything OK? Is it Miriam?'

'There's no change. I'm going to see her this afternoon.'

'Do you want me to go with you?'

'No. Thank you, though.'

'OK, just let me know if there's anything I can do,' I say, still idly scrolling Lenny's Instagram account.

'Actually, I wondered if you fancied dinner tonight. I wanted to thank you properly for all your support.'

'There's no need.'

I go back to the beginning of Lenny's timeline and am about to come off my laptop when I notice a photo of Lenny cuddling a girl with black hair extensions and false eyelashes. At first I assume it's just another shot of him and Cassie, but the girl's eyes are smaller and her eyebrows less aggressive. The more I look the more I realize, it's not Cassie.

'But I'd like to. It would be good to see you. Are you still there, Ally?'

The girl is sitting on Lenny's lap. They're in the front passenger seat of a car.

'Yes.'

'Is that a yes you're still there, or a yes you'd like dinner with me?'

'Sorry?'

'Dinner tomorrow night. At the Albion. At 7 p.m.?'

'Right.'

Even under all that Rimmel, she can't be more than fourteen years old. I'm guessing this is the girl Lenny cheated on Cassie with.

'So, er, shall I see you in the Albion at 7 p.m.?'

'Yeah. Sure.'

I ring off, my attention still on the photo of Lenny Russo. His hand is resting on the girl's thigh and vivid purple love bites blotch the side of his neck. He's grinning triumphantly into the camera as she gazes lovingly at him. Underneath are the hashtags: #love, #couplegoals and #theoneforme. Give me a break.

I have some degree of sympathy for Cassie, who doesn't hold back in the comments section, her vitriol aimed squarely at the mysterious girl who she threatens to 'shank' for 'stealing her man'. Lenny, meanwhile, escapes her wrath, apparently entirely unaccountable for his actions. I check the date and time of the photo. It was posted five hours before someone set fire to my cabin and murdered Jay Cox.

56

She refused to come at first, but I told her that I wouldn't be asking if it wasn't important. She hesitated because she knows my history and what happened to another SIO who declined to listen to me when I told him Pascoe was a killer, but that doesn't mean she has to be gracious about it.

'This had better be good.' DI Harriet Moore sweeps into the cabin. 'Have you any idea how far it is from Exeter to Bidecombe?'

'Seventy-eight miles. And I promise it is.'

'OK, what have you got?'

She follows me into the cabin. I pass her my phone. On it is the photo of Lenny Russo and the unknown girl.

'I'm fairly sure the fingerprints found on a spray can lid at Bidecombe Supplies and on the black holdall at the slaughterhouse belong to the boy in the picture.'

Harriet enlarges the photo, homing in on the boy's face. 'Who is he?'

'His name is Lenny Russo.'

As revelations go, it's a pretty bloody good one and well worth the petrol money, but Harriet is wary. 'And how do you know all this?'

'Lenny Russo is or was going out with Cassie – who is Karyn Dwight's foster daughter – until he cheated on her. Karyn got Lenny sent back to a care home in London when she discovered they were in a relationship.'

'I see. So, no love lost there.'

'No, but their relationship continued with Lenny visiting Cassie as often as he could. The last time was a week ago.'

'So he was here the night Bidecombe Supplies was broken into.'

'Precisely. Karyn suspected it was him. She didn't say anything as she's still trying to patch up her relationship with Cassie.'

'OK. Well, the first thing we need to do is pick this Lenny kid up.'

'Geoff Conway who runs Whitebeam House might have an address for him in London.'

'Great, I'll swing by there now. And we need to have another chat with Cassie.' She looks at me. 'Seems we might have been a bit hasty dismissing her.'

This is as close to an apology as I'm going to get, but I didn't ask her here to score points.

'I still don't know what, if anything, she told Jay the night he died, but maybe it's something to do with Lenny Russo. When Cassie saw this photo on Instagram, she went ballistic. I'm wondering if she told Jay something she shouldn't to get back at Lenny. Something that cost him his life.'

'OK, we'll bear that in mind. Once we confirm Lenny Russo burgled Bidecombe Supplies we can question him about the slaughterhouse and find out what's been going on there. Thanks.'

'No problem.'

She hands my phone back to me and I'm about to put it

back in my pocket when I stop myself. Harriet has nudged the image and it's no longer Lenny's face that is magnified, but the dashboard. I enlarge it further.

'What is it?'

'I'm not sure.' I pass the phone back to her. 'Hold that for me. I need to check something.'

Mildly piqued at being told what to do by a subordinate, Harriet takes my phone whilst I flip open my laptop. A few clicks later, I have what I'm looking for. I angle the laptop towards her.

'Take a look at this.'

She squints at the screen. 'What am I looking for?'

'See that in the corner?'

'It looks like an air freshener in the shape of a rose.'

'Now look at the photo on my phone.'

Harriet takes it and holds it against the computer screen. 'It's the same car, but where did you get that photo on your laptop?'

'You.'

'What?'

'It's a still from the film you sent me.'

'What film?'

'The film shot by one of the tourists who discovered Miriam wandering across the moor the night she murdered Gabe.'

Harriet turns back to the image on the laptop. 'So let me get this straight. We have a family of tourists, the Brookes, I think they were called, heading home from their holiday late one night when they come across an old lady holding a knife who has just murdered her son, a man who it transpires is a paedophile and is also quite likely involved in drug running. A few days after Gabe is murdered, this Lenny Russo kid is photographed in the exact same car.'

'Yes.'

'And this is the same Lenny Russo whose fingerprints you believe are on a holdall containing £180,000 in an old slaughterhouse. And who broke into Bidecombe Supplies.'

'Yes.'

'And who was going out with a young girl, Cassie, whose foster mother is Karyn Dwight aka Gabe Narracott's ex-fiancée, and who is currently shacked up with Tony Cox, a known drug dealer.'

'Yes.'

She shakes her head.

'But we interviewed the Brookeses. He's a driving instructor and she's a receptionist at a spa. Their statements checked out. They'd been staying at a self-catering apartment in Bidecombe. They got a cheap deal before the season started so they decided to take their daughter, Natasha, out of school and go for it. They couldn't have been more normal.' I have the impression Harriet is talking to herself as much as anyone. 'They called it in, for God's sake. They didn't have to do that. They could have just left Miriam on the moor. They even waited for us to arrive. The mother, Jo, was really worried about her.' She closes her eyes and sighs. 'How the hell did we miss this?'

'It could all be perfectly innocent. Maybe Lenny's related to the Brookes family, and he told them what a lovely place Devon is, so they decided to come and check it out for themselves. It's possible they don't have anything to do with any of this.'

'I think you and I both know that's bullshit.'

57

Megan's face appears on my screen. She's alone. Just as I'd hoped. I don't want Julian and Cam listening in to this conversation.

She quickly dispenses with my enquiries about how she's getting on with her usual 'fine' and our conversation lapses into the silence I've been waiting for.

'There's been some progress on Jay's case.'

'What is it?'

'I can't say too much, but things are starting to move quickly.' This is how it happens in investigations. They can appear to slow to a dead stop and then from nowhere new information reignites them. 'Do you mind if I ask you some questions? The police might want to talk to you as well.'

'OK.'

'Did Jay ever talk to you about a boy called Lenny? He was Cassie's boyfriend.'

'Not really no. I mean she was really into him and then he went and cheated on her with some girl back in London. Jay said she was really upset about it. He thought that was the reason Cassie wanted to hang around with him. To get back at this guy for messing around.'

'And Jay was OK with that? I thought he hated her. Cassie did get rid of the picture of his mum.'

'He did, but he said it suited him to make her think he liked her. It made it easier to get what he wanted out of her.'

'What did he mean by that?'

'I don't know. Mum?'

'Yes.'

'Penny called me. She said you're investigating what happened to Jay.' She still can't use the word 'murder'. 'She said that if anyone could find them, it'd be you and that when you did, I could come home and the two of us can get on with our lives.'

'She shouldn't have said anything. Sorry.'

'It's OK. I'm glad she did. I wanted to say thank you.'

'That's OK, but, you know, there's no guarantees.'

She smiles. 'I know.'

But she's not listening. In her mind, it's a done deal. Now I'm involved, Jay's killer will be caught. I hope for both our sakes she's right.

***

As I walk into Kebabulous, the smell of grilled meat doesn't so much pique my nostrils as slam into them, reminding me I haven't eaten all day, but my hunger isn't the only reason I'm here.

'Ally!' booms Ali, the owner, endlessly amused that we share the same name. 'Long time no see.'

'Indeed.'

'Chicken shish with extra garlic sauce?'

'Please.'

While the skewers of meat sizzle on the grill, he selects a pitta bread, which he slices down the middle with a flourish and fills with an array of salad items from the trays in the chiller in front of me.

'We hear about Jay. Very sad. He came here a lot. He'd get his kebab while he waited for his girl to see the doctor.' He's talking about Megan. She wasn't Jay's 'girl' but he's in full flow so I don't correct him. This is going to be easier than I thought. 'People tell me bad things about him, but, you know, he was always very polite to me.'

'That's good to hear.'

Ali nestles the grilled chicken on the salad and slathers the lot in garlic sauce. 'He would always say our Jemmy Twitchers are the best in North Devon.'

'He's right. Ali, were you working the night he died?'

'Yes, you and me, Ally, we're always working.'

'And Jay came in about 8 p.m. right?'

'That's right.'

'How did he seem to you?'

He slides my parcelled kebab towards me. 'Not happy, but not sad either. Like I tell the police.'

'What do you mean?'

'Like he had a lot on his mind.' Ali taps the side of this head with his forefinger. 'So, I asked him if he was OK. He said he feel a lot better in a few hours, but there was something he needed to do.'

I hand him my tenner. 'Did he say what that was?'

'No, but he was nervous.' Ali thinks about this for a moment. 'No, he wasn't nervous. He was . . . scared. Enjoy your kebab.'

58

Harriet calls just as I walk back into the cabin, kebab in hand.

'I thought you might like to know – we've had the photo on Instagram and the still from the film examined,' she says, not bothering with pleasantries. 'And it's definitely the same car.'

I appreciate the call. She doesn't have to tell me anything. She froze me out of the investigation when she found out I'd slept with Kit and she knows I'm leaving the job, but Lenny Russo and his link to the Brookeses' car are down to me and one thing I've learned about DI Harriet Moore is that she has a strong sense of fairness.

'What now?' I ask, mobile wedged between my chin and shoulder while I unwrap the paper and slide my kebab onto a plate.

'We've spoken to the owner of the car, Dean Brookes. He denies knowing Lenny Russo or that he was ever in his car. He says lots of cars have plastic rose air fresheners attached to the dashboard. When I asked him if he'd visited here before his recent holiday, it was like I was asking him if he'd ever been to fucking Narnia. Never heard of North Devon until a couple of months ago, apparently.'

'Do you believe him?'

'Nope. We've got ANPR showing him driving along the link road into North Devon towards Bidecombe six months ago.'

'What does he have to say about that?'

'Someone must have ringed his plates.'

'He's got all the answers, hasn't he? Have you examined his car?'

'Not yet. He won't tell us where it is. Says he sold it to someone down he pub but can't remember who.'

'That old chestnut.'

'Not very original, is it? But we really need to find it. Want to know something else not very original about our Dean?'

'Go on.'

'He's got a criminal record.'

'What for?'

'Murder.'

'You're kidding.'

'Nope. It was some kind of gang initiation in the West Midlands about fifteen years ago.'

'A gang initiation?'

'Yeah, a drive-by shooting. Dean Brookes drove up to this random man in the street and shot him dead, although he never coughed to it. Never said a word from the moment he was arrested.'

'And they let him out?'

'Yeah, well, life rarely means life these days, does it?'

'Is he still involved in gangs?'

'I see where you're going with this. Gangs equals drugs, but he swears he's a reformed character and that we're harassing him. He also reckons he should be up for a Pride of Britain award.'

'Oh?'

'Apparently, he could have left Miriam in the middle of the road, but he didn't. Like all good citizens, he called us.'

'What a hero.'

'Not even a runner-up. His girlfriend, Jo, made the call, not him. If you watch the film, you can see our Dean isn't too happy about that. Now we know why. Anyway, I'm not buying any of his crap. We'll keep digging. We'll get there in the end.'

'Harriet, thanks for telling me this. I think you should know that I've spoken to Megan. She told me that Cassie was really upset about Lenny cheating on her and that Jay thought she was hanging out with him to get back at him in some way, which worked for Jay as it meant it would be easier to get what he wanted from her. I still don't know what though, but Cassie definitely knows something.'

'OK thanks. We'll bear that in mind when we speak to her again. And don't worry about Lenny. We're on to him, Ally. It's only a matter of time before we pick him up.'

59

Just as I finish my kebab, my phone buzzes again. This time it's a FaceTime from Julian and Cam. I let it ring until I can wipe the grease from my fingers. By the time I join them they're mid-conversation. When they realize I'm online, their expressions change to delight and I'm subjected to an onslaught of waves and hellos, but it's too late. I've already seen the frowns.

'Sorry to call you out of the blue, Wish.'

For fuck's sake, stop calling me Wish.

'Is everything OK?'

'It's nothing to worry about. Everything's great.' Cam's side glance suggests otherwise, but I let them play out their little charade. 'We just wanted to have a quick chat with you.'

'Good, there's a couple of things I'd like to talk to you about too.'

Julian looks to Cam to take over in a move that couldn't be more rehearsed. What the hell is going on with them?

'Megan and I have gotten pretty close over the last few days. She's opened up a lot to me.'

What am I meant to say to this? Well done on becoming my daughter's confidante.

'OK.'

'Yah, she told me what you've all been through these last few months. It sounds terrible.'

'It was, but we're getting over it.'

'Yes, your friend Penny called her and told her you're going to find the person who killed her friend. Megan was very excited by the idea, but you're not actually on the case, are you?'

'I'm just making sure every avenue is explored, that's all.' I shrug. 'It's no big deal.'

'So the police are still investigating this?'

'Yes, of course they are.'

Neither of them says anything as if they're waiting for an explanation, but I don't owe them one. Finally, Cam speaks.

'Do you feel it's rational to be doing what you're doing?'

Christ, is she counselling me?

'I . . . I don't know. I've not really thought about it.'

'And in some way, it's a totally normal reaction. Your friend clearly meant a lot to you both.'

'His name is Jay and, yes, he did.'

'But equally. There are some red flags.'

'What red flags? I'm a CSI. It's what I do. The police are always short-staffed. I'm just an extra pair of eyes.'

'But you're still on compassionate leave.'

'So?'

'So, you need time to process what happened to you and to Megan last year. It'd also be good for Megan to see you addressing your issues.'

'I don't have any issues. Is this about the counselling thing again?'

'It might help.'

'Help what? Look, the only issue I have is you filling her head with nonsense about living with you permanently and going to college in London.' Julian shifts in his seat. 'So, it's true then?'

'Not quite,' he says. Cam shoots him a look, but he ignores her. 'It was Megan who asked if she could move in with us.'

'What?'

'She also asked if there was a college nearby that offered a photography course.'

'And you didn't deter her?' I ask, pushing aside my hurt that my daughter wants out of her life with me.

'Megan is nearly sixteen. She's old enough to make her own decisions about her life. We . . . we all need to respect that,' Cam chips in.

'We, meaning me.'

'Isn't that why she's here in the first place?' says Julian. 'Why she doesn't want to go home? You don't trust her to make the right choices.'

'I'm doing what's right for Megan.'

'Are you? Or are you doing what's right for you?'

60

The Albion is crowded tonight and it takes me a few minutes to locate Kit. He's talking to someone at the bar who I recognize immediately. I slide in next to him.

'Hello, Gavin.'

'Hello, Ellie. How are you?'

'It's Ally and I'm good. Found any nightjars recently?'

'Not yet, but it's only a matter of time. Anyway, I'll see you later, mate.' Gavin drains his glass and leaves.

Kit frowns at me. 'You know each other?'

'A little. Clearly not enough for him to remember my name.'

Kit laughs. 'Can I get you a drink?'

'Sounds good.'

'Bill, a pint of Sam's for Ally and the usual for me. Are you OK bringing our drinks over to our table?'

'Sure.'

'You know you've been here too long when you're on first-name terms with the landlord, don't you? And "the usual"? You're definitely sounding like a local.'

'I'm beginning to feel like one again. I wasn't sure you'd come tonight.'

'Oh?'

'You sounded a bit distracted on the phone.'

'Yes, sorry about that, but you have my full attention now.'

We find a table.

'How's Miriam?'

'Still no change.'

'I'm sorry.'

'Thank you. Even if she survives the stroke, it's going to be a long road to recovery.'

'Yes, I guess it will be. When Megan was in hospital last year, I learned that all you can do is take one day at a time. Just concentrating on the here and now, and not thinking about the future made it easier to cope.'

'It must have been really tough.'

'It was, especially in the early days when we didn't know if she'd be left with permanent brain damage.'

'But she got better?'

He wants me to tell him Megan is restored to the girl she was before she was attacked, but that's not true. Megan will never be the same. That day in the woods altered her path through life for good. But this isn't the time for that conversation. He's searching for some vicarious reassurance that Miriam will come through this.

'Pretty much.'

'That's good.' He smiles and takes a sip of his drink. 'So, how do you know Gavin?'

'A blind date,' I reply, also relieved the subject has changed.

'Really? I take it that it didn't go so well.'

'Do they ever?' I shrug. 'How about you? How do you know him?'

'I met him four, five years ago, helped him get some

accounting work with the Clevedons when he was going through a rough patch.'

'Oh?'

'Yeah. He was involved in a car crash, got banned for drink driving. He lost everything, but he got help and he's good now. I had no idea he was here.'

'He's staying in one of Will Sneddon's cottages, doing some work locally.'

'Maybe I should have a chat to him then.'

'About the farm?'

'Yeah. Mum isn't going to be well enough to run it for a long time, if ever.'

'You don't want to take it on?'

'No. I thought about it, but too many memories and I don't need the stress. It'll take a lot of money to turn it around with no guarantees it'll pay off. Besides, Mum's long-term care will need paying for, but I can't just sell it to anyone. It's been in the family for generations.'

'Couldn't Sammy buy it off you? He's family.'

'We've talked about it. He's definitely interested, but he needs to talk to his bank. Till then it's down to me, so it looks like I'll be here for a while.'

'Is your boss OK with that?'

'Mike? Yeah, he's fine. He's told me to take as long as I need.'

'And Georgina?'

'She's already set her sights on someone else. What about you? How do you feel about me hanging around a bit longer?'

'Doesn't sound like I have much choice,' I joke. Bill arrives with our drinks and places them in front of us. 'But you'll have to kick the G&Ts into touch. We don't stand for that southern nonsense around here. It's cider or exile.'

Kit smiles. 'Cider it is then.'

We both take a drink.

'I hope it all works out for you, Kit.'

'Thanks. You OK? You seem a bit wound up.'

I thought I'd hidden it, but I'm touched he noticed.

'It's Megan. She wants to live with my ex full-time.'

'I didn't think they knew each other that well.'

'They don't, but anything is preferable to living with me.'

'I'm sure you're not that bad.'

'It seems I am. My ex and his wife think I should get counselling.'

'Counselling? What for?'

'They reckon it'll be good for Megan to see that I'm getting help, but counselling is the last thing I need right now, believe me. What I need is for my daughter to come home.'

'I'll drink to that.' He tips his glass towards me and takes a sip. 'I know you have a lot on, but have you given any more thought to . . . us?'

'Let me get my daughter back first.'

61

I declined Kit's offer to walk me home. I knew if he did, he'd wake up in my bed tomorrow morning and that's one complication I can do without. Besides, there's something comforting about Bidecombe's damp and dark streets at this time of year, as if we're all revelling in the empty off-season silence.

Seven Hills Lodges is in complete darkness. Penny is at Will's and there's no point switching the lights on when there's only me here at this time of year. I slide my phone out of my pocket and tap the torch on, but as I pass Penny's house I hear a fox raiding the bins, searching for titbits for its young, no doubt. Too tired to go and shoo it away, I carry on. There's another sound. This time it's a bin lid slamming shut, but the more I think about it, the more it sounds like a door closing.

I cut the torchlight and dip behind a tree, letting the seconds pass. I peer around the trunk just in time to see a shadow pass in front of the reception window. It seems I'm not the only one who knows Penny spends her nights elsewhere.

The back door isn't locked. That doesn't surprise me. I've told Penny a million times to lock her door at night, but she tells me it's her way of proving to herself that she's no longer scared her ex is going to carry out his threat to kill her in her bed, but Ian isn't the only criminal out there.

I'm about to make a move when an owl shrieks, startling me and sending me back behind the tree where I berate myself for behaving like a bit-part player in a B-movie.

I compose myself once more and quickly cross the path, entering the house through the kitchen door. There's just enough moonlight to make out the table and the units. There's no one here, so I move towards the front room, staying close to the doorjamb, away from what little light there is. I pause for a moment, straining to interpret the slightest noise above the sound of blood throbbing at my temples. I'm sure I can detect the shallow breaths of another presence. I know the drill. I should get out and call the police, but the blue line is at its thinnest at night and by the time they get here, whoever it is will be long gone.

I step into the darkened living room. My one advantage is that I know the layout of Penny's living room and just inside the doorway is a dolphin cast in bronze. A symbol of friendship and loyalty, I gave it to Penny on her fortieth birthday. I pick it up by its tail and raise it above my head, my eyes desperately trying to search out unfamiliar shadows, dark forms that shouldn't be there, but I can't make anything out. Everything is as it should be and I'm beginning to think I imagined it all when a figure appears in the doorway to the reception and rushes towards me. I shout out and take a swipe at them but miss. Before I can go again, I hear a click and the main light goes on, momentarily blinding me.

'Ally, what the hell are you doing?'

Penny's horrified eyes are fixed on the metal dolphin I'm holding aloft.

'Oh God, Penny. I thought you were an intruder.' I lower the dolphin. 'What are you doing here?'

It's only then that I notice her face is blotchy and her eyes shot through with red. She's been crying.

62

It's 8 a.m. I'm spooning coffee into a mug, desperately trying to inject some enthusiasm for the day into myself, having spent most of the night comforting a distraught Penny. At first, I thought Will had hit her, but it turned out she had finished with him when he refused to admit to her that he'd set his dogs on Gabe's flock and she decided a relationship based on secrets and lies had no future. I know that feeling.

When my phone goes off, I fully intend to ignore it and all calls until the caffeine kicks in, but it's an unknown number, which means it's probably Harriet. I can't help myself. You can take the girl out of CSI, but not the CSI out of the girl, it seems. As usual, she doesn't bother herself with pleasantries.

'Thought you'd like to know we found Brookes' car in a lock-up in South London.'

'And?'

'And it gets better. In the boot was a stash of cocaine. Estimated street value of around £200,000 which, if memory serves me right, is roughly the amount that was recovered from the slaughterhouse.'

'That is good news. What's our friend Dean got to say about it all?'

'Nothing. He's got himself lawyered up to his eyeballs, but this is London. Like I said, you can't scratch your arse without being filmed and the council have just, very helpfully, installed some lovely new CCTV for their lock-ups after a spate of vandalism, which means we have footage of our Dean in glorious technicolour driving the car into his lock-up. He can say no comment until the cows come home, but he isn't going to be able to wriggle out of this one. At the very least, we're looking at intent to supply . . .'

'What about Cassie?'

'Yeah, we picked her up too, but she's still saying nothing. Tough cookie, that one.'

'Did you find Lenny?'

'Yes and no. He left care some time ago. We managed to track him down to a halfway house, but he wasn't answering his door. We got the caretaker to let us in, but there was no sign of Lenny.'

'Any idea where he might have gone?'

'No, but that isn't all. There had clearly been a fight of some kind. Furniture turned over. Lamps smashed. God knows how no one heard it. And there was blood. A lot of blood.'

'Lenny's?'

'Who knows? Probably. It doesn't look good for him, Ally, and Dean Brookes already has form for murder. I hope for Lenny's sake he got away and that we find him first.'

63

I have little time to consider the possible fate of Lenny Russo because as soon as Harriet rings off, my phone goes again. This time it's Bernadette. Clearly, one in-person visit to Seven Hills was more than enough.

'Is it sorted?'

'Sorry?'

'Megan. Is she coming home?'

'Not yet. No.'

'I thought as much.'

'She needs time.'

'What she needs is to be home.'

'Maybe it's for the best that she's with Julian.'

'Best for her, or best for you?'

'What do you mean by that?'

'Well, it solves the problem of sorting yourself out, doesn't it?'

'I've no idea what you're talking about.'

'I asked Megan if there was a reason why she didn't want to come home.'

'And?'

'She said that you wouldn't leave her alone. It was why she

liked having that Jay chap with her. She said it was the only time you gave her any space. She thinks you haven't got over what happened to her last year. That you're overly protective.'

'Can you blame me? She almost died.'

'No, but you're pushing her away.'

'Julian and his wife Cam said the same thing.' I let out a long sigh. I'm tired of fighting Bernadette.

'What is it?'

I brace myself for derision. Counselling, in Bernadette's world, is for the weak.

'They think I should see a counsellor.'

'So, see one.'

'Really? I thought you'd be against all that.'

'You don't know everything about me.'

'But there's nothing wrong with me.'

'Well, that's a matter of opinion, isn't it? Besides, this isn't about you. This is about getting your relationship with Megan back on track and if that means telling some quack how traumatized you were when your pet rabbit Fluffy died then do it.'

'I never had a pet rabbit called Fluffy.'

'Precisely. Honestly, Aloysia, I sometimes wonder how you ever got into Oxford.'

'Maybe it was because lying to a psychiatrist wasn't in the entrance exam.'

'Look, Megan may go and live with them to do her college course and that's fine, but now is definitely not the time to make that decision.' Christ, my own mother is giving me parenting advice. That's how bad it's got.

'I don't seem to have much choice, Mum. She's there. I'm here.'

346

'You always have a choice. You're her mother, for goodness' sake. She needs you even if she can't see it. And you need to do whatever it takes to get her home, Aloysia.'

The line goes dead and I slide my phone into my back pocket, but something obstructs it and I remove a card that's been there since the owner gave it to me. I stare down at Lisa Kendrick's name, written in loopy handwriting and followed by a string of letters. Underneath there's a phrase in italics – *When it's time to move on*. Isn't that exactly what I've been trying to do? Move on? Isn't that why I'm resigning from a job I love? Why I've let Kit into my life? Why I'm not fighting Megan on living with Julian?

I'm about to toss the card to one side when I notice the faded picture behind the writing. It's of a pine forest, just like the one on my living room wall. Sinking into the green velvet sofa, my gaze fixes on the tall pines, haloed by the sun, its shafts bursting through the tall trunks. It's then that I realize we've all been had.

***

I grab my phone and call up the photo of the girl sitting on Lenny Russo's lap. Granted, it doesn't look great, but there's nothing to suggest there's anything untoward going on. Megan and Jay would lie all over each other, but they weren't going out. It's just what today's teenagers do. What's more mystifying is why there was only one photo of the couple when there were dozens of Lenny and Cassie.

The girl is tagged so I go onto her Instagram too, but to my surprise, there are no photos at all, and the account was only created a few days ago. For a fledging relationship, I'd expect their timelines to be littered with PDAs. But it's the hashtags that make me really suspicious. They only appear under the photos of Lenny and this girl. There are none under the ones of him and Cassie and yet they were together for a few years. And what teenage boy uses hashtags like #couplegoals anyway?

I take another look at Cassie's comments. They're extreme even for a teenager. The whole thing is fake. Lenny didn't cheat on Cassie and Cassie didn't break up with him. Any interest she showed in Jay was feigned. The whole thing is a set-up to make the police, Dean Brookes, whoever, think Devon is the last place Lenny Russo would run to.

64

It's 1 a.m. I've been here for two hours and I'm not sure how much longer I can hang around without a suspicious resident calling the police on me. I'm mulling my options when the door to Tony's house opens and Cassie appears in a pink puffer jacket carrying a plastic bag. Gingerly she closes the front door behind her. She doesn't want Tony to know she's snuck out.

DI Harriet Moore is right. It is very difficult to avoid the authorities in this country. We Brits are the most surveilled people in the world. There's a camera on practically every street, shop and road in England, tracking our every move. And then there's our phones, our greatest friend and worst enemy. They'll take you to places you've never heard of and then secretly tell those you don't want to find you that you've arrived. Technology catches criminals and even provides a digital trail to seal their fate. It's only a matter of time. But there's little tech in the countryside. I know that. I suspect Lenny knows it too.

I slide down into my seat as Cassie walks past the car, but there's no need. Her hood is up and her head is down. Wherever she's going she wants to get there quickly.

She reaches the corner and that's my cue to get out of the car. She takes the right turn through the estate. At the end, there's just open fields. Beyond that, Bidecombe Woods where Jay was living, where Geoff, the care home manager, said his kids would often go because it was a Wi-Fi signal dead spot and they couldn't reach them there, where I'm pretty sure Lenny Russo is lying low.

I can't risk crossing the field. It's too open and partly illuminated by a streetlight. Cassie only has to glance behind her and she'll clock my silhouetted form so I wait for her to disappear into the woods. I have to hope I'll be able to find her, but by the time I reach the trees, there's no sign of Cassie. I stand still, straining to hear human sounds above the shrieks of a vixen out to attract a mate.

There's a crack, followed by several more that are too heavy-footed for a woodland creature. I turn in the direction of the sounds and am rewarded with a glimpse of an iPhone light bobbing through the undergrowth. It's moving surprisingly quickly and I struggle to keep up without making too much noise.

The light stops and I slow my pace, making sure not to brush the branches or stumble in the bracken, until Cassie's pink puffer jacket comes into view. I'm just a few metres away from her. Maybe she's seen me, but she turns around suddenly and I dart behind a tree and wait.

I hear whispered voices and dare to peer around the tree trunk. Cassie has been joined by someone. A boy. He turns and in the light of her iPhone I see his bruised face. It's him.

Cassie opens the plastic bag for him, and he grins and takes out what looks like half a packet of biscuits and a can of drink.

They hug each other in what is a surprisingly touching gesture. Two kids seeking solace in each other.

He releases her and melts into the undergrowth. Cassie picks her way back through the woods towards the housing estate. I let the minutes pass before returning to my car, parked a few streets away from Tony's house. I take my phone out of my pocket and dial Harriet's number.

'You need to get the dog unit out. I've found Lenny Russo.'

65

It's late afternoon. I'm not sure what I'm doing here, but Harriet wouldn't take no for an answer. 'I know you're resigning and all that, but you're still a CSI at least for a few more weeks and I want you there. You bring something different to the party, Ally, but the truth is we wouldn't even be having this briefing if it weren't for you. Just one condition, I'm trusting you not to share the findings with anyone.' Anyone meaning Kit Narracott. I said yes because, well, what else am I going to do with my time? And she's right. This is my shout.

The atmosphere in the briefing is different to last time I was here. Then it was downbeat, solemn – the enormity of such a grim task weighing heavily on all those present. Today there's a relaxed air. Good news has that effect. It doesn't last, of course, but for now they will make the most of it.

I take up my position at the back of the room. The chatter naturally subsides and, in what feels like perfect timing, Harriet enters the room followed by DS Whitely.

'Afternoon, everyone.' A few people respond with an 'Afternoon, boss', or 'Ma'am.' 'Well, this is my favourite kind of briefing because this is the one where I say we got our man, and you can all feel very smug.' I assume the 'man' she is referring to is Dean Brookes and the reason we've got him is because Lenny Russo has spilled an entire crate of beans on his drugs operation. When I called it in last night, Harriet didn't hesitate. She sent in the dog unit as I waited by the edge of the woods. Half an hour later, they were frog-marching Lenny Russo to the nearest police car. 'Anyway, I'll cut to the chase. We now have further confirmation that Miriam Narracott killed her son, Gabe.'

Surprised murmurs ripple through the assembled crowd. Mine among them. I thought I was here to be told that a major drugs ring had been busted.

'Don't keep us in suspense, boss,' a voice says from the back of the room.

'It seems Lenny Russo called at the house the night of Gabe's murder.'

'Is he the kid who was photographed in Dean Brookes' car?' says the same voice.

'The very same. Thanks to Ally, we picked him up last night, hiding out in some woods in North Devon. Anyway, according to your man, when he knocked on the door, Miriam answered, still holding a knife. Lenny says he noticed blood on the blade and when he looked down the hallway, Gabe's body was lying on the kitchen floor. He panicked and ran. Remember the shoe mark that forensics lifted from the farmyard that matched the one outside the slaughterhouse? They belong to a pair of trainers owned by our Lenny, who was kind enough to be wearing them when we arrested him.'

'What was he doing there in the first place?' asks someone else.

'Good question, and another reason why he ran. He was there to drop off drugs at the slaughterhouse and collect money owing from a previous drop-off. The money came up short, by around £20,000, so Lenny went to the house to speak to Gabe, which is when he saw Miriam.'

'So, this Lenny's a courier for Brookes?'

'Yep. Brookes gave us nothing when we interviewed him. Swore blind he'd gone straight although local intelligence reports suggest he was back to dealing. Fortunately for us, Lenny proved to be a little more talkative. He admitted working for Dean and running the line into Bidecombe so he could get to see his girlfriend, Cassie.'

'But how did Dean know Gabe Narracott? And how did he persuade him to use his place as a trap house and launder his money for him?'

'Well, Lenny also revealed that Dean once told him that he knew North Devon because he had also spent time at the children's home there when he was a kid. Geoff said they encouraged the children to make friends with the local children. He even dug out a photo taken before the incident and guess what – there's Gabe standing right next to Dean. What we don't know is how Lenny was able to persuade Gabe to get involved in his little drugs racket.'

'Maybe he knew Gabe was a paedophile,' says a female detective.

'Well, the photo was taken just before the incident involving Gabe so possibly, or maybe he'd heard Gabe was struggling financially after he lost his flock. From what locals have told us Gabe's money troubles were quite well known. That's one we're still working on.'

'So, once Lenny brought the drugs into North Devon, who distributed them?'

'Again, we don't know for certain, but we think his girl-friend, Cassie, was involved, probably with the help of Tony Cox.'

'No surprises there.'

'Cassie came here with her foster mother, but the relation-ship broke down. Since then, she's been running wild. She's part of the drugs scene in Bidecombe. Lenny, who she met at the care home, admitted introducing her to Brookes, who we think then groomed her to run the Bidecombe end for him.'

'A regular little production line. So were any drugs found at Tony's house?'

'No. The searches turned up diddly squat. Maybe he knew we were coming, but he managed to get rid of any drugs.'

'This Cassie's a bit young to be running an op like this, isn't she?' says Henry.

'They start them young these days.'

'They do, but I agree with you, Henry, she is young to be given this level of responsibility, but, if someone else is involved, we haven't found them, and Cassie isn't giving anything away.'

'So, Gabe's death had nothing to do with drugs then?'

'No. Miriam killed Gabe and then followed Lenny out the front door, which is why it was left open. As you know, she told us as much herself before she had a stroke, but it doesn't hurt to get it confirmed once and for all.'

'Why did she do it? She doted on her son, didn't she?'

'I guess we'll never know. She's unlikely to fully recover from the stroke so she's never going to stand trial, so that's it. That's the way it goes sometimes. What's it called, Occam's Razor, when the most obvious answer is the correct answer?'

The mood is jovial as everyone files out of the briefing room amid a serious debate about which pub should be rewarded with their business.

'I hope you'll join us for one, Ally,' says Harriet. 'After all, this is thanks to you.'

'Thank you, but I ought to be getting back,' I lie: an empty cabin is all that awaits me.

'OK, if you're sure. I'll call Kit Narracott and break the news to him about Miriam. Until then, I'd appreciate it if you didn't say anything.'

'No, of course not. Have you made any headway with the Jay Cox case?'

'No. Nothing yet, but now this one's as good as done, I can put some more bodies on it.'

'Cassie hasn't said anything, has she? About what she told Jay?'

'She swears she didn't tell him anything.'

'And Lenny?'

'He says he's never met Jay and CCTV has him in London the day of Jay's murder. But this is far from over and we're investigating every angle. I want to find Jay's killer as much as you do and, if we get something, I promise you'll be the first to know.'

'Thanks.'

I leave the briefing room and return to my car. A huddle of officers are already ambling towards the exit and their hostelry of choice. DS Whitely is among them. When he sees me he detaches himself from the group and ambles towards me.

'Are you sure you don't want to join us? You've earned it.'

'No, but thanks anyway.'

The truth is I don't feel like celebrating. Not while Jay's killer is still out there. I get back into my car and am about to turn the ignition on when my phone rings. It's an unknown number, but it can't be Harriet. I just left her. Either way, I take the call.

'It's a match,' the voice says.

66

I must have dropped off because I wake up to find myself slumped over the dining table. My cheek is smarting from resting on the cold, hard laminate and my lower back aches from being hunched over in an odd position all night. I straighten myself, raising my hands above my head in the hope it'll ease the soreness. I could do with a coffee, but it'll have to wait.

Next to my laptop, my notepad is covered in scribbles and arrows. I reacquaint myself with my findings, such as they are. There are a lot of questions and the name of the one person who can help me with the answers. I'm just waiting for him to come on shift.

A check of the clock on the kitchen wall reveals its 9.30 a.m. I can't wait any longer.

'Derek? It's Ally Dymond.'

'Ally. How's life in the land of sheep rustling?'

'If only that was all we had to deal with.'

'You don't fool me. Anyway, what can I do for you?'

Derek is a CSI in the East Midlands. They don't have sheep rustling there. I met him at a seminar on a new fingerprinting technique some years back. He's been a CSI forever and I often call him for advice. Today I'm after information.

'I wanted to pick your brains about a murder fifteen years ago in your neck of the woods.'

'I'll do the best I can.'

'The Glenn Manston case. A lad called Dean Brookes, or Carter as he was then, was convicted of murdering a middle-aged man on his way home from work. He shot him in the street.'

'Oh yeah, I remember it. Weird one. It was a hit. The killer was a young lad who didn't seem to have any connection with the victim. He was living in Devon somewhere, not far from you, I think. He'd just moved there, but he was originally from London, a small-time drug dealer, involved in gangs. Nasty piece of work.'

'So he travelled just to carry out a murder.'

'Yeah.'

'Was his victim involved in drugs?'

'If he was, he hid it well because we didn't find any evidence for it.'

'So, what was this kid's motive?'

'No idea. In the end we thought it might have been some kind of gang initiation. There was a spate of them at the time. Random drive-by killings. The bloke he killed was just unlucky. Wrong time, wrong place.'

'How did you find Brookes?'

'Well, normally, as you know, these kinds of murders are a nightmare to solve. What's the stat? Eighty per cent of killers know their victim. But we picked this lad up on CCTV and we did a national TV appeal on *Crime Time* UK. A detective in London recognized him and called in.'

'And he had no connection with the victim? Or the area?'

'No, not as far as I'm aware.'

'Thanks.'

'Are we done? How did I do? Have I passed?' He laughs down the line.

'Top marks, but I've just got one more question for you. Easy one, this one.'

'I like the easy ones.'

'I can't find anything online about it. Do you know why that is?'

'I do. Our local paper is family owned and the old editor is an old stick-in-the-mud, so it didn't go digital until eight years ago. The case was all over the papers and local news, but you'd have to sweet-talk the archivists at the news offices to get them to dig it out for you.'

'Thanks, Derek.'

I get up to make that coffee. I've a long morning stretching ahead of me.

***

Three hours and six black coffees later, the archivist at the *Solihull Gazette*, a lovely lady called Maureen, has answered my questions. I thank her profusely and make a mental note to send her a bunch of flowers. She'll likely never know it, but Maureen who owns a Tabby called Loopy has just solved a murder.

I'm about to call Harriet with the news when a message on my laptop invites me to join Megan on Zoom.

'Hi, Mum.'

'Hi, love. This is a lovely surprise. Everything OK?'

'Yeah. Of course. Just fancied a chat, that's all.'

'Great. Megan, I hear you're looking at a college near Julian's and you're thinking of living with him permanently.'

Megan blushes. 'I didn't realize you knew.'

'It's OK. I just wanted to say if that's what you want, you've got my full support.'

'Thanks, Mum.'

'Julian and Cam also said that one of the reasons you didn't want to come home is because I'm too overprotective.'

Megan winces.

'Really?'

'Yes, but it's OK. It's all good. It's taken me a while to accept that they're right. I do need to trust you more. I know counselling has been good for you so I've decided to get some too.'

'You don't have to do that, Mum.'

'Yes, I do. I need to sort myself out, for both our sakes, so I've booked a session. I probably should have done it a long time ago. Megan, I'm so sorry for everything and I promise when . . . if you come home things will be different.'

'Thanks, Mum, but it really wasn't that bad. I kind of over-reacted. I'm sorry too. I was so angry with you about not letting me go to school and then when Jay died, it all got too much.'

'How about we start over?'

'Actually, I was thinking about coming home anyway.'

'Has something happened?'

'No. It's been great here. I've really enjoyed it and the local college looks good.'

'But?'

'Well, the boys are really loud and want to hang out all the time. They're up at six every morning and Julian and Cam are so enthusiastic about everything I'm worn out. I miss the quiet.'

'I understand.'

'And I kind of want to see my new bedroom and the en suite. I've been thinking about how I'm going to decorate it if that's OK with you?'

'Of course. It sounds like a great idea!'

'I also thought we could go prom shopping on the weekend, if you're OK with me going.'

'Of course. Why don't we go to Exeter and make a day of it?'

'That would be brilliant.'

'When you're back, we can have a really good chat about you going back to school and what you want to do afterwards. I'm open to anything including you living with Julian while you do your photography course, if that's what you want.'

'Thank you.'

'How about I collect you tomorrow afternoon? Do you want me to tell Julian?'

'No, I'll tell him. And, Mum?'

'Yes?'

'You really don't have to do the counselling if you don't want to.'

'It's all booked now and, anyway, I apparently have some unresolved issues to do with a pet rabbit called Fluffy.'

'What?'

'Nothing. I'll be there tomorrow.'

'Thanks, Mum.'

'I've missed you, Megan.'

'I've missed you too.'

My smile remains long after our call ends. My daughter is coming home.

67

The waiting room at Lisa Kendrick's is empty and I take a seat while Fran buzzes her to let her know I've arrived. A few moments later, Lisa and her megawatt smile appear in the doorway to her office.

'Ally, lovely to see you, come on in.'

I follow her into the office where Freud is in his usual position on the sofa.

'Can I just say well done for taking me up on my offer. The first step is the hardest step of all.'

'Thank you. It's Megan's doing really. She says it worked for her.'

'Thank you. How is Megan?'

'She's still at her father's. They seem to be getting on well. It all worked out in the end. In fact, she's coming home tomorrow.'

'Great. Take a seat and we'll get started.'

I sit next to Freud while Lisa sits opposite me, a large notepad resting on her knee, pen poised.

'There's a few things I need to run through with you.'

'OK.'

She outlines issues of confidentiality, the timing of the

sessions and, of course, payment. Every time she pauses for a response from me, I nod and tell her everything is fine.

'Great. We'll use the first session to assess your needs, expectations, your reasons for seeking counselling, that kind of thing. I've had a look at the forms you filled in for me online, so I'd like to begin by asking you what you expect from therapy?'

My hand runs the length of Freud's glossy coat. She smiles at me.

'Take your time. I know how difficult this is for you.'

It is, but not for the reasons she thinks.

'The thing is, Lisa. I'm not here for counselling.'

'Oh?'

'I'm here to tell you I know you killed Jay Cox.'

I promised Harriet I'd keep Lisa talking, just until cavalry arrived, but as soon as I saw her, I knew that wasn't going to happen. This is personal.

'Sorry?'

'You heard me.'

'What are you talking about? I don't even know Jay, other than he was your daughter's friend. You're not making any sense.'

'Then let me spell it out to you. Jay saw a girl, Cassie Warnock, coming out of your office late at night. Now, to anyone else that wouldn't mean anything, but Jay grew up in a drugs house. To him, when a person visits a property at odd hours, it means only one thing: drugs. Anyway, it was enough to make him suspicious, so he followed Cassie. Ali, the kebab shop owner, told me Jay bought a kebab most evenings while he waited for a girl to come out of counselling. I thought he meant Megan, but her appointments didn't match the times

364

Jay was there and then I showed Ali a photo of Cassie. It seems she was a regular visitor to your office.'

'What? That's rubbish, as well as being defamatory.'

'Well, here's a little more defamation for you. Cassie was couriering the drugs from Slaughterhouse Farm, the centre of a drugs ring run by your mate, drug dealer and convicted murderer Dean Brookes, or Dean Carter as you probably remember him.'

'Stop this, Ally, right now. I don't know where you got these ideas from, but they are complete nonsense. It's not rational. Let's put this to one side and focus on the real issue here, which is the guilt your feel over what happened to your daughter and the damage it's done to your relationship.'

'Keep your counselling bullshit to yourself. This isn't about Megan; this is about you. I know you met Dean when you were teenagers. There's even a photo of the two of you on Bidecombe Quay, taken by Geoff, the manager.' It was the luckiest break of all when I asked Geoff if I could see the photo that Harriet mentioned in the briefing. On the back row was Gabe, towering over everyone, including the two people next to him: Dean and Lisa. Geoff didn't recognize her, but I did.

'Is this some kind of sick joke?'

'Not at all. As it happens, I don't find murder very funny. The thing the police couldn't work out is how Dean persuaded Gabe to use his farm as a trap house, but that's where you come in, isn't it?'

'What? No.'

'Gabe came to you for counselling about his predilection and you told Dean Brookes, who used it to blackmail him. And it was all going great until Jay came along. Megan probably

365

told you how Jay was desperate to prove to me he was going straight. What better way than to bust open a drugs ring?'

'This is ridiculous. I want you to leave now or I'll call the police.'

I pick up the phone receiver and offer it to her.

'Go ahead.' She doesn't take it and I put it back down. 'I think Cassie refused to tell Jay what was going on, so he broke into your office and found the drugs for himself. You walked in and caught him. I'm guessing you pretended to be as shocked as he was to find drugs on your premises, but you also knew he'd tell me, so you gave him a can of Coke laced with heroin, and sent him on his way, knowing he'd be out cold when you came calling with your petrol can.'

'This is total guesswork. You can't prove any of it.'

'But I can. You see, I've saved the best till last.'

'What?'

'When you got to Seven Hills that night you couldn't find my cabin, could you? You got my number from Megan or Cassie, but I swapped them after Cassie showed up. I don't like people knowing where I live.'

'So?'

'So you went to the wrong cabin first and that's when you pressed your head up against the window, trying to see in and leaving a very lovely impression of your forehead in the process.'

'Forehead?'

'Yes, and the thing with foreheads, believe it or not, is they're a bit like fingerprints in that they're unique. And yours even comes with a scar.'

'But you can't date fingerprints or foreheads.'

'That's true, but unfortunately for you those cabin windows were cleaned the day before Jay was murdered. When I saw the scar on the impression I took, I remembered the scar on your forehead. I'll be honest, I wasn't holding out much hope, but a friend compared the impression to the photo on your website and confirmed it was a match.' I've no idea if this will hold up in court, but more importantly neither does Lisa. 'What I couldn't understand is why you'd want to hurt Jay, not until I uncovered your connection with Dean Brookes.' She doesn't say anything. The shock of being found out does that to you. And that's OK because I have plenty to say. 'You know what? Jay was no saint, but he was beginning to get his act together after a pretty shit start, and then you do this.'

Lisa bites her lip, trying to restrain her tears, but they fall anyway.

'I didn't want to do it, but it was the only way. I've built this practice from nothing. I've done so much good. I've helped so many people. And then Dean shows up out of nowhere threatening to tell the truth about my stepdad if I don't hand over my clients' names. I had no choice.'

'And what is the truth?'

'Dean and I met on holiday. He was besotted by me. Followed me around like a little puppy. I won't lie, I enjoyed the attention. By the end, I knew he'd do anything for me, and I wanted to teach Glenn, my stepdad, a lesson. I never meant for him to kill him.'

'But he did, and he kept your name out of it.'

'Yes.'

'And then he came out of jail and called in the favour.'

'Yes. He said he just needed help to get started so I gave

him the names of people who were vulnerable, people who could be groomed into helping him. I told him about Lenny. But then he needed a place in the town to store the drugs, a place the police would never think to look. A few weeks ago, I told him I wanted out for good, so he came down and threatened to hurt me if I did anything to jeopardize his operation. I was terrified.'

'So you killed Jay Cox who was about to do just that.'

'I'm so sorry.'

But her apologies are beginning to grate.

'What for? Murdering my daughter's friend or getting caught?'

'I never meant for any of this to happen; I'm just trying to tell you that I had no choice.'

She'll get life, of course. But it isn't really life. It's fifteen to twenty years maximum because she'll be a model prisoner. And then she'll be out. Her whole life ahead of her. No doubt she'll write her story, explaining how she's really the victim in all of this, get 'her side' across. Some will sympathize. Others will hate. But it doesn't matter because she gets to carry on living.

'Someone once told me you always have a choice.'

'I can tell you're angry, Ally, and I don't blame you.'

'Too fucking right I'm angry. You set fire to my home. You killed my daughter's friend. How else am I meant to feel?'

She nods. 'I'm sorry.'

I want to slap her. I want to make her suffer for the hurt that she has caused, but I don't.

'It doesn't matter anyway. The police will be here any minute.'

'The police?' She seems surprised. 'OK. Just let me tell Fran to cancel my appointments.'

She gets up from her chair and goes behind her desk where she presses the intercom and instructs Fran to clear her diary as she's not feeling very well. She stares at me, but stays where she is. I'm still thinking this is an odd move when her hand moves swiftly to the top drawer and before I realize what's happening, she's opened it and grabbed a handful of what looks like tiny white sweets wrapped in cellophane, but they're not sweets. They're drugs. She crams as many as she can into her mouth; her cheeks begin to bulge with the lethal pellets.

'Shit.'

I lunge across the desk, but Lisa steps back beyond my reach, grabbing a silver paperknife. She backs into the corner, knocking over her chair. The noise rouses Freud and he leaps off the sofa, yapping between the two of us, but Lisa's eyes remain trained on me. Mine are on the knife in her hand, but when I inch towards her, she jabs the blade at me, rooting me to the spot where I can only stand by and watch her kill herself. After several attempts, she swallows the bolus of drugs in her mouth and smiles.

'Let me die, Ally. You know you want to.'

'What?'

'You want me dead. You want revenge for what I did to Jay. I understand that and you're right: I deserve to die.'

'I didn't say that.'

'You don't need to. I can see it in your eyes.'

Her forehead glistens with sweat, the first protests of a poisoned body. Next, her stomach appears to clench and she winces with pain. The drugs are taking effect.

'Thank you for giving me a way out.' She gasps. Her body

is failing her, and she leans against the wall to prop herself up. 'This way, we both get what we want.'

'No!' I fling myself at her, knocking the knife out of her hand. Grabbing a clump of her shiny chestnut hair, I push her head down towards the floor. The move takes her by surprise and she's unable to resist. Her weakened body crumbles and I collapse on top of her. She writhes beneath me, trying to shake me off, but she's not much bigger than I am and I use my weight to pin her to the ground. The effort saps her energy, and a stillness comes over her as she pauses to gather her strength. This is my chance. I yank her head backwards; she screams out in pain. But I'm not listening. I'm looking at her mouth that is a gaping hole. I have to do this. It's the only way. I ram two fingers deep inside her wet throat which closes around them, and she begins to gag. It's a terrible violation and I want to snatch them back, but I don't because in that moment I want Lisa Kendrick to live.

Unable to swallow the obstruction in her throat, Lisa's body starts to shudder and shake. Freud dances excitedly around us like it's some game. She begins to choke and, eyes bulging, her stomach heaves. When I think she's about to spew, I withdraw my fingers and push her off me just as she leans to one side and her mouth expels a yellow slurry of half-empty cellophane bags. She continues retching until there is nothing left, and her body is spent.

I keep her arms clasped behind her back in case she tries to re-ingest the drugs, but she doesn't move and the two of us lie there panting, enveloped in the stench of Lisa's vomit, repelling Freud who has slunk into the corner.

I lean over and put my lips to Lisa's ear. 'You have no fucking idea what I want.'

68

Two weeks later

Megan emerges from her bedroom dressed in a long-sleeved fitted lace cream dress that ends above the knee; even as a small child she was never one for those princess dresses with their satin bodices and copious amounts of pink floor-skimming netting. She's wearing the brooch Bernadette gave her when she came by earlier. It's two dolphins, one gold, one silver. She told Megan that my dad, her grandad, gave it to her as a symbol of their love. Bernadette is right: there is so much I don't know about her.

Megan's pale red hair is pinned back in a messy bun at the nape of her neck, apart from several strands teased out to soften her face. She's wearing make-up too, just enough to enhance her hazel eyes and high cheekbones. She has Julian to thank for those. I realize in that moment that she's no longer a child, but a young woman on the threshold of adulthood. She's already been through so much in her short life, and I can't remember ever feeling this proud of her. So far, touching all the pine trunks at Seven Hills, she hasn't had another seizure. The tests are clear, suggesting she fainted in the shop that day.

'Don't you like it?' she says, mistaking my expression for disapproval.

'No, I don't like it,' I say solemnly before bursting into a smile. 'I love it! You look amazing.' She rewards me with a hug. I never want to let her go, but I do. I have to.

'The car's here,' I say, glancing out of the cabin window. Crawling up the narrow pathway towards us is a stretch limo. Hanging out of the window are several of Megan's old school friends including her best friend, Helena, waving furiously at us. Megan doesn't know I called her and asked her if Megan could go with her to the prom. She didn't hesitate to say yes.

'Hurry up, Meg, we'll be late!'

Megan returned from Julian's and went straight back to school. Despite her reservations, her friends were beside themselves to see her, welcoming her with squeals of delight when I dropped her off at the school gates. I got a text from her telling me she was going into Bidecombe with Helena. She had slotted back into her old life as if she'd never been away. I don't know what she'll do next, but whatever it is, it will be her choice, not mine.

'Are you ready?' I ask.

Megan nods and I open the front door for her. She pauses in the doorway. 'Mum?'

'Yes?'

'Thank you.'

'What for?'

'For not giving up on Jay.'

'That's OK.'

'We did all right by him, didn't we?'

'I think so, love.' The previous evening, we had gathered in the park and released some Chinese lanterns in Jay's honour. There weren't many people there. Jay had more enemies than friends. We raised a can of Dr Pepper to him, and Megan said a few words about how he'd helped her to recover and how he was happy and on a new path when he died. In among my sadness over the loss of such a young life, I felt intense pride at my daughter's compassion for her friend. She still has a long way to go. She's convinced she's to blame for Jay's murder because it was her who told Lisa that Jay had moved in with us and that he was keen to prove to me that he'd put his druggie past behind him. She also told Lisa he was spending time with Cassie because he thought she knew something that could incriminate his dad. She'll take some convincing that this isn't her fault, that she didn't kill Jay, that Lisa used her to get to him, but I'll get there.

Jay's dad, Tony, didn't say anything at the service. In fact, it was only afterwards that I realized he'd been there the whole time, leaning against a tree trunk. He came up to me and for a moment I thought he was going to launch into a tirade, but he just nodded and went on his way. On the fringes of the group was Karyn Dwight, as immaculate as ever. Next to her was Cassie, black mascara trails on her cheeks. In her own way, I think she liked Jay. She's no longer seeing Tony. She and her foster mum are making another go of their relationship. Despite Cassie's involvement in the county line, the police didn't press charges. The line between criminal and victim is sometimes a fine one. Besides, Brookes was the man they wanted. And Lisa Kendrick. Lenny has been charged with burglary and numerous drugs offences.

'You still OK to do this?'

'Yes.'

I follow Megan out onto the veranda where we are immediately blasted by the Beatles' 'And I Love Her'. Penny's eyes widen when she sees Megan and she mouths 'beautiful' before stepping forward and throwing her arms around her. By the time she releases her, her tears are in free fall, and Will slides a comforting arm around her shoulders. They're back together and Will has just about forgiven me.

It turns out that Jonny Ingham did ask Lobby Rix if Will Sneddon was responsible for destroying Gabe's flock. Lobby said it wasn't him, but a man whose name meant nothing to me. I've never been happier to be wrong about something. Maybe, there is such a thing as a one-off. I've apologized a hundred times to him and Penny, and she's been gracious enough to shrug it off as her friend just looking out for her. Emma is here too. She has declared herself single for the foreseeable future. I never told Will about Emma's liaison with Sammy in the barn. Some things are better left unsaid.

Julian holds out a red velvet box. 'I've got you something, Megan.'

His eyes are full of love and pride for his daughter. When I asked him if he wanted to be here for her prom, he told me he wouldn't miss it for the world. I'm getting used to the idea of him being in her life.

Megan opens the box and her eyes light up at the bracelet; gold hearts linked together by a chain. She looks at me as if to ask me if it's OK for her to accept it. I smile.

'It's beautiful, Julian.'

He puts it on Megan's wrist, and she holds it up for inspection.

'Thank you, Dad.'

Julian's chest visibly swells. He glances at his boys who are doing tumble turns over the railings and have declared that their house is boring and they want to live in a cabin in the woods with Meggy and Aunty Ally. I know what's going through his mind. This is his family now. And it's my family too. It just took a while for me to get my head around it. Cam is here, of course. I'm warming to her. Someone once told me that the road to hell is paved with good intentions. Cam's is paved with a desire to fix everyone. I can relate to that.

I also invited Bernadette. For all our disagreements, she loves Megan and she loves me, in her own way. Her determination to dislike Julian crumpled in the face of his charm and obvious wealth and he won her over in an indecently short space of time. Julian won me over when she made a crack about my sub-standard parenting and he told her I was an amazing mum and Megan was a credit to me.

Julian pops the cork on a huge Champagne bottle and sloshes the fizzing liquid into a tray of glasses held by Cam. We raise our glasses to Megan. She takes a quick sip and gets into the limo. Instantly, her head pokes through the sunroof, still holding the glass of Champagne. Grinning so hard her cheeks must hurt, she toasts us as the limo rolls back down the hill towards the site's exit. Our reward for enduring a cold, bleak winter has been an unseasonably warm April with days of unbroken blue skies, as if winter used up spring's cloud quota, and I watch as the slowly setting sun threads Megan's hair with gold and casts the warmest of glows across her face. Seconds later she sets off.

Julian turns to me, his eyes glassy with tears.

'Thank you so much for letting me and Cam into Megan's life, Wish.'

'Thank you for being there when she needed you.'

He presses his lips together, closes his eyes and nods. I give him time to reclaim his composure.

'But if you want to stay in her life, please stop calling me Wish.'

'Fair enough.' He grins. 'Look, we're having dinner at the Sea Grill on the quay. We'd love it if you'd join us.'

'Yes, Ally, please come,' says Cam.

'Thank you. That's really kind of you, but I've got plans of my own tonight.'

69

The sledgehammer thwacks the arm of the chair, splitting it in half. Another swing and the chair's legs buckle, and it collapses into kindling on the kitchen floor of Slaughterhouse Farm.

I was with Kit in the Albion when Harriet called to tell him that Lenny Russo was able to confirm that Miriam killed Gabe and the case was closed. He just nodded and said a part of him accepted that was the case some time ago, he'd just hoped it wasn't true. He asked her if she had any idea why she did it, but the best she could come up with was that Miriam lost her temper after she discovered the images on the computer in the Slaughterhouse. Harriet told him not to let it eat him up. The best thing Kit could do now was to be there for his mum, who has been moved to a nursing home. He nodded and said that that was at least some comfort.

It was me who asked Kit to meet in the Albion so I could give him the answer he had waited so patiently for. I told him I was ready to give our relationship a go. I have no idea what the future holds. There is an undeniable spark between us but whether it fizzles out or ignites into something more meaningful, only time will tell. I'll give it my best shot. We're taking things slowly, so slowly I haven't told Megan yet. Not until there's something to tell.

While he sorts out who is going to run the farm, Kit has moved into the farmhouse, but he can't bear to be surrounded by the furniture that reminds him of what took place there, which is why, with Megan safely at the prom, I'm here wielding a sledgehammer.

Kit appears by my side just as I take another swing, recoiling at the noise.

'Wow, remind me never to get into an argument with you.' He laughs.

'Let that be a warning to you,' I say, pointing my sledgehammer at the splinters of wood.

'It's nearly dark. How about we finish up here for today? I'll take the furniture to the dump before it closes and grab us some fish and chips on my way back.'

'Sounds good. Do you want to pick up some ciders while you're at it? It's about time we educated you in the ways of the pressed apple.'

'Sure.'

He bundles the wood as if it were matchsticks and carries it out into the yard. Through the gloom, I watch him load it onto the back of his truck. The sun has yet to set, but it has already abandoned this corner of the valley.

I'm about to turn my attentions to another chair when my phone goes. Leaning the sledgehammer against the sofa, I ease the phone out of my jeans pocket.

'Ally, hi.'

It's Harriet who, unusually, is full on with the pleasantries.

'Hi.'

'How are you?'

'Er . . . good, thanks. You?'

'Good. Good. Sorry to call out of the blue and this is a bit awkward, but I figured you ought to know.'

'Ought to know what?'

'The DNA came back from the used condom we found in the barn at Narracott Farm. It doesn't belong to Gabe Narracott, but it does belong to someone closely related to him.'

'Yeah, sorry. I know.'

'You do?'

'I should have told you that I found out Emma Sneddon was seeing Sammy Narracott, Gabe's cousin, behind Will's back.'

'She might well have been, but it wasn't Sammy Narracott she was having sex with in the barn. It's closer than that. Unless there's a secret brother somewhere else, the DNA belongs to Kit Narracott.'

'Kit?'

'Yes.'

Kit. My mind begins to race, trying to unravel the implications of this until the truth dawns on me. Emma was waiting for *Kit* that day by the barn. When I saw her in the pub with Sammy, she wasn't begging him to go out with her, she must have been pleading with him to speak to Kit. Outside Lisa's, Emma assumed I was talking about Kit, but looking back I don't think I mentioned his name.

'Sorry to be the one to tell you. I just thought if you're still seeing the guy, you really should know the truth about him.'

'Yes. I should.'

'Anyway, I'll leave it with you.'

'Thanks. One more thing before you go, Harriet.'

'Yes.'

'What's Kit's DNA doing on the database?'

'Drink-driving conviction about five years ago. He was four times over the legal limit at eleven in the morning. That's some drink problem he's got there. He should have gone to prison, but he agreed to rehab instead. Guess he lapsed.'

Harriet rings off. Drink-driving. Sleeping with his boss's wife whilst also having sex with a girl almost half his age. What else don't I know about Kit Narracott?

I call Bill, the landlord at the Albion. I'm lucky. He's around and he confirms what I've already begun to suspect. I ring off just as the back door to the farmhouse opens. Kit pauses in the doorway to brush the dust from his jeans.

'Any more furniture for the dump? I've got room.'

'Er. Yes.'

'Great.' He looks at me oddly. 'You OK? Did you hurt yourself?'

My gaze shifts from his concerned frown to the white doorframe behind him. They're gone now, of course, scrubbed clean by Kelvin's Clean Team, but I remember exactly where those bloodstains were and now, I know why their location bothered me so much. Three stab wounds. Two different heights of blood spatter. Two different people.

I see it all as if it's a film playing out before my eyes. Miriam stabbed Gabe twice low down, but Kit, who is at least a foot taller than his mother, delivered the fatal blow. When Lenny came to the door, Kit must have stayed out of sight. All Lenny saw was Gabe's body in the kitchen and Miriam with blood on her nightshirt.

380

Kit follows my eye to the doorframe. His frown deepens.

'Are you sure you're all right? You look like you've seen a ghost.'

'You were here.'

'What?'

'The night Gabe was killed, you were here.'

'What are you talking about?' He laughs. 'I was pissed as a fart in South Devon, remember?'

'No, you weren't. Georgina must have lied for you, for some reason, because you've been sober since your drink-drive conviction. I checked with Bill; you only ever drink tonic. Is that how you met Gavin Baxendale? You were in rehab together?'

Kit raises his hands. 'It's not what you think.'

'What were you even doing here? I thought you were done with the farm. You said you never wanted to come back.'

'I didn't. I came to ask for some money.'

'But you said you didn't need money. Mike Clevedon paid you well.'

'Things were getting awkward with Georgina. I wanted my own place, but I needed an extra £50,000 to set myself up. I thought my criminal record might cause problems in getting a mortgage so I asked Mum if she'd sell off some land to release some equity.'

'And what happened?'

'She said no. She said I'd abandoned her, that I didn't deserve a penny. She kept going on about how Gabe was the only person who'd never left her. So, I told her what kind of a man her precious son was and the real reason I left.'

'You told Miriam her son was a paedophile? You knew?'

'Yes. It was after Dad died, I was going through the accounts when I noticed a file I didn't recognize so I clicked on it and that's when I saw these pictures.'

'Why didn't you tell the police then?'

'I know I should have done, but when I found out I just wanted to get as far away as possible. I had no idea Mum would react the way she did when I told her. I'd never seen her that way before. She went mad. She just grabbed a knife and went for Gabe. Before I knew what was happening, he was lying in a pool of blood by the back door.'

'That's not what happened though.'

'Yes, it is. Mum told DI Moore she did it. I know I should have said something about being there, but I just panicked.'

'You're lying. The spatters on the door are too high for it to be Miriam. The final stab wound, the one that killed Gabe, was you, Kit.'

I tug my mobile out of my back pocket.

'What are you doing?'

'Phoning the police.'

'Why?'

'Because you killed your brother.'

'Christ, Ally, he was a paedophile.'

'It doesn't matter.'

'But no one's going to miss him. The world's a better place without people like my brother.'

I stop dialling. He's right. Gabe Narracott is no loss.

'No one needs to know, Ally. Please.'

Slowly, he reaches for my phone. No, this isn't right. I snatch it away from him.

'But I know.'

I make it to the first nine, but he knocks the phone from my hand, and it clatters to the floor.

'I can't let you call the police,' he says, daring me to pick it up. I don't move. I only have one thought screaming inside my head: nobody knows I'm here. I've got to get away.

I grab the sledgehammer; Kit goes for it too and we end up grappling for control. I yank it as hard as I can, and he lunges towards me. Keeping my eyes fixed on his, I ram my knee up into his crotch. He gasps in pain and momentarily loses his grip. I snatch the hammer from him and take a swing at him. The metal head glances his shoulder, toppling him sideways, but a kitchen counter breaks his fall, and he quickly rights himself. There's not enough space to take another swipe so I lob the hammer at him, scoring a blow to his chin. This time he goes down.

I grab the few seconds I have and run out through the open back door into the dusky farmyard, but there's no safe hiding place for me here. Kit knows these outbuildings better than anyone, and there's no point hitting the roads on the off chance of a passing car. There won't be any. With darkness falling, my only hope is the woods. If I make it that far.

I throw myself over the five-bar gate into the fields and make a dash for the woods, stumbling over the uneven ground, passing the barn where Emma and Kit had sex. At the edge of the woods, I risk a backward glance. Kit's already over the farm gate. I've fifty metres on him, max. Diving into the undergrowth, I veer left to right, avoiding the paths, hoping to shake him off. I've no idea where I'm going, but the failing light is my friend. The deeper into the woods I go, the darker it gets, the more chance I have of giving Kit the slip.

Finally, exhaustion sets in, and I dip behind a tree, its girth wide enough to conceal me while I gulp back silent breaths to ease the tightness in my chest. My heart rate levels, but I'm not safe. Not yet.

Through the trees, the slaughterhouse sits in the clearing like a malevolent toad lurking in the shadows, waiting for its prey. A place of abject misery, where animals had their throats cut, where cash was traded for drugs, where images of abused children were viewed, the slaughterhouse is no refuge.

Beyond it is the main road, but that will leave me exposed. Kit will find me in no time. My only hope is to try and make it to Will's farmhouse about a mile away on the other side of the woods.

I listen out for sounds more human than animal, but apart from the distant coo of a pigeon and the light rustle of a breeze in the trees, there's nothing and I dare to hope I've lost him. I'm about to make my move when I hear a crack, nothing specific, but it was made by a boot not a paw. It's him. I know it.

I risk a look and my breath freezes in my mouth. Peering into the undergrowth, Kit's crouched figure is less than ten metres from me. I watch him for a few moments, scared that even the slightest movement of me retreating behind the tree will attract his attention. He pivots on his foot, scanning the thick bracken, but it's too dark. There are too many shadows.

Eventually he gives up and heads for the road on the other side of the slaughterhouse. I wait until he's out of sight before I begin to pick my way through the thick brown mesh of bracken and bramble. When I look back all that's chasing me is the gathering gloom. The diminishing light filtering through the woods guides me out and towards Will's farm. It can't be far. Once I'm clear of the woods and on Will's land, Kit won't risk following me there. I hear a distant hum. It's coming from the electric wire that marks the boundary of Will's farm. I'm almost there. I can't help myself. I pick up the pace, but it's some moments before I register the swishing sound is my jeans brushing against the nettles that have crept across my path.

Kit is too far away to hear, but I still leap over the remaining undergrowth. The hum grows louder. The edge of the woods is less than twenty metres away. I've made it. I'm safe. Then from behind a tree, Kit steps straight into my path. I slam right into him.

'You didn't seriously think you could outrun me, did you, Ally?'

I pull away. All I can do is run back into the woods, but he's on me in seconds, grabbing my waist and dragging me to the ground. The impact winds me, leaving me battling for breath. Kit throws me onto my back and sits astride me, but I don't recognize him any more. His face is hard, determined.

'Kit. Stop.'

But he doesn't, instead he uses his weight to pin me down, clamping my wrists together and pegging them to the ground above my head with one hand. The other closes around my throat and his fingers begin to squeeze. I try to swallow, to cry out, to make a noise, any noise, but no sound comes out.

He continues to apply pressure. I look directly into his eyes, appealing to his humanity, but he has none. This is the face of a killer. There is nothing I can do. My attempts to twist myself out from underneath him exhaust me and use up what little oxygen I have. My body relaxes. It knows I can't fight it. My one thought is of Megan in her prom dress, the evening sun radiating behind her, grinning like the stick figure she drew of herself on the wall of our old cabin. I don't want to leave her. Not yet.

Suddenly, Kit's eyes bulge and his body tenses. I don't know what this means, but he's shaking his head as if trying to rid himself of some irritant. As he does this, he loosens his grip and my wrists spring apart. Fighting to contain them again, Kit lowers himself towards me. This is my chance.

Clamping his head in my hands, I ram my thumbs deep into his eye sockets, pressing his soft eyeballs back into his head as hard as I possibly can. He cries out, releasing my neck so he can use both hands to pull mine away from his skull. My fingers are wet with his sweat and when his head jerks back, my grip finally slips.

He grabs my neck again, his thumbs crushing my windpipe. The veins in his neck stand out with the effort. He wants this over. My hands alternate between trying to beat him off and trying to claw his fingers from my flesh, not making an impression on either. Finally, they flop to my sides and the sky begins to close in. I fight to keep my eyes open as if it will make any difference. The darkness is coming for me.

Without warning Kit's head suddenly bounces towards me; his eyes roll up into his head. He lets go of me and slumps to one side. I push him off and he tumbles lifelessly to the ground. He's out cold. Dead, for all I care, but even with my lungs burning and my throat on fire, I'm taking no chances so I scrabble backwards along the ground until I'm clear of him, propping myself up against a tree. It's then that I realize I'm not alone.

Dressed in khaki and draped in netting sown with green

plastic leaves, Gavin Baxendale is standing in front of me, holding a huge black rock. Behind him is a small hide no more than a metre off the ground, camouflaged and blending perfectly into its surroundings. He looks at Kit and drops the rock as if it's suddenly combusted in his hand. Then turns to me, horrified, and confused.

'I was just out looking for nightjars.'

Kit

The police came for her in the middle of the night, dragging her from her bed. It was only a few weeks after she had lost Billy and she was weak, but they didn't care. They threw her into a police cell where they left her all night. No one told her until the next morning it was because of Ralph. When they told her what he'd done and how she'd helped him, she threw up, but they just chucked a cloth at her and carried on.

She wanted to tell them they were wrong. Ralph wasn't like that. She wasn't like that. He'd never hurt a child, and neither would she. She loved children. But it was even worse than that. Ralph told the police that she had led him on.

They told her she was pure evil and that she should never have children because she was sick in the head. They called her a nonce, a pervert, names she didn't even know the meaning of. She was no better than that Myra Hindley, that terrible woman who kidnapped and tortured children. They'd both rot in hell. They questioned her for hours in a windowless room until she wasn't sure if it was day or night. She told them over and over that she'd never do anything like that. She loved children. Didn't Ms Winters tell her she had a way with them? She was a natural.

Ms Winters. That was it. That was the answer. Ms Winters would tell them the truth, but they ignored her pleas and carried on calling her names, and as much as they hurt, it was the thought that she had let her beloved Ms Winters down that really destroyed her.

In the end, they said if she told the truth, she could go home. But she didn't know what the truth was any more, and her mind started to think that maybe they were right. Maybe she did those terrible things, and she was the wicked girl they said she was. That was why she'd lost Billy. She wasn't good enough for him.

They helped her write her statement, admitting what she'd done. She'd feel better for getting it off her chest, they said, and then she could go home, but they didn't release her. They put her back in the cell and left her there alone. Then the next day the detective told her he wasn't going to charge her and she was free to go. Just like that.

Ralph got three years and the nursery was closed down. The trial made the news, but because she was never charged her name stayed out of the papers. That didn't stop the gossips. Father wanted her out of the house. Mother kept quiet. It was Robbie who said she shouldn't be punished because of what some posh boy had done and for once the rich kid got what was coming to him.

She never told anyone about what happened, not even Silas, until that night.

It was 1.30 a.m. in the morning. She'd heard noises and thought one of the dogs had got shut in a room. When she went downstairs she found Kit climbing through the kitchen window. He'd snuck out to hang out with his friends. He was only about nine then, but she was so angry with him she slapped him hard across the cheek. She'd never hit either of the boys until then. Kit held his reddening cheek, the hurt in his eyes fighting off the tears.

'What did you do that for?'

She felt terrible and she tried to console him, but he shrugged her off.

'I'm sorry. I'm scared something bad will happen to you.'

'Why would it?'

And then it all just came out. She hadn't meant to tell him, but she couldn't help herself.

'I fell in love with a boy called Ralph Foxton. He dumped me when I got pregnant and went to university.' Kit didn't react and she realized it was too much for his nine-year-old brain, but she couldn't stop herself. 'I lost the baby. Billy, I called him. It was a terrible time, but it got worse. After Ralph went to university, a parent of one of the pre-school children at the nursery said Ralph had hurt him. It was my fault. I let Ralph in after my shift ended, and the other staff had gone. It was his idea. I thought it was so we could be alone together, but I was just an excuse. He'd send me to the other side of the nursery to fetch something. I never suspected a thing. For a while the police believed I did it too, but I didn't. I swear to you, Kit. You believe me, don't you?'

The little boy nodded at her, watching her tears drip onto her cheeks.

'That's how I know what's out there, Kit. I'm just trying to keep you and Gabe safe.'

'I can look after myself,' Kit said.

'You need me too, but Gabe isn't like you. He's so trusting. I can't let him out of my sight, but I'll make it up to you one day, Kit, I promise.'

But she had been wrong all along. Gabe didn't need protecting from the world, the world needed protecting from him.

It was Kit who told her the truth. She hadn't heard from him since he asked her for all that money. Gabe had already turned him down.

He told her that she owed him the money for all the time she had spent with Gabe and not him, she but said no. She didn't want him to buy a place somewhere else. She wanted him to come home. Then he showed her photos he'd found on Gabe's computer, told her that was the real reason he left all those years ago.

Gabe didn't say anything at first. Just like when he was a child and struggled to take things in, like words had left their meaning behind and it took a few seconds for it to catch up. When it did, he denied it all. Said it wasn't his laptop.

At first she didn't believe Kit until she realized it was because she didn't want to, just like she hadn't wanted to believe the police officer when he told her Gabe had been photographing young girls in the park, just like she hadn't wanted to believe it of Ralph. But she knew it was true. Of course it was. This was her punishment for letting Ralph do what he did. She lost Billy, but Gabe had lived and look what he had become. It had taken his brother to show her what he really was.

'Mum, what are you doing?' She'd never seen fear in his eyes before. 'Put the knife down. Stop. This isn't you. You're a good person.'

All her life, she'd been told she was good, but that wasn't true. Men just told her that because she always did what they wanted her to do. But that didn't make her good. It just made her obedient, bending to the will and whims of others. She saw that now, but it wasn't too late. For the first time in her life, Miriam would stand up for herself and do the right thing.

70

'Where the hell are you? Sounds like you're in a wind tunnel.'

'I'm at Breakneck Point.'

'Aren't we all?' Harriet laughs. 'Anyway, I won't keep you long. I wanted to let you know we charged Kit Narracott with murder.'

'No surprises there.'

'It seems he planned it too. A couple of months ago, he met Gabe at a market in South Devon. According to a farmer who knew Kit their conversation got a little heated and he overheard Kit asking for money.'

'How come this didn't come out in the original investigation?'

'Kit wasn't a suspect. He was supposedly blind drunk and ninety miles away when Gabe died, remember? And his girlfriend at the time corroborated his story. Plus, as you say, he was well off and didn't want the farm. He had no motive.'

'So why didn't this farmer come forward?'

'He lives in deepest Devon and doesn't bother himself with the news, only interested in weather reports, apparently. It's only when we started asking around the markets that we came across him and he remembered the argument.'

'So Kit was telling the truth when he told me he went to Slaughterhouse Farm to ask Miriam for the money.'

'Yes. What he didn't tell you is that he'd cooked up a plan to show her what kind of a man Gabe really was. He bought a laptop in South Devon some weeks ago. He gave the shop owner Gabe's details but when we showed him a photo of Kit, he identified him. Then he loaded it with indecent images and drove to the farm and pretended it was Gabe's.'

'So Gabe wasn't a paedophile?'

'No, he wasn't.'

'But isn't that how he came onto Lisa and Dean's radar?'

'No, Lisa said Gabe went to her because he was suffering depression over his financial situation.'

'I don't get it though. Why was Miriam so quick to believe Gabe was a paedophile and why did she react so strongly? She adored him.'

'Well,' says Harriet in a way that suggests she's very pleased with herself. 'It seems that in the 1970s Miriam was implicated in a child sex abuse case at the nursery where she worked. The owner's son, Miriam's boyfriend at the time, was found guilty. They were seeing each other at the time, and she let him in to the building after everyone had gone home, which gave him his chance. But she was never charged. When Kit told her about Gabe, we think it might have triggered something, and she went for him. Then she either took the blame for Kit, or she genuinely believed she killed her son. I think it's the latter.'

'Go on.'

'We think Kit let her believe she'd killed him, knowing he was still alive. Then Lenny shows up. Obviously, at first, this is the worst thing that could happen, but Kit sees it's a young boy, so he opens the front door, letting Lenny see Gabe's body and Miriam with his blood all over her. Terrified, Lenny runs away and Miriam, traumatized by what she's done, follows him into the night.'

'But Miriam was found with the knife.'

'Yes, we think Kit then went back and stabbed Gabe, caught Miriam up and slipped the knife into her hand. It's dark. She's in a catatonic state. It's unlikely she'd even remember him doing it. Then he goes back to the farmhouse, cleans himself up and anything he's touched and makes sure Gabe's prints are all over the laptop.'

A shudder runs through me.

'Christ. He put his brother's prints on the laptop post-mortem.'

'Yes, then hid it in the slaughterhouse.'

'Ready for him to find accidentally if the police didn't find it first.'

'Exactly.'

'Jesus, that takes some mind.'

'It certainly does.'

'But how did he persuade his girlfriend to give him an alibi?'

'He didn't have to. When we spoke to her again, she admitted that she was passed out through drink that night so when he told her he'd never left her side, she had no reason to disbelieve him.'

'Christ. OK, but what if Miriam had come out of her catatonic state and told the police Kit had been there too?'

'She thought she'd killed Gabe. Kit was betting on her keeping him out of the picture. If she implicated him, they would lose the farm, a farm that's been in the Narracott family for generations.'

It all makes sense, but the criminal justice system isn't built on sense.

'But with Miriam on death's door and Kit sticking to his story, you can't prove any of this.'

'No, we can't. Not at the moment, but we'll keep at it. According to his ex-wife, Kit absolutely hated his brother, always did, because he was Miriam's favourite. He was also very bitter that his mum sided with his brother over the farm, hence the drinking before he was caught drunk behind the wheel and why he hired someone to destroy Gabe's sheep.'

I flush with embarrassment even though I've apologized a dozen more times to Will. When Jonny Ingham told me that a man called Chris Stathmore paid Lobby to set his dogs on Gabe's sheep, it meant nothing to me. It was only when Harriet repeated it to me that I remembered Kit worked at a sheep station in Australia called Stathmore and Kit is a derivative of his full name – Christopher. Kit won't admit to it, of course, but it's too much of a coincidence and, either way, it puts Will in the clear.

'So, watch this space because we're not done with Kit Narracott yet.'

'Christ, how could I have got Kit so badly wrong? I didn't see it in him. I should have listened to you. You warned me about him.'

'Don't beat yourself up about it. Kit's a very charming and persuasive individual and, besides, if you'd listened to me, we wouldn't have caught him and he'd have got off scot-free, having not only murdered his brother, but had him labelled a paedophile as well.'

'Some consolation, I suppose, for being a shit judge of character when it comes to men. Seems to be a recurring theme in my life.'

'It's never too late to change. Anyway, you'll also be pleased to hear we've charged Lisa Kendrick with Jay's murder.'

'That's good, at least.'

'Yeah. A lot easier this one. She just told us everything we wanted to know. You were right. She was storing the drugs for Brookes and it wasn't just Cassie dropping by for late night visits, there were others too. She was supplying most of Devon. We need to keep an eye on her though. She tried to take her own life again last night even though we've got her on suicide watch. You did well there. If you hadn't intervened, those drugs would have killed her.

'Anyway, the other reason I'm calling is to talk about your resignation.'

'What about it?'

'I want you to withdraw it. It's not too late. I understand your reasons, but I think you'll regret it. You're a brilliant CSI, Ally, and I don't think you'll be happy doing anything else which is why I'd like you to come back to Major Investigations.'

'Major Investigations?'

'Yeah. Why else do you think I asked for your input on Gabe's case? I like to try before I buy.'

'You did a good job of not showing it.'

'I know. And I know you've got childcare commitments, but I reckon we can work around that, maybe look at a job share. I've got to clear everything with the boss, of course, but either way I want you on board. You've solved two murders in less than a month. I'm not letting you go now. How is Megan, by the way?'

'She's really well, back at school and revising hard for her exams.'

'Great. Wish I could say the same about my eldest. Lazy sod. Anyway, think about it and get back to me when you've decided.'

She rings off. Major Investigations. There was a time when I'd have jumped at the opportunity to go back.

'Ally.'

A familiar voice startles me from my thoughts.

'Liam.'

'Penny said I'd find you here.' Before I can stop myself, I throw my arms around him, leaving him mildly shocked. 'I should go away more often.' He laughs.

'Sorry. It's just really good to see you. When did you get back?'

'Just now. Penny told me what happened. Seems I missed all the action.'

'Yes, it's been a little busy around here.'

'How's the throat?'

Self-consciously, I touch my neck. Even though the redness has faded, the memory hasn't.

'Better.'

'And you found the person who killed Jay.'

'Thanks to your friend.'

As soon as I saw the forehead impression on the cabin window, I knew if anyone could help me, it would be Liam.

'My pleasure. Weird to think it was Megan's counsellor.'

'I know.'

'And poor Jay. He really didn't deserve that.'

'No, he didn't.'

Our conversation drifts away until the only sounds are the seagulls overhead and the waves below. But I'm tired of the silence between us, tired of not saying what needs to be said. Liam deserves the truth. Then at least he'll understand why I said no to him, and we can get on with our lives.

'Liam. There's something I need to tell you.'

He smiles at me. 'It's OK. You don't have to say it, Ally. I already know. I've always known.'

'What?'

'Curiosity got the better of me. After Pascoe's body washed up on shore and his suicide note turned up, I went back into the girl's account and read the messages between you and Pascoe, arranging to meet here at Breakneck Point.'

'Oh God. Is that why you left?'

'No. I left because you turned me down, remember?'

'But you asked me out even though you knew what I'd done . . . what I am.'

'Yes.' Liam's eyes trace my face. 'Because what you are, Ally, is a mother who would do anything to protect her child and a CSI trying to stop a killer. That's all. Nothing else.'

'Do you really believe that?'

'I wouldn't be here if I didn't.'

'But you don't know the whole story.'

'I think I do. Penny told me what happened with Tony and how it shook you and that you weren't sure you could trust yourself any more.'

'What? Why did she tell you that?'

'Because I told her I knew you'd killed Pascoe and that she'd helped you to escape. It took me a while to work it out, but it's the only way you could have done it, but that doesn't matter. The point is Tony Cox is still here, isn't he?'

'It isn't just Tony. When I was in Lisa's office and she'd taken the drugs, there was a moment when . . .'

'Stop.' He squeezes my arms gently and tilts his head so he's looking directly into my eyes. 'Listen to me, Ally. You're a CSI. You and I know you could have got away with killing them both and no one would have suspected a thing, but you didn't. You chose to let them live. You don't need to be scared of yourself.'

'Then why haven't I had the nightmares and the panic attacks like Penny? There's been nothing. It's like it never happened.'

'Not everyone suffers from PTSD. The fact you haven't had any symptoms doesn't mean anything. It certainly doesn't make you a psychopath . . . Ally, you're not Pascoe.'

Hearing Liam say those words sends a sudden wave of relief crashing over me. He's right. I'm not Pascoe.

'Thank you.'

'And PTSD can strike any time so keep an eye on yourself, OK?'

'I will.'

His hands fall to his sides, and I find myself wishing they hadn't and that he'd just pulled me towards him and taken me in his arms instead. 'Now, did I hear you say you're going back to work?'

'I don't know. Whatever you think of me, I still crossed the line, remember?'

'Then cross back. God knows they need you.'

'So much has happened. I need some time to think about it. But what about you? What are you doing here?'

'Well, I was about to sell the Coffee Shack, but my girls begged me not to. Turns out they really like their time down here with me and apparently I'm a much nicer person when I live in Devon, so I called it off.'

'I'm really glad.'

'Me too. Anyway, I thought I would celebrate by having a cup of coffee with my favourite CSI. Join me?'

'Of course. Only make mine a chococino.'

'Deal.'

I let him go on ahead while I hang back for a few moments. There's something I need to do. Rummaging in my pocket, I fish out the small black button that has lived there for the past eight months. Pascoe's button. I give it one final look before tossing it into the void.

Epilogue

The Georgian pile that is Haywards Lodge is no longer the country seat of the Mayforth family and my red Volvo joins a line of parked cars, next to the sign for the reception.

As I stroll across the gravel, a familiar figure emerges from the front door and skips down the steps.

'PC Rogers. I almost didn't recognize you in your civies.'

'Dymond, good to see you.'

'So, they do give you time off then?'

'Occasionally.' He grins. 'I'm here to see my old mum.'

'Everything OK?'

'Yep. Eighty-eight and still beating the pants off the rest of them at Bridge.'

'That's good to hear.'

'But what about you? What are you doing here? It can't be your mum – I heard Bernadette was still doing a sterling job of ensuring everyone who parks on her street is in possession of a valid residents' parking permit.'

'That sounds like Bernadette.' I laugh. 'I'm here to see someone else.'

***

The carer leads me into a room with floor-to-ceiling windows. In front of them. Miriam Narracott is sitting in a wheelchair, hands on her lap, palms down as if someone has positioned them there. Dressed in a flowery blouse, cardy and skirt, her hair is neatly brushed. She doesn't look up when I enter the room but continues to stare out through the French windows to a place well beyond the neatly trimmed lawn and ornamental urns.

Against the odds, she survived the stroke. Physically, she has recovered enough to be moved to a home providing round-the-clock care, but she remains paralysed and unable to communicate; it is anyone's guess how much she's able to take in, but I have to try. For her sake.

When Harriet told me what happened to Miriam when she was younger, I couldn't get it out of my mind. She said that Miriam was never charged which means, originally, they suspected Miriam was involved. I also couldn't understand how something that had happened so long ago could lead to her attacking her son, so I went to the police archive and requested the file. Pouring over it I quickly realized that Harriet only knew part of the story.

'Hello, Miriam. My name is Ally Dymond,' I say, taking a seat next to her. 'We met when you were in the hospital.' I don't mention I was with her son Kit at the time. The less said about him, the better.

'I hope you don't mind, I've been looking at the old police file about what happened at the Ladybird Nursery when you worked there in the Seventies.'

The file was thick with various forms, black and white photos, and tattered statements; two of which stood out. The first was a confession from Miriam Barker. I read through it. I recognize police speak when I see it. Few words in it were hers. Truths and falsities woven together until it was almost impossible to tell them apart. Yes, she let Ralph Foxton into the building. Yes, it was her idea to do what they did to the boy. Jesus. But this was the Seventies. Suspects didn't have an automatic right to a solicitor and if you didn't ask, the police didn't offer. Deprived of sleep and locked in a windowless room with two detectives who had pre-determined her guilt, Miriam didn't stand a chance. My guess is she was threatened and abused until she told them what they wanted to hear, admitting anything and everything on the lie that if she did, it would all go away.

'What I couldn't understand is why the police let you go when you confessed to the crime. Then I came across another statement. The detectives also interviewed Ms Cynthia Winters, Ralph's mother and your boss. She thought very highly of you, Miriam, and she never believed you were guilty. She said you were incapable of hurting anyone and that you had a bright future ahead of you before you met Ralph. She deeply regretted asking you to tutor her son. She said that if anyone was to blame it was her, for bringing Ralph Foxton into this world in the first place.'

It was a startling admission by Ms Winters, but her statement went further, much further. 'Ms Winters told the police that you couldn't have committed the crime because you weren't there. She checked the date when it happened against the staff roster. You were working the early shift. It was your co-worker, Rachel Montgomery, who let Ralph into the nursery. He was seeing her too, but Rachel was never questioned and when Ralph was interviewed again, he changed his statement, saying no one at the nursery knew what he was doing.'

I couldn't fathom why the police had ignored such vital evidence until I delved a little deeper into Rachel Montgomery's background and discovered she was the daughter of Jeremy Montgomery, Barnston's mayor, who likely used his influence to keep his daughter's name out of the proceedings. And they call it the good old days, but not for Miriam. She has carried the shame of being blamed for a crime she didn't commit all her life.

'The point is, Miriam, you had nothing to do with the crime at all.'

But that isn't the whole reason I'm there. Buried deep in Miriam's confession was another paragraph, a paragraph that suddenly made sense of it all.

'The thing is, despite the police, you must have known you didn't do those terrible things, but I couldn't work out why you couldn't put it behind you. Why, it came back to haunt you years later. And then I found it.'

I can only guess what the detectives said to her. Maybe they told her she was a monster, not fit to be a mother, that she was no better than Myra Hindley, the Moors Murderer, a case that had happened a few years previously but still lingered on the nation's conscience, and that if they had their way she'd be swinging from a rope. I don't know, but whatever they said, it did the trick because Miriam uttered the most heart-wrenching words I've ever read in a statement. Words that could only have belonged to her.

Yes, yes, I did it. I know that now because it's why Billy

*didn't want to be born to me. That's why I lost him. He knew
what I was.*

There it was. Her trauma laid bare in a police interview
room all those years ago. Miriam had had a miscarriage before
she was arrested and in forcing a confession from her, they
had convinced her that losing her baby was evidence of her
guilt. No wonder she didn't want to have more children. No
wonder, when she did, she was overprotective, suspicious of
all, constantly living in terror that someone would harm them,
only for Kit to mislead her into thinking she hadn't raised
a potential victim, she'd raised an abuser.

I take Miriam's frail, weightless hand in mine, wondering if
she'll respond to the gesture. She doesn't and I can only cling
to a distant hope that she can hear me and take some solace
in what I am about to say.

'Miriam, I'm so sorry you lost your baby, but that wasn't
your fault either. None of this was.'

It's then that I remember I'm still holding the bouquet of
tiny purple flowers I brought for her. I look down at the wilting
stems in my hand. Violets. I remember a young man once told
me they were a symbol of innocence.

Acknowledgements

Writing acknowledgements is something I look forward to for two reasons. Firstly, it means I finished the book which still never feels like a foregone conclusion. Secondly, it enables me to draw back the curtain and shine a light on all those brilliant people who got me to the end. So, here goes. My first thank you goes to Lucy Morris. Your wisdom, your easy humour, your guidance, not to mention an unsurpassed skill at selecting amazing eateries makes you an agent amongst agents. A huge thank you also to everyone at HQ Stories. Cicely, I couldn't have wished for a better editor. Your unerring support, gentle suggestions and positivity go a long way to reducing the fear of waiting for those editorial notes. I hope you never have to keep sheep in your spare room but if you do, they will be the best looked after sheep ever. A big thank you also to the brilliant Becca and Sophie, and more latterly Sarah and Janet. Thank you for shouting so loudly about my books. My thanks too to Anna for her wonderful cover design.

Twitter gets a bad rap but without it I wouldn't have met other writers who have provided me with a community I never thought I'd be a part of. You are an amazing bunch. Brilliant books. Brilliant people. Yes, I'm talking to you – Debuts22,

Screenwriting for Authors and the original September tribe! Thank you for making me feel I belong. I'm privileged to be a part of your journey.

Thank you also to the army of book bloggers and reviewers. Your generosity is awesome. As someone who is just starting out, I am forever in your debt.

Choosing character names is always difficult for me so I'd like to say a special thank you to the three Carolines, Bernard R, Emma C and Jonny B who lent me their names for characters in *Slaughterhouse Farm*. You got off lightly, Bernard. You were almost a rabbit.

I am lucky enough to have a huge extended family cheering me along the way. Thank you for buying multiple copies and for the photos of my book on bookshop shelves. I never tire of them.

Finally, I want to thank Richard: my science consultant, my proof-reader, my pop-down-the-Spar-for-M&Ms guy, my court jester, my hand holder, my everything.

Don't miss the next gripping instalment in the CSI
Ally Dymond series…

DEVIL'S ROCK

A remote island off the North Devon coast, Devil's
Rock is home to few inhabitants. The rugged
coastline has a history of smuggling and shipwreck,
but there has never been a murder – until now.

When the body of Kieran Deveney is found on
Devil's Rock, two islanders confess to the killing.
Both claim they acted alone, and neither can be
convicted while the other stands by their story.

The team is relying on CSI Ally Dymond to
uncover the evidence that cracks the case. What
she finds is a community awash with secrets.

Shortly after she arrives, the island is hit by a storm that
prevents anyone from leaving. But it's not the treacherous
weather that Ally fears, it's the people she's trapped with…

Coming soon in hardback, ebook and audio.

ONE PLACE. MANY STORIES

If you were hooked by Ally Dymond's latest shocking case, find out where the story began in *Breakneck Point*

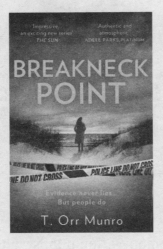

CSI Ally Dymond's commitment to justice has cost her a place on the major investigations team. After exposing corruption in the ranks, she's stuck working petty crimes on the sleepy North Devon coast.

Then the body of nineteen-year-old Janie Warren turns up in the seaside town of Bidecombe, and Ally's expert skills are suddenly back in demand.

But when the evidence she discovers contradicts the lead detective's theory, nobody wants to listen to the CSI who landed their colleagues in prison.

Time is running out to catch a killer no one is looking for – no one except Ally. What she doesn't know is that he's watching, from her side of the crime scene tape, waiting for the moment to strike.

Out now in paperback, ebook and audio

ONE PLACE. MANY STORIES

Bold, innovative and
empowering publishing.

FOLLOW US ON:

@HQStories